GOLD DIGGER

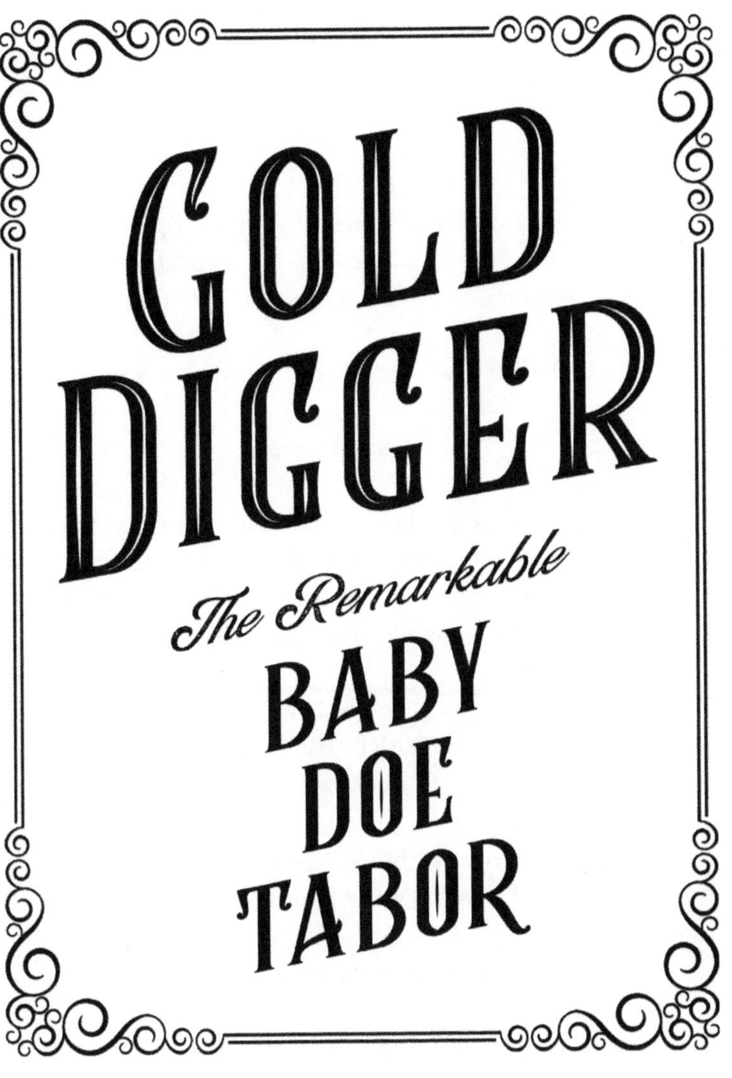

GOLD DIGGER

The Remarkable BABY DOE TABOR

REBECCA ROSENBERG

LION HEART
PUBLISHING

This is a work of fiction. Names, characters, organizations, places, events, and incidents are either products of the authors imagination or are used fictitiously.

Published by
LION HEART PUBLISHING
California

Paperback ISBN: 978-0-578-42779-9
Ebook ISBN: 978-1-7329699-0-2

Cover Design by *the*BookDesigners

Cover Image: Painting of Baby Doe Tabor by C. Waldo Love.
Used with permission. Scan #10027230. History Colorado.

Printed in the United States of America

To my parents
who ventured west with us
to prospect gold and ghost towns.

And to Pamela,
who shared Gold Digger from the beginning.

Part One

I had a grand dream of my Harvey Doe.
He was with us in our home— my Mother was with us,
dear Harvey sat at the Piano as he always did
and all at once he sang a grand rich operatic song
his beautiful voice was strong full… and swelled out in great volume
it was glorious
… he was so happy handsome and grand

—Baby Doe Tabor's Diary, Colorado Historical Society

1

Trans-Continental Railroad, April 1878

Tumbleweeds scraped across the Colorado prairie as Lizzie looked out the window of the Pullman railcar, rushing along the rickety tracks, too fast, too far, ever farther away from her family.

The ache under her breastbone deepened as she remembered Da back at the train platform, dour as a pallbearer. Ever since the Oshkosh fires ripped through their haberdashery, their theater, and even their home, the light went out of his Irish eyes. He should have hugged her and wished her Godspeed, but he just pressed a cameo locket into her palm.

On the train, Lizzie opened the locket hanging over her heart, staring at her parents' faces.

"You are such a tease." Harvey Doe, her husband of two weeks, reached across and caressed her décolletage like it belonged to him, which maybe it did.

A bead of irritation trickled down her neck, the July morning already stifling. "My stars, are you as ravenous as I am?" Lifting a profusion of red-gold locks, Lizzie fluttered a peacock feather fan. "I'll go find out when breakfast is served." Maybe fresh air would clear away her homesickness.

"Elizabeth McCourt Doe, just sit there and look beautiful." Harvey's bowler hat topped dark blond curls framing a face so thin-skinned his blue veins showed through. Lizzie's father had tailored his natty three-piece suit to perfection. His starched shirt still held its press for the third day on the Union Pacific, headed west to Central City, Colorado. "No wife of mine will be wandering around the train looking the way you do."

"What's wrong with how I look?" She leaned over to the wall mirror and pinched her cheeks for color. Her beauty was a gift from God, Mam said, a gold-plated guarantee she'd marry a gentleman of means and wouldn't have to take in mending. She tied her hat ribbon under her chin, her bosom inches from Harvey's eyes, wielding her power over the boy.

He pinned her to the seat, sweet-clover breath close to her own. His trembling fingers traveled down her face, pulling back her curls until it hurt and kissing her breathless.

"Lizzie, I'll make you the richest woman in Colorado. I swear I will. The Fourth of July gold mine will strike it big. Just wait and see."

Richest woman in Colorado. He said it again. She didn't need to be the richest, just enough to pull her family back from the precipice.

"But, we'll be back for Christmas?" She spread her fingers through his hair.

"Sooner, if I can help it."

The train porter strutted down the aisle ringing his brass bell, wearing the same blue uniform with frayed cuffs he'd worn the whole trip. "Breakfast is served…in a quarter hour," he said, his Southern cadence melodic to her ears.

Harvey traced the crocheted trim on her plunging neckline with a bitten fingernail.

"Enjoying the scenery?" the porter asked.

Harvey retrieved his hand and studied it for a hangnail.

Lizzie laughed. "Why, yes, we are, Mister George."

"Just plain George." He pointed to the nametag on his lapel.

"Seems like all the porters are named George," she said.

"They calls us that after George Pullman, inventor of this here sleeper car." He smiled.

"George it is, then." She gazed outside the window, bothered he wasn't allowed to use his real name.

Two bare-chested men rode horseback on a barren hill. "Land 'O Goshen." She pressed her palms on the window. "Are those real Indians?"

"Pawnee, I reckon." George plucked whiskers on his chin, eyes fixed on the horsemen. "Pawnees looking for a Morning Star sacrifice. Not a subject fit for ladies."

"You have to tell me now," she said, irked when he looked to Harvey for permission.

"She won't leave you alone until you do," Harvey said. "She questions everything."

"Don't say I didn't warn you." George's voice dropped an eerie octave. "When the morning star rises, a Pawnee brave shoots an arrow through the heart of a young woman."

She felt the soft spot between her ribs where the arrow could penetrate.

"Then, the Pawnee carves a star around her heart and lays her in the field to drain her blood out to nourish the prairie."

"You're trying to spook me." Lizzie hiccupped and grabbed the Dr. Mackenzie's Smelling Salts from her handbag.

"Indians aren't the only varmints in the West," George nudged Harvey. "Keep her away from bandits like Jesse James. They'll steal a girl out from under your nose." Lizzie swallowed a hiccup and changed the subject. "What's the next stop, George?"

"The Mile High City."

"He means Denver," Harvey said, puffing out his chest.

"Why do they call it that?" she asked.

"Denver's a mile higher than sea level," George said. "Don't you feel it? Hard to catch your breath." He continued down the aisle, ringing his bell.

Ready for breakfast, Lizzie and Harvey jostled through the narrow passageway of the train. Her shoulders bumped one side, then the other, until the end. Harvey insisted she jump first between the railcars, so he could help if she had trouble. It scared her, all right, the whirring of wheels on tracks, the link-and-pin coupler holding the cars together, the ground rushing below.

She jumped before she dared think of the consequences. The impact of the metal floor on the balls of her feet sent a whoosh of exhilaration through her. Harvey stood on the opposite platform, watching the flickering tracks below.

"Just jump," she shouted above the roaring train.

He squeezed his eyes closed and leapt, one boot landing on the platform, the other skidding off the edge. Panicked, she pulled him to her, his heart flailing against her own.

The sweat on his lip belied his smile. "See? You did just fine," he said, opening the door.

His bluster annoyed her, but a fight wouldn't help her find out more about the mine. Why did his eyes glaze over whenever she brought up the subject?

As they passed through the dining car, folks turned to stare. She'd grown used to people's reactions to her over the years, and now her boyish husband seemed to amplify the effect. All eyes devoured the fetching damask gown Mam had sewn for her trousseau.

Mam. Lizzie swallowed hard as her fingers grazed the real silverware, crystal, china, smoothing the white linen, while, back home, her mother struggled to put food on the table.

They'd left behind the abundant Oshkosh trees that cradled the sky with lush foliage. Trees were scarce here on the western plains; the bleak horizon stretched a hundred miles in every direction. Even the sky's color had changed from eggshell blue to a vibrant turquoise that hurt to look at it.

A sizzling platter of pan-fried steak and eggs arrived at the table. "Ohhhh. That smells divine." She took a bite, mulling over what she wanted to ask him. "You never told me how your father found the mine."

"Always the questions." He tweaked her chin.

"Maybe if you answered I wouldn't have to pester you."

"Okay, okay." He held his palms up. "Father met this prospector,

Jenkins, who needed money to build a mine, so he backed him."

"But why is he sending *you* to the mine?" She bit into the steak, too tough to chew.

He pushed eggs around his plate. "Some things are better left unsaid."

"Tell me," she pushed.

"My father wanted us out of Oshkosh, okay?" His face reddened.

"What do you mean?"

"Father never even mentioned the mine until I told my parents I was marrying you, and mother left the room in a conniption. Then he poured me a Glenlivet and said, 'Time to cut the apron strings, son. Take your beautiful bride out west for a honeymoon and work the gold mine until your mother simmers down.'"

She nodded slowly. "Your father is a smart man." What a relief to get away from Mrs. Doe who never looked Lizzie in the eyes. Her backbone stiffened. She'd make a good wife and strike it rich at the same time. "What makes your father so sure we'll strike gold?"

"Father says Central City is the richest square mile on earth." Harvey leaned back, elbows splayed, hands behind his head. "He'll meet us there after he finishes up some business in Denver."

"What will he want me to do?" Lizzie said, anxious to get started.

"Stay home and sit pretty, most likely," he said.

"Come on, Harvey." She laced her fingers with his. "I'll do anything to help." Anything to help her family.

He kissed her knuckles. "You can count the gold."

"I'll be good at that." She smiled; the bookkeeping she'd done for Da would come in handy.

As the train pulled into Denver's outskirts, the double-time pace of the city thrilled her. Hundreds of carriages, supply wagons, horses and buggies traversed the brick street. A milk wagon dodged the streetcar running down a wide boulevard flanked with stores.

"George was right about the altitude." Harvey jerked his collar, sucking in dry, sparse air.

His mother had warned about his asthma, instructing Lizzie to distract him from his tight chest. So, she read the signs on the storefronts. "Robertson Art Gallery. Larimer Butter & Cigars, Walker Whiskies & Wines. Whoa. Look at that one, House of Mirrors."

A revolving red light glared off a million mirrored tiles behind a woman in a lacey bustier gyrating up and down a brass pole.

Lizzie had read about tainted women in the Bible, but never imagined them so…striking.

"House of Mirrors." Harvey's eyes bulged. "We don't have places like *that* at home."

"Because we don't need them, do we?" She turned his head and kissed him with all the fervor she could muster. The best kiss they'd had, ardent and satisfying.

Afterward, Harvey's eyes still followed the red light.

At the foothills, they transferred to the *General Sherman*, a narrow-gauge train just three feet wide to squeeze through the steep and winding mountain tracks. American and Colorado flags fluttered from the locomotive, black smoke billowed from the smokestack, the bell clanged.

Harvey heaved trunks to the porter, then doubled over, wheezing. "I can't go on."

"The train is leaving, we have to go." Lizzie helped him up the steps, determined not to turn back. She settled him on the front-row bench, and the train lurched forward. Rubbing Harvey's back soothed him.

After a few miles, his breath resumed a halting rhythm and he patted her hand. "You're a good wife, Lizzie."

She smiled, things would be fine. Never mind the altitude zinging her eardrums with pain.

They passed a waterfall cascading down jagged rocks and plunging to the river. "Ever see anything so glorious?" She turned to

Harvey, but he slept, bowler tipped over his forehead, sweet mouth pursed for a kiss.

Mam was right; she could learn to love this boy. Harvey Doe, son of the mayor of Oshkosh, had walked into Da's haberdashery, proud and flirtatious, bragging about his father's gold mine in Colorado. Mam had set her cap for him right then. Not-for-nothing had she coddled Lizzie, excusing her from chores, and dressing her like a porcelain doll. Harvey Doe was the *gentleman of means* she'd been groomed for.

Lizzie figured they'd return to their families after a few months at the gold mine, and with the money she brought back, she'd help Da open a new haberdashery.

As the train threaded Clear Creek Canyon, sheer rock walls rose like a formidable fortress, grand and terrifying, nothing like the gentle hills of Wisconsin. Layers of rock ranged in color from blood red to charcoal to gold. One enormous peak overlapped the next, obscuring the distant view. The majesty of it all cracked her heart open as surely as if the Pawnee had, pouring her hopes onto the magnificent mountains.

When the conductor called the next stop was Central City, Harvey stretched and smiled, apparently feeling better.

The train pulled around the last bend, whistle shrieking through the canyon. They chugged to a halt, billowing clouds of steam.

Breathless and light-headed, Lizzie rushed to see the legendary Central City. Her new home. *Her gold mine.* Raising her petticoats to step down, she imprinted the red soil with buttoned boots.

The sulfuric breeze seeped into her lungs. Ramshackle buildings had been thrown up haphazardly over the rising slopes. Piles and piles of discarded ore littered the barren hillsides. Pine trunks had been hacked at their base, clear-cut for lumber. The stench of burning garbage and burping fumes gagged her. She pulled out her rosary beads and prayed for strength.

If this was the richest square mile on earth, it certainly didn't look like it.

2

Turquoise Lake, Colorado, May 1878

Horace Tabor grabbed his gold pan and snuck out of the Tabor Mercantile while his wife instructed new prospectors on the importance of Dentacura for tooth hygiene, Gowan & Stover's Miners soap for scouring ore from skin, snakebite kits for rattlers, iodine and tourniquets for frostbite and gangrene.

Out back, the ferocious current of the Arkansas River beckoned Tabor like a seductive siren. Kicking off boots and socks, he slogged through freezing water, searching for the one thing that would save him from the dull life of a merchant and keep Augusta happy at the same time, if such a miracle was possible. How many times had she said luck had passed him by? But *Lady Luck* could change on a whim, and that old stinging in his tailbone lured him deeper into the river.

He goose-stepped from rock to slippery rock to a pool formed by a crevice of granite. As he dipped his pan into the silt, sunlight glared off the dappled water, making it impossible to see the bottom. But, soon the reflection parted like theater curtains, revealing thousands, no, millions of shiny flecks glittering like midnight stars on the sand. A burning prickle shot up his tailbone to his brain. Scooping ore into his pocket, he dipped his pan again.

"You have to choose, Horace. Me or the gold." Up on the riverbank, his wife flapped her arms like a scarecrow in a windstorm.

Caught red-handed doing what Augusta strictly forbade, he dropped his gold pan and it skittered down the river. Lunging forward to recover it, his feet slipped. His long legs flew up and his tailbone cracked on the boulders. Pain shot up his backside. The powerful current submerged him under water, pummeling his back along the jagged bottom. Water flooded his throat, scrubbing his lungs. His head rapped against a rock, and the world went dark.

Tabor awoke in a beaver dam, twigs poking his sides.

"Horace, grab this." Augusta braced herself on a tree trunk, holding out a pine bough.

He pulled himself up by the branch, hand-over-fist. Forcing his feet underneath his legs, he launched himself onto the riverbank, wet and lifeless as a dead trout.

"Serves you right for running off and leaving me and Maxcy to mind the store."

"I was getting water for camp." He propped himself up on his elbows, feeling foolish.

"You can't hornswoggle me." She waved his gold pan. "You promised to give up prospecting."

Tabor sighed. Sure, he wanted to tell Augusta what he'd seen, but first he had to make sure his eyes weren't tricking him. For twenty-one years, he'd tried to live up to his promises when she followed him for the gold rush, and for twenty-one years, he'd come up short. She'd led the privileged life of a quarry owner's daughter, a debutante, no less, when Tabor worked for her father. The man never forgave Tabor for luring her west. Back then, Augusta believed in him with a determination that made him believe in himself. While he prospected, she ran a mercantile, supplying whiskey, coffee, vittles, and mining equipment. But after two decades of futile prospecting, Augusta insisted he quit.

The ore he discovered today would redeem his sorry soul and give her everything she deserved.

The glow of sunset softened Augusta's wrinkles. Silver streaked her coal-black hair, caught in a tight knot at the back of her neck.

She'd long since given up frivolous grooming and pretty clothing, preferring to accomplish one more task before nighttime prayers with their son, Maxcy.

Tabor leaned in and brushed a wet ringlet from her forehead. "You said I have to choose between gold or working with you in a musty mercantile?"

She swatted at him, but he caught her arm mid-air, drawing her strong body down to a cushion of pine needles. "I choose you, Augusta." He kissed her hard. "But I wouldn't turn down gold if it hopped into my pan."

She wriggled free and stood above him. "You're just like your pa. Bad Luck Tabor follows you wherever you go."

The woman had a way of sucking the nectar right out of him.

After she stomped off, he rubbed the ore between his fingers, slippery and elusive. Didn't feel like gold. Scooping it out for closer scrutiny, his palm began to tingle. Didn't look like gold, either. The ore was *silver.*

"We'll just see about Bad Luck Tabor," he said. He'd promised Augusta a better life out west. Looked like he could finally make good on that promise.

Tabor stepped out of the mercantile to the wrap-around porch for a breath of fresh air, but none was to be had. Thunderclouds crackled over the Sawatch Mountain Range. A dozen high-strung men played poker like it was their last game. The smell of desperation mingled with electricity in the air. Fingers drummed tabletops. Muddy boots rocked in agitation. Cards shuffled, clay chips clacked, swear words flew.

Tabor flipped his lucky silver dollar, which landed on *Lady Luck* as it always did, like some riddle to figure out. On one side of the coin, things were mighty good. Gold Fever had heated up like, well, a fever. Never mind honest gold claims were few and far between. Their little mining camp had grown from a handful of prospectors to five-thousand folks, throwing up shacks and tents anywhere they damn pleased. As a result, Tabor Mercantile thrived, selling everything Augusta brought in from Denver, two wagonloads a week, which Tabor and Maxcy hardly unloaded before the contents sold: whiskey, tents, picks, pans, salt-bacon, beans, more whiskey.

But, on the flip side, their success left Tabor no time to develop the silver claim he'd staked. He'd followed those promising flecks on the Arkansas River to an outcrop of rose quartz with gray-white streaks. *Silver.* Ordinarily, prospectors ignored metal other than gold, but he'd staked the claim, barely able to write *The Matchless Mine* on the ledger, his arm stung so. The prickling ricocheted from his funny bone, straight through his heart. *A lucky streak.* He called his lucky streaks *Matchless,* that crazy-bone feeling when nothing and nobody could beat him.

Now he needed someone to mind the mercantile post office, so he could work the Matchless Mine before someone jumped it. He scanned the gamblers for a candidate.

At the next table, Scrawny Sullivan swept poker chips toward his belly like a chipmunk hoarding acorns. "Too bad for you, Duggan. I win again."

"Leave those chips lay." The gunslinger lifted Scrawny by the neck, feet dangling like a hanged man. "I ought to snap your neck."

"Let me go."

Duggan dropped him in a heap. "Give me my money."

Scrawny rubbed his throat. "It's mine, now."

Duggan reached back and drew his Remington revolver.

Tabor jumped up.

Just then, Augusta stuck out her head from the store. "What's all the ruckus? We're conducting business in here." She gasped to see the revolver. "Holy Jehoshaphat."

Tabor shielded Scrawny and Augusta. "Calm down and give me the gun."

Duggan's face purpled, body bristling. "Scrawny cheated. You know I hate cheaters."

"Somebody grab his gun," Augusta yelled, but the crowd backed away.

Tabor stepped closer. "Duggan, you came here with your wife for a new start."

Duggan's knuckles whitened around the gun. "She's having a baby. We need that money."

Sweat drenched Tabor's back as he stepped toward him. "I'll be damned if we have another killing this month." He held out his palm. "You're a good man, Duggan; make the right decision."

The gunslinger blinked and shuddered. "I needed to win today, Mr. Tabor. I had to win, and he stole my money." His arm fell to his side and Tabor took his gun and handed it to Augusta.

"Lock this in the safe."

"Thank you, Lord." She rolled her eyes skyward and took the revolver inside.

"Scrawny, give him back his money," Tabor said.

Sullivan hugged his burlap bag. "It's mine."

"I bet that ace of diamonds came from your sleeve," Tabor said, playing a hunch.

Sullivan's shoulders slumped and he handed over the bag. "I ain't drawn a paycheck since Pickering Mine shut."

"See that?" Tabor clapped the two men's shoulders. "You're both down on your luck. Don't take it out on each other next time."

Augusta returned, signaling thumbs up.

Tabor gave each of the men a silver dollar. "Get yourselves cleaned up and report back here six in the morning."

"What for?" they asked in unison.

"You need jobs, don't you?"

They nodded.

"Scrawny will be the postmaster and Duggan the sheriff." His tailbone prickled; his luck was changing. Matchless Mine was within his reach.

"Imagine that, I'm a postmaster." Scrawny hooked his thumbs under suspenders.

"A gunslinger for a sheriff?" Augusta huffed. "Bad idea."

"We *need* someone tough." David May glanced sideways at Duggan. "We can't keep living this way, cheating, stealing, gun fighting and claim jumping." Tabor respected May, a Jewish merchant who planned to open stores from Leadville to St. Louis.

"Shut your trap, May. This ain't no Sunday school." Chicken Bill bobbed his red head. "Hell, it's a mining camp."

"Not for long," Augusta pointed to the long wagon train winding down the mountainside.

"People are invading our camp by the thousands," said Winfield Stratton, the weasel-eyed prospector. "And when the railroad gets here, God help us."

"Well said, Stratton." Tabor had grubstaked him for years; maybe now he'd pay him back by taking charge of this mess of a mining camp. Thunderclouds spattered their first raindrops. Chickens in the road squawked and scurried for shelter.

"Tabor." Stratton's eyes crossed. "What are you daydreaming about?"

"Chickens running around with their heads cut off," he joked.

"You know who stole my chickens?" Chicken Bill said. Men threw poker chips at him.

"This is serious, Horace." Augusta pushed up her pince-nez glasses. "We have to protect what we've built here."

Tabor held up Stratton's arm. "I nominate Winfield Stratton for mayor. All in favor, say 'aye'."

Not a man raised his hand.

David May stood, nervous but resolute. "Tabor, before you came here no one talked to each other. You brought us together right here at the mercantile."

"You helped me homestead land for the church," Father O'Mannie said.

"You grubstaked most of us," said Stratton.

"I nominate Horace Tabor for mayor," May said. "All those in favor?"

"Aye."

"Aye."

"Aye."

A dozen *ayes* knocked Tabor flat as an avalanche would.

"Congratulations." Stratton shook Augusta's hand. "Your husband is our new mayor."

She hooted. "If that doesn't make a stuffed bird laugh."

"Now you can stop all the hollering and shooting at night, Mayor." David May clapped his shoulder. "My missus needs her sleep."

Chicken Bill butted in. "Jesse James jumped my claim. You gotta lock him up."

"Shut down that whore crib, won't you, Mayor Tabor?" Father O'Mannie said. "Those girls flaunt their bodies like it's France."

That lucky tingle in his tailbone turned stone cold.

3

Leadville, Colorado, May 1878

Before dawn, Tabor and Maxcy sat on the mercantile steps whittling pine, waiting on a supply wagon that was due sometime before noon, no telling when. Tabor inhaled the green smell of kinnikinnick, cogitating on how to get his son working at the Matchless Mine and give him elbow room from his mother. Of course, working alongside Maxcy would complete Tabor's dream.

A lark trilled from an aspen branch. The stirring melody drew his gaze to the jagged silhouette of the mountain against the brightening sky. The Matchless Mine lay up there, untouched since he'd become mayor of the mining camp they'd named Leadville.

"You miss prospecting, doncha Pa?" Maxcy peeked through unruly curls.

He nodded. "I reckon I do."

"Is that why you hate being a postmaster?" Maxcy hacked at his wood.

"Scrawny's helped with the post office." Tabor whittled the nut between his chipmunk's paws. "But mining gives me a chance to achieve something bigger with my life, something important. Don't you want to feel that way?"

Maxcy slashed at his carving. "Ma says that's The Fever when you talk like that. She says you'll die from The Fever like your pa."

"Pa didn't die of fever." He died a drunk, but Tabor refused to spook Bad Luck Tabor on his son.

Maxcy tossed his wood in the dirt. "I'm n-n-no good at whittling." His stutter had gotten worse. "How'd you l-learn it?"

"It's all how you look at things." He dusted off Maxcy's discarded pine, peering at it from every angle. "If you look carefully, you see things beneath the surface that no one else can see."

Maxcy cocked his head. "Like c-conjuring?"

"Some call it that, but I like to think of it as *envisioning*." He handed him the wood. "Ever dream something would happen before it did?"

"If I d-did, Ma would say the d-devil got to me," Maxcy said.

"You have to trust your instincts, son." He noticed a dawn blush to the sky. "Hey, the morning star's rising. Make a wish."

"Naw." Maxcy straightened up. "I'm too old for wishes."

"Never too old for wishing." But was that true? At forty-seven years old, his own wish of mining eluded him like a mirage. Every day seemed lost to mail sorting, listening to people's problems, and trying to keep up with the needs of a town. So much to do but never what he wanted most. The orange sun crested the Sawatch mountains, and the morning star vanished from view.

Two bearded men trudged up the rutted road toward them, mighty odd at this early hour. They wore layers of ragged clothing and carried large packs on their backs: pans, picks, shovels, bedrolls, canteens. Tabor recognized the German prospectors he'd grubstaked, Rische and Hook. They'd be looking for more supplies, but he'd have to refuse. Augusta cut off his grubstaking, said people took advantage of his generosity.

The Germans ran toward them. "Vee struck it, Mayor Tabor. Vee struck it."

Tabor thrust a finger to his lips. "Shhh. Rische. Keep your voice down. News like that could start a riot." He smiled; these coots had brought him plenty of fool's gold before.

The prospector opened a burlap bag. "Hold your hands out, boy." He poured rocks into Maxcy's palms.

"Doesn't look like gold," his son said, eyes clouding over.

"It's worth something, isn't it?" Rische asked.

Tabor studied the rocks and his stomach leapt like a rainbow trout. *Lead and silver*—no question about it. He rubbed the Morgan silver dollar in his pocket and Lady Luck grew hot between his fingers.

"Maxcy, wait for the supply wagon while I check this out."

"I can't unl-l-load the wagon alone, and it l-leaves for Aspen by noon."

Tabor weighed the consequences: facing Augusta's wrath versus chasing down a glimmer. "Gotta trust your instincts, son. I'll be back before you know it."

They reached a three-foot post stuck in the ground with the required claim notice nailed to it. Tabor ripped it off. "It's in German. You can't stake a claim in German."

"That's all we write, Mayor." Rische shrugged, and Hook scratched his head.

Tabor glanced back toward town; maybe it wasn't too late to get back before the supply wagon arrived. These geezers wouldn't know silver from pyrite. Even if they did, a spot this close to town should have been discovered by now. Mines dotted the hills around them, morning sounds of picks hitting rock, whirring rope hoists hauling buckets of slag, and the constant ear-shattering blasts of dynamite. Too close for comfort.

"How'd you find this place, boys?"

"Remember last week when you smuggled us supplies and a jug of whiskey, right under your wife's nose?" Rische chuckled. "We climbed Fryer Hill and drank the whole jug right under this pine tree. When the sun came up, we started digging."

"Sure you boys didn't steal those rocks from one of the other mines?" Tabor asked. Salting mines with rich ore was a popular swindle.

"Would we do that you?" Rische pressed his hand to his heart.

Grabbing his pick, Tabor climbed into the hole. "Show me the ore."

Hook pointed out a faint gleam in the rock. Tabor hacked into the wall, revealing more glistening rock, silver mixed with lead. Blood charged his veins like triple-X tequila. "Haul this dirt out so we can take a better look."

Rische sorted out the silver bearing rocks, depositing them in a wooden cart above the hole.

Hook shoveled slag into a pile, whistling a tune.

Tabor put his old back into it, chopping into rock as if thirty years younger. His chest prickled with exhilaration. Sparkling rock fell in chunks, unlike any he'd seen. Wait 'til he told Augusta. She'd prance like a filly in springtime, and see him for the man he was, instead of Bad Luck Tabor, son of a drunk.

After a couple of productive hours of picking and sorting, they stopped to rest.

"Did you name this claim, boys?" he asked, swigging from the canteen tasting of copper.

"Little Pittsburg, after our home town," Rische said.

"Little Pittsburg. Fine name." Taking another mouthful from the canteen, he felt guilty about missing the mercantile shipment. Hell, Augusta wouldn't care when she heard they were rich.

He searched for the gleam where he last picked. "Lost sight of the vein, boys. See anything?"

For the next hour, the men hacked at every glint and found nothing but rust-colored earth.

Energy deserted his body, replaced by the searing pain. Fooled, again. His luck never changed. Isn't that what Augusta would say?

Frustrated, he hacked until he couldn't lift the pick another time. "It must've been a small pocket, fellas. It's gone."

Hook wiped his glasses and searched the rock wall.

Tabor patted his shoulder. "You keep the silver we found."

"Equal partners, Mayor," Rische said. "We owe it to you."

A vicious prickle ripped through Tabor's spine. He spun in the opposite direction he'd been digging and yelled at the rock wall. "Dammit, what am I not seeing?"

Rische stabbed his shovel in the air as if fighting demons. "Who are you talking to, Mayor?"

"Silver." Tabor brushed away dirt on the far rock wall exposing a five-inch band of silver. "Hey, hey, hey there. It wasn't a pocket, after all. Looks like a motherlode."

Rische frowned. "What kind of ore is *that*?"

"A motherlode is the *source* of a vein, silver or gold." The charge in Tabor's spine drilled deep within him, stinging and satisfying.

He lifted his pick, but his back muscles seized up something fierce. Bending backward to stretch, he caught sight of a figure silhouetted on the hillside above, peering down at them with oversized field glasses, lenses glinting in the sun. Tabor waved at the black form, but the specter disappeared behind the hill.

Tabor rehearsed how he'd tell Augusta the good news. He'd promise her a raccoon coat for the winter, and maybe even some pearls, if the motherlode proved strong.

When he walked through the door, the smell of vittles on the stove gave him stomach pangs. "Smells delicious." He set his gunny sack on the table.

"Supper's over." Augusta glowered at him. "Maxcy unloaded the supply wagon himself.

Maxcy patted his back, repeating the standing joke between them. "You know what Mark Twain says about mines, doncha, Pa?"

"A mine is a hole in the ground owned by a liar," Tabor answered.

"Ain't it the t-t-truth, Pa…" Maxcy laughed.

"Don't use *ain't*," Augusta said. "It *is* the truth. Your pa is living proof digging holes instead of working for an honest wage."

"Only, this time, I'm not lying." He poured the gunny sack of rocks on the table.

Augusta leaned forward, hands hovering over the slick gray rocks. Lifting her pince-nez glasses, she pinched her eyes closed then opened them again.

"I told you grubstaking would pay off," he said. "Now we can hire help for the mercantile, so you don't have to work so hard."

Augusta's eyes watered as she turned to him, and he opened his arms to hug her. But she grabbed the broom instead and swept the rubble off the table, crashing to the floor.

"Fool's gold, for fools. We'll go broke giving supplies to everyone who says they struck it."

He picked up a chunk from the floor. "It's silver, Augusta, and the U. S. Treasury's buying silver to mint Morgan silver dollars."

"A silver vein, Pa?" his son asked. "C-can I help?"

"Absolutely, Maxcy. You'll manage the mine eventually. But there's a lot to learn." He winked at Augusta. "Like the difference between fool's gold and silv—"

"Stop it, Horace." Her fist landed on the table. "I am not losing Maxcy to your shenanigans. Someone has to run the store and post office, and it's obviously not you."

"Ma, it's a great opportunity," Maxcy said. "Pa said he'd make me manager of the mine."

"If you want to be manager, then, congratulations, Maxcy." She smiled stiffly. "I'm making you manager of the Tabor Mercantile."

"Really?" Maxcy raised his chin and pulled back his shoulders. "But, that's Pa's job."

"Not anymore." She dragged her skirt through the slag. "Now clean this dirt up."

Tabor snorted. "Hells-Bells. She fired me."

4

Central City, Colorado
May 1878

"This place is something else," Lizzie said, opening her parasol against the blazing sun.

"Something like Hell," Harvey choked out.

The mountains had been hacked for the riches they harbored, now left barren and scarred. The disfigured earth kicked up tufts of dust. Her head pounded from disillusionment.

"Load our trunks back on the train," he barked at the porter and grabbed her hand.

She wanted to flee this awful place as much as he did. But she couldn't. Her fortune lay in those mountains. Her family's redemption. Maybe she was dreaming, but they *had* to try.

"If we leave now, you'll sit behind a desk at your father's lumber yard, and I'll get fat with babies." And Da would never rebuild his haberdashery. "The Fourth of July is the chance of a lifetime. We have to give it a go." She kissed him with a passion not to be confused with affection.

"Whoa, girl. You cross-lots to get what you want, don't you?" He pointed at her. "Better *not* get fat."

The hired buggy driver with hound dog jowls, loaded their trunks on the back of his rundown rig. Harvey slid in beside her, and the sway-backed horse slogged up the hill.

A horrific clash turned Lizzie's attention to a large warehouse, doors wide open. No sooner had the clanking ceased than it began again. Iron collided on rock, rhythmically smashing her eardrums. Yellow smoke billowed from chimneys smelling of acid and rotten eggs.

"What are they doing in that building?" she yelled to the driver.

"Hell's Gate, they call it," he said. "The mill crushes the rock, and the smelter melts down the ore." He whirled a whip, and the buggy pitched through discarded slag. Clapboard houses and lean-to shacks were scattered to the outskirts of the city and farther to the top of the ridge, shattering her dream of the gingerbread Victorian she'd pictured for their honeymoon.

They passed St. James Methodist, where a couple of young women in calico dresses hung kitchen towels on a line to dry, watching her with sun-worn faces. Maybe they could be friends.

Downtown, two main roads intersected brick and stone buildings. Lizzie felt a ray of hope when she read the sign on a three-story building. "McFarland's Temple of Fashion, Dry Goods & Carpets. A monument to denim jeans, tin pans, and mechanical contraptions."

A dizzy diversity of men traversed the cobblestone streets, alarming and mesmerizing in their coarseness. Buckskinned Indians carried beaver pelts dangling from tree limbs across their shoulders. Miners in threadbare denims and crumpled hats rode wagons headed up the mountain. On the boardwalk, a cowboy in chaps stepped aside for a gunfighter, holster slung low on his hips.

She elbowed Harvey's ribs. "Guess this is what they mean by the Wild West. What's that Indian wearing?" She pointed to a small man in a pointed straw hat, pushing a cart up the road.

"That's a Chinaman. Father calls them Celestials from the Celestial Empire. Says they work cheap in the mines."

"Never thought I'd see men from China in Central City." She took a whiff of smelling salts.

A newsboy's cry interrupted her thoughts. "Hot off the press. Silver strike in Leadville. Read all about it. Leadville mayor strikes it rich."

A ragged miner handed the newsboy a coin for the thin tabloid.

The boy hollered with new fervor. "Mayor Tabor strikes it rich. Silver strike in Leadville."

Shop owners bounded out of their stores. Men jostled around the boy to buy a newspaper.

Lizzie tapped the driver's back. "Could you pull over, please? I'd like to buy that paper."

The buggy swerved to the side of the road. She lifted the train on her skirt and jumped down. The men parted for her, mouths dropping open as if beholding an angel from heaven. She handed the boy a nickel and rewarded the crowd with a smile. She felt every man's eyes trailing her as she boarded the buggy, exposing her petticoats and bloomers.

"Lemme see more of that purty leg," a short, sturdy man heckled.

Harvey jumped from the buggy. "Apologize. That's my wife you're talking to."

"Apologize for what? Admiring an ankle? Get back on that buggy, Peachfuzz." He pitched his thumb at a tall Chinese man. "Or Chin Lin Sou will stuff your broken body in a cart and run you back on the rail you came in on."

Chin Lin Sou stood six-foot-six, if he was an inch. Menacing arms flexed under his buckskin shirt. Bear claws hung from a leather cord around his neck. Lizzie noticed with surprise that his eyes were blue. Ice blue.

Harvey turned toward the buggy, and she was relieved. But, then, he spun around and cuffed the heckler's jaw. The man squatted low and propelled his leg into Harvey's belly.

"Oaff." Harvey grabbed his stomach and fell on the cobblestones. The crowd swarmed in from every direction pummeling him with a frightening fervor.

"Do something," Lizzie said to the driver.

"I'm not getting myself kilt," he said. "If your rich boy survives, it'll be a miracle."

She lifted her skirt to jump out, but ruffians grabbed at her legs, leering with missing teeth and salacious smirks. The driver beat them back with his crop, which only inflamed their lust. They rocked the buggy, and she clutched the sides not to fall into their grasping arms. She couldn't see Harvey in the frenzy, just Chin Lin Sou standing head-and-shoulders above the fray, staring at her with those disturbing eyes.

Suddenly, Chin bent over the thrashing bodies and picked up Harvey by his armpits. Carrying him above their heads to the buggy, Chin plunked him down beside her. Then, raising his face to the sky, he howled and yipped like a coyote, then slapped their horse on his haunch.

The buggy lurched and Harvey fell back on the seat, his fine pleated shirt filthy and buttons ripped off. Maroon bruises blotched his face. Blood dripped from a gash on his cheek.

"Never seen anything like it," he said.

"The crowd or the Chinese man?" she asked.

"I'm talking about *you*." He poked her chest. "Those varmints never saw a woman like you." Grabbing her handkerchief, he swabbed his neck. "This isn't Paris, Lizzie. You can't wear clothes like that around here. You'll get yourself ravaged and get me killed defending you."

His logic galled her. "No one asked you to belt the guy."

"You're so naïve. Those men would sooner jump your bones than look at you, Lizzie."

"That's ridiculous," she said. But maybe he was right. All those grimy hands wriggling around her ankles made her feel…unclean. Working in Da's haberdashery had not prepared her for the lust of deprived men. Cheeks burning hot, she hid her face in the tabloid that started the trouble.

Reading about the silver strike absorbed her attention as the buggy slogged up the hill. A strike of a pick and rich ore poured from the rocks. Astounding.

The Teller House stretched the entire block and soared four stories high, accentuated with red brick arches. Lizzie smiled. This town couldn't be all bad with a hotel like this.

A striking man swung his stiff leg across the portico, sporting a stylish ebony and mother-of-pearl cane. His slicked-back hair revealed a widow's peak under a hat her father would call a gambler's skimmer. His waxy skin looked like he'd just shed a layer. His mustache gleamed, thin and black. A leather bolo tie hung from a turquoise stone at the collar of his pleated white shirt.

"You must be Mr. Doe." He shook Harvey's hand, but his eyes never left her face. "Welcome to the Teller House, the grandest hotel in the Rockies. I'm the manager, William Bush." His voice dripped with confidence and honey. "And this lovely creature must be Mrs. Doe." Bowing low, he kissed her hand, his lips sparking on her skin.

She pulled back her hand.

"Static shock, from the altitude and dry air," he explained, green eyes glittering up at her.

"Since when does air shock a person?" She fluffed her curls, masking her distress.

Mr. Bush's eyes devoured her hair, her face, the cameo locket resting between her breasts.

Harvey cleared his throat.

"Something wrong, Mr. Bush?" she said. "Or does everyone in this town misbehave when they see a woman?"

"Pardon me. We're unaccustomed to such loveliness in the mountains." Bush rapped his cane against the baluster and strutted down the portico, Harvey and Lizzie followed in his wake.

"A little Teller House history," Bush said. "When President Ulysses Grant visited Senator Teller, we laid silver bricks on the street." He pointed his cane to the cobblestones below. "But, since Grant demonetized silver in the Panic of 1873 and made gold the only legal tender, he ignored our silver path and entered through the back door."

Lizzie brandished the tabloid. "But they're minting silver dollars again, right? That's why this silver strike is causing such a stir."

He spun around to assess her. "A woman who reads the newspaper." He snatched the tabloid from her hands. "What silver strike?"

"We stand by gold," Harvey said.

Lizzie darted him a warning look not to talk about their gold mine. She certainly didn't trust the hotelier to keep the news to himself. "Weren't they processing gold by the railroad tracks?"

"Just enough gold to keep the rumor mills burning." He scanned the newspaper. "I'll be damned, old man Tabor struck silver. Republican cohort of mine." His nostrils flared, and he swatted his lame leg with the paper. "This calls for a drink. Will you join me?"

Harvey touched his jaw and winced, his eye was swelling. "I hope you mean something stronger than tea."

Bush snorted. "Do you favor whiskey, Mr. Doe?"

"Father and I drink Glenturret."

Bush held open the lobby door for her. "Ah, yes…you are clearly a man of fine tastes."

Floral rugs covered parquet floors. Overstuffed armchairs and settees surrounded low mahogany tables polished to a shine. Lemon and linseed oil scented the air just like their furniture back home, bringing on a pang of homesickness.

"What would give you pleasure, Mrs. Doe?" Bush said. "Whiskey? Or will it be tea for you?"

His words wielded a double-edged meaning, but she wouldn't let him ruffle her.

"I prefer *Irish* whiskey," she said. "But a glass of sherry would be divine."

Bush relayed the order to a bartender in vest and shirtsleeves, filling bowls with cherries and olives, then peered back at her. "Please, make yourself comfortable."

Lizzie sat on the overstuffed sofa, spreading her skirts around her ankles, pretending to ignore his blatant leer.

The bartender brought a tray of crystal glasses and served them amber liquors.

Bush held up his glass. "To the good old days of gold."

Lizzie tipped her glass. "What do you mean, good old days?"

But Bush read the newspaper, leaning his cane against the bar. "Tabor, you son of a gun."

At close range, Lizzie realized his cane had eyes that matched his own; hard and glinting emerald eyes above sharp fangs. Stripes ran from the top of the head down the diamond-patterned shaft and ended with a pointy crosshatched tip of a rattlesnake. Diamondback Rattler.

The hair on her arms rose.

"I'd like to go to my room and freshen up," Lizzie said.

"Of course, you would. I upgraded you to the Columbine Suite. Your trunks have been taken up." Bush held out his arm, smelling of bay rhum and something musky.

"I'll leave you to your preparations, my dear." Harvey raised his second glass of Glenturret, his bruised eye swelling.

A good wife would put ice on that, but right now the exhaustion of the trip and emotional drain of leaving home crashed in on her like coal down the shoot. A bath and nap and she'd rebound. As Bush lead her past the front desk, Lizzie noticed a telegram with her name perched up on the call bell. "What is this?"

"This came for you this morning."

Her heart stuttered. Only her family knew where to reach her. The seal had already been broken. The teletype words stood stark against the white page.

"DA LAID OFF **STOP** DESPERATE **STOP** SEND MONEY FOR RENT **STOP** CLAUDIA"

After the fire, Da had found a job, but now he'd lost it. So dire before, what would her parents do now? His eyes were going, and he had a hump on his back from bending over his work. She should have stayed home and taken in mending. Or, she could have worked in the theater downtown. Here, she only had the mine. Here, she only had Harvey, who didn't seem up to the task. The mine had to pay off. It had to. She'd put up with these wild men and air so dry it sparked, whatever she needed to, but she had to make that mine pay, no matter what.

"Not a problem, I hope." Bush's black eyebrow arched.

"Nothing I can't fix." Stuffing the telegram in her handbag, her resolve stiffened her spine. "But you could do me a favor." She mustered a fetching smile.

"Of course, Mrs. Doe."

"Make sure my husband doesn't drink too much. We're meeting his father early to inspect our mine, and I don't want any excuses."

"Whoa. Whoa." Mr. Doe commanded the horses to stop at a mound of rocks just like many they'd passed on the steep mountain trail. He'd changed his top hat to a miner's slouch but wouldn't fool anybody with his hundred-dollar suit and shined boots. The man wore ambition like a uniform. Mr. Doe was The Boss. From lumber baron to mayor to gold miner, his plans brought success. Hopefully, some of his drive had rubbed off on his son, but Lizzie had her doubts.

Mr. Doe jumped down from the buggy and Harvey followed, leaving Lizzie to jump down on her own.

"Harvey, where are your manners?" Mr. Doe held out a strong hand for her. "May I?"

She stepped down gracefully, holding her parasol against the sun.

Harvey wheezed with new allergies that bloomed with alpine wildflowers. "I can't breathe. We're over nine thousand feet elevation."

"Slow deep breaths," she whispered.

Mr. Doe rolled his eyes. "Lizzie, I'm counting on you to keep Harvey on the straight and narrow. It's going to take a lot of single-mindedness and gumption to make the mine profitable."

She tilted her chin up. "Don't worry. I'll be right beside him, no matter what." She handed Harvey a handkerchief for his dripping nose.

Mr. Doe pointed out a couple dozen miners pounding nails into a long, narrow contraption, pumping water from the river, sorting rocks into piles. "We count on Cornish and Welsh miners for expertise. Mining's in their blood. But we import Chinese for labor." He pointed out a crew wearing conical hats hauling wheelbarrows of rock.

An older man walked to greet them, a torn oilcloth jacket covering a mud-splattered shirt. "Mr. Doe. Thank the Lord." He lifted a crushed felt hat off his pale forehead, the rest of his face fried to leather by the sun. "When you didn't answer my telegrams, I didn't know what to think."

"Mr. Jenkins." Mr. Doe shook his hand. "I brought my son Harvey to help you out. And this is my daughter-in-law, Mrs. Doe."

Jenkins squinted in the harsh sunlight. "All due respect but this ain't no place for a tenderfoot. And sure-as-hell no place for a woman."

"I beg your—" she started.

Harvey squeezed her arm. "Let Father handle this."

"What's this about needing new equipment?" Mr. Doe said. "The sluice box should be producing by now. Show me what needs to be replaced."

"It's not that we have to replace the sluice box." Jenkins swallowed hard. "We need to go at the gold a whole different way."

Mr. Doe's face reddened. "What are you trying to pull? We had a deal."

"I can still triple your money, just need a little more, that's all." Jenkins patted the long wooden chute zigzagging down the mountain, water flowing through it from the creek above.

"Is this the sluice box?" Lizzie asked.

"Yes'm. Those young'uns, Stefan and Günter, shovel river gravel into the top, water washes it over these wooden rifles and catches the gold." He plunged his hand in the water and delivered a gold pebble to Lizzie.

She admired the glow. "How much is this worth?"

"Well, an ounce of gold pays nineteen dollars," he said.

"Land O'Goshen," Lizzie said. "That would pay my family's rent."

"This spring, we cleared a thousand dollars a month. But last month, we were down to half that. Looks like we've played out the sluice. We need to start hard rock mining."

Mr. Doe's eyes narrowed. "What's it going to take?"

"We have to dig down into the mountain and build a mine shaft. We'll need dynamite, lumber, and manpower. But the Chinese work cheap, so that's not a problem."

"How do you talk to them?" Lizzie asked.

"See Chin Lin Sou over there?" He pointed to a man who towered over the others. "Chin manages the Chinese in Central City—all three hunert of them."

A shiver sizzled through her. The man who humiliated Harvey.

"We'll need sledgehammers, steel drills, mules, powder kegs, ore carts," Jenkins continued.

"How do I know it'll be worth my investment?" Mr. Doe asked.

"Never pays to throw good money after bad," Harvey said, kicking his foot into the dirt.

"It will be worth it," she reminded him.

"Take a look for yourselves." Jenkins led them up the mountain.

Lizzie climbed after him, rocks bruising her feet through her thin soles. Holding up her skirt and parasol got heavy but she wouldn't let Mr. Doe and Harvey pass her, wanting to be first to see what Jenkins would show them.

Finally stopping, Jenkins swung his arm up like a vaudeville showman to reveal a wall of crystal sparkling in the sunlight.

Lizzie gasped. "Is that gold?"

Mr. Doe took off his hat, hands burrowing through his hair, and stared at the wall. "Son of a gun." Squeezing his eyes closed, then he stared again.

Harvey caught up, bending over and gulping for air.

"When quartz and iron pyrite are found together, there's always gold," Jenkins said.

Mr. Doe rubbed his chin. "Hard rock mining is a lot more than we bargained for."

"We can handle it." Lizzie wove her hand through Harvey's arm. "Can't we, darling?"

He blew out his cheeks, then let them go slack.

"What's it going to be, son? Have you got it in you?"

She caressed Harvey's dimpled chin. "Of course, he's got it in him. Don't you, darling?"

For the next two weeks, they developed a plan with Jenkins. The preparations exhilarated Lizzie and she absorbed all she could. Mr. Doe had a way of asking the right questions and making smart decisions. So much to learn. Harvey seemed excited about the gold, but when she pressed him for opinions about equipment or methods, he told her to leave the details to Jenkins. When she asked Jenkins her questions, he answered eagerly, like Da always did about tailoring. His enthusiasm worked like a tonic on her homesickness.

When it came time for Mr. Doe to get back to Oshkosh, Lizzie wanted to squeeze the last bit of knowledge from him, so she arranged a farewell dinner at the Teller House.

"Famous rainbow trout and McClure potatoes for the table," Mr. Doe ordered.

"Excuse me." Lizzie stopped the waiter. "I had my heart set on buffalo steak." Tilting her head to her father-in-law, she used her charm like Mam taught. "You don't mind, do you, Mr. Doe?"

He laughed. "A woman who knows what she wants and how to get it." Turning back to Harvey. "The blacksmith is making you eight-pound hammers to double jack."

"Double jack?" Harvey bit his lip.

"Two miners working together," Lizzie explained. "One holds the drill steel to the rock, while the other strikes it with a heavy hammer."

"Use the burly guys to hammer and the puny sorts to light dynamite," Mr. Doe said. "They run quicker."

Harvey drained his Glenturret and raised his hand for the waiter.

A commotion at the bar caught Lizzie's attention, William Bush in the middle of it, wagging his cane in the air. When she heard him mention Tabor, she couldn't sit still, hungry to hear about the silver strike. "Pardon me, I'm going to the powder room." She guided her ruffled train through the tables.

"I'm telling you, it's just Tabor's luck, dammit," Bush said to a handful of bankers and shopkeepers. "Take poker. Old man Tabor plays like he doesn't care a hoot, but somehow his cards magically fall into place." He rapped his cane on the table. "Tabor pretends to lose occasionally, but it's only to win the rest of the games and empty your pockets." His drunken cronies jeered.

Bush threw back a tequila. "Remember in '73, when Tabor brought the Republican Convention to Central City? The floor collapsed, and two-hundred men dropped into the basement. Not a scratch on any of 'em, lucky for Tabor. They should have hung the bastard. I was the only one to break a leg and I've been paying for his bad judgment ever since."

Bush's envy and rage for Tabor amused Lizzie, but then, his bloodshot eyes caught her in their crosshairs, traveling slowly down her body as an intimate sneer curled his lips. Despite the warning bells in her head, a thrill spiked up her core.

"Carry on, boys." He swaggered toward her.

"I didn't know there was entertainment in the bar," she said.

"Why, Mrs. Doe, you look absolutely ravishing." Leaning too close, he took her hand and kissed it. Shocked her again.

Altitude, her foot. And his scent, something animal.

She inhaled. "Bay rhum, but another smell I can't identify."

"Snake oil," he said, goading her, but she refused to bite.

"Mayor Tabor must be quite a man to get you so riled up."

Bush scoffed. "Tabor's a washed-up prospector who has the

luck of a fool who doesn't know when to quit."

"So, he's tenacious. I admire that."

"I see." His eyes flared in surprise and desire, his voice hushed and excited. "You didn't come to Central City to play house, did you, Mrs. Doe? A wimp like Harvey couldn't snag a beauty like you on his own."

His insolence shredded her nerves and she slapped him.

"Bulls eye." He smiled seductively. "You are what we call a gold digger."

She wound back for another slap, but he caught her wrist and squeezed until it throbbed.

"Don't worry, you came to the right place. We're all gold diggers here." Enfolding her arm, his hand covered hers as if sealing a secret pact between them as they walked back to the table.

"You don't know anything about me, Mr. Bush," she seethed.

He patted her hand. "I have a second sense about things."

"Do you read palms, too?" Yanking her arm from his grasp she stomped to the table, his snide laugh following her. What was it about him that drew her like a magnet and repelled her at the same time?

Mr. Doe held up his fork with a glistening piece of fish. "Mr. Bush, I was saying how remarkable the rainbow trout is. Even the fish here lead to pots of gold."

Bush held out her chair.

"Sit with us, Mr. Bush," she said, reversing her strategy. "Tell us more about Tabor's big strike." The buffalo tasted wild and juicy.

Bush rolled his eyes. "Don't want to interrupt your dinner."

"Nonsense," her father-in-law said. "We all want to hear about the strike."

Bush pulled out a chair. "Well, Tabor's always been a fool for grubstaking prospectors that he never hears from again. But this time, two German geezers came back to share a big silver discovery."

"See, Harvey? The Rocky Mountains are flush with ore," Mr. Doe said.

"From the newspaper account, Tabor made it look easy," Lizzie said.

Bush lowered his eyelids half-mast. "If you saw Tabor, you'd think different. The man's bent over from panning gold, his fingertips fell off from frostbite, and he's deaf from dynamite blasts."

"Sounds like hell." Harvey covered his face with his hand.

Steak caught in her throat and she swallowed hard. "You can't scare us off, Mr. Bush."

He pushed back his chair. "Have a good trip back to Oshkosh, Mr. Doe." He pointed at Lizzie. "Steer clear of miners and barflies." Swinging his stiff leg across the room, his rattlesnake cane tip pierced the planked floor.

"I've been thinking." Mr. Doe lit a pipe, smelling of rich tobacco. "If you kids make a go of the mine, you can have the deed as a wedding present." He puffed his pipe.

"You'd do that for us?" Lizzie couldn't believe it; her own gold mine. "I'll do whatever I can do at the mine."

"Your wife is a firecracker, isn't she?" Mr. Doe drew deep from his pipe, sucking the air right out of the room. "The mine is no place for a woman."

Harvey squeezed her knuckles, and she pulled away.

"There must be some way I can help."

"You, charming lady, can help by making a good home for my son: cook hot meals, wash the laundry, clean the house."

The hair bristled on the back of her neck. "You want me to stay home all day while Harvey works at the mine?"

"How callus of me." Mr. Doe laid his pipe aside. "A young girl alone in a strange mining town." He shook his head. "But it's only a few months. I'm sure you can find yourself a woman's group or charity work."

Harvey's hand covered hers like a snuffer on a candle flame. Only, she wouldn't be snuffed.

"What time does your train leave in the morning?" she asked Mr. Doe.

Harvey would be a pushover compared to his father.

5

Leadville, Colorado, June 1878

Tabor searched for William Bush through clouds of cigar smoke wafting between trophy heads of moose, mountain lions, and coyotes, poised to pounce from the walls of the Silver Dollar Saloon.

He'd been surprised when Bush agreed to meet about a job offer, since they hadn't talked since the Central City fiasco. He still felt guilty about Bush's leg, and this job could make it up to him. Thanks to mining profits, Tabor had started a dozen businesses and things were spiraling out of control. *Bad Luck Tabor* would bring him to his knees if he didn't hire a business manager.

He spotted Bush playing poker in his damask vest, ruffled shirt, and string tie. Poker chips piled around him like a fortress. Hadn't changed a lick.

"Showing these fellas how it's done, Billy?" Tabor sat next to him. "Deal me in, boys."

He rubbed Lady Luck on his silver dollar, feeling warm and generous as a lady should. Studying his cards, he fed a chip to the pot. Jack of clubs and an ace, two, four, and five of diamonds.

Next round, he traded the Jack and turned up the new card. Three of diamonds. "Steel wheel." He slammed his hand on the table.

Bush shook his head. "Never could beat your game."

"Keep trying, Billy, my friend. Maybe someday you'll beat the master."

"Breaking your luck gives me something to live for," Bush joked.

"Gentlemen, if you'll excuse us, we have business to discuss." He found a table out of earshot. "We'll have to drink bourbon since the water will kill you. We need holy water."

"Okay, I'll bite," Bush said. "How do you make holy water?"

"Boil the hell out of it." Tabor laughed. "Seriously, ore processing chemicals are seeping into the water, burning eyes, and eating holes in stomachs. Twelve have died this year already."

Bush cocked his hat over one eye. "So, you're spending your fortune on holy water?"

"Started the Leadville Water Company, drilling wells, building pipelines and holding tanks."

Bush's eyes chased the curvaceous saloon owner. "Now there's a project I'd take interest in." Dolly's bosom overflowed a laced-up corset, her hips bounced to the lively piano tune.

"How's your lovely wife, Marianne?" Tabor asked.

"She keeps a clean house," Bush deadpanned.

"Ah, a respectable woman, like my wife. Why can't respectable women be built like Dolly?"

Dolly set drinks and a bottle on the table, a rose tattoo on her breast. "On the house, Mayor, after all you've done for Leadville." She rubbed against him like an alley cat.

"Is Shorty Scout back?" he asked and turned to Bush. "Her boyfriend's the best game tracker in the West."

"He's hunting with Buffalo Bill." Her painted lips pouted.

"Knowing Shorty Scout, he'll bring back a caribou to mount on your wall." He pressed a silver dollar in her palm, and she swayed back to the bar.

Tabor poured Bush a bourbon. "So, what's it going to take to steal you away from the Teller House?"

"I'm not a miner," Bush said.

"Don't need to be. Lou Leonard manages my mines." He drank, and the whiskey shot straight to his brain. "Listen, Billy, I've run from bad luck my whole life, but with your help, I might just outrun it this time." *Bad Luck Tabor.*

"What bad luck? You just struck silver."

He slapped the table. "Yes. Yes. That's it, Billy. Silver changed everything. Now the name Tabor will stand for something, big things: water companies, fire stations, railroads, insurance and real estate companies. Silver mines planted all over God's green earth. Are you with me?"

"Depends." Bush's eyes narrowed. "I want my own hotel. Finer than the Teller House."

"We'll build it, then. Leadville needs a luxury hotel." He reached to shake Bush's hand, and it shocked him something fierce. "Hope that's a good sign."

A ruckus kicked up outside the saloon doors. "Mayor. Mayor Tabor. Call off your goon."

Tabor rushed out and saw Marshal Duggan shoving Rische.

"Your partner shot Winnemuck in the foot."

"He was spying on us with field glasses," Rische said. "Trying to steal our silver."

"Winnemuck was delivering this subpoena." Duggan handed Tabor a document and pushed Rische toward jail.

The subpoena claimed the Little Pittsburg was mining a Winnemuck silver vein. His stomach tightened. Damned if he'd let Winnemuck horn in on his silver. But another voice echoed like a train whistle through a canyon. *Bad Luck Tabor, Tabor, Tabor...*

He returned to the dim saloon and tripped over Bush's cane. "That cane of yours is lethal." Picking it up by its rattlesnake fangs, the shaft pulled apart in his hands, revealing a concealed sword.

Bush jerked it away and closed the sheath, a cane once more. "What's all the commotion?"

Tabor turned over the subpoena. "This lawsuit claims that since the Winnemuck mine is older, our silver vein is theirs."

"We need a map of Fryer Hill."

Tabor fished one out of his pocket and slapped it on the table.

"Just happened to carry a map?" Bush spread it out.

A jolt of pride rocked him. "Hey, some people study the Bible. I study mine maps."

"What if the surrounding mines get wind of Winnemuck's lawsuit?" Bush studied the map.

"If mineral rights belong to the oldest mine claim, I don't own a doggone thing."

Bush rapped his cane on his snakeskin boots. "This lawsuit will take some fancy footwork."

"Never been a good dancer," he admitted.

"Don't worry, I'll take the lead." Bush swaggered to the door, saluting two fingers to his hat.

Tabor saluted back, amazed Bush jumped in to help him. He'd feel even better if he didn't stand to lose everything he'd worked for. Just hoped Bush knew what he was doing.

6

Central City, Colorado, July 1878

The flat above the feed store was far from what Lizzie imagined for her first home. Cook-stove, cast-off table and chairs in one room, a bed in the other, their travel trunks for side tables. She cracked open the window to let in morning air. At least the view made up for it. A waterfall tumbled down to a clear pool under her window where deer, mountain goats, and fox came to drink.

She heard the mining wagon pulling up on the street.

"They're out front, Harvey. Time to go." She hoped her blue gingham dress would do for the mine; it was the plainest she'd packed in her trousseau.

Harvey grabbed his muslin lunch sack. "Where do you think you're going?"

"You don't expect me to sit here." She hated the whine in her voice.

He counted ten dollars from his pocket and handed it to her with a list. "Go to McFarland's and pick up these supplies for Jenkins. And get me a proper lunch pail, won't you? They make fun of my sissy sack." He jumbled down the stairs but turned back at the landing.

Her heart skipped. He remembered their morning kiss. She started down to meet him.

"And don't get all gussied up." Wagging his finger. "You cause enough talk around town." He ran to the wagon and she looked after him. Their morning kiss had disappeared after the first week Harvey worked at the mine.

"You can count on me," she called after him and took a dollar out to save for her family, a familiar ache set in. According to Claudia's last letter, Mam had gone half-crazy with lonesomeness for Lizzie, her favorite offspring.

She watered a geranium like Mam kept on her windowsill. The spicy smell took her home, Mam telling tales while she braided Lizzie's hair.

Pulling open her dresser drawer, Lizzie reached under petticoat for the Celtic rosary beads Mam gave her, hidden from Harvey's critical Protestant eyes. Picturing her mother's smile, she kissed the Mother Mary medallion, symbolizing the moon's feminine strength. Mam had told her, "The silver moon rules ocean tides and passage of time. Silver is the metal of your soul." She couldn't let her down, but what could she do stuck here at home?

Mr. Doe had made her duties clear. "Hot meals, clean laundry, babies, charity..."

Going out by herself in Central City was quite different than in Oshkosh. Hungering eyes of men on the streets devoured her like a rabbit on a campfire. Retreating deeper into her bonnet against the leers and whistles, she finally ducked into McFarland's. Still not a woman in sight, she searched crammed aisles for obscure items on her shopping list, overwhelmed by boilers, hobnailed boots, sugar-crystal candy, helmets with carbide lights, picks, sledge hammers, rope, chain, buckets and ladders. Crates of dynamite lined the wall, roped off and signed, 'KABOOM. Step Carefully'.

When she located an item in the maze, she felt a small victory and checked it off the list. Oats for mules, candles, a dozen 'S' hooks, four hardhats made of felt boiled in resin. She spied a small pair of overalls and added it to her pile on impulse, perfect for her five-foot frame, then found boy's lace-up boots, plaid shirt, and slouch hat. When she changed Harvey's mind, she'd have something to wear to the mines.

Something else Harvey wanted? A lunch pail. Wasn't it right by the hardhats?

Searching, she pushed past a couple of mountain men with her head down and bumped into a tiny woman examining a tin box, her hair pulled into a tight bun.

"Oh. Excuse me." The woman's yellow gingham dress was not flattering to her sallow complexion. "We're twins."

The woman's brow wrinkled.

"Both our dresses are gingham." Lizzie laughed, but the woman didn't smile. "Is this a Cornish lunch pail? It looks so complicated."

"Not in the least," the woman said, picking up the tin. "Miners hang the pail in the mine and light the candle below. By lunch time, their pasty and tea are warm."

"Ummm, makes me hungry for corned beef and cabbage pasties. Oh, I'm Lizzie Doe. My husband and I moved here from Oshkosh to manage his gold mine." That ought to warm her up.

"I'm Marianne Bush." The woman curtsied.

A sharp rap-rap echoed on the linoleum floor, accompanied by an oddly familiar scent.

"This is my husband, William Bush."

His snake cane advanced on her, fangs bared.

"Why, Mrs. Doe, a pleasure to see you again," he said in that honeyed voice. "The Does stayed at the Teller House, dear. How's the gold mine going?"

"We started hard rock mining. They sent me to buy supplies." She bit her tongue. Why tell him anything? Mam said a man with a widow's peak couldn't be trusted.

Bush's mouth curled. "Marianne, you should invite Mrs. Doe to your sewing circle to meet other women."

"We haven't seen you at church," she said.

"St. Mary of the Assumption?" Her chest filled with hope for friends. She'd missed the sweet comradery from back home.

"St. James Methodist." Marianne's eyes flashed. "*All* of us are Methodist."

Bush's cane struck the pickle barrel. "It's not a religious sewing circle, is it, Marianne?"

"Not exactly." She dropped her gaze to the floor. "But, it sounds like Mrs. Doe is busy."

Lizzie pulled her shoulders back and smiled. "I'd love to join you."

"I'm better at design than sewing," Lizzie confessed to the five women gathered in a circle with fabric trailing from their laps. "But I did bake snickerdoodles for you girls." Praying they wouldn't recognize cookies from Wimburger's Bakery, she passed the sugary aroma under their noses. She'd tossed out her own burnt cookies for the racoons.

Joining the sewing group had taken some sting out of her homesickness, and she learned more about mining through their gossip. They gathered in Minnie Bueler's front room, sitting in an odd lot of rocking chairs, benches, and milking stools. She could see through the log slat walls, making it hot in the summer, but Lizzie relished their company.

"I really shouldn't." Marianne took a cookie. "Mr. Bush complains I haven't lost the baby fat from our last child."

"How can he complain when he's the one who got you in the family way?" Lizzie said.

All eyes turned on her.

"Don't take me wrong," Lizzie said. "You look fine, Marianne, especially for a woman with three babies." Passing the cookies, she scrambled to make it right. "I'd have a baby, but then I'd never get to work in the mine."

Minnie shook her finger. "Women are bad luck in mines."

"Miners are very superstitious." Peggy Sue knitted with baby blue yarn over her growing belly. "Besides, who'd want to work in the mine? Have a baby. I'll teach you to knit."

A disturbing prickle sprouted in Lizzie's abdomen, a longing she didn't recognize. The mine has to come first. The few dollars she'd sent Mam wouldn't feed a mouse. The rent was due and Da hadn't found a job. They'd be out on the streets, if she didn't send more money. "What if I get pregnant anyway? Then I *can't* work in the mine." The prickle turned painful.

"You could try the sponge." Marianne's cheeks colored. "Mr. Bush won't allow it."

"What's the sponge?" Lizzie asked.

"Prevents babies," said Velma, the preacher's daughter.

"Where do you get them?" Lizzie asked.

"Behind the counter at McFarland's," Velma whispered. "You have to ask."

Lizzie pictured McFarland smirking at her request.

"Besides, working in a mine is not worth breaking your back for a dollar a day." Minnie whistled through the gap in her teeth when she talked. "We'd go broke if not for high-grading."

"High-grading ore is stealing," said Velma's sister, Kitty.

"Owners expect to lose ore," Minnie said. "Otherwise why would they pay so low?"

"Lizzie's a mine owner," Kitty said. "Enough sinful talk of stealing and making babies."

Shocked that miners would steal from owners, Lizzie would ask her later about high-grading.

Velma interrupted her thoughts. "What did you think of our church?"

Enduring the sermon had made her bottom numb. "Your father gives a doozy of a sermon."

"He speaks the Word." Kitty looped the yarn around the needle.

A strip of fabric fell from Marianne's lap, and Lizzie retrieved it. "Starting a new project?"

"A flag for the Teller House, since Colorado became the thirty-eighth state last year."

"Looks like you have your hands full," Lizzie said. "May I help?"

Marianne raised an eyebrow. "I *could* use the help. I need to finish it by Labor Day."

Lizzie organized the materials, seven red stripes, six white stripes, and thirty-eight stars. But as the work progressed, the quiet got on her nerves.

"Can I teach you a game we played as kids?" she asked. "It's called Truth or Lie."

"Count me in." Minnie tossed aside the shirt. "My eyes are buggy."

"Someone tells a story that's hard to believe. If you think it's true, shout out *Truth*. If you think it's false, shout *Lie*. I'll go first." She racked her brain for an exciting subject. "Jesse James lives outside Leadville with his gang. Truth or lie?"

"Truth," Marianne said. "Jesse James drinks whiskey with Mayor Tabor."

The ladies clucked their tongues.

"Tabor drinks with Jesse James?" Lizzie asked. Tabor's legend grew bigger every day.

"Mr. Bush says they're thick as thieves." Marianne punctured fabric with her needle.

"I've got one." Velma's cheeks colored. "The preacher's daughter loves a Jewish man."

Kitty threw a basket at her and calico squares flew in the air. "I'll get even with you."

"It's true." Velma wagged her finger at her sister. "Kitty loves Jacob Sandelowsky."

"I just think he's handsome," Kitty said. "Is that such a crime?"

"Not at all." Lizzie toyed with her. "It's no crime for a Jewish man to be handsome."

Minnie and Velma burst out laughing and the rest joined in. They laughed at each other and themselves, until their cheeks glistened with tears.

Kitty slumped. "But father says it's a sin for a Protestant to marry a Jewish man."

"You'll find someone." Lizzie patted her hand.

"My turn." Marianne smiled secretively. "He has a *little red heart* on his arse."

"Who does?" Peggy Sue asked.

"Mr. Bush." Marianne pressed a hand over her mouth.

"Come on." Lizzie taunted. "A birthmark on his arse? Is that all you've got?"

"He, he makes me do wicked things in bed." Marianne's eyes opened wide, and the girls gasped.

"Like what things?" Lizzie squelched a titter, dying to hear more.

Marianne stood, dropping red and white stripes to the floor. "You tricked me, Lizzie. After I invited you into my circle you goad me to say evil things." Tears gushed onto her cheeks. "I thought we were friends." Gathering her skirts, she ran out the front door.

"That was cruel, Lizzie," Peggy Sue said.

"Downright spiteful," Minnie agreed.

"It was a *game*." She looked to Velma and Kitty to defend her. "You can't blame Marianne for what she said."

"Oh, we don't blame Marianne," Velma said, and buried her head in her work.

She pressed her hand to her chest. "You can't blame me."

"It's not your fault," Minnie said. "Catholics are raised different."

Church bells chimed on the hill. Lizzie piled Marianne's materials neatly in her basket. "You're right, Minnie. Catholics go to confession. I'm going to confess I have no idea what happened here." As soon as Lizzie closed the door, she heard them buzzing.

Weeks passed, and Marianne didn't return to the sewing circle. Lizzie took over sewing her flag, as impossible as the task was, painstakingly sewing the stars and stripes with tiny stitches. Da would be amazed at her handiwork. When she finished, she'd bring it to Marianne to make amends, though she still didn't know what for.

No one in sewing circle was in the mood for Truth or Lie. She tried to spark conversation, asking questions about the mines or their families. Their one-word answers turned her heart as cold as her untouched plate of snickerdoodles.

When, at last, she finished the flag, she baked a fresh batch of cookies and walked to the Bush's Victorian home, the closest thing to a dream house she'd seen in Central City.

Sweet-smelling hollyhocks lined the flagstone walkway leading to the spindled porch. An empty rocking chair teetered back and forth. Inside, a baby cried. A twinge of remorse roiled in her belly. Marianne had her hands full, and she'd made it worse.

She knocked. A gap opened in the lace curtains and closed again, followed by footsteps and rustling.

"Marianne, I finished the flag." She waited, but the door remained closed. "I never meant to hurt your feelings." A dark cloud covered the sun and made her shiver. Even the heavens disliked her. She left the folded flag on the rocker with the cookies.

The next afternoon Lizzie went to Minnie's house as usual, but the window shades were drawn. Walking home she passed Marianne's Victorian. Joyful laughter wafted through the windows, hollowing her out like a rotten log.

Without the sewing circle, Lizzie wanted more than ever to be part of the Fourth of July, and schemed up a plan: delicious meal, hot bath, and then she'd convince Harvey how valuable she'd be at the mine.

Lizzie's budget couldn't stretch to buy beef, so she bought venison, which had to cook all day to make tender. She poked the deer meat. So tough. How could she make a decent meal?

Problem was, the recipe Mam sent didn't include her cooking skills. Slicing her fingers with the dull knife, she chopped onions, potatoes and carrots, ruminating over Mam's letter asking for more money. Lizzie's brother Peter had left their parents for a theater job in Chicago, just like him to shrug responsibility. Didn't Mam know how tough it was to make ends meet here?

She stirred fiercely, grabbing the boiling pot and searing her hand. Tears sprang to her eyes as she sucked the blistering fingers.

Later, from the window, she saw Harvey climb off the wagon, barely able to lift his weary legs to the ground. Her heart ached. Nothing in his upbringing prepared him for such back-breaking work.

His step dragged up the stairs. The door opened, his eyes downcast. Mud caked his denims.

She hugged him and led him to the sink. "Come wash up for supper."

Red soil embedded cracked fingernails and the crevices of his palms, unyielding to lye soap.

"I've got a nice stew for you." She ladled it into his plate, smelling of sage and dried chilies.

He dropped into a chair and ate in silence, shoulders drooping.

"How's the progress at the mine?"

"Can't you see I'm too tired to talk?" He shoveled food into his mouth without commenting on the taste. After supper, he stretched out on the bed.

She lay beside him and rubbed his head. "I could come help."

He closed his eyes. "Maybe not. Now shut up."

"Don't be like that, Harvey. We're on the same side here." She went to wash the tin plates and think of a better strategy.

Harvey opened one eye. "They think I don't know beans."

"Who?" she asked.

"Günter and Stefan." He propped himself up on his elbows. "Günter says to hand him a red-headed woodpecker saw. I search the tool chest, trying to figure out which one it is. Meanwhile, they're bouncing their boiled hats together, guffawing, having themselves a gay ole time."

"Red-headed woodpecker saw? Really, Harvey?"

His cheeks colored. "They say the only things going for me are Daddy's bank account and my baby-doll wife."

She brushed a smile away.

"Jenkins told them, 'That's two more things than you hoodlums got going for you.'" He covered his face.

She filled the half-barrel tub with warm kettles of water and helped him into the bath, lathering a washrag with good lavender soap.

"Let me start with your handsome face." Oily ore pitted his pores. "You even look like a miner. Your father would be so proud."

He sank deeper in the tub, and she rubbed his newly-muscled back.

"Harvey, have you heard of high-grading?" She lathered his scalp with her fingers. "High-grading's when miners slip gold in their pockets. It's common practice."

"How can I watch what goes in their pockets?" he grumbled.

"I can be your extra set of eyes." She tipped back his head and poured warm water over his dark blond curls. "That way, we'll get all that's coming to us." She held up a towel as he stepped out.

Pressing his naked body against her, he kissed her hard. "I want all that's coming to me." He pushed her onto the bed, hovering above. "You *do* have a point, Lizzie."

"I do?" Her goal within grasp, she lifted her face for a kiss.

"You *do*. But Jenkins is my extra eyes." He dropped down, crushing her.

This was his idea of passion? Anger pulsed at her temples, but she wouldn't let it stop her, blowing a warm breath into his ear. "Tell me Jenkins cares more than I do, Harvey." Nibbled his ear-lobe. "*Nobody* cares like I do."

7

Denver, Colorado, August 1878

"All rise," the bailiff commanded. "The honorable Judge John Dennis Fitzgerald."

Bush still hadn't arrived at the courthouse. He'd assured Tabor everything was in place, but his confidence eroded when Bush didn't show.

Tabor's lawyer stood and gestured for him to do the same. Towering oak panels dwarfed the restless crowd. Gaslights cast a fevered glow on the faces of miners, politicians, and reporters. The landmark case would determine what dictated mineral rights in a mine: vertical borders or the first mine to work a vein, even if the vein ran into another claim.

Judge Fitzgerald entered the courtroom wearing a powdered wig and rectangle glasses dangling off his nose.

Tabor folded his clammy hands on the table, rubbed shiny by countless other chumps who'd sat in his seat. Inhaling odors of cigar smoke and castor oil, he loosened his collar, and prepared for the fight of his life. The Little Pittsburg, lynchpin to his wealth, made all his other mines and businesses possible. Losing it now would destroy everything he'd achieved.

Lewis C. Rockwell, the high-faluting Denver lawyer Bush hired, combed shiny fingernails through lamb chop sideburns and read his scrawled notes.

Tabor's new fortune lay in Rockwell's ability to decipher that gibberish. Money-grubbing Winnemuck and his Leadville lawyer sat across the aisle, looking mean as Frank and Jesse James. Tabor popped a licorice not sure his city lawyer was tough enough for this mountain-man fight.

The cracking of the gavel sounded a lot like hammering the lid on Tabor's coffin.

The Judge peered through cloudy glasses at the papers in front of him, making sure the court was paying full attention. His nose was swollen and red like he'd been stung by wasps.

"I have to say, it's an abomination you lawyers would waste this court's valuable resources with such a clear-cut case," he said. "In fact, there *is* no case. Not only does the Winnemuck Mine own most of the vein in question, it predates Tabor's Little Pittsburg by several years."

Tabor jumped up. "We discovered that vein, not Winnemuck." Rockwell tugged his coattail.

The gavel cracked down. "Counselor control your client."

"Won't happen again, your honor. But, Winnemuck vacated his mine years ago."

"Still, the Winnemuck Mine has the first claim on record." The judge seemed ready to get back to his Irish coffee.

"But, your honor, a silver vein can branch out in different directions," his lawyer said.

"Your point?" The judge glanced at his timepiece.

Rockwell brought forward a document. "This map shows that Horace Tabor owns four mines bordering the Winnemuck."

Bully for you, Rockwell. Full steam ahead.

Judge Fitzgerald's eyebrows shot up. "Doesn't impress me. This case is solely between the Little Pittsburg and Winnemuck. And, since the Winnemuck was owned first, it takes precedence."

"With all due respect, your honor, see the mine on the far side of the vein? It's the New Discovery, bigger than the Little Pittsburg and Winnemuck combined, and it predates them both."

Tabor waved his hand for Rockwell's attention, but the lawyer stared straight ahead. He should keep quiet about the New Discovery. The owner would love a piece of this action.

The judge coughed. "This discussion requires the owner of New Discovery to be present."

Everyone talked at once, yet Tabor heard only the thud of his heart.

"Order in the court. Order in the court." The gavel pounded.

"Excuse me, Judge." Rockwell pointed to the back of the courtroom, where a distinguished white-haired gentleman stood. "Senator Chaffee purchased the New Discovery."

"I had first dibs on that mine," Tabor said, as Chaffee walked to the bench. His hair had turned white since they'd met at the Republican convention, but he possessed the same honest eyes, blue as the Colorado sky. He handed the judge a paper.

"You bought the New Discovery?" Judge Fitzgerald asked.

"Yesterday, your honor."

"What's *your* claim on the silver vein running between the Little Pittsburg and Winnemuck?"

"Not my concern, sir." "I sold the New Discovery this morning."

Tabor's gullet burned.

Judge Fitzgerald's glasses clattered to the podium, and he fumbled to put them on. "Let me get this straight. Yesterday you bought the New Discovery for fifty thousand, and today you sold it for one hundred thousand? Quite a profit in a day. I can't make out the signature of the buyer."

"I sold the New Discovery to Horace Tabor." All eyes in the gallery swung to Tabor.

He shook his head. "I think I'd remember that."

"Highly irregular," the judge gurgled, his wig askew. "Counselors. My chambers. Now."

"What in thunderation is going on?" Tabor asked Rockwell.

"Ask Billy." The lawyer snapped his case closed and followed the judge.

Senator Chaffee, dignified in his ditto suit and winged collar, caught Tabor's eye.

Was that a wink?

After the recess, Judge Fitzgerald slammed the gavel on his podium. Tabor scooted to the edge of his seat, his future at the mercy of the soapy-eyed judge. Where in tarnation was Billy?

"I've studied the Fryer Hill maps carefully," the judge said. "With the addition of the New Discovery, Mr. Tabor owns every mine bordering the Winnemuck."

Chaos erupted in the gallery, and the judge pounded his gavel.

"This court has decided the equitable solution is to combine the claims of both parties and divide shares proportionate with their ownership. Tabor at ninety percent and Winnemuck ten percent." He pounded his gavel. "Court adjourned."

Tabor expelled a great gust of air.

"Congratulations." Rockwell pumped his hand. "A great victory."

Tabor heard the metallic tap of Bush's diamond-studded cane.

"Brilliant strategy, Bush." Rockwell clapped his shoulder. "Wish I'd planned it myself." He closed his briefcase and left the courtroom.

"Did you enjoy the dance?" Bush smiled.

Tabor wanted to throttle him and hug him. "Why didn't you explain what you were doing?"

Bush caressed the snakehead of his cane. "What you don't know keeps you innocent."

"And you say you're no good at gambling." Tabor shook his hand.

"Never said that. I said I can't beat *you* gambling."

"You forged my signature on the deed?" His belly tightened.

"No, sir." Bush held up his palms. "After you read Rockwell's contract you signed a signature page."

Tabor ran the scenario in his mind. "That's when I bought the New Discovery?"

"By the way, you owe Senator Chaffee for the mine."

"You're the one I owe, Billy." His voice caught in his throat.

"As your business manager, I'm taking commission on the mine deal," Bush said.

"Commission?" Confusion clouded his gratitude.

"Ten percent off the top." Bush cut through his fog with razor-sharp clarity. "Because thanks to me, you still own your mines." His eyes narrowed to slits.

Like staring down a rattler.

8

Central City, Colorado, September 1878

Now Da was helping Claudia and Mam take in mending and laundry. Lizzie couldn't stomach the thought of her proud Da, sleeves rolled up, wringing out wet long johns.

Redoubling her efforts to get to the mine, she tried a different tack with Harvey. "I could collect the ore, sort it, and take it to the assay office to be measured. Then, we would make money on all the minerals, copper, silver and lead…not just gold."

For once he didn't argue and when morning came, Harvey's attitude softened.

"If you think you know so much about mining, prove it." He grabbed his miner slouch. "Better hurry, the wagon's waiting."

She leapt into a plaid shirt and overalls, pulling a hat over her hair.

Harvey stood by the wagon, shaking his head. "You look like a blasted beggar." He jumped into the wagon and pushed to the front.

Glancing down at her overalls confirmed his insult. No longer beauty queen of the Oshkosh parade, no longer the winner of the ice pageant, no longer the pride of Da's eye. But she *was* on her way to her gold mine. She pulled herself up into the wagon, smiling at the miners. They tipped their hats shyly and made room for her.

The wagon passed Minnie's house, where she shook her rug out on the front porch. Lizzie waved at her with a big smile, but her friend ignored her. Gulping down crisp mountain air, she turned to the miners. "So how deep is the main shaft now?"

"About twenty-five feet, ma'am." Günter stared at his lap.

"What types of ore are we finding?" Lizzie glanced back, and Minnie stared after the wagon. Gawk all you want, Minnie. At least she wasn't home doing women's work. Her stomach twisted. Women's work? What made work men's or women's, anyway? Made no sense. No sense at all. She shook the nonsense from her brain and asked about the ratio of quartz to gold.

At first, the miners seemed reticent, throwing Harvey nervous looks. But, Lizzie kept asking questions and, soon they shared what they knew about the stubborn ore and how they extracted it.

"Unfortunately, it's a horizontal vein trapped in layers of hard granite," Günter said. "We'd need to build another shaft to get at it proper."

"Sounds expensive," she said.

Harvey's mouth twisted.

The wagon reached the mine, and she heard mules braying and screaming as if in great pain. Jenkins had tethered a rope around the belly of a blindfolded mule, whose ear-splitting shriek set off the rest of the herd in a horrifying cacophony.

"Why is Jenkins doing that to the mules?" She brought her hand to her throat, which ached with their screams.

"Has to hoist them down the mine shaft to haul rock," Harvey said.

"Blindfolded and trussed like a turkey? That's heartless."

"Hold your tongue, Lizzie."

"It's hurting them, Harvey. We can't—"

Gunshot echoed through the pines, and she riveted toward the sound. A young miner jammed a shotgun against his chest, tears streaming down his cheeks. A mule lay in a heap with its hide torn with buckshot, blood gushing over white bone. The shooter doubled over and retched.

"What are you doing?" she yelled and jumped out of the wagon.

"Sorry you had to see that." Jenkins scratched his head. "That mule was so afraid of the dark he kicked against the shaft and broke his leg, hollering the whole way. Had to shoot him. Scared the other mules sumpun fierce."

Jenkins lowered the pulley, and the next mule thrashed against the ropes, black lips quivering over mossy teeth, shrieking from the pit of his stomach.

Lizzie turned to Harvey. "This can't happen at our mine."

"Quit acting like a girl." Harvey scoffed. "There're lots of things you shouldn't see, but if you're bull-headed enough to be here, you have to swallow it." He pushed past her toward the headframe and climbed into an ore bucket the hoist man held steady.

She ran after him. "But how do they get the mules out?"

A bitter smile stiffened his lips as they lowered him into the shaft. "They don't come out until they die."

"That's brutal, Harvey," she yelled. "Cruel and heartless." But he disappeared. Shaking with anger, she turned around. The miners shook their heads.

"Come on." Jenkins grabbed her arm. "I'll take you back to town."

She jerked away.

"I didn't leave everything behind to sit in a strange flat and do nothing." Her knees locked. "I'm staying, Mr. Jenkins. Put me to work."

He lifted his hard boil and wiped grimy sweat off his brow. "Chin Lin Sou is over in the sorting shed. He'll show you what to do."

Chin. Her temples throbbed. "Can't I work on my own?"

He shook his head. "If you stay, you work with Chin."

Shoving her fist into her pocket, she ran her rosary through her fingers and stepped toward the shack. She stopped at the door, heart pounding in her throat.

"Go on now," Jenkins said. "He doesn't bite."

Pulling open the splintered handle, she peered into the darkness, smelling minerals, laundry soap, and tobacco. Those same bear claws dug into Chin's chest. Maybe he'd killed a bear for them.

Chinaman. Chink. Celestial...offensive terms folks called Chinese men imported for labor.

"Jenkins sent me to sort ore." She hiccupped, throat tightening. "You understand English?"

He separated rocks into three burlap bags. "Gold rocks here. Silver here. Rest there."

"I'm not afraid of the Chinese, if that's what you think." Though, in truth, she was petrified. She'd never seen a Chinese person and now she worked with one.

"Then we're even." He bared white teeth. "I'm not afraid of Lady."

Pulse drumming in her ears, she forced herself to sort rocks in the dusty twilight of the shack, watching Chin watch her, strange blue eyes glued to her every move. Was he suspicious because she was a woman? Two eyes, two hands, the desire to work, what was so different between them? The irony wasn't lost on her.

Hours later, her back cramped from bending over. Black dust coated her larynx. She choked and gasped, sucking for air, desperate to free her clogged throat.

A large hand covered her face, smothering her with a handkerchief.

She panicked, kicking and screaming as loud as she could. "Harvey! Jenkins! Save me!"

Chin jumped back, holding the handkerchief over his nose like a bandit. "See, Lady? Mask helps with the dust."

"You were helping me breathe?"

Jenkins pushed open the door. "Something wrong, Mrs. Doe?"

She coughed, embarrassed. "Coughing fit, that's all."

Chin handed her a tin cup of water, and she drank it sheepishly.

"I want to show you something," Jenkins said. He led her to the headframe above the shaft and climbed into the ore bucket. Reaching for her, he smiled like the devil inviting her to hell.

The smell of dank earth made her skin crawl. "No thank you, Jenkins." She turned away. "I should get back to my job."

"Thought you wanted to be a hard-rock miner," Jenkins teased.

"I don't need to climb under a mountain of rock to help." She walked back to the shed. Yet, Jenkins was offering exactly what she'd longed for, a chance to be part of the Fourth of July. If she wanted safe, she should have stayed in Oshkosh.

She ran to the headframe. "Wait, I'm coming."

Climbing into the bucket, she gripped the sides for dear life, as the rope lowered them into the darkness. The temperature plummeted, raising goose bumps on her arms. A wet mineral smell clung to her sinuses, and her stomach somersaulted. The bucket hit bottom with a jolt.

Lanterns lit halos along a chiseled tunnel creating a spellbinding sanctuary. She was witnessing God's creation from the beginning of time. Molten minerals mixed together, then hardened to precious ores deep within Mother Earth. A netherworld of which she'd never dreamed, now held the answers to her future. Adrenaline pumped through her veins. This was where fortunes were discovered or lost. Would they strike it big, or go bust like so many?

A sharp bray broke her spell. "These poor mules will never feel the warmth of the sun or smell fresh grass again," she whispered.

"They get used to it," Jenkins said.

A crack of steel on rock jabbed her eardrums. Barely visible by candlelight, she made out Harvey at the end of the tunnel holding a drill steel in place. His brawny partner battered the steel with an eight-pound hammer, pelting rocks at them.

No wonder Harvey was spent. A lump formed in her throat.

Jenkins leaned to her. "Mighty rich vein they're digging on. Can you see it?"

Harvey's partner hit the drill steel again, and she detected a glimmer which made her shiver.

"That's deep enough," Jenkins told them.

Harvey and his partner scrambled into the mining cage, while a small wiry man plugged a stick of dynamite into the hole.

Jenkins tugged their own rope, and their bucket rose to the surface. Up top, dirt-faced comrades beckoned them to take cover behind trees. "Ten, nine, eight…" they shouted down the seconds. Jenkins found a wide trunk and pushed her behind him.

"Five. Four. Three."

She glimpsed Harvey in the clearing. "Take cover," she yelled, but he waved her off.

"Two. One."

Nothing. A full minute in silence.

"The fuse must have gone out." Harvey shrugged and walked to the shaft.

"Don't go out there," she yelled.

A low rumble rippled underground and broke through the earth's crust with a thunderous explosion. Boulders erupted from deep within the mountain, spiraling in every direction, raining rocks on her head.

Harvey's body shot through the air and splatted against a cedar. She jumped up, but Jenkins held her back. Breaking away, she ran to him, ground quaking and rumbling.

"Darling, are you hurt?" No answer. She picked up his head, wet and sticky with blood. Suddenly, she was back in Oshkosh, at that picnic by the stream, his head resting in her lap. The golden boy with a gold mine, the answer to all her problems.

"Lizzie?" His eyes flickered open. "Lizzie are you alright?" His head fell back on her breast, and she rocked him.

"Dear God, what have I done?" Her gut wrenched. "What have I done to you, Harvey?"

When the last blast subsided, she heard the mules scream.

The mine closed for a day, and she soaked Harvey's gashes and bruises in lavender salt. She made a picnic by the waterfall. Harvey couldn't hear for the ringing in his ears but seemed to relax in her arms. Deer came to quench their thirst in the pool, and the aspen glittered like golden coins in the setting sun. When Harvey fell asleep in her lap, she watched the moon and stars rise, bright and promising as they'd ever been. They were in this together, no matter what.

They waited at the window for the assay clerk to weigh their ore. Lizzie had taken over sorting, so Chin could manage his men. Now, Harvey would see the difference her efforts made.

The clerk counted money into her hand. "One hundred sixteen dollars, Missus Doe."

"Are you sure?" The sum would barely cover expenses. "What about that big gold nugget?"

"Turned out to be pyrite. Better luck next week." He closed the assay window in their faces.

Harvey gnawed a hangnail, while Lizzie swallowed hard and tucked five dollars in her pocket for her family. Of course, Mam thanked her for sending money but never failed to ask if Lizzie couldn't send more, like she was holding out on them. The burden weighed heavy on her.

They walked back to the wagon where the miners waited to be paid, jockeying for position, sprucing up the best they could.

"Don't spend it all tonight, Stefan." She handed him ten dollars.

"I'll try not to, but the dealers are slick, and I'm still learning faro."

"Just realized who you remind me of," Jenkins said, rubbing three-day whiskers. "My neice back in Oklahoma. Same big round eyes."

"Eyes like a baby deer." Günter buttoned his pay in his pocket.

"A female deer is a doe," Lizzie instructed.

"Then you look like a baby doe," he said.

"Baby Doe," Jenkins nodded. "The name suits you."

"Baby Doe," Stefan repeated. "We've got the prettiest girl in Central City."

"It's *me* who's got the prettiest girl in Central," Harvey said. "Don't you hooligans forget it." He yanked her toward home.

"Let them have their fun. God knows they work hard enough." She squeezed his hand, trying to lighten his mood.

"Hard rock mining's a heck of a lot tougher than sluice-box mining," he said, as they climbed the stairs to their apartment. "Father has no idea what I'm up against, tunneling into granite, mucking out rock by the ton, moving mountains to get the gold." He opened the door, and she felt the wood stove. Stone cold. Lighting new kindling, she lifted a pot of chicken from the icebox to the stove top, then rifled through the mail.

"Hey, you haven't read your mother's letter." Lizzie gave it to him, and he tore it open.

"Why didn't you tell me I had a letter?" As he read, his eyes grew wide, and he smiled. "How fast can you get us ready? Mother got me a job in Denver for the winter."

"But the mine just got going. What about the miners?" What about money for her family?

"Damn, woman. Do you have to ruin everything?" He grabbed his coat and jerked open the door. "I'm telling Jenkins we're shutting down for the winter."

Lizzie sat down, chin in her calloused palms. She was as dog tired as Harvey. Maybe a break would do them all good. Denver, the Mile High City, sounded like heaven about now.

By his third week in Denver, Lizzie had ironed all the suits Harvey hadn't worn since Oshkosh and found his favorite red polka-dot bowtie. Her husband looked more dapper than ever. She kissed him and handed him a lunch sack of boiled ham and candied ginger, delicacies from Larimer Street. Seeing Harvey happy again eased her guilt of leaving the mine early, and his generous salary meant she could send more money to her family. Mam wrote that her contribution would pay for Christmas dinner, and Da found a part-time job with another tailor.

After cleaning their flat, Lizzie dressed in a rose-colored frock from her trousseau, a pleasure she never allowed herself in Central City. What a shame she had to cover the dress with Claudia's hand-me-down overcoat.

Heavy snow fell, and gusts of wind blew up her skirt, making her wish for her long johns. She stopped by Churchill's to see if Harvey wanted to splurge and have supper out. The sophisticated products for sale at Churchill's put McFarland's to shame: Ellis & Flint Oysters, Towles' Log Cabin Syrup, cherry toothpaste patronized by the Queen, fine brandies, Irish wool.

"Ah, Mrs. Doe, a sight for sore eyes." Mr. Churchill wiped his hands on his shop apron, embroidered with Churchill's logo. "I just sent a letter to Oshkosh about Harvey's performance."

Her stomach fell. "I'll talk to him, Mr. Churchill. Whatever it is, I'll take care of it."

The shopkeeper laughed. "On the contrary, my dear. I wrote, 'Harvey's charming personality makes him a favorite among customers.'"

"I'm sure Mr. Doe will be pleased." She glanced past him. "Is Harvey in the storeroom?"

"Oh, he left early." He folded a denim shirt. "Mr. O'Toole wanted to hear him play piano, so they went to Gahan's Saloon."

Why didn't he fetch her? Harvey spent all his free time at Gahan's, playing popular tunes at their upright piano.

She forced a laugh. "How silly of me. It's Harvey's night out. What am I thinking?"

"No need to worry about that boy." Mr. Churchill swept the floor. "You should hear how he talks about you. Baby Doe, the Belle of Central City, he says."

Baby Doe, the name he loathed. She gritted her teeth. "Nice to see you, Mr. Churchill." Pushing the door, glacial air seared her cheeks.

Marquee lights blazed on the theater down the street, and she went to see what vaudeville act was playing. In the flush years before the Oshkosh fires, Da had built a playhouse next to his haberdashery, and she'd fallen in love with theater. Lizzie acted, while her brother was stage manager. Peter loved to play practical jokes, like when he pretended the curtain wouldn't close, and she was forced to curtsy until the audience tired of clapping.

"Sorry, no work for extras." A brocade-vested man polished glass on a Vaudeville poster.

She pulled her shoulders back. "Excuse me?"

The man did a double take and smiled broadly. "We don't need extras this week, but if we did, I'd sure hire you."

Light flashed from across the street as a mirrored doorway opened, catching the last rays of sunlight. Harvey rushed out, red polka dot bowtie dangling, pulling on his overcoat against the blowing snow. Tugging his bowler low, he checked right and left, and his eyes stuck on hers. His face turned as red as the revolving light over the door.

Seeing him, Lizzie dropped her handbag, spilling her compact and change purse on the boardwalk. She bent to gather them up, heat flushing through her body.

Harvey dodged a carriage as he crossed the brick street. "Lizzie, what are you doing here? You shouldn't be in this part of town. It's dicey on this part of Larimer." He hustled her away from the mirrored door.

Turning back, she read the sign on the awning. House of Mirrors. Proprietor, Mattie Silks. The same den of iniquity they'd seen from the train when they first pulled into Denver.

"The question is what were *you* doing there?" she said.

"Mr. Churchill gives me a package to deliver on Thursdays," he said, tugging his bowler.

"Oh, really? Mr. Churchill said you were at Gahan's."

His cheeks splotched red. "Now you know what I have to put up with. The poor fellow is losing his marbles."

"What does House of Mirrors buy from Churchill's?"

"I don't know...all sorts of things," he sputtered and tugged her along. “Soap and perfume, I suppose. The ladies look forward to it.”

“The ladies?” She stopped him, tugged his lose tie. “Why is your tie undone?”

“They were teasing me. You know, razzing the delivery boy?” He gulped. “All I wanted was a signature for the package, but they were cooing and smiling, running their fingers through my hair. What was I supposed to do? The ladies are customers.”

“They’re no ladies, Harvey.” She tied his tie tight, not to be undone again. “Tell Mr. Churchill to find someone else to deliver to House of Mirrors, understood?”

9

Leadville, Colorado, October 1878

"That town meeting would have lasted till midnight if you hadn't rescued me," Tabor said to Bush as they passed Tabor Mercantile. The new manager was climbing the ladder to turn off the gas lamps. That used to be Tabor's job and sometimes, afterwards, he'd watch the sunset with Augusta. Hadn't watched a sunset with her in a coon's age, too busy with their own lives. He missed those sunsets, a riot of color or pastel silhouettes of clouds and mountains.

Bush stepped off the boardwalk.

"Where are we going?" Tabor asked.

"Tabor Mining Exchange," he grumbled. "Senator Chaffee and that hot-shot banker showed up, demanding I fetch you like I was a trick dog."

"Like them, much?" Tabor quipped.

"They sniff around you like bloodhounds tracking a wild boar."

"Then cook the bloodhounds a steak." Tabor needed to set him straight. "Turnbull and Chaffee put my mines on the stock market, and that's what's funding our new hotel."

Bush tipped his gambler skimmer. "Boar steaks, coming right up, Boss."

Tabor smiled, pleased to have him by his side. "Ah, Billy, the world has changed, and we need to change with it. Mining used to mean swirling a pan on a mountain stream. Now it means selling stock, investors, dividends, politics and greased palms…not much about the actual silver. We need Chaffee and Turnbull to navigate those treacherous waters."

Pulling open double doors carved with bulls and bears, Tabor breathed in tanned leather and beeswax wood polish. He'd built the Mining Exchange as a private club for mine owners to discuss issues: mine safety, unions, and East Coast bankers who lobbied to demonetize silver to inflate gold prices. His hand ran along the brass railing of the oak bar, boasting imported liquors waiting to be poured into lead-crystal tumblers. Beveled mirrors reflected tufted red leather furniture, and a fire blazed in the stone hearth.

The banker, Turnbull, and Senator Chaffee played poker at a game table, inhaling Tabor's fine Virginia cigars. Turnbull chomped on his, extracting tobacco like an exotic salad.

By contrast, Senator Chaffee appeared the consummate statesman. His top hat sat on the sideboard, and his white hair shone in the firelight, his mustache meticulously groomed. His oval lenses reflected a pair of jacks. Tabor always won when he played the senator.

"Ah, the Silver King, himself." Chaffee laid down his cards.

"Hail the King." Turnbull exhaled blue smoke and coughed.

"Billy, fetch the tequila," he said. "We're in Lusty Leadville, for God's sake. Get rid of the nooses around your necks and kick up your heels."

"The situation in Washington is dire, Mayor Tabor." Chaffee lowered his patrician cheekbones to peer above his lenses. "The Silver Purchase Act is in danger of being repealed."

"Not going to happen," Tabor said. "Silver pulled us out of the depression and built railroads across this land. Just ask farmers and factory owners; they need silver to fuel the economy. And America's rich with silver."

Turnbull's jowls reddened. "Open your eyes. World trade is demanding gold, not silver. If the president vetoes the Silver Purchase Act, silver won't be worth the expense to mine it."

"East Coast Republicans are against silver," Chaffee said. "We need a strong Republican Party in the west to change their minds. If you want to keep your fortune, you'll run for governor."

Tabor threw back a tequila, feeling it burn his gullet.

"People trust you," Chaffee said. "Pulled yourself up by your bootstraps from prospector to shopkeeper to millionaire. Look what you've done with Leadville since you've been mayor."

"Sorry, my mines need attention." Soon they'd elect a new mayor, and he'd pursue mining full bore. He needed to lighten this conversation. "Say, know what happened to the Republican when he knocked on the pearly gates?"

They puffed their cigars impatiently.

"Saint Peter told the Republican he could choose between heaven or hell. So, first, he goes down to hell, and his Republican friends are playing cards and drinking whiskey. Beautiful women serve oysters and steaks, and the devil cracks jokes."

Turnbull downed a second tequila.

"The next day, he visits heaven and sings with the angels." Tabor grinned. "When Saint Peter asks the Republican where he wants to go, he says he'll go to hell with his friends. And presto—" He snapped his fingers. "He's in hell, but it's a burning shambles. His friends wear rags, the women are hags, the food's moldy, the drinks rotgut. So, the Republican asks, 'What happened since yesterday?' The Devil says, 'Yesterday, I was campaigning. Today, you voted for me."

Turnbull choked on his whiskey.

"Run for governor, Tabor," Chaffee said.

He lit a cigar. "Barking up the wrong tree, boys." No way could he lead the state. Sure, things had improved lately, but Bad Luck Tabor lurked over his shoulder, waiting to take him down.

Bush nodded at Turnbull. "These men are offering you power over your own fate, Boss."

His hackles reared up. "That was me saying no, wasn't it, Billy?"

"You said you wanted to outrun your bad luck," Bush said. "Here's your chance."

Tabor's teeth clenched together. How could Billy expose him like that?

"No one else can save silver from certain death." Chaffee's cool eyes assessed him.

Fire ignited in his belly to fight for silver: what it meant for America and for himself. Silver had given him power over his fate, Desire popped and crackled below his ribcage. It was a fight he wasn't prepared for, a fight he might lose.

"You boys are giving me heartburn. Got any honey, Billy?" What about his fifty-or-so mines that needed him sorely?

His friend brought him a piece of honeycomb from behind the bar. The golden wax tasted tangy and sweet. "Sorry, gentleman." He licked his fingers, smiling. "Hell, my wife would leave me if I take on another darn thing." Expecting a laugh, he got none.

Turnbull stood over him. "Your wife? That's your lame excuse?"

"Let's all calm down." Chaffee pulled the banker to his seat. "The convention's next week. Just let me introduce you to some folks."

"Sorry, boys, can't make it. But let me help out another way." He nodded to Billy. "Write these gentlemen a check for five-thousand to the Republican Party of Colorado."

Senator Chaffee clinked his glass. But Turnbull followed Bush to the roll-top desk, slipping a hundred-dollar bill in his coat pocket.

After the politicians left, Tabor turned to Bush. "What was the hundred for?"

"Hell if I know." His eyes shifted. "But I never refuse a hundo thrown my way. Do you?"

"Silver miners are responsible for the vast wealth of this country." Tabor pounded his fist on the podium at the Republican Convention. "But we're treated like second-class citizens. Miners deserve health insurance and pensions. And, we need to keep the value of silver strong, so miners make an honest wage." Delegates cheered and whistled.

His heart thrashed like a bobcat in a trap. When he refused to run for governor, they begged him to run for lieutenant governor. Augusta was all for it, since she'd taken up with the Pioneer Ladies Society, serving punch in the back of the ballroom. Felt good to have her on his side for a change.

Close to the stage, Senator Chaffee, Turnbull, and the new gubernatorial candidate, Frederick Pitkin, stared at him like the goose who laid golden eggs. Of course, the Republicans needed his money, but they sure-as-hell didn't need a broken-down miner for lieutenant governor.

He continued his speech. "But, if you doubt what we can do for miners, just take a look at Leadville, which grew from a mining camp to a city of forty thousand in three years." His pulse pounded in his throat. "Now, we have sheriffs and a jail, a fire house, gas lights, telephones, banks, running water, and garbage collection."

Waves of applause washed over him as he made his way down the platform.

Pitkin shook his hand, his palm as soft as Augusta's churned butter. "Mayor Tabor, I'd be pleased if we could be partners."

"Hold on there, Pitkin. I already have a wife," Tabor deadpanned. "But if you'll promise to hold your tongue better'n she does, I'll join the ticket as lieutenant governor."

Pitkin coughed. "I heard you're from back east, too. I was a Wesleyan crew paddler while I earned my undergraduate. My law degree is from Albany Law School. Where do you hail from?"

"I was hailing gold from the South Platte River, while you were paddling through college."

"Ah, yes, a prospector. God blessed you with mines in Leadville."

"Well, if God showed up as two German prospectors needing a handout, then, yes, God blessed me." His humor stank like a sulfur geyser, and just as unpredictable. "Don't get me wrong. I'm a church-going man. Hell's bells. I've donated to every damn church in Leadville."

"All the silver in the world can't buy a ticket to heaven." Pitkin's tiny eyes pierced him. "If you're the great savior of the West, why couldn't you stop the Utes from killing two dozen soldiers near the Continental Divide?"

"If you are talking about the Meeker Massacre, white men were the savages there."

Pitkin's face flashed red. "You're calling our soldiers savages?"

"First off, we sent Preacher Meeker to the Ute reservation with no experience and even less sense. Meeker plowed under the Ute's sacred buffalo hunting grounds and forced them to farm it. When the Utes refused, he called in the cavalry. Hundreds of soldiers descended on the reservation, guns blazing." He shrugged. "The Utes just defended themselves."

Pitkin yanked Chaffee's sleeve. "This redneck mountain man can't be trusted to run a state."

"What state are you talking about, Pitkin?" he said. "I'm talking Colorado, not Connecticut. Tabor *is* Colorado, and a snot-nosed eastern lawyer won't get elected governor without him."

Pitkin's eyes rolled to heaven.

"You look skittish as a newborn colt," Tabor said. "Can I buy you a whiskey?"

Pitkin buttoned his waistcoat. "I don't drink."

Tabor snorted. "Sure you want to take on Colorado? This state is as wild as the Utes and the buffalo, but it's miners who made this country rich with silver. We need to protect their rights."

Chaffee nodded. "No one says it better than you, Tabor."

"You need someone who speaks their language," Turnbull told Pitkin.

Augusta arrived and shoved a newspaper at Tabor. "Horace, why are they calling you a polygamist?"

"Give me that." Pitkin snatched the paper and read.

Tabor shooed it off. "Reporters making up skilamalink."

Pitkin crumpled the newspaper. "What are you trying to pull, Chaffee? Colorado will never be taken seriously if it's lumped with polygamists."

"Tabor is footing the bill of this campaign," Chaffee said.

"For God's sake." Pitkin walked off, and Turnbull and Chaffee chased him.

"Pull out of the race, Horace," Augusta said. "I won't have you destroy the Tabor name."

"Tabor is *my* name, isn't it?" he said, irritated as hell.

She thrashed through the crowd.

He called after her, "My name to do with as I damn well please." Though she didn't turn around, he was sure she heard him. Maybe for the first time ever.

10

Central City, Colorado, March 1879

Tabor took Pitkin to Central City to meet with Senator Teller, Colorado's most influential Republican. They climbed the Teller House steps when a young fellow passed, about Maxcy's age. His bowler topped blond curls framing an innocent face darkened with minerals.

"If you're asking for money, don't count on it," the boy said. "Teller is a tightwad." He walked on, shoulders slumped, hands stuffed in his pockets.

Tabor felt his despair. "I'll be right up," he told Pitkin, and went to find the boy.

Out on the portico, Tabor couldn't see the fellow. The barn across the street advertised *McClary's Livery & Feed, Carriages to Idaho Springs, Pine Creek, Yankee Hill, and all points of interest.* A buggy burst through, the driver snapping the reins. "Out of the way. Got a train to catch." The buggy knocked the boy to the cobblestones, flat on his back, wheezing.

"You all right?" Tabor offered a hand. "Gotta watch where you're going around here."

"I'm *going* to Dostal Alley Saloon." He tried to stand straight, but the task proved too much.

"Are you a miner, Mister…?" Tabor asked.

"Harvey Doe," he said, eyes watering. "*Owner* of the Fourth of

July mine." He winced. "Until the bank shuts us down, that is."

Tabor looked up at Teller's office, the lamplight lit. "I have a meeting right now, but I'd like to talk about your mine."

"You know where to find me." He hobbled down the road.

Tabor joined Teller and Pitkin but kept picturing poor Harvey Doe. One more broken-hearted man who'd come west for a dream that eluded him. Tabor had a soft spot for down-on-their-luck prospectors, seeing as he'd been one most of his life. An hour passed before he could duck out of the meeting.

When he found Harvey, he wished he hadn't. Skunked and slurring, the young man spewed self-pity to anyone who'd listen. Didn't even notice when Tabor sat on the next barstool and ordered a sarsaparilla.

"The miners think *Baby Doe* is one of those patron saints," Harvey whined. "It's her fault they don't work harder, mooning around her. So damn humiliating watching her work in the mine, dirt-faced, dressed in overalls."

"Tell me something new, Harvey." The barkeep chiseled his molars with an ice pick.

"They think Baby Doe can do no wrong," Harvey said. "The assay man teaches her to get extra yield out of the ore. The smelter processes her ore first. When our miners quit for higher wages, she's the only one who can convince them to come back."

"Sounds like quite a woman," Tabor said.

"Who assed you?" Harvey nudged the man on his other side, dressed in chaps and vest. "You don't look like an undertaker, Cady. Anyone tell you that?"

"Two tequilas," Cady ordered. "You have to chase that beer with tequila."

"It's the other way around," Harvey said, taking another gulp.

"Couple of these and you won't care who chases who." Cady tipped his glass to a moose-faced dancehall girl. "And you won't care what she looks like, neither."

Harvey tossed down the shot. "Whoa. Burns my eardrums."

Rubbed his ears. “Dynamite destroyed them, ringing so loud it wakes me up.”

“I wouldn’t complain about waking up aside Baby Doe,” Cady said.

“Stuff it, Cady.” Harvey’s forehead plunked down on the sticky bar.

Tabor tried to lift him. “Where does he live? I’ll take him home.”

The bartender shook his head. “Let him sleep it off. Wouldn’t want his wife to have to deal with him like this.”

Harvey’s curls soaked up beer on the bar.

Anguish oozed from Tabor’s gut, remembering his father’s head laying in a puddle. But there was no saving Pa, no matter what he’d tried. Maybe, this fellow was not too far gone. He tucked a business card into Harvey’s coat pocket.

Since Harvey was meeting with Senator Teller, Baby Doe took over his job of hauling slag in a wheel-barrow, only able to remove half as much as he usually did. She prayed he secured the loan from Teller, because they’d run out of dynamite and couldn’t break through to the new vein.

When Harvey didn’t show up for dinner, she ate by the window, watching for him in the path from Dostal Alley, even darker on the moonless night. He’d frequented the saloon since they’d come back to Central. Liquor turned him into a grizzly at night and a sloth during the day.

Hearing a commotion outside, she tried to get a better view. A wild animal with ferocious antlers attacked his prey below. Hooves stamped, heaving great clouds of dust. With a loud hissing and clicking, the animal’s body undulated faster and faster until it seemed to burst into flames, tramping around a huddled victim. With a flash it disappeared, leaving a plume of smoke.

What kind of animal was that? A lone figure crawled down the path.

"Harvey?" She ran down the steps and helped him up, smelling of horse muck and beer. He doubled over and retched.

She helped him upstairs. "What was that thing?"

"He said, be good to lady."

"It spoke to you?"

"Said he'll kill me next time." He lurched and retched again.

Drunk talk. She hoisted him up to the apartment and flopped him into bed. Maybe it was a bear? With antlers? Undressing him, she found a card in his pocket. Mayor Horace Tabor, Leadville.

The Silver King was at the Teller meeting?

Soon, Harvey was snoring. Wondering about Tabor, she undressed and backed into bed.

Harvey flailed his arms around her, and she felt him hard against her backside. He moved onto her body, searching, kneading, pinching.

"Stop it, Harvey. You're hurting me." Kerosene on a flame.

He pulled her hair back and plunged into her. "No one else has this *Baby Doe*. This Baby Doe is all mine."

She should have bought the sponge at McFarland's.

In the morning, Harvey couldn't recall the animal attack, but admitted he didn't get the loan.

"Was Horace Tabor at the Teller House?" She showed him the business card.

Harvey grimaced. "I seem to remember his showy mustache."

She slipped the card in her drawer, hoping Tabor's luck would rub off on her.

After church service, Mrs. Teller announced a fundraising campaign for a new Central City Opera House featuring music from the miner's homelands of Wales, Ireland, and Germany. With her love of theater, Baby Doe was first to volunteer. Afterall, the miners were as homesick for their Motherlands as she was. Moved by their sad songs, folktales, and wistful stories of their mothers and lovers, Baby Doe knew the opera house would bring them a piece of home. Maybe for her, too.

Crossing Lawrence Street with Mrs. Teller's plans under her arm, she rehearsed her sales pitch, oblivious to the hubbub of wagons, buggies, and horses. Her dainty heel stuck in the rutted road and she fell. A strong arm swept her up, bringing her inches from enormous brown eyes.

"Oh, my goodness." A twinge shot through her ankle and she faltered, clutching the drawings. "Ow. Must have twisted it."

Smelling of chalk and roasted coffee beans, he carried her to the Shoofly Saloon.

"Not a saloon. Who do you think I am, Mister?"

He whisked her into the dark interior and set her down on a settee. "Richcreek, you here?"

A double-chinned man barged through a swinging door holding his blood-drenched hands high. Startled, he wiped his hands on his apron. "Sorry. Just butchering a deer."

"Mrs. Doe turned her ankle in the street."

Mrs. Doe. He knew her name.

Richcreek left and returned with ice and a clean bar towel. "I sent my dish washer to fetch Doctor Wilson."

Her rescuer examined her ankle with his fingertips, which hurt like the dickens. His jaunty derby hid most of his fine dark waves. A dotted silk vest and plaid four-in-hand tie set off his sack suit to perfection, totally out of place for a mining camp. He was a gentleman, like Da.

"How do you know who I am?" she asked.

"All due respect, ma'am." His eyes shied away like she was too bright to look at. "Central City doesn't have women like you." He wrapped ice around her swelling ankle with care. A lock of hair fell softly on his olive-skinned forehead.

"We all know who you are." Richcreek held out a plate of fried doughnuts dipped in sugar. The aroma made her stomach gurgle.

"You gentlemen have me at a disadvantage." She took a donut. "Mr. Richcreek, is it?" The sugar tantalized her. "Oh my, delicious." She licked her fingers. "But who are you?"

"Jacob Sandelowski, but everyone calls me Jake Sands."

"Ah…" The Jewish man Kitty was sweet on. She could see why. "Sands Haberdashery?"

He tugged his lapels. "Finest clothing in the West."

"I was coming to see you." She raised the plans. "I'm raising funds for the opera house."

Sands shook his head. "Who'd go to opera in Central City?"

"Not just opera. Vaudeville, plays, musical reviews, magic shows."

The door burst open, daylight shone through bandy legs. "Someone call for a doctor?" His whiskey voice grated on her ears.

"We sent for Doctor Wilson," Richcreek said.

"Got a problem with me?" His hand hovered near his gun holster.

Sands stood by her, strong and steadfast.

Richcreek's brow sprouted sweat. "The young lady's ankle looks mighty poorly."

The intruder zigzagged toward them, duster coat flaring behind. He sat by her feet, staring at her with rheumy eyes. "Well, if it isn't Baby Doe, Belle of Central City."

She frowned. Sounded like the title on a dime novel.

He adjusted his holster with a shaky hand. "I'm Doc Holliday."

Sands moved closer.

"The gunfighter in the newspapers?" She'd read such grisly tales about the desperado.

"I'm harmless, unless you cheat at cards." Doc held her foot and bent it up.

"Ow."

"Now rotate it."

She winced.

"Not broken, but too sore to walk for a good while. Keep it iced and elevated." He coughed and spit blood into his handkerchief. "Double whiskey, Richcreek." He noticed the rolled-up parchment in her hand. "Whacha got there?"

"Plans for the Central City Opera House."

"My mother sang in the opry." His raspy voice almost purred.

She spread the drawing on the table, pointing out the curved balustrade, private boxes, and ample stage. "A Denver architect designed it."

Yellow dew oozed from Doc's pores. Between whiskeys, he gulped from a laudanum bottle.

Her stomach clenched remembering the last article she read. Reportedly, Doc Holliday had warned a card shark to stop peeking at the discard pile. When he refused, Doc jabbed a knife in his abdomen and spilled his entrails to the floor.

"I love opry," Doc said, rubbing the handle of his six-shooter. "How much do you need?"

She cleared her throat. "We're asking each business for five hundred dollars."

Sands scoffed. "You'll have a hard time squeezing that kind of money."

Doc drew his gun and spun it on his trigger finger. She felt Sands stiffen.

"How about a game of faro?" Doc said. "Losers donate to the opera house."

"That's generous of you, but—"

Doc flicked his gun at Richcreek. "Deal the cards."

Richcreek dealt, and color drained from Sands' face.

Only when Doc drew the winning card, did he replace his gun in the holster, his bushy mustache hiding a devious smile.

"Pay the lady, boys." He rolled up the architect drawing, put it under his arm, and stood.

"I need to take the plan back." She reached for them.

But Doc swaggered out with those bandy legs, waving without

turning around.

"What's he going to do with those drawings?" she said.

"No telling." Sands blinked long eyelashes, longer than a man had the right to. "Doc's clock is ticking. Tuberculosis does strange things to a man."

Her ankle throbbed. "I better get home. My husband will wonder why church took so long."

With Sands' arm firmly around her waist, she hobbled out the door.

They passed St. James Methodist just as the preacher's daughters stepped out.

"Velma and Kitty, so nice to see you," she said.

Kitty glared at Sands' arm around her. "You stole my—but he's Jewish and you're Catholic. And you're married." She stepped backward, pointing. "You, you, you…harlot." Lifting her skirts, she ran inside the church.

"You can burn in hell." Velma wagged her finger and went after her sister.

Baby Doe's stomach hardened against their attack. Much as she'd tried, these women had never really been friends. For better or worse, she'd chosen her path, and it didn't include them.

"What was that all about?" Sands held her tighter.

"Sounded like religion, didn't it?" Something twinged in her belly. "Where can I find Doc?"

11

Leadville, Colorado, July 1879

While Bush snoozed under his gambler skimmer, Tabor drove the buggy down to city hall, wrestling with misgivings about moving to Denver to be lieutenant governor. How could he leave the Rocky Mountains? He'd come here with a gold pan and a dream to put *Bad Luck Tabor* behind him for good. How long would his luck last when he left?

He drew the alpine air deep into his lungs, scented with blue spruce, columbine, sage and freedom. "I'll miss this air when we move."

Bush raised an eyelid. "You can order air whenever you want, now that you're lieutenant governor."

He laughed. "Thank the Lord."

Bush picked up *The Denver Tribune,* which arrived by Pony Express each morning. "Whoa, did you read the front page? 'Mayor Tabor leaves Leadville with an organized government, bricked streets, gas and water works. We hope he delivers such prosperity to the rest of Colorado.'"

"I could do with a little sainthood," Tabor said, noticing his friend's green gills. "You must have burned the midnight oil after I left." There'd been something about that woman at the Silver Dollar last night. Lorinda. Her black hair and pale skin attracted and repulsed Tabor, reminding him of his mother who left him so long ago. She even walked like his mother, cat-like and seductive.

But the more tantalizing Lorinda became, the more he avoided her.

"Why'd you leave?" Bush straightened his bolo tie. "Lorinda and Elsie danced the flamenco, roses in their teeth, taps on their shoes, a dervish of carnal excess."

"The finale was too much." The whirling scene had turned lurid when the women fell together, lips hungry for each other. "I had to get out of there." Why did his mind replay that old fabricated memory? Just a child when he opened the pantry door, there was his mother, stained lips and ivory skin pressed against another woman. He loathed the lurid fantasy.

"At least you could have kept me company," Bush said.

"Need an alibi for your wife?" Tabor jerked the reins.

"Don't cry for Marianne. She's got everything she wants. Beautiful home, three daughters."

"Ah Billy, what it must feel like to be you, without a concern in the world."

"We're cut from different cloth. You live to make a better world. And I live to live it up."

Tabor laughed. "You can twist the rattle off a snake and call it a massage."

A crowd gathered at City Hall to pay tribute to him. Miners, bankers, businessmen, firemen on the fire wagon he'd donated, Tabor Electric workers, the Carbonite Chronical reporter, churchgoers, even red-light girls. He swallowed hard, searching the crowd for Augusta and Maxcy.

The horns of the Elks' band squawked in the morning breeze. The city board lined up to shake his hand, men who'd supported him during the tough first years of Leadville. Last in line was Father O'Mannie, eyes brimming. "You moved heaven and earth to make us proud of Leadville."

Six white horses pranced down the cobblestone street pulling a wagon festooned with roses. Maxcy sat on the bench behind the driver. "Take the seat of honor, Pa. It's your shining hour."

"Where's your mother?"

"She'll meet us later." Maxcy pulled him aboard. "The whole city's here to honor you."

Except Augusta. A hollow tribute without his wife by his side. She was still stewing about the polygamy claim like it was his fault. If she saw this, her frown would change into a smile…but she was home, probably darning socks.

The parade stopped at the grange. Men slaved over smoking barbeque pits, and the smell of molasses on roast hog made him hungry. Children scampered through a hay-bale maze. Pumpkins and gourds decorated long tables. Scarecrows perched gaily in the corners. Swaths of orange calico scalloped the rafters. The Elks' band broke into a polka, and ladies lined the walls, eager to dance.

"Where'd you run off to last night?" Lorinda whispered in his ear. "Come on. They're waiting for the guest of honor to start the dancing." The temptress pulled him into the middle, black hair caressing her bare shoulders. The music lifted his spirits, not to mention the alluring Lorinda in his arms, dancing, laughing, so full of life. Soon the floor swirled with ladies and Cavalry men.

When the song ended, he walked Lorinda off the dance floor.

"I'll get us some punch." Her fluttering eyelashes clumped like mating mosquitoes. He watched the swish of her hips until a finger jabbed his side.

"And you wonder why they think you're a polygamist," Augusta said.

His brain muddled. "Certainly, you don't think—"

"It's in your bones to philander, I suppose."

He grabbed her shoulders square. "Don't say things you don't mean."

Her lips trembled. "Your mother left your pa, didn't she?"

A rabbit kick to his gut. "You think I'll leave you?" He pulled her close, her taut body quivering. "I'm here, Augusta. I'm not going anywhere."

12

Central City, Colorado, September 1879

Feeling nauseous and plum out of energy, Baby Doe paid a professional call to Doc Holliday at the Teller House.

"You're pregnant," Doc said, confirming her suspicion.

Afterward, she tiptoed down the back stairs, her knees quivering so badly she feared she'd tumble head-over-heels into the saloon below.

Doc's heavy boots clomped on the steps behind her. "You forgot this." He handed her the architect drawing. "I turned over thirteen thousand dollars in your name."

She clutched the railing, her head fuzzy and throbbing. "For the opera house?"

Doc twirled his six-shooter. "Fancy gun slingin' and a few faro wagers, and we've got ourselves an opry house."

"That's incredible, Doc." Her head spinning, she faltered and lost her balance.

"Easy now, little filly." He helped her reach the bottom stair.

She clutched the railing, head pounding and utterly drained.

"Go home and get in bed," he said, and swaggered to the bar.

She teetered through the lobby, woozy, skin filmy with sweat. A kaleidoscope pattern dissolved her vision, and her limbs gave out, falling to the floor.

A harsh odor scoured her sinuses. A blurred form waved

smelling salts under her nose. Gambler hat, bolo tie, furrowed brow…William Bush?

Behind him, a door opened, and Marianne appeared. "William, they're ready to start. Heavens to mergatroid." She retreated, slamming the door behind her.

"How do you feel?" Bush laid his cool hand on Baby Doe's forehead.

"I must have fainted." Then she remembered her diagnoses and shuddered.

"Let's get you out of the saloon." He helped her into a meeting room filled with town folk and set her in a chair by the door. "Rest here awhile, then I'll drive you home."

Marianne's glare burned across the room, making her feel even hotter in the stuffy room.

William Bush introduced the speaker, Lucy Stone from the *Suffrage Journal*, a simple woman with a bun of dark hair and wearing a plain muslin dress.

"Young women today have no idea the price that has been paid for rights we take for granted." Her passion shone through her mousy appearance. "The right to education and free speech was hard fought by brave women. When Mrs. Tyndall of Philadelphia increased her husband's Chinaware business, sending ships to China and enlarging warehouses, the fact was quoted as a wonder. And when Doctor Elizabeth Blackwell hung her shingle in New York City she blazed a trail for women physicians. Women have gained the right to education and to participate in most professions." She pulled back her shoulders. "Now, we must fight for the right to vote."

Baby Doe clapped, amazed at this woman's fire. Why shouldn't women vote when the outcome affects women as much as men?

A man jumped up. "A woman's place is in the home."

The audience spoke all at once.

"Women's vote will sink the men's vote and there'll be chaos."

A rotten tomato landed on Lucy's chest. She raised her fist, eyes flashing. "Fight for the women's vote."

Bush shuttled Lucy out. "Better save your talk for city folks."

Baby Doe followed them out to the lobby, still dizzy and holding the wall.

"We won't back down until women are equal," Lucy said.

Women are equal. Women are equal. Women are equal. The idea thrummed through Baby Doe's head like a rosary, giving her strength and courage.

"I told you to stay in bed." Doc Holliday grabbed her arm and ushered her out the door.

Bush's eyes tracked her, probably thinking the worst.

With no loan from Teller, the Does were forced to move to a cheaper room in Blackhawk, the smelting town by the railroad tracks. Dirtier. Lonelier. Uglier. The constant clank of stamp mills crushing rock fought with the scream of locomotives reverberating off canyon walls. Mining and human waste polluted creek water. Toxic coal dust and sulfur clogged her lungs.

Against Doc's orders, she kept working at the mine until one October afternoon, she cramped and felt blood seeping from her body. She searched for Harvey, but he was down in the shaft, so she hitched a ride on a wagon back home.

She laid on the lumpy straw mattress, feet up on the headboard, as Doc had instructed to save the baby. She had to tell Harvey about the baby now. Maybe the news would lift his spirits. But, she knew it wasn't true. The evening shadows deepened her depression. Soon, she heard the wagon wheels creaking, delivering miners back to Blackhawk.

Harvey pushed the door open and leaned against it. "Where'd you run off to? I needed you at the mine. There was an accident."

Her stomach wrenched. "What happened? Is everyone okay?"

"The east shaft collapsed." He coughed, struggling to catch his breath.

She poured him water, but he waved it away.

"We dug out until dark," he said. "They were gone when we found them."

"What do you mean, gone? Who's gone?" A wave of nausea overwhelmed her, and she collapsed into a chair.

"Jenkins and Stefan died." Harvey fell to his knees. "Lew Cady has the bodies."

She gasped and clutched his nape. "No… it can't be." Gulping air to keep from vomiting. "My God, Harvey. It could have been you. Why was Jenkins down the shaft with Stefan?"

"My asthma got so bad I couldn't breathe."

The horror dawned on her. "You made Jenkins take your place?"

He buried his face in her skirt, wailing. "Father will have a conniption."

She gripped his shoulders and shook him hard. "Stop it, Harvey. You have no right to feel sorry for yourself."

He stood and poured a whisky and drank it down. Then poured another.

She swayed. "They died for *us*."

"They knew the hazards." He picked up an opened envelope, shaking it. "Mother wants me to come home for a few weeks. She's ill."

Lizzie held her burbling stomach. "We can't just leave, Harvey."

"Mother sent one ticket." He held it up, shook his head. "There's no money for another."

"You're not leaving me here." A thrust in her abdomen made her moan.

"Quit whimpering," he said. "There's nothing we can do until I get more money."

She wouldn't tell him about the baby when he acted like this.

"If I take care of Mother, she'll take care of me." He rubbed his fingertips and thumb together. "I'll be back for Christmas dinner and we'll finish what we started."

He was abandoning her. "Do you even love me, Harvey?"

"Of course, but we need more money, and I'm going to get it."

He lifted the trunk to the floor and flopped on the bed. "Quit pouting and send me off with a little sugar."

"You'll get sugar when you come back." She stomped off to the kitchen.

Not a star lit the black sky out the window. She pulled rosary beads through her fingers praying for Stefan and Jenkins. She'd give them proper funerals at St. Mary of the Assumption.

Harvey would be gone at least a month. The baby kicked, and she rubbed her belly. At least she'd have company.

When would the blizzard end? The fire had long since gone out, but the snow had drifted so deeply against her door that Baby Doe couldn't get out to gather more wood. She curled up under her bearskin, clenching her teeth so they wouldn't chatter. The wind shrieked, frightening her. She tried to calm her nerves by talking to the baby. *Don't worry, little one.* The two of them had grown so close, alone in the rattletrap town of Blackhawk.

Her stomach growled. A quarter loaf of bread left, but no cheese, and the water had frozen in the bucket. Must make it through this storm.

A noise on the stairs. *Harvey?* It had only been two weeks. Outside her door, something gnawed and scraped, huffing and growling. She searched for a place to hide, but where?

A tremendous force heaved on the door. Boards bulged but didn't give. Another powerful thrust and the door broke open, slamming into the wall. A towering animal burst into her room bringing the blizzard with it. Vicious antlers flailed about, gnarled hooves stomped the floorboards, bear claws dangling from its neck. Its undulating body shimmied toward her, picking her up. She kicked and screamed, beating the creature's back until it howled.

Jake Sands answered his door and shut it again. The antlered giant forced the door open, barreled across the room, and lay Baby Doe on a settee. His iridescent wings spread wide as he bowed and backed out of the room.

"What the devil was that?" Sands closed the door against the ogre. "Did he hurt you?"

"That's our Chinese foreman, Chin Lin Sou." So strange, how could she explain? "He saw my door snowed in and rescued me." Threading her rosary through her fingers, she gave a prayer of gratitude. Without Chin, she would have frozen before the sun came up.

"Does your foreman always wear that costume?" His mouth twisted.

How outlandish this must be for him, here in his cozy house, playing chess by himself in front of the crackling hearth.

"I don't understand it, but Chin told me the costume brings him extraordinary strength. He embodies the mystical Chinese protector, Pixiu, a winged sea-dragon who craves silver and gold."

"Now I've heard the whole megillah." His eyebrow arched. "But, why did he bring you *here*? Where is your husband?"

"His mother called him back to Oshkosh." Sands frowned, and she realized she made a mistake in asking Chin to bring her here. "I didn't know where else to go," she admitted, shivering in her nightgown and pulling the bearskin under her chin.

Sands brought her a cup of tea and a porcelain pitcher of hot water to bathe. "Take your time. I'll make up the spare room."

Dipping the towel in the water, she felt steam rise and curl her hair. Her belly gurgled with life and she warmed it with her hand. She couldn't go back to that shack tomorrow, or ever.

Sands returned, shielding his eyes. "Mrs. Doe, you—"

Covering her threadbare nightgown, hardly concealing swollen breasts, she pushed her pride aside. "I need a job, Mr. Sands. At your haberdashery. I worked in my father's store in Oshkosh."

"A woman in a haberdashery?" He shook his head. "Not in this town."

"I'm knowledgeable in fabrics and measurements. In fact, I've designed and tailored suits for my father," she exaggerated.

He kneeled beside her, his scent warm and reassuring, like chestnuts roasting. "You need someone to take care of you. When will Harvey be back?"

Pain knotted her abdomen, and she flinched. "I can take care of myself." And my baby.

He stroked his chin. "I could use some help here until my new store is built in Leadville. I'll be gone much of the time to supervise."

"I'll require two dollars a day," she said.

He straightened. "You drive a hard bargain."

Independence took root in her, strong as a weed. "And five percent commission on sales."

"Whoa. You cross-lots, don't you?"

Another jolt to her abdomen made her buckle.

"What is it?" Sands touched her arm.

He'd never hire her if he knew she was pregnant. "Just excited to get started."

Sands Haberdashery smelled of men's cologne and wool, reminding Baby Doe of happier times before her father lost his Oshkosh store. She created new displays and reorganized the ledger. She practiced measuring and fitting suits, happy she hadn't grown large enough for anyone to notice. In fact, Senator Teller and his cronies insisted Baby Doe fit them for new suits, even though their measurements were the same as the last time Mr. Sands fitted them.

Her paychecks grew with commissions, and she sent money to her family, though Mam complained she should have come home with Harvey. *A woman's place is with her husband.*

She'd love to tell her side of the story, but Harvey would be home in a week, and what good would it do to stir the pot?

But Christmas came, and Harvey didn't. Instead, a letter waited for her at the post office. A fifty-dollar bill fell from the envelope.

"Dear Lizzie,

I'm sorry I haven't written much. I've been so busy. Father sends his best and $50 for expenses. The landlord will have to wait for the rent when the Fourth of July comes through. Speaking of the mine, I've been meeting with father's bank and several investors, so I'm hoping someone will invest by spring.

Mother says I'm the best medicine she can have. She's not in favor of my return. I must admit it's an easier life here. Of course, I miss my sweet Baby Doe and count the days until we're together again.

Your husband,

Harvey Doe"

The writing blurred. She rolled the fifty dollars with other money she'd saved.

Her entire body ached. A long day in the store had worn her to the bone. Black clouds heaved a heavy, wet snow. Climbing the narrow stairs to her apartment, she imagined herself a princess, high above the world, protected in her tower. What a strange thought.

She fed the stove, watched coals ignite the wood's rough edges. She stared at the fire too long, deciding sleep would be better than eating. Her face burned, and temples throbbed. Mam's voice cautioned, "When a person's sick, make sure the bed points north and south to guard against evil spirits." She pushed the bed parallel with the mountain range outside her window and burrowed under the bearskin.

From the corner of the ceiling, she viewed herself on the bed, curled into a ball, teeth chattering. Every muscle shrieked with pain. "Don't worry *little one*, the bearskin will save us. Devils and demons ravage our bodies, but they can't touch our souls."

A fevered sleep devoured her, until ice pelted the window panes. Her raw throat begged for water, but the pitcher on the table was too far to reach. She couldn't move. Spirits screamed in the black night, but the bearskin shielded her. Her eyelids shut tight against the nightmare and she succumbed. Her abdomen buckled and twisted in anguish. Lifting her pulsating head from the pillow, she fell back, the bearskin swallowing her whole.

Sometime later, light hit her eyelids. Her tongue lay thick and swollen, and her lips split and peeling. She needed water.

Pushing aside the bearskin, she pulled her feet to the wood floor with all the effort she could muster. A hot current flooded her thighs. Her feet, so far away, stood in a red puddle. A tremendous wrench in her uterus made her gasp. Another yank followed the first, then another, wracking her body in powerful waves. She tried to clear her mind. Heat a kettle of water. Find a knife.

There was no time. As swift as it was agonizing, she expelled a dark, curly-haired baby boy.

Warmth radiated through her body as she reached for her son, recollecting Mam's warning to protect newborns from the Evil Eye. "God Bless It. God Bless It." Her heart beat against him, hands stroking his blue body. Her breath caught in her throat, waiting for his wail. But none came.

A retch of her womb pitched her to the fluid floor. She clutched her son tight against the fall. The force ripped afterbirth from her insides as a butcher's knife scrapes fascia from meat.

Spent and shivering, she lay in the waste.

Still, her son did not cry, his dark eyes staring at her.

A feral howl erupted from her throat. Once she started, she could not stop.

Her eyelids were glued closed, but she forced them open. Ice daggers hung outside her window. So cold. She trembled, sodden cloth swaddling her skin, her son lay still on her chest.

A knock shook the door.

Unable to lift her head from the floor boards, she moaned.

"Mrs. Doe, are you there?"

Mr. Sands. Her womb convulsed.

"Baby Doe?" He pushed her door open and his gaze dropped to the floor. Blood and vomit pooled around her expelled body tissue on the wood planks. He gagged and held his stomach. Then, touching the stove, he shoved wood in and lit it.

Spasms wracked her body and she grasped the baby to her.

"I had no idea," Sands said, shoulders quaking. "No, not true. I just couldn't admit it. Harvey Doe should be lynched."

He lifted her to the bed and wiped blood from her face and arms with the sheet.

She buried her cheek against the infant's head, weakly humming her Mam's Irish lullaby. Holding him warmed her as no fire could. A boy. Harvey would love a boy.

Sands pried the burden from her. "I'm so sorry."

"No, you can't take him. He's mine." Her fists pummeled his legs. "No. No. No. No."

Sands shook his head. "He's dead."

"No." Unable to stand, she reached for her son as Sands took him away.

For two weeks, Baby Doe lay in bed, not eating, not talking. The place the baby had occupied had been scoured clean, not a trace of warmth left inside her.

"Let me wire Harvey," Sands said. "He'd want to know."

She climbed out of bed, tottering on unsteady feet, awakening to an ache that wasn't physical. "I need to see my baby." She pulled on a coat over her nightgown. "Take me to my son."

Sands tried to reason with her, but she stood her ground, shaky as that felt. Eventually, he gave in, helping her to the buggy. "He's buried on Boot Hill."

The horse pulled them up the steep dirt road above Central

City, stark and desolate, mines abandoned for the winter. White-trunked aspen swayed like skeletons against the winter sky. Melting snow revealed piles of slag, and steaming trash heaps smelled foul.

"Tell me about my boy," she said, desperate to hear every detail.

"I hired the undertaker, Lew Cady, to build a tiny pine casket." They stopped at Boot Hill and Sands helped her down from the buggy.

"That drunkard, Cady? The news must be all over town."

"Cady won't say a word. He hates your husband, for some reason."

Flurries blew sideways over Boot Hill, dropping wet clods on their heads.

Sands wrapped his scarf around her bare neck and pointed. "Over there. That little stone by the tree." Purple crocus sprouted through the snow around the tiny mound.

He helped her across the crusted snow. Kneeling, her finger traced the chiseled cross.

"My son." The baby had been her comfort. Without him, she was alone. "I wanted you so."

Sands shuddered beside her.

For the first time, she thought of Sands discovering her bloody body clutching the dead child. She rose and held his hands, gazing into his eyes, brown and warm as chocolate. "I'll never forget what a good friend you've been, Mr. Sands."

He blinked back tears. "I wanted…I'm so…"

She touched his trembling lips. "Let's not speak of it again."

The tiny stone looked as forlorn as she felt. No son. No husband. No gold mine. The harsh truth gutted her hope. Nothing left to do but go back to Oshkosh. But what was there for her?

A bolt of survival shot through her spine. "Take me to Leadville to see your store."

"Harvey will expect you here, guarding the Fourth of July," Sands said.

"Harvey deserted the mine, just like he deserted us." A putrid taste puckered her tongue.

He tapped his clean-shaven chin. “A change of scene might do you good.”

“Tomorrow.” She turned away from the grave. “Take me to Leadville tomorrow.”

Part Two

Dream of Beautiful Tabor...magnificent looking tall straight & big & so happy & well. He had on a high black new silk hat & rich new overcoat black velvet collar & his hair black & mustache black & perfect his face white & so handsome...
Then he said to me "Can't I see you tonight?"
"Oh yes Oh yes"

—Baby Doe Tabor Diary, Colorado Historical Society

13

Leadville, Colorado, January 1880

Nothing less than a miracle.

Baby Doe kissed her rosary and thanked the Lord above. The dark cloud that hung over her in Central City blew away in the bracing wind on their two-day climb over the Rocky Mountains. The struggle with the Fourth of July, her deserting husband, the desperate lack of money...she would leave it all behind, and forge a life of her own, without the heartaches. The only raw spot left was her unfulfilled love for her baby son.

The sign at the edge of Leadville claimed an altitude of 10,200 feet, almost double Denver's. In this rarified altitude, she felt positively effervescent walking down Harrison Street on Jake Sands' arm. Her chest quickened with the honky-tonk music and laughter rollicking out of every bar door, the jolliest from the Silver Dollar Saloon. The rough mining camp had transformed into the richest town in the West with Tabor's famous silver mines. She counted her lucky stars to live here now, with a great job, no less. Wait until Da heard this.

Mr. Sands held open the door of the new Tabor Grand Hotel. She noticed congratulatory nods and meaningful winks thrown his way, acknowledging him for his new companion. The attention didn't bother her, it felt good to be out of mining togs and in a beautiful dress again. Meanwhile, Mr. Sands seemed to walk taller, shoulders back, a syncopated rhythm in his gait. He deserved to be happy after all he'd done for her.

She squeezed his arm. "I never expected a hotel like this in Leadville."

A coy smile formed on his lips. "Perhaps you'd like a glass of sherry?" He led her to a Queen Anne loveseat by the window.

"Do you feel it, Mr. Sands?" She plumped a cushion inviting him to sit beside her, why not?

He sat close enough for her to smell his spicy cologne. "Please call me Jake."

"Jake." She liked the decisive bite of his name. "This feels like heaven, Jake. Like we're floating on fluffy pink clouds."

"Oh, I get it. The altitude's made you loony." He circled a finger around his ear.

A uniformed waiter approached them. "My name is Chicago. Whaaat kan I get for you sir?" Flat Midwest vowels clashed with his highbrow delivery. His pasty complexion, hair slicked from a middle part, and penciled mustache could not belong to a mountain man.

"Two glasses of sherry, please, Chicago."

"My treat," Baby Doe added. The waiter scowled and disappeared.

Jake's face reddened. "It's a man's place to pay."

"Let me do this small thing." She took his hand. "You've lifted an avalanche off of me, one boulder at a time."

He scoffed. "You women and your rights. Do you think it's easy to take care of yourself?"

"I'm ready to try." Conviction sprung up in her, hungry as a mountain lion. "Living under a husband's care almost killed me. I'm determined to go it alone and see how I do."

Jake lowered his head, then gazed up through dark lashes. "It doesn't have to be that way."

He was sweet on her! She assessed him with fresh eyes. His suit skimmed his body to a tittle, the calling card of a tailor, Da had said. His muscular arms came from twenty pushups executed before the store opened, besides lifting fabric rolls and restocking the shelves. She respected Jake's work ethic, his efficiency at accomplishing tasks. Just the kind of man a woman could count on. But she wasn't about to lose her new-found independence.

She turned to a brass urn of peacock feathers. "I always wanted to own a peacock when I was little. I've still never seen one, have you?"

"Never have." Jake's eyes danced.

"Did you know peacocks symbolize resurrection?" Plucking a feather from the urn, she tickled his cheek, then felt a pang of guilt for flirting with him. But why should she? "I feel better than I have in a year."

"Do you really? I feel the same way, Mrs. Doe."

"Baby Doe," she corrected. "Call me Baby Doe." Her finger traced the green eye of the peacock feather, willing it to see good things for her future.

The waiter delivered the sherry.

"To resurrection." Sands clinked her glass, light sparking his eyes.

"To resurrection." She drank a toast to her rebirth. She'd been given another chance, and this time she'd let no man control her.

Bush polished the brass wall placard with his sleeve. THE TABOR GRAND HOTEL, William Bush, Proprietor. Big-wigs and boot-lickers now sidled up to him like he was Buffalo Bill. Orphan boy finally makes good. He laughed scornfully. Never mind that without Tabor's money, he'd still be a glorified clerk at the Teller House. The name of the hotel irked him, but Tabor convinced him it would draw more folks. The man's ego was growing as big as his bank balance.

After shaking hands and giving tours all day, Marianne had excused herself to the powder room, and he allowed himself to revel in his accomplishment. Six months of elbow grease and greasing palms had finally paid off.

His headwaiter served drinks to a couple sitting by the window. They looked familiar. *Baby Doe.* Drinking sherry in the lobby of his hotel like the day she arrived at the Teller House.

What was she doing in Leadville? And with the tailor? He looked like a schoolboy with his first crush, and she looked…ravishing. The only word that ever fit her. What happened to the mining overalls? Bush snorted. Not that overalls ever diminished her incandescence.

She laughed a glorious trill of notes, lilting down the scale. Her delicate hand held a crystal glass, pinky finger crooked invitingly. Purple lace skimmed bare arms, her bodice gathered around brimming breasts. No, this cherub had not been mining. Warmth rippled through his loins.

Marianne returned, neck blotched red. "What is *she* doing here?"

"It's been a long morning," Bush said. "You should go home."

"I wouldn't think of leaving before saying hello." His wife crossed the room, and he limped after her, skewering the Persian carpet with his cane.

"Jacob Sandelowsky." Marianne curtseyed. "Welcome to Leadville." Then, she reared her hand back and slapped Baby Doe. "That is for Kitty." She barely paused before slapping her other cheek. "And this is for me."

Baby Doe held her face, smiling. "I take it you won't be inviting me to your sewing circle."

Pivoting on her toes, Marianne walked out of the lobby.

"Come back and apologize. Mrs. Doe is our guest," Bush called after her.

"Don't bring her back," Baby Doe said. "We're not meant to be friends."

"My deepest apologies," Bush said. "My wife suffers from pregnancy lunacy."

"Maybe you should stop having children." She smiled slyly, catching him off guard.

"Bring our guests Veuve Clicquot champagne," Bush ordered, and Chicago ran off.

"That would be lovely. I'm parched from the excitement." She presented her gloved hand, and Bush kissed it.

A static shock stung his lips.

"You'll get used to it." She winked and laughed, sharing their private joke.

"So I've heard." He laughed. How she'd changed in the past two years, her desperation and struggle replaced with joviality and poise. And where was her husband? Jake Sands must pay for her company. She'd never be with him otherwise.

"You've been busy since you left Central, Mr. Bush." She waved the peacock feather around the room. "The hotel is a wonder."

"Isn't it?" Bush viewed the room through her eyes, leopard chairs, potted palms, globe chandeliers…then back to Baby Doe, looking like she was born to such luxury.

She caught him staring, and he turned away. "When will my suit be ready, Mr. Sands? It's way overdue."

"You missed your fitting appointment." Sands' eyes crinkled. "Perhaps you'd like to reschedule with my assistant."

"Why should I settle for your assistant? I want *you* to fit my suit."

"Then you'll be missing something." Sands patted Baby Doe's hand. "She's outstanding. Catered to the elite at her father's haberdashery."

She laughed as if he'd told a riotous joke.

Bush rapped his cane on the marble floor. What was it between these two?

Tabor searched out a quiet spot in the lobby behind a low hanging palm frond, away from the irksome attention of constituents.

"Can I get you something, Mr. Tabor?" asked Chicago.

"Just resting my bones." Tabor shook his head. "Wait until you get to be my age."

"I should be so lucky at your age, sir." He rushed off to another table.

Folks' reactions to the hotel amused him. The eclectic design took some getting used to. Fluted Corinthian columns, bamboo bookcases, Japanese screens, Florida palms in Delft pots, peacock feathers in brass urns. Augusta wouldn't like it. She wouldn't come to the opening, too busy in Denver with her Pioneer Ladies.

"Boss, over here." Bush waved from a divan by the window. "I want you to meet someone."

Tabor recognized Jake Sands, the new tailor in town. A girl sat next to him wearing an exuberant brimmed hat, waving a peacock feather to punctuate her point to Sands, who followed her every move. She must be an actress, he guessed, or Sands' daughter playing the lady? Curiosity got the better of him, and he crossed the room. He wished she'd take off the enormous hat.

Bush said something, and she laughed, sounding like sleigh bells jingling on a snowy path. She set her hat on the table, and Tabor finally saw her face, fresh and dewy like Palisade peaches, eyes shimmering like amethysts, golden curls cascading to her creamy shoulders. Tabor swayed, losing his balance.

Bush grabbed his arm. "You all right, Boss?"

"Forgive me." Tabor shook his head, trying to recover. "I thought I knew you or should know you. Maybe from the stage?"

"I love the theater, but I'm not an actress."

Her voice sounded like the round notes of a baby grand.

Bush stepped in. "Mrs. Doe, may I present lieutenant governor Tabor."

"Your reputation precedes you." She presented her hand and he kissed it, couldn't let go.

"A reputation's like a shadow," Tabor said. "Just can't shake it."

"Although, you're nothing like I was told." She examined Tabor's fingers. "Your fingertips haven't fallen off from frostbite." She smoothed his coat between his shoulders. "And your hunchback has disappeared." Her gaze met his. "And you're so much younger."

He laughed. Her humor delighted him, hadn't seen much of that of late.

Bush cleared his throat. "Crazy what people say, isn't it? Mrs. Doe is the *Belle of Central City*. You heard the story. Beautiful damsel who works with her husband in the mine?"

Oddly disappointed at her marital status, Tabor said, "I think I met your husband once outside the Teller House. Is he here with you?"

She examined the eye of the peacock feather. "He's back east caring for his ailing mother."

Tabor ogled Sands. "What man would leave his wife in the Wild West, prey to bandits, desperados, and tailors?"

Her eyes flashed. "A man who cares for his mother, wouldn't you think, Mr. Tabor?"

"You got me there," he admitted. "I try real hard never to think of my mother."

"What a shame. A mother's love is the best in the world," she said wistfully, caressing his hand with the peacock feather with a delicacy that stopped his heart.

"Allow me to clear up any misunderstanding," Sands said, replacing the feather in the urn. "Mrs. Doe agreed to assist me in the new store until her husband returns. In fact, she'll assist with your Cavalry uniforms, lieutenant governor. I just haven't been able to get down to Denver to buy fabric."

"We need those uniforms. President Grant arrives in three weeks," Tabor said. "Perhaps I could accompany Mrs. Doe to buy fabric." His head buzzed with the possibility.

"You have to plan the president's visit," Bush said. "I can accompany Mrs. Doe."

Tabor clapped him on the back. "You're training hotel staff this week."

"Chicago can cover it. We wouldn't want Mrs. Doe thrust onto the streets of Denver alone."

Sands put his arm around her shoulders. "Mrs. Doe doesn't need a trip to Denver just yet."

"Gentlemen, please." She shrugged off Sands' arm. "I do not need anyone's help in Denver. I am fully capable of riding the train and purchasing fabric on my own."

"Of course you can," Tabor said, admiring her gumption. Why couldn't Maxcy find a woman like this?

"I have business in Denver," Bush said. "I'd be honored to offer you a ride in my coach."

The beautiful Mrs. Doe leaned to Tabor as if they were alone. "Can you guarantee my honor in Mr. Bush's hands?"

"You have my word he won't touch a hair on your head," Tabor answered.

"Then it's settled." She smiled at him. "I'll bring back the fabric and start straight away, so you'll have the uniforms in time."

"Excellent." He should be pleased, but somehow, he'd lost the showdown to Bush. But what were they fighting for?

On the last day of their journey to Denver, Bush was determined to crack Baby Doe's reserve. She'd avoided his questions, swinging the conversation to Horace Tabor. How long did it take Tabor to strike silver, when he'd married, how strange that his eyes gleamed like amber?

"Only around you," Bush told her, and she'd laughed.

He needed to steer clear of that malarkey. "Sorry about last night's boarding house. There's not much between Leadville and Denver."

She'd twisted her hair into a chignon; a netted hat screened her eyes.

"It's no match for the Tabor Grand Hotel, that's for sure."

"A beautiful hotel fit for a beautiful lady." His cliché made him cringe. She was just a woman, a woman he'd lusted for since their first meeting. "So, is it true you trained as a tailor?"

"I worked in Da's clothier since I was fourteen," she said. "Loving political debates and the smell of shirt starch."

"Instead of baking bread and churning butter?" he joked.

"Is that all women mean to you?" The carriage swayed, and she braced herself.

"There are other attributes I appreciate." He laughed. "Why hasn't Harvey come back yet?"

Her lips jutted defiantly. "I don't care if he never comes back." She peered out the window.

He admired her resolve. Harvey was never man enough for her.

When Bush saw the tall buildings of Denver, he broke the silence. "I booked two rooms at the American House. They have a great steak house, and I know how you like buffalo."

"How thoughtful." She kept staring out the window as they turned on Larimer Street, with dancehalls, theaters and 'houses of ill repute'.

Baby Doe shrieked. "Oh. Oh, my Lord in Heaven." She pointed to a man half-a-block away, blond curls sticking out of a jaunty derby. He followed a red-headed woman in purple satin toward a mirrored door. "It's Harvey. Stop the coach."

He recognized the gaudy entrance too well. "I thought you said he was in Wisconsin."

"That's Harvey, I'm telling you. Please. Stop the coach."

The coach continued, and she yelled out the window. "Stop – this – coach – at – once."

The driver pulled aside, and she tugged open the handle and ran toward the man. "Harvey Doe. Harvey, stop."

The man tugged his bowler down and ducked into the mirrored door.

The door closed as she reached it, her lovely image distorted in the mirrors.

Bush ran to fetch her, wanting to save her from the vulgar sight.

"I'll go in and check for you."

But she grasped the door handle and stepped inside.

He followed her, accosted by bitter opium smoke and memories he'd rather forget. Tinny notes of a worn-out player piano dragged and sped up maniacally. Gilded mirrors of every dimension covered the walls and ceiling, reflecting half-dressed girls fondling old men's laps. Liquor bottles littered the bar. Girls with flabby thighs gyrated to the erratic music and made sucking and kissing sounds to lure men to indulge.

A young waif doused in Florida toilet water rubbed her breasts against him. "You're back."

Pushing her aside, he followed Baby Doe down the hallway of mirrored doors.

She picked up a red polka-dot bow tie from the floor and pounded on the closest door. "Harvey, I know you're in there. Come out and face me."

An orange-haired woman wrapped in a kimono poked out her head, spewing profanities that stopped when she saw Bush. Just his luck, Mattie Silks, owner of the establishment. The bed rustled behind her, covers pulled up hastily.

"Well, well, what have we here?" Mattie perused Baby Doe's attributes. "With that face and figure you could do a hell of a business." She cocked her finger. "One thing you have to learn is the customer always comes first. Give me a minute to finish him off and we'll have a drink together." Closing the door in their faces, her voice drifted through the door. "Now, where were we? I was the dancehall girl and you just struck it rich."

Bush unsheathed his cane, his sword blade glinting in the mirrors. He'd kill the bastard.

Baby Doe flinched at her distorted reflection in the mirrors, flashing red with the lights. She staggered backward, and a customer caught her. "You must be new to the house."

Bush swung his sword to the man's neck. "Hands off or I'll serve up your head on a platter."

Baby Doe turned and ran out.

"She's a lady." He sheathed his sword and ran after her. She didn't deserve this.

Even with everything Harvey had put her through, Baby Doe never considered divorce. A sin she wasn't prepared to commit. But witnessing him at the House of Mirrors changed her heart. She purchased fabric for the uniforms, then asked Bush to take her to a lawyer.

"Don't try to talk me out of it," she said, expecting a fight. But he drove her to a brownstone office on Fourteenth Avenue, and she was grateful. Hard enough to bury her dream, once and for all.

Lawyer Amos Steck answered the door. "Well, Mr. Bush. Come in. Come in." Red bags hung below his eyes, magnified with thick lenses.

"This is Mrs. Doe," Bush said.

"Pleased to meet you." She swallowed the lump in her throat.

Steck offered chairs. "How's your boss doing? Tabor's crazy to take on Colorado with the railroads blowing each other up and Indian massacres. He's likely to get killed if—"

Baby Doe interrupted. "I'm here to secure a divorce from my husband." She squeezed her rosary beads.

Steck lifted his glasses and rubbed his eyes. "There's only one divorce granted for every thousand marriages. You can bet your bottom dollar it's not granted to a woman. We don't let women vote, why let them divorce?"

The injustice throbbed at the back of her head. "Then this case will set a precedent."

"Her husband deserted her," Bush said. "We just caught him in the red-light district."

"Women *should* have the same rights as men, but they don't."

Steck polished his glasses with a handkerchief. "It is impossible for a woman to get a divorce."

His attitude annoyed her. "Obviously, I came to the wrong lawyer." Wrapping her rosary around her fist, she walked toward the door.

"What God hath joined together, let no man put asunder," he said.

She spun around. "God would never want me shackled to a man who deserted me and bedded a whore." She'd said the rosary until God answered her, so definitive and just.

"Society will never accept a divorced woman."

"I won't stay married to him." If he wouldn't do it, she'd find someone who would.

"You're a strong-minded young lady." He handed her a form. "This is a divorce affidavit. Include all the dirty details, or I can't make it stick. Desertion. Non-support. Adultery."

Each ugly word punched her gut.

Steck offered Bush a cigar. "Care to join me outside?"

"I'll stay with Mrs. Doe," Bush said.

"No, I have to do this on my own," she insisted.

He sighed and followed the lawyer out.

Gripping the fountain pen, her ribs squeezed her heart until she couldn't breathe. So much deceit and weakness. She'd seen Harvey as her savior, and that was her sin. Never again would she surrender her will to a man. If that's what marriage offered, she'd have none of it.

As Amos Steck asked, she detailed Harvey's non-support, his adultery, his abandonment, but there was more that was too personal to share. His jealousy, his whining, the sniveling mornings, the sullen suppers. How many nights he'd come home drunk and surly, just to rut her like a wild boar, dirty and screaming, then silent.

By the end of the document, her fingers cramped, and she was spent.

Last night in her prayers, God told her he'd forgive her the sin of divorce, when she forgave Harvey. She doubted that day would ever come.

Back in Leadville, Baby Doe wrote her family about the divorce and her decision to move back to Oshkosh. Mam wrote back immediately.

"After all the effort and attention I poured into you, Lizzie, you repay me by divorcing Harvey Doe? You are a disgrace. Divorce is a sin against God and the Catholic Church, so you'd better make a life for yourself there."

Baby Doe felt like a boat that had come loose from its moorings, untethered from the last thing that felt safe—her family. Maybe she'd been wrong to think of them as her port. Her first memory was Mam's hand running through her curls. *Beautiful girl, beautiful girl.* So many tender memories...how her mother painted her eyes and cheeks with pots of color for communion, while other girls went plain-faced. And when she competed in the skating championship, Mam made a skating dress scandalously short to feature her legs.

Her mother, always coddling, prodding, correcting. Baby Doe had thought it was love. She opened her cameo locket and stared at her parents' faces, scrambling to make sense of it. Everything she'd been taught felt false now. Yanking the necklace off, she threw it in a drawer.

The next Sunday, Baby Doe sat in the front pew of Annunciation Church, letting the priest's Latin and heavenly bells loosen her grief and guilt. Feeling better after the service, she joined the congregation for punch and cookies. Maybe she'd meet new friends. But the church ladies huddled around the punch bowl threw her dark looks.

Baby Doe took a ginger snap and struck up a conversation. "Wasn't that an inspiring sermon? Love one another, Jesus said."

She bit into a ginger snap and smiled. "These are delicious. Which one of you made these cookies?" From now on, she'd employ the grace of God to lessen the disgrace of a divorced woman.

Billy Bush made daily visits to the haberdashery, offering her wicked humor and fresh gossip. She looked forward to his company but drew the line when he offered an apartment.

"No one needs to know," he said.

"I'll know," she answered and continued to pay exorbitant rent for her small room, preferring the hotel's safety to the lecherous streets of Leadville.

Burying herself in her job, she found solace in checking in shipments, stocking shelves, and measuring wealthy men for new suits. Except when they pestered her with invitations for buggy rides and dinner. Some didn't bother to couch their advances, offering clothing, jewelry and money. Rebuffing them exhausted her and turned her heart stony.

One afternoon she was unpacking shirts into the armoire, admiring their pleated bibs, when Harvey's father walked in.

"Hello, Lizzie." Mr. Doe took off his fedora, perspiration beaded his face. "How's my daughter-in-law?"

She shook her head. "What are you doing here, Mr. Doe?"

He handed her a letter in Harvey's handwriting.

Dear Father & Mother,

I'm heartbroken about my sad, sad loss of my darling Babe, but it wasn't my fault that I went into the House of Mirrors. I was trying to find a man to sell my mine for me. I pray you get Babe to come back to me for she's all I have in this world. Hoping you'll look into this sad affair.

Your Loving Son,

Harvey

"There's a beautiful white Victorian in Oshkosh for you two," Mr. Doe said. "Harvey is managing my lumber yard."

He offered what she craved most. Home. Family. Respectability. *But, Harvey?* "Your son was dismal at mining but worse at marriage," she said.

"You're as stubborn as Harvey said." He held out a gilt-edged parchment. "At least take this old deed I found in my safe-deposit box. Troy Gold Mine. Worthless, I'm sure, but maybe you can sell it. You have to support yourself."

She waved off the deed, not wanting his charity. A familiar customer waved back and smiled that lecherous smile she got so often. She took the deed.

Mr. Doe glared at the man. "Be a good girl, Lizzie."

Bitterness coated her tongue. "I *am* a good girl, Mr. Doe. Always have been. Your son did not change that."

14

Leadville, Colorado, July 1880

Tabor's insides curdled with the gush of steam as he watched the Leadville, Colorado & Southern engine pull into the train station. "God help me," he prayed. The telegram he received a month ago had begged no response.

From the office of President Ulysses S. Grant

To Lt. Governor Horace Tabor

The President would like to visit Leadville for a tour of your silver mines. His train arrives eight o'clock on the evening of July 30, 1880.

The setting sun scorched the peaks of the Sawatch Mountain Range, ribbons of magenta and orange reflected off Lake Turquoise. Augusta and Bush stood with him at the head of the reception line. Five thousand citizens anxiously awaited the president. The Elks' band held brass horns high. Five church choirs filed into the risers. In the front row, Mrs. Doe stood out like a blooming rose.

He nudged Bush. "I think I should join the choir."

Bush shook his head. "You're not Catholic."

"The president's visit has to go smoothly." Tabor repeated for the hundredth time. "Wall Street is so volatile that a bad report will send silver stock plummeting. Reporters will descend on us like vultures on carrion."

"Then they'll love the beef we're serving at the banquet," Bush joked.

He laughed. "I couldn't do any of this without your help, Billy."

The hotelier canted his gambler skimmer. "Then I'll expect a raise in my paycheck. Marianne's in the family way again."

Tabor studied him. "You have enough girls to start a convent."

"I'm trying for a son like Maxcy."

"Nothing like a son." Tabor saluted Maxcy, leading the cavalry.

The train doors opened, belching out half-a-dozen Pinkerton agents in coal-black suits. *Hail to the Chief* played as the president stepped down in his stove-pipe hat, meticulous beard and three-piece suit. His left eyebrow cocked as if he understood things others never could.

"Mr. President, it's an honor to have you visit Leadville." Tabor shook his hand.

"Ah, Mr. Tabor, the *legendary* Silver King," the president said, puffing his loamy cigar.

His snide tone reminded Tabor only too well of the president's previous visit to Central City, when he shunned silver in favor of gold. Acid ate at Tabor's stomach, and he popped a licorice.

The president surveyed the turquoise sky silhouetting the mountain range. Smoke swirled from rooftops, kerosene lamps lit windows. "Not bad for the end of nowhere. Not bad."

Augusta chortled, and Tabor saw she was about to tell him off. "Mr. President, I'd like to introduce my wife, Augusta Tabor."

"Mrs. Tabor." The president blew cigar smoke away from her. "I'm sorry my wife couldn't make this trip. Julia loves star gazing, and I daresay your evening sky would thrill her."

Her mouth twisted. "Can't say we have much time for stargazing out here," she said, as the cavalry horses strutted toward them. "That's our boy leading the Tabor Cavalry."

The president winked. "He takes after his mother."

Her proud smile took Tabor by surprise. Not much made her happy these days.

The cavalry looked sharp in the uniforms Mrs. Doe had designed: short coats and gray jodhpurs with red stripes. Tabor stole a glance at her radiant face. *A perfect mountain rose.*

Maxcy shouted an order, and the cavalry shot a twenty-one-gun-salute. The acrid smell of gun powder hung in the air. President Grant saluted them, and Tabor's chest swelled.

A hundred-voice chorus sang "My Country Tis of Thee" like a choir of angels. Tabor tried to pick out Mrs. Doe's voice, but couldn't. A visit to Annunciation Church wouldn't hurt.

But the heavenly serenity shattered when the platform started shaking. Torches flickered through the trees. Yips, hoots, and hollers pierced the air. Indians swooped in, flashing horse manes and flared nostrils in the torchlight.

Looked like the Meeker massacre all over again.

Tabor pushed the president behind him and Pinkerton's surrounded him. People screamed and covered their heads in fear of being scalped.

Tabor grabbed Edison's new-fangled microphone. "Nothing to worry—" Damn thing wasn't working. He thumped and jiggled it, still nothing.

Bush flipped a switch on the amplifier and nodded. "You're on."

"Calm down. Calm down everybody." Tabor's voice blared, loud and distorted. "Everything is under control." Sweat dripped down his neck. "We invited the Ute Nation here to dance for President Grant, their great champion."

At least the president couldn't accuse Leadville of being boring.

Indians planted cattail torches in the ground, stinking of burning bear fat. Squaws in beaded buckskins faced braves decorated with brilliant feathers.

"Greetings, Great White Chief," a young Ute woman said in precise English. "I am Amitola, granddaughter of Chief Ouray. We are honored to perform the Spring Bear Dance."

The dancers shimmied and swayed, white buckskin moccasins padding the dusty ground.

"In springtime, two braves came upon a bear in the woods," Amitola began. "They drew their bows and aimed to kill. But the bear charmed them, dancing on his hind legs, wiggling and scratching his back against the bark. Amused, the braves spared his life, and the bear taught them this dance. Bear spirit brings us strength, wisdom, and survival."

Braves hung their costume feathers on a cedar tree.

"They're shedding tensions built up over winter," Tabor told the president, as touched by the ceremony as when he first learned of it.

If only I could get senators to do that." The president smiled."

A spotted Appaloosa galloped in with Chief Ouray, feathered headdress flying, festooned in beaded buckskins. His horse reared high on his hind legs, and the crowd gasped.

Chief Ouray raised his ancient head. "Long time ago, Utes had plenty. Antelope and buffalo so many Ouray can't count. In the mountains, deer and bear everywhere. In the streams, trout, duck, beaver. Utes happy. White man came, and now Utes go hungry. Old man weak for food. Squaw and papoose cry. White man grows a heap. Red man—soon die all. Remember the Utes."

"We haven't kept our promises, Mr. President," Tabor said, the injustice weighed on him.

A burning bottle flew from the crowd and broke on Chief Ouray's appaloosa.

"Utes must go," a man yelled from the crowd. "Utes must go." Strident voices joined in. "Utes must go." A dozen burning bottles flew and smashed on the stage, flames ripping along the platform, reeking of kerosene.

Cavalry men jumped off their horses and wrestled down angry rioters. Pinkertons shielded the president from spewing glass and fire.

"Take the president to the hotel," Tabor told the Pinkertons.

"You shouldn't have invited the Utes," Augusta said. "You were asking for trouble."

"Go with the Pinkertons," he said. "You'll be safe."

She rolled her eyes but left with the president's detail.

Tabor turned back to the rampage. Fire had jumped to the choir risers and people screamed and pushed. On the front row,

Baby Doe helped an old woman to the ground. But a spark caught her pink ruffled hem and sizzled up the skirt.

"Mrs. Doe." Tabor sprang toward her, but Bush held him back. "No time for damsels in distress, Boss."

Sands reached Baby Doe and snuffed the flame with his coat. Tabor's head shimmied, trying to focus. The president needed attention.

From the bottom of the Matchless Mine shaft, Tabor looked up thirty feet to blue sky, trying to calm his palpitating heart. Searching for fresh air untainted by minerals, he detected a hint of blue spruce. He closed his eyes and drew it into his lungs. But with eyes closed, he heard the groan of timber straining against rock, gravel breaking away, the drip of ground water…causing his heart to race. He'd never gotten over his claustrophobia in the mines, but the big ore was buried under a mountain. Why would God make it easy?

He longed for the old days of prospecting when mining meant wading in mountain streams, filling his pan with sand, and swirling pebbles until flecks gleamed on the bottom. That was the life.

He heard the president and Lou Leonard talking from somewhere down the tunnel. "But are the miners safe down here?" the president asked.

Tabor's stomach churned and he popped a licorice. *Safe*? Just last month, a timber slipped and crushed his foreman's leg. Poor guy wouldn't walk again.

The walls closed in, collapsing his lungs, had to get out of here. "Mr. President, you are in good hands here. I'll see you at the dinner tonight," he called to them, and heard an affirmative response. He yanked the rope to signal the hoist man. The squeal of the coiling reel heightened his panic. What if it broke? Each pull brought him closer to the surface. *Closer to oxygen.*

At the top, Maxcy helped him out, peeking through a lock of chestnut hair. "I wanted to apologize to the president for not weeding out the Indian haters at the rally."

Tabor scoffed. "Wouldn't be the Wild West without a skirmish, now would it?" He clapped Maxcy's shoulder, surprised how strong it had become. "Come on, son. I know just what we need." Grabbing pans from the shed, they headed to the Arkansas. But the easy manner between them had grown stiff over the past few years, and the silence made him antsy. Maybe a joke would help.

Tabor glanced sideways. "A barber asks a man; how would you like your hair cut?"

"In silence," Maxcy answered.

"Guess I need some new material."

"Wouldn't hurt," Maxcy said, laughing.

At the river, they yanked off boots, rolled up their trousers, and waded in. The icy water shocked Tabor's ankles as he navigated the river stones. He pointed out a shallow spot, and Maxcy scooped sediment and swirled it just like he'd taught him. Aspen glimmered under the vibrant sky, the scent of pine, clean and pungent.

"Eureka." Maxcy held up a tiny gleaming nugget, his smile shining bright.

"That's my boy," Tabor said, thumbs up, smiling until his cheeks ached. He wanted to freeze this moment with his son. Proof positive there were things much more valuable than gold.

15

Denver, Colorado, September 1880

A dirty squall blew in the carriage window, kicked up by the flurry of wagons and buggies on the Denver street. Tabor choked. It'd been a grueling two months residing over the state senate. All he wanted was to head back to Leadville with Augusta and look at a new mine for sale.

Mansions lined the leafy avenue, each more elegant than the next. A far cry from the ramshackle cabins they'd lived in. The Tabor mansion soared three stories high, lined with shuttered windows. He swore there were rooms he'd never seen.

The coachman opened his carriage door. Pete was a young black man from Aberdeen, cousin of his butler, Samson. His eyes rarely met Tabor's, a vestige of a southern upbringing. The liberal West would do him good.

In the front yard, Augusta bent over, ankle deep in soil. Her milk cow, Black Beauty, stood tethered to the railing, chewing grass.

"What in tarnation are you doing?" he asked.

"What's it look like? I'm planting potatoes, beans, tomatoes, and corn."

"First the cow, now a farm in front of our mansion? I'm lieutenant governor for God's sake."

She clucked her tongue. "You bought your office with a fat check to the Republican Party."

He sighed. "Let's not squabble. I'd like to take you up to Leadville with me. There's a new mine I might buy." The lucky itch stung strong this time.

"I don't have to witness you throwing away money. Make sure there's enough for Maxcy when he's married."

"Maxcy's sweet on someone?" Why hadn't he told him?

Augusta wiped her brow, streaking dirt across her forehead. "If you paid him any mind, you'd know he's courting Louella Babcock."

He watched Augusta dig, hurt Maxcy hadn't confided in him. "Come up to Leadville with me, Augusta. Just you and me like old times."

"Old times? I liked the Tabor of old better than the overblown fancy man I see before me."

Frustration burned his gullet. "Can't you just enjoy it? We've got nine million in the bank."

She tried to step onto the porch, but her boots stuck in the mud.

He laughed and lifted her out. "Will you come if I buy you new gardening boots?"

Augusta swatted his arm. "Wash up. There's pot roast for supper."

"I love Martha's pot roast," he said.

"I let the cook go. Don't need her."

He sighed, feeling them drift ever farther apart. "Sure you won't come with me?"

She shook her head. "Who'd milk Black Beauty?" The cow bellowed, and Augusta petted her. "Don't fret, now, Beauty. He'll get his head out of the clouds someday."

Tabor stepped off the train and breathed in sagebrush and pine, his tension easing until he saw his managers waiting on the platform.

"What was that telegram about selling the Matchless Mine?" he asked.

"The silver is mined out," Lou said, looking worn as his mining denims.

"Sell it, Boss," Bush said. "Get rid of it while we can."

"It's the Matchless, Billy. The first mine I staked in Leadville."

"But it's worthless. And with a hundred mines now, we need the cash."

"Always bellyaching for cash." Tabor lengthened his stride. "What about the Chrysolite?"

"This month's dividend is two-hundred thousand," Lou said. "Good time to sell shares."

"There's your cash, Billy," Tabor said.

Leadville's new mayor headed straight toward them, surrounded by a hornet's nest of complaining citizens. Tabor wasn't about to get sucked into Leadville's problems.

"Catch up with you boys later." He backed into Sands Haberdashery and bumped into something. A mannequin fell to the floor.

"You could have just asked her to dance." Baby Doe's hips swayed, hands on her tiny waist.

Was she flirting with him? Tabor picked up the mannequin, brushing her off.

"Did you come to see her?" She laughed. "Or did you want a new suit?"

The mayor's crowd buzzed passed the door, and Tabor sighed. "You read my mind."

"I read measuring tapes." She measured his leg length. "Taller than most." Stretching the tape around his waist. "Is that House of Creed cologne you're wearing?"

"Picked it up in New York on my last investor trip."

"My father used to sell Creed." She noted the measurements on an index card. "That should do it. Would you like to look at fabrics?"

He pulled a poker face. "Choose something that makes me look younger, slimmer, and more commanding."

"Absolutely. I have that magic cloth right here."

Her wit raised his spirits. "Perhaps we could look at swatches over dinner at the Saddle Rock?" It popped out before he could reel it back.

"I have to mind the store." Her voice fell flat.

Jake Sands walked over. "I'm sure we can accommodate Mr. Tabor, can't we, Mrs. Doe?"

Her forehead gathered like thunderclouds, then relaxed. "Splendid idea. I'll gather swatches and meet you at the restaurant." She walked back to the storeroom and he stared after her. Something about her made him happy.

Sands cleared his throat. "She'll meet you at the Saddle Rock, Mr. Tabor."

"Oh, great, thanks." Tipping his hat, he left.

At first, Baby Doe was miffed Sands insisted she come, and even more miffed Tabor requested the meeting. Why couldn't he look at swatches at the haberdashery? Did he think his money granted privilege? And she was the privilege?

Then she'd realized it gave her a chance to sell Tabor the mine deed Mr. Doe gave her. And for that, she'd changed into a nicer dress, ochre brocade that matched the color of her hair.

She walked into the Saddle Rock greeted by the delicious smell of garlic, glowing kerosene lamps, and cheery red-checked tablecloths. Tabor was talking to the new mayor seated with the sheriff. When they noticed her, his face turned red as the tablecloth.

"Oh, Mrs. Doe, I didn't expect you," he said. "Is Mr. Sands bringing the fabric swatches?"

She held up the swatch book. "You'd prefer to work with Mr. Sands?"

"Not at all." He helped her with her cape and hung it up.

"Benvenuta, Signorina." The owner, Batista led them past leather booths along one wall.

Tabor greeted town folks along the aisle with a hearty laugh that brought smiles to their faces. He didn't introduce her; why would he? She was a mere shop girl as far as he was concerned.

"Buon Appetito." Batista handed them menus, winking at Tabor before leaving them alone.

"What was that ruse in front of the mayor?" she asked.

"I wanted to preserve your reputation."

"Poppycock, I'm a divorced woman. There's nothing left of my reputation or men wouldn't gather around me like flies on horse muck." She shielded her hot cheeks with her menu.

A stocky, dark-haired waiter appeared.

"Renzo, how's Filipa treating you?" Tabor asked.

Oblivious to his question, the waiter grinned at Baby Doe.

Tabor took their menus and handed them to Renzo. "Two Hangtown Fries. And ask Batista to bring up the Pouilly-Fuisse from my stash." Aromas of fried onion and potatoes wafted from the kitchen. "Their Hangtown Fry beats all."

Irritation needled up her chest. "What if I preferred a steak?"

He signaled Renzo, but she stopped him. "I'll try the Hangtown Fry. I've never had it. In fact, I've never been here. I eat in my room."

"I should have asked what you wanted," he said. "I'm sorry."

"No, you're not. Rich men always get their way."

"Not as often as you think." His face drooped in such profound sadness, it made her want to cheer him up. What made him so unhappy, when he had everything going for him?

She tweaked his suit sleeve. "As your tailor, I should advise you that hopsack is most unfitting for a man of your stature. Don't you read *Harper's Magazine*?"

"You don't appreciate my rough-hewn charm?" His smile chased away those sad lines.

"Oh, but I do," she said. "And your wicked humor."

"My humor is God-awful, and you know it." He laughed.

She lifted the ring of swatches to the table and leafed through them. "Maybe we should choose a Tiger's Eye tweed to go with your eyes?"

"I'm sure whatever you choose will be perfect." His hand covered hers.

She should move but it felt so warm and comforting, something she hadn't felt much lately.

Renzo came to pour the Pouilly-Fuisse, gazing at their hands until the wine overflowed. "So sorry, Mr. Tabor." He wiped up and scuttled away.

She laughed and held up her glass.

"To peacocks." He clinked her glass.

"Why peacocks?" The wine tasted fresh as melon.

"You seemed fascinated with peacock feathers when I met you at the hotel."

"I used to dream of having a pet peacock," she said.

"Nothing's stopping you, the world is your oyster. Speaking of which, here they are."

Renzo presented steaming dishes smelling of earth and sea.

"There are oysters in Hangtown Fry?" she asked.

He leaned forward. "A prospector in Hangtown, California struck gold and wanted the most expensive meal possible. So, they fried eggs with oysters and salt-bacon. Best taste in the world."

She took one bite, then another. "Delicious." Better than a cold dinner in her room.

Tabor scooped up eggs on sourdough toast. "You mentioned loving the theater."

"You remember a lot about that day." She eyed him, suspicious, but flattered. "I helped design sets and costumes for my family's theater next to our haberdashery."

"Sounds like you'd like to go back."

Her heart contracted. "My family doesn't speak to me since the divorce."

"What a shame. A mother's love is the best in the world," he repeated the phrase she'd said when they met. How cruel she'd been to him.

"I deserved that." She swallowed a lump.

"I didn't say it to be unkind." He covered her hand again. "In fact, I admire your respect for your parents. I'm sure they'll come around with a daughter like you."

His hand was almost twice as big as hers, freckled and tan...a gold band on his finger. She withdrew her hand.

He cleared his throat. "What happened to your Fourth of July mine?"

Her gut hardened. "Foreclosed. The First Leadville Bank owns it now."

He flinched. "That's my bank."

She handed him the deed she brought. "Perhaps you'd be interested in buying the Troy Mine. My father-in-law gave it to me as alimony."

He barely glanced at the paper. "Let's ride out and take a look."

She shook her head. "Mining has brought me nothing but misery."

"You should know what you're selling."

He had a point. Besides, a day with the Silver King could be educational, at the very least. "Tomorrow is Sunday, my day off, if you want to see the Troy," she said. "Strictly business."

16

Leadville, Colorado, September 1880

The mountain air bit brittle with cold, and the sun cast an orange hue to the dawn as Tabor pulled the buggy around to the hotel promptly at seven o'clock. Baby Doe was waiting for him, her breath forming clouds. Her serviceable wool coat, work boots, and cotton duck skirt dampened his glamorous image of her.

"I see you dressed up for the occasion," he teased.

"Sorry to disappoint you, but this isn't a social engagement."

Bad start. He snapped the reins, urging the horses to a gallop. What had he gotten himself into? If her mines were bust, she held worthless paper. If they were rich, she didn't have money to develop them. He turned the puzzle over in his head, searching for a solution.

As the sun arched higher in the sky, she gazed out at a meadow of wildflowers. "I love those white and lavender trumpet flowers."

"Columbines," he said. "Nothing better than a field of wildflowers to make my day."

She looked at him sideways, like she didn't know what to make of him. What happened to the glib girl at the Saddle Rock full of piss and vinegar? He tried another tack.

"Won't they miss you in choir, today?"

She scoffed. "The director will be happy. She's fit-to-be-tied to let a divorced woman sing for Annunciation Church. Father

O'Mannie makes her."

"It's unfair for people to judge without knowing the circumstances." He drove on in silence before daring to ask his question. "Do you mind me asking what happened with your husband?"

"No use hashing over the past." She lifted her chin. "What's important is to look forward, learn to be happy by myself, and earn my own way."

He laughed. "Wish more people thought like you."

She smiled, then glanced away. Maybe she'd warm up with the sunshine. They crossed a rough bridge built over a narrow point in the river. White water tumbled through giant boulders.

"The evergreens here are so different than in Oshkosh," she said. "Colorado blue spruce is my favorite." She gazed at the layers of mountain rock: red limestone, gray granite, sparkling quartz. "Truly God's country. No wonder people flock here."

He laughed. "If you think people come for scenery, you're much too innocent to live here."

"Of course, they don't come for the scenery, but it gets under your skin, doesn't it? Could you ever move back east?"

"I could never leave Colorado." Of that, he was certain.

The horses headed up a steep slope, and he consulted the map. "Around here somewhere."

"Heaven and stars!" She pointed out a deteriorating wood A-frame with a landslide above caving in on it. "I hope that's not it." She jumped out of the buggy and headed over to the shaft.

Catching up, he pounded rotting headboards. "This mine hasn't been worked in years. Not safe to go in."

"Could there still be gold?" She gazed into the abyss, darkness swallowing her voice.

"They wouldn't abandon it if there was gold left, but maybe—" He picked up a shimmering rock. "Silver. See if there's more."

They surveyed the ground around the mouth of the shaft. Sparkling gray rocks lay everywhere. Tabor took off his hat, breezed his hands through his thinning hair, then shook his head.

"Worthless. It's salted." He watched to see her reaction.

"A salt mine?" Her shoulders dropped. "Why'd Mr. Doe say it was gold?"

"You passed the test." Tabor laughed. "Let me explain. This miner, Chicken Bill, duped me into buying his mine by spreading silver ore all over the ground. It's called 'salting'. When I saw all the silver here, I had to make sure you didn't salt it."

Her forehead wrinkled. "You thought I was trying to swindle you?"

"Can't be too careful when it comes to mining." He studied the silver rock, a sting shooting from his funny bone through his shoulder. "I feel it all right. Haven't seen this much silver all year."

"So, you'll buy the deed?" Her face brightened.

"No."

Her eyes blazed like the hottest part of a flame. "Why did you agree to come, if you aren't interested in the mine?" She stomped back to the buggy.

He smiled at her feisty spirit. Better let her cool down, before making his offer. He picked wild flowers along the way, rock roses, columbines, verbena; nature's beauties, like her.

She stood by the buggy, arms crossed, tapping her toe. "Take me home, Mr. Tabor."

"I'd work this mine quick before another prospector jumps you." He held out the nosegay.

She eyed it suspiciously but took the flowers. "You know I have no money."

He tipped his hat back. "You think I came all the way up here without a motive?"

"Should've known your help came with a price." She held out the bouquet but he held up his palms.

"Hear me out. I fund the mine operation. If there's no silver, you owe me nothing. If we strike it, I get half."

She cocked her head. "Sixty/forty and you have yourself a deal."

He hooted. Her offer was downright insulting, but the dimple in her chin overruled logic. "Remind me not to play poker with you." They shook hands.

"The flowers sealed the deal." She sniffed the nosegay, gazing at him through the petals, so brilliant and beautiful he made himself turn toward the buggy and lift out a picnic basket.

"The hotel made us lunch." He spread a blanket and set out miner rolls of sliced beef and cheese on sourdough. Then he opened the bottle of Pouilly-Fuisse. "You liked the wine."

She crinkled her nose. "I love everything French."

"You'll have to go someday." He poured wine into glasses and handed her one.

"To our partnership," she toasted and tasted the wine. "Melon and orange blossom."

He laughed. "And here I thought it was only wine." He suspected her thirst for knowledge went deeper than wine. She took on the world with a bravery he'd rarely seen, man or woman.

A loud warble interrupted his thoughts, he searched for the lark and pointed. "Watch him."

The striking black and white lark soared so high it became just a speck. Hovering there for a moment, it spiraled down toward earth at breakneck speed. Inches from the ground, it swooped upward and flew into the air once more with a triumphant trill.

Tabor threw back his head and laughed. "I have to admire courage like that."

She clinked his glass. "To reckless dare-devils."

"Don't you know it," he said, astonished she saw him for who he was, without judgment.

Bush brought the financials for their monthly meeting, not that Tabor ever paid attention. Expenses had outrun income since he'd been on board.

"The numbers show you're expanding too fast," he explained, as Tabor tapped his toes to some unheard beat. "There's no choice but to close down businesses and consolidate the mines."

Tabor drummed his fingers. "There's nowhere to take a lady for entertainment."

Bush did a double-take. "You have the attention span of a squirrel. Maybe I should bring acorns next time."

Tabor spun the dial on the safe and took out a scroll. "We need an opera house with first class shows next to the hotel."

"Your money's making you reckless, Boss. You can't build everything that crosses your mind." On the other hand, why object when Tabor's hair-brained schemes lined his pockets?

"I sent for Baby Doe to give a woman's perspective," Tabor said.

Baby Doe. Heat prickled Bush's chest. The bright spot of his day was when he stopped by Sands' haberdashery to see her. "Why not get Augusta's opinion?"

"Didn't you say Baby Doe raised money for the Central City opera house?"

She burst through the office door, her churned-butter complexion pale. "I came as soon as I got your message. What happened, what's wrong?"

Tabor spread the scroll on his desk. "I want your opinion on these theater plans."

"This is urgent?" Her cheeks colored. "I was with a customer."

Her perfume cleared Bush's head like smelling salts. It wasn't a theater fueling Tabor's passion; it was Baby Doe.

Tabor shrugged. "We're starting construction soon, and I want to make sure it's right."

"I appreciate your help with the Troy Mine, but if you think I'm at your beck and call you're mistaken." Turning to leave, she noticed the plans on Tabor's desk and moved closer. "You're actually building a theater?"

"Three-stories high, constructed of stone and brick." Tabor pointed out the details. "Modern plate-glass storefronts flank double doors, which open to an impressive lobby. There's a wide staircase to the balcony. I hope you'll design the usher uniforms."

Her fingers glided over the drawings. "Hummm."

"My suite on the second floor will have seven arched windows facing the mountains."

Bush never heard Tabor brag like this. "Sounds like a fortune."

"Thirty-thousand, but the builder said it'd take a year to build with the snow coming soon. So, I doubled his fee if he finishes before snowfall."

"Outrageous," Bush said. "I'll negotiate a better price."

Tabor waved him off, watching Baby Doe.

"Why is this store marked Sands Haberdashery?" She pointed to the plan. "Mr. Sands didn't tell me we were moving."

"Wouldn't you enjoy being near the theater?" Tabor grinned.

Frowning at him, she huffed. "Money can't buy everything, Mr. Tabor." She stalked out the door.

Tabor shook his head. "She's something, isn't she?"

"Some kind of trouble." Bush expected his ready laugh, but Tabor just gazed at the door.

17

Leadville, Colorado, November 1880

Baby Doe fumed as they packed the haberdashery fixtures into the wagon. Tabor hadn't been around for two months, but he'd have to show up for the theater opening, and when he did, she'd give him a piece of her mind. Sands could no more afford to move into that huge store than to thread a camel through a needle's eye. Where did Tabor get off manipulating everybody at his whim? And what about her mine? He'd roped her into that deal, too.

Sands closed the wagon gate and brushed his hands together. "No turning back now. Let me buy you dinner."

"I'm tuckered out." She was starving, but Sands couldn't afford restaurants any more than she could. "I'll just go rest up for tomorrow."

"Come on, you have to eat. I'm too worked up to turn in now."

She could never disappoint those big brown eyes, now ringed like a racoon from the strain of the new store. As they walked to the Saddle Rock he raked his hand through his hair and chattered nervously. "If we watch expenses and sales are good, we should be able to make it in the new space. You've developed quite a following of businessmen."

She squeezed his hand. "The store will be a big success." Brave talk masked her anxiety, the loss of her father's haberdashery still haunted her. She couldn't let that happen again.

"When Tabor told me how much you wanted it, I signed the

lease on the spot," Jake said.

She stopped, curious people passing them. "You did this for me?"

"I respect your opinion, Baby Doe." Sands' face colored. "Don't you like the new store?"

She sighed. "I love it." Taking his arm, they continued down Harrison. "One lie begets another," Father O'Mannie would say at confession. She should have learned that by now.

"I have a surprise when we get to the restaurant." He fairly skipped.

At the Saddle Rock, the fried-onion smell reminded her of dinner with Tabor, igniting her ire all over again.

Batista raised a quizzical brow. "Signorina, you lika the Hangtown Fry?"

"Colorado lamb chops, please," she said.

"Make that two," Sands said, and Batista went running. "Now close your eyes, Baby."

Playing along, she covered her eyes.

"All right, now look."

A small velvet box sat on the table. "What's this?" She opened it. A gold bracelet, studded with three tiny diamonds, lay on white satin. "Jake, no. I can't." Her hand flew to her chest.

His face crumpled, and she couldn't bear his disappointment.

"Ohhh. It is absolutely stunning." She slipped on the bracelet.

"I ordered it from Kilpatrick Jewelers in New York. Eighteen-carat gold with real diamonds. Look, here's the receipt." He showed her a folded paper.

"Jake, darling, I don't need the receipt to know how valuable it is." Turning her wrist, the diamonds glinted in the gaslight. "I've never had anything so beautiful."

"Sands Haberdashery could be yours, too." He covered her hand. "We work so well together, it's meant to be. I've tried to give you time, but…I hope you'll consider marrying me."

Both hands engulfed hers now, those practical hands that never stopped, so dependable and true. Jake had been there in her direst times. Her father would love her marrying a tailor.

She slipped from his grasp. “Jake, you’re the dearest friend I have, but I’m not ready to marry again.”

He stuffed his hands in his pockets. “I thought you were.”

“I may never be ready.” Her struggle with Harvey had suspended her heart like a fish frozen in a pond. “But I’ll tell you what, you’ll be the first to know when I am.” She took off the bracelet, but he stopped her.

“Keep it, Baby. Nothing’s changed between us. Accept it as a token of my…friendship.”

“It’s gorgeous.” She admired it.

Bush walked through the front door, just as the waiter delivered lamb chops and sweet potatoes to the table.

“Mrs. Doe.” Bush tipped his hat. “I’m surprised you’re not at the church auxiliary, decorating for Harvest Fair, seeing as it was your idea.”

Her heart sank at the auxiliary’s snub. Ever the divorced woman. “But they don’t know my plans. Hay wagons and scarecrows for the grange, pumpkins and cornstalks lining the boardwalk.”

“They finished the grange.”

Her throat closed. “Good, that leaves me less to do. I’ll set up the farmers’ market, games, and horseracing.”

“Stunning bracelet.” Bush took her hand and studied the diamonds. “A special occasion?”

“That doesn’t concern you,” Sands said.

“I almost forgot, Baby Doe,” Bush said. “Tabor wants to meet you about the Troy Mine.”

Her stomach flip-flopped.

“Troy Mine?” Sands asked.

“Harvey’s father gave me an old claim as a divorce settlement.”

“What does Tabor have to do with it?” He wiped his mouth with a checkered napkin.

“We’re partners. He’s developing the mine.”

His eyes bulged. “You’re partners with Horace Tabor?”

Sands’ misery turned her insides to mush. “Excuse us, Billy.

We'd like to enjoy our dinner."

Tipping his hat, Bush left their table. Sands laid his napkin across his unfinished plate.

"The last thing I want to do is hurt you, Jake," she said. "But I will not feel guilty for supporting myself. You, of all people, should understand that."

Sands promoted Baby Doe to manager of the new store. She wrote her family her proud news and enclosed her whole paycheck, thinking that would break their silence. But no return letter. Her family's judgment weighed on her, but she had to make a new life for herself, and she was grateful to Sands for the opportunity.

Unpacking a crate of taffeta opera gowns, she hung the intricate beauties on a rack to steam their wrinkles, their richness a stark contrast to the worn work dress she wore. Would she ever afford such frothy confections? Her mother's promises about her beauty paving the way to riches had been nothing but a cruel fairytale.

A long-nosed man wearing a sombrero entered the haberdashery, followed by Tabor with his commanding stride and confident air, holding a nosegay of wildflowers, like at the Troy Mine. The new suit she'd tailored skimmed his shoulder blades without a wrinkle, and the trouser crease broke at the ankle, draping perfectly on his long legs. No sign of the mountain man he once was.

He brought her flowers…her insides boiled with conflicting emotions. At first, she shrugged them off as excitement over the Troy Mine, but she found herself recounting what he said, how he looked, and even how he smelled. His generosity, honesty, and even his humor impressed her. She'd never met someone like Tabor, a man's man, strong and confident. Maybe he hadn't gone to college or traveled the world, but his innate intelligence and common sense made up for that. Thoughts she shouldn't have about a married man.

"Mr. Sands—" Tabor shook Jake's hand like an old friend. "Meet Jack Langrishe, writer, director, and star of our show at the Opera House. His costumes didn't make it from Deadwood. Fix him up, won't you?"

He strode to her and presented the nosegay. "Congratulations, Baby Doe. Quite an accomplishment to become manager of this establishment." He looked around the store.

"The building improvements were much costlier than we bargained for," she said. "I believe you should compensate Jake."

His mouth pursed comically, eyes dancing. "How about a tour?"

She led him through the store, proudly pointing out all the special features. "Modern plate-glass display windows, stamped-tin ceilings, handsome shelving lining the walls, parquet floors, oak tables to display merchandise with drawers underneath."

Tabor shook his head, his eyes wide. "A marvel what you've done with this place. The finest store in Leadville."

Warmth spread through her body, their effort rewarded. But it wasn't enough. "Two thousand dollars should cover Jake's building expenses."

Tabor's brows flew up, but he smiled and shook her hand. "A bargain."

Heat rushed her cheeks. "And what ever happened to the Troy Mine?"

"We hired a foreman and seven miners," he said. "They're pumping out ground water now. We should hear something soon."

His report knocked the wind out of her. "Since I hadn't heard from you, I thought you'd forgotten all about it."

"The senate was in session," he said, staring at her with those amber eyes. "But I would never renege on a deal with my partner."

"It's good you're back," she said. "The miner's union has been wreaking havoc at the mines, looting, setting fires, blocking mine entrances so no one can work. They're getting ready to target your Matchless Mine."

He sighed. "The union wants salaries raised to three dollars a day and eight-hour workdays instead of ten. It'll bankrupt the mines." He tugged at his mustache. "How'd you hear about this?"

"The union boss was in here shooting off his mouth, paying no attention to me."

"What man on earth wouldn't pay attention to you?" His eyes grazed her worn cuffs, and she clasped her hands behind her.

He cleared his throat. "I'd like you to be my guest for the grand opening of the Tabor Opera House."

"I'd love to come," she said, a little breathless.

He reached into his vest pocket. "Tickets for you and Jake."

How foolish to think he was asking her. "Very generous." Tucking the tickets in her pocket, she stared at the nosegay.

He picked up a new gown by the hanger. "What are you recommending for women to wear to the theater opening?"

The saleswoman in her surfaced. "The green silk is outstanding. See the ruched layers and the way the bodice hugs so nicely?"

"Wrap it up, will you?"

"What size?"

His eyes traveled from her face to her feet. "She's about your size."

Her chest tightened. He compared her to Augusta. "Your wife will love it." She wrapped the dress in fancy tissue, tearing it with trembling hands. He'd flustered her, that's all. She'd go to his confounded opening with Jake and have a grand old time.

18

Leadville, Colorado, December 1880

Fancy hand-tooled boots twitched and jerked as the buffalo skinner dangled from the noose in front of the courthouse, his neck snapped in two. Baby Doe pressed her fist to her mouth, her heart skipping beats, and pushed past the bloodthirsty crowd. The buffalo skinner had stolen his partner's hides. The judge ordered his hanging today, regardless of the Tabor Opera House opening. Jake Sands stood in front of the theater tapping his foot.

"I forgot about the lynching." She breathed deep to calm her nerves.

Sands stared at her with a curious mix of awe and betrayal.

"What?" She glanced down to see what he gawked at. "Oh, the dress. I bought it with my mining dividend." Almost the truth. The dress had been delivered to her room with a note, *Your first Troy dividend.* Green silk rustled under her hands like crisp hundred-dollar bills. She should've refused Tabor's gift but convinced herself she'd earned it.

"You were meant for beautiful clothes," Sands said.

"You look dapper yourself." She took his arm, determined to enjoy the evening. "Shall we?"

The Tabor Opera House rose three stories high with arched windows facing Mount Massive and Mount Elbert. Light shone from Tabor's suite on the second floor, and she looked to see if he would pass. Should she thank him when she saw him?

Inside the lobby, a young usher handed her a program, wearing the uniform she'd designed, scarlet jacket with double-breasted brass buttons and black satin stripes down the trousers. Her chest expanded, inhaling smells of beeswax and varnish.

Soon, the lively crowd pushed them through swinging doors into the expansive theater, glowing with gaslights. Dignitaries and townspeople craned their necks, taking in the ceiling frescoes, crystal chandeliers, gleaming gold leaf trim. A white and gold balustrade bordered the balcony; thick red carpet ran down aisles of gleaming hardwood.

"Now I've seen the elephant." Sands rolled his eyes. "Who is Tabor trying to impress?"

"I wonder." She recalled those afternoons with him, his long fingers grazing the architects' drawings, the eager timber of his voice describing every corbel and baluster, the keen gleam in his eyes assessing Marshall Field's furnishings. *What do you think, Baby Doe? Cherrywood or oak? Damask or tapestry? Cast iron or wood?* He'd listened to her opinions, which spurred her to make other suggestions. Those exhilarating exchanges ended abruptly when he left town.

Had Tabor felt the same way, or had she imagined it? Her hand slid across the cast-iron chairs, upholstered in scarlet velvet. "Eight hundred and fifty seats," she said.

"Doesn't look that big to me." Jake frowned.

Gaslights flickered three times. "Come on, our seats are down in front."

The eight-piece orchestra played a bouncy tune. On stage, golden ropes held back heavy red velvet drapes, revealing a painted backdrop of the Rocky Mountains.

A murmur arose from the audience, and all heads turned. Horace and Augusta Tabor walked down to their private box followed by a spotlight. Baby Doe's stomach fluttered. She reached for Jake's hand to ground herself. Solid and warm. His smile so tender.

The audience clapped, but no sound reached her ears. She watched

Tabor, bigger-than-life in his sharp black suit, waving to the crowd.

Augusta's eyes darted through tiny spectacles, and her gray topknot pulled her forehead tight. Black taffeta covered her from jawbone to bony wrists.

Sound returned to Baby Doe's ears, and she gasped for air.

"Are you all right?" Sands steadied her.

The lights lowered and the orchestra's rousing tune called their attention to the stage. Jack Langrishe made his entrance in leather chaps and vest adorned with grommets and leather laces.

"Where'd you find that getup?" Baby Doe whispered to Sands.

"The buffalo skinner they hung today." A sly smile crossed his lips. "His last wish was to die in new clothes. So, I outfitted him and used his clothes for Langrishe."

She tried to focus on the stage instead of Tabor. The comedy kept her laughing until her stomach ached. Jake squeezed her hand, and she squeezed back. So long since she laughed like this.

When the lights went up for intermission, she snuck a gaze at Tabor's box. Empty.

A uniformed page startled her, handing her an engraved invitation. *Please join us for the grand opening party at the Tabor Hotel ballroom.*

"What's that?" Sands asked.

"An invitation to the opening party, but we can't go." She shrugged her disappointment. "The haberdashery's open after the show."

"Go to the party. I'll mind the store. Have some fun."

She plucked business cards from Sands' coat pocket. "I'll hand out our cards and be back in an hour." She kissed his cheek, giving him no chance to change his mind.

Baby Doe's spirits rose with the scent of cedar boughs decorating the ballroom. She passed out business cards to men in dinner jackets, who were only too happy to receive them, nodding appreciation, and following her with their gaze. Recognizing two sopranos from Annunciation Church, she walked toward them, cards in hand. They ducked behind a fan, eyes narrowed in disapproval. Baby Doe stopped in the center of the room, isolated by her past.

Her customer, John Burke, offered her a glass of champagne. A slob, but unmarried, at least.

"Is Mr. Sands here?" he asked.

"He's minding the store." She drank half the glass.

Burke's features crowded the middle of his face, thin strands of hair swept over his glistening head. Tailoring his suits posed a peculiar problem. With his waist circumference twice that of his chest, she debated whether his trousers should be belted above or below his girth.

"That pinstripe suit looks handsome on you," she lied, finishing her champagne.

Burke laughed, his teeth caulked with cream cheese. "I'll be sure to let my tailor know." A waiter exchanged their empty glasses for fresh ones. "Veuve Clicquot from France. Only the best for Tabor." He toasted. "To the filthy rich."

His toast rankled. "Isn't it rude to disparage our host while drinking his champagne?" she asked. "Don't we Americans believe in climbing the ladder of success?"

"Not on the backs of others. Tabor built this town on the broken bodies of miners. They make two dollars a day while he builds an opera house, by God."

William Bush strutted over. "Mr. Burke." He kissed her hand. "And his lovely date."

She handed him a business card. "I came to promote Sands Haberdashery."

"Got any real booze here?" Burke asked, and Bush directed him to the bar.

"Saved my life," she said, laughing.

"John Burke's harmless."

"Even weasels wreak havoc."

"Come on, let me introduce you to the rest of the animals." He bowed to a thin matron dressed in black. "Mrs. Tabor, may I introduce Mrs. Doe."

Baby Doe balked but managed to curtsey. "I've heard so much about you."

"Excuse me. The Boss is calling," Bush said, leaving her to fend for herself.

Augusta lifted her chin to look through lenses perched on her nose. "If you heard about me from Mr. Bush, I apologize. He knows I don't approve of him."

"Mr. Steck told me about your work on women's suffrage." She sipped her wine.

"Well, Amos is a great lawyer." Augusta scanned the room. "Which one is your husband?"

She hesitated. "Actually, Mr. Steck arranged my divorce."

Augusta coughed. "A crying shame for a woman so young."

Heat rushed her face. "The shame was to stay with my husband so long. He abandoned me."

"I see. You're brave to be alone."

Her words kicked up a tornado of misery. "Not so brave." Pressure built behind her eyes.

Bush and Tabor joined them.

"Heh, heh, this is a party, not a funeral." Tabor turned to his wife. "I hope you've been pleasant, Augusta."

"She's been nothing but kind," Baby Doe said. "Just got me missing my Mam." She tried to smile. "The opera house is spectacular, Mr. Tabor."

"I disapprove of theater," Augusta said.

"I know, theater is a sin." Tabor laughed. "Mrs. Doe's dress is gorgeous, isn't it, Augusta?"

"Sands Haberdashery." Baby Doe whirled around to show him the full skirt and plunging back. Half-way, she realized she'd been too brash.

Augusta's eyes darted from her to Tabor and back again. "You two have met before?"

He straightened his shoulders. "I'm helping Mrs. Doe with a mine her husband left her."

"Then it was no coincidence Amos Steck granted your divorce." Augusta clenched her teeth.

"Let's not embarrass our guests," Tabor said.

"*You* are the embarrassment, Horace." Augusta turned and left.

"Dance with me." Bush pulled Baby Doe to the dance floor.

"What are you doing?" she said to Bush.

"Saving Tabor's reputation."

She swayed and dipped under his smooth guidance. "I didn't mean to make Augusta upset."

He shook his head. "She's unhappy with Tabor. She preferred the pioneer life where she could keep him under her thumb."

Guests watched them dance and whispered to each other.

"The whole room is jealous of me dancing with you." His breath warmed her ear.

"Why do you say that?"

"Don't play coy. I have the most beautiful woman in Colorado in my arms." He swung her around in perfect cadence to the music.

How wonderful it was to dance like this. Tabor moved to the bar, his eyes riveted on them.

"I've wanted to dance with you since you showed up at the Teller House," Bush whispered.

"Watch out what you wish for, it can come back to bite you." Snapping her teeth playfully, she spied Jake Sands standing at the ballroom door, glum jaw and half-lidded eyes. She dropped Bush's arms. "I promised Jake I'd be back in an hour." Glancing at the doorway, Sands had gone.

Bush opened his pocket watch. "The store's closed now. I'll walk you home."

"Get back to the party," she said. "My room is just downstairs."

"If you insist—"

"I do." He kissed her hand and left.

Retrieving her coat from the valet, she felt a paper in her pocket.

"Dear Baby Doe,

It troubles me to see you alone without protection, yet so many ready to pounce at the slightest chance. I'm willing to make you an offer, with all the benefits that come with that. Sit down and write me as you would your best friend. If I should have the pleasure to hear from you, I will write you a more interesting letter.

Your staunch admirer,

—John Burke."

His letter hollowed her out as every other admirer's letter had. And yet, on dark and lonely nights in her room, she reread each letter, one by one. She crumpled Burke's note in her pocket, vowing to make it on her own without a man's help.

19

Leadville, Colorado, February 1881

A series of blizzards left Leadville blanketed under four feet of snow. No customers walked into the haberdashery. Sands would close for the winter if not to keep her employed. Her salary was a burden she didn't want him to bear. If she sold the Troy Mine to Tabor, she could make it through the winter without Sands' paycheck.

Bush arranged a meeting for her, with a warning. "Watch yourself with Tabor. He can have any g'hal in town at a flip of a silver dollar."

At the appointed hour, she climbed the sweeping staircase to his suite, gaslights burning bright. She felt light-headed and anxious. Hopefulness or nerves? She hadn't seen him since the opening and missed his assuring presence. The wild town felt safer when he was around.

The carved double doors of his suite were closed, so she knocked. He opened them with a curious smile and glanced down the hallway. Chestnut hair waved behind his ears, gold-flecked eyes gleamed. His Creed cologne smelled like wind off snow-capped mountains.

"Come in," he said, in a throaty voice.

Inside his suite, candles burned halos on the arched windows and a chandelier cast a glow. A bear rug lay in front of a crackling fire. A silver bucket chilled Veuve Clicquot champagne. The room oozed...*romance.*

"There must be a misunderstanding. I asked for a business meeting." She moved to leave.

"Please stay." He touched her arm, and she hesitated.

What did she have to fear, after all. Tabor was her partner, not a lecher. She took off her cape and hung it on the coat tree. "I came to discuss the Troy Mine."

"We shall." He offered a chair. "But I was hoping you'd join me for some champagne first."

"Celebrating something?" Brushing past him, she sat on a velvet window seat, a niggling pressure building in her chest.

"You could say that." He lifted the bottle from the sweating silver bucket. "I wanted to thank you for tipping me off about the miner's union. I was able to negotiate, and they didn't strike the Matchless Mine." Holding the cork, he twisted the bottle, releasing a gasp. An expert. Bush had bragged about their antics with showgirls, claiming Tabor's motto was, "Champagne all around."

He poured the golden liquid into coupes and handed her a glass, his touch sizzling up her wrist like a dynamite fuse.

"To avoiding a strike, Mr. Tabor." She drank the entire coupe, and he poured her another.

"Please, call me Horace." He sat next to her on the window seat.

"I prefer Mr. Tabor." Scooting away. "I'm not one of your g'hals."

"How could I confuse you with a g'hal? I've never seen you kick up your heels." He studied her. "Divorce must be tough on a young woman."

"How many divorced women have you met?"

"Only one, come to think of it."

"And most likely, you'll never meet another. I'm a non-entity. An unspeakable." She drank.

"I've had my own trials with marriage." Sticking his finger in the candle flame, he winced but didn't move. "I thought a silver strike would make up for everything my wife found lacking in me."

"Silver didn't help?" She rubbed soot off his finger.

"Made it worse." Frowning at Augusta's portrait in a gilded frame, he laid it face down. "Poor and happy one moment, rich and miserable the next."

Bringing his finger to her lips, she kissed it.

His brows arched.

"I had the same dream as you," she said. "I thought a gold mine would solve all my problems, but it didn't happen that way."

He poured more wine. "I say, if money can buy it, you don't have a care in the world."

"A rich man's motto if I ever heard one." She let go of his hand.

"Think about it," he said. "Important things aren't about money. Health. Friendship. True love. If you don't have those, money can't buy them for you."

His wisdom drew her to him. She kissed his lips, lightly at first, then, unable to hold back, she kissed him again. His groan shook her to her senses. *A married man.*

She pulled away. "Too much champagne." But wine had nothing to do with how she felt. Tabor understood her better than she understood herself. He'd dreamed the same dreams, and they'd disappointed him, too. He knew the heartache of conquering a mountain, no matter the difficulty, no matter the danger, no matter what rational people said. He knew.

Tabor retrieved a burlap sack from his rolltop desk. "You wanted to know about the Troy."

She sat upright. "Yes, I want to sell you my half of the mine."

"Now, that would be plain fool hardy." Opening the sack, he poured sparkling gray rocks onto a tray. "The Troy struck high-grade silver ore at seventy-five feet."

"You must be kidding."

She rushed into his chest, his strong arms and bracing scent enveloping her. Her lips brushed his sideburns, sparking temptation.

He turned to her, and she was ready. His warm lips worked like a tonic, releasing tension and loneliness. Kissing him again and again, powerful sensations flooded her body. She floated blissfully down a river...then, the current turned deep and violent.

She pulled back, gulping air, needing to gather her wits. Picking up a rock, she smelled it, willing the mineral scent to clear her senses. "Looks like pure silver."

"Now you won't have to live on Sands' paychecks," he said, pleased with himself.

Her hackles prickled. "Remind me not to tell Billy anything."

Tabor caressed her cheek, reassuring. "You've struggled long enough, Baby. I've deposited your dividends into your bank account. You can leave Sands whenever you wish."

Something didn't add up. "Where did this ore come from?" She let the rock slip from her fingers. "The Troy closed down for the winter."

His Adam's apple rose and fell, sweat beaded his forehead. "I told Billy you'd see through this ruse. The Matchless is still working. The silver came from there."

"I cannot be bought." Her head throbbed with anger and champagne as she crossed toward the door and put on her cape.

Glancing back, she saw his head hanging down, caught in a lie. She let herself out, heart knocking against her chest, mad at herself more than anything. Tabor had wormed his way into her heart with his pitiful story of unrequited love and wrong turns, expecting she'd swallow the tale whole. He'd played her. Billy was right about him.

Outside, freezing wind chafed her cheeks, yet the imprint of his lips kindled her longing. Confused, she rehearsed her confession to Father O' Mannie all the way to Annunciation Church.

20

Denver, Colorado, March 1881

Working at home in his mansion, Tabor rubbed his eyes good and hard. If he could forget Baby Doe, he might make sense of these papers. The latest miner union demands could bankrupt the industry. He'd been their champion, supporting insurance and wage increases, but the more he gave, the more they demanded. Just as he needed to finance the Windsor Hotel for Maxcy.

Still, he thought of nothing but her. Her fervent kiss rocked him to his core, in stark contrast to her beautiful face when she left, stricken white by his dishonesty.

Augusta carried in a tea tray to his study. "I baked those molasses cookies you like."

"Set them on the table." He studied the union demands, searching for a compromise.

"Can't you take a minute for your wife?" Her voice trembled. "We haven't talked since I got back from Aunt Flossie's funeral."

"I'm sorry. These papers give me a headache." Setting the file aside, he gave her his full attention. She still wore her mourning dress, the bleak color aged her. Corkscrew curls on her temples did nothing to soften her expression, so different than Baby Doe's ready smile.

"What are you working on? Not another fool mine, I hope." She peered over the top of her pince-nez glasses and poured tea.

"Augusta. It's what I do. I mine." The cords in his neck stretched tight as banjo strings. "Maybe you've noticed I'm rather good at it."

"A fool and his money are soon parted." She clucked her tongue. "Come drink your tea."

He sat in the settee by the fireplace. She placed two lumps of sugar and cream in the tea and handed him a cup.

"I like it black," he said.

"That's no way to drink tea."

He stared into the milky liquid, trying to think of a subject they wouldn't argue about. "Did you hear about that new dance hall in Leadville?"

Her mouth puckered. "How can I uphold your reputation in Denver with stories circulating about your wild women?"

"The cavalry boys take me dancing. Doesn't mean anything." He smiled. "Maybe you shouldn't sleep in the servants' quarters instead of our bedroom."

"It's closer to Black Beauty. You know how lonely my cow gets at night."

His laugh tasted bitter. She'd rather sleep with her cow than him. "Say, what were you digging for in the moonlight? Don't tell me you're planting more corn."

"Not corn, money. I bury big cans of money for a rainy day."

"We own two banks, for God's sake."

"If our money is in the bank, you'll use it to buy another mine."

He laughed. "If it makes you feel better, Augusta, bury trunks of cash."

"You go through money like toilet paper. There'll be nothing left for Maxcy."

"Don't worry. I'm buying the Windsor Hotel for Maxcy to run."

"You have to stop, Horace." Her shrill voice unraveled. "You're out of control." Her arm flailed against the china teapot, crashing on the floor. Shattered pieces surrounded them. "I suppose you'll just buy me a new teapot, won't you?"

"I'd dance barefoot on these shards, Augusta, if it'd make you happy." He picked up pieces and stacked them on the tray. "Tell me about your aunt's funeral. How's your father taking it?" He pictured his father-in-law who drove the quarry like a slave boss.

"He was fit-to-be-tied when they read her will. Aunt Flossie left everything to…What do you remember about your mother?"

…her scent of jasmine, her velvety voice, her cool hand on his neck. "Not much, she left when I was twelve. Did you hear something about her at the funeral?"

"Father made me promise not to say anything until he contests the will."

"What does my mother have to do with it?"

Her lips clamped together.

"You're siding with your father against me?" Her betrayal clawed at his chest. "Come to think of it, I can't remember the last time you sided with me."

She picked up the tray and left his office.

He poured a whiskey, drank it, felt the burn in his gullet. Poured another. Her dishonesty disgusted him. But he was no saint. He'd been dishonest with Baby Doe and it backfired. He prided himself for being an honest man but, the more he stewed on it, the more he realized he'd been dishonest for years. That sneaky kind of dishonesty that starts with one harmless lie, then another, until you can't tell lies and truth apart. He'd been lying all along, leading Augusta to believe he could be the man she wanted. Worse that that, he'd lied to himself, trying to make things work. But, by fifty years old, a man ought to own up to who he was and live with the consequences.

Tabor pulled down a trunk from the closet and started packing up his office.

"You bought the Windsor?" Bush perused the opulent hotel, his temples throbbing. "We shouldn't be expanding with the union threatening to shut down the mines."

"Leave the miners to me." Tabor thumbed his chest. "You handle the finances. The Windsor runs in the black, unless we screw it up."

The hotel covered an entire block in the heart of Denver. His boss's holdings grew faster than he could record. The more money Tabor made, the more he gambled on new prospects. Wasn't fair to have his dumb luck.

"Will you teach Maxcy the hotel business?" Tabor frowned. "I want him to manage the Windsor."

Stunned and flattered, Bush answered, "I'll teach him everything I know."

"Good." Tabor collapsed on a leather divan. "I'm moving into the penthouse."

A waiter interrupted. "What can I get you to drink, gentleman?"

"Sarsaparilla," Tabor said.

"Double Scotch whiskey, neat." Bush brushed the waiter away as panic set in. Turnbull had told him Tabor was their leading candidate for the U.S. senate. If he separated from Augusta, the Republicans would drop him, and Bush's kickbacks would end. "You can't do this to Augusta. You've been together so long."

"Twenty-two years now." He squeezed his eyes. "For twenty-two years, she convinced me she was the only thing that stands between me and *Bad Luck Tabor.* Twenty-two years, she reminded me that my pa suffocated in his own drunken vomit."

The waiter arrived and set drinks on the table.

"Bring the bottle," Bush told him and turned back to Tabor. "You can't desert Maxcy."

"Maxcy should stand by his mother. She'll need him." He shoved a leather portfolio at Bush. "Take Augusta a hundred thousand in government bonds. She can live on the interest."

"Generous." Bush swallowed a mouthful of whiskey. "But the Republican Party won't see it that way. They want you to run for U.S. senator, but if you do this, they'll revoke your nomination."

"A man has a right to live life the way he sees fit," Tabor said.

"The party will just have to accept me as I am. If they don't, they won't get my contribution check." Tabor play-punched his arm.

Bizarrely happy for a man about to lose his family and political career. The reason hit him. "Don't tell me it's Baby Doe."

Tabor' eyebrow arched. "This has been brewing for a long time." He didn't deny it.

Bush should have stopped his lark earlier. "You have to listen to me, Boss. Since the very first day Baby Doe arrived, she needled me with questions about your silver strike." Heart palpitating, he scrambled for something more. "And Marianne has heard horrible things about her."

"Pay no mind to the rumor mill."

"She heard Doc Holliday treated Baby Doe for the clap." Bush set the hook, and Tabor swallowed it, his Adam's apple waggling.

Bush reeled him in, fabricating more lies. "Baby Doe entertains more sugar daddies than all the whore cribs put together. She'll take your money and run."

Tabor stood. "I'm going to forget you said all that." He clapped down hard on his shoulder. "I gave you a job to do, didn't I?"

"Right away, Boss." He stood and saluted his gambler skimmer. "Just don't want to see you throw your life away over a woman like that." He bolted before Tabor could retort. Turnbull would know how to stop this thing.

21

Leadville, Colorado, April 1881

Baby Doe would quit the haberdashery when Sands returned from his buying trip. Just wasn't sure where she'd go. Not Oshkosh, with her family still not talking to her. Maybe Denver. She enjoyed the city when she was there. Maybe work at the theater on Larimer.

She loved her job, but it wasn't fair to Jake. He hadn't brought up marriage again, but his actions gave him away. His face lit up when she came through the door, he followed her as she created new displays, not to mention his shy invitations to dinner.

She wished she could return his affections. Why reject a steadfast suitor like Jake yet still be ruminating about Tabor?

Closing the haberdashery, she dropped the skeleton key in her handbag. Scents of pine, sage, and wildflowers reminded her of Tabor. "Stop that right now," she scolded herself.

A month had passed since that last night. She'd thrown herself into work, read the Bible, and said extra rosaries. And yet, when her shipment of House of Creed cologne arrived at the store, she brought a bottle home and kept it on her nightstand. When she awoke from forbidden dreams entwined with Tabor, she opened the bottle of Creed and breathed in the scent.

Images whisked through her brain: his rakish smile holding up a silver nugget, his confidence shaking hands with President Grant, the naked longing in his eyes by candlelight.

Reaching her room, she couldn't wait to slip into bed. A note peeked from under her door.

"Meet me in my suite at seven. –Horace"

Her head reeled. Father O'Mannie commanded her to stay away, allowing God to forgive her. But she had to see him one more time before she left Leadville. Dressing in a gorgeous sapphire gown, she tightened her corset until she couldn't breathe. Let him suffer.

He waited at the door of his suite.

Her breath hitched, a deep ache within her ribs.

Dressed in a dark suit, white tuck shirt, and black string tie, his long fingers drummed the door frame. He enclosed her hand in his. "I left Augusta."

"No." Chills quivered through her but Father O'Mannie's face flashed in her head. *Go child and sin no more.* Her heart churned under her ribcage. She steadied herself on the door frame.

"Not your fault, Baby, believe me. Augusta and I were over the day I struck my first silver vein. It was never the same after that."

"I can't be in the middle, Horace." She turned away, but he grabbed her waist.

"You're not in the middle." He drew her close. "You're the only."

She couldn't move. Couldn't breathe. The man she obsessed over for so long stood right in front of her, offering himself. Every cell in her body said…yes.

Feeling woozy and not trusting her limbs, she walked away and sat on the settee. "This is moving too fast, Horace. What made you leave Augusta?"

"I was in New York for two weeks promoting the mines. Every time I talked about Leadville, I thought of you." He poured Veuve Clicquot and handed her a glass. "And soon it didn't matter what I was talking about, I was hearing your voice, your smart ideas, your laugh. When I gave up trying to forget you, the truth became very clear." He took her hands. "We need to be together."

"That's impossible." Wiggling free, she grabbed her champagne. "You're the most famous man in the West." She finished the glass, hoping to calm her nerves.

"You're letting that stop you?"

"I'm afraid." Why did she always choose the one man who would make life a living hell?

"You've never feared anything. What are you afraid of?"

A hysteric giggle rose in her throat. "The wrath of God, your wife and son, my family, the city of Leadville, the state of Colorado…"

"You're overthinking this." Tabor poured champagne. "Don't we have a right to be happy?"

Simple question. Complex answer.

He leaned close. "Are you happy when you're with me?"

She thought about it. "More alive than I've ever felt, excited for what comes next."

"I like that answer." He kissed her, tasting of licorice. The brush of his mustache on her mouth made her quiver.

"Will you still feel this way when the firing squad gets hold of you?" She drowned the image with champagne.

The saddest smile bloomed on his lips.

She had to hug him close, her hands stroking his back muscles, so strong, yet vulnerable. Tucking her face into his neck, she inhaled his scent, that powerful scent. Her lips moved on his, searching, wanting. His limbs wrapped her in warmth that penetrated every part of her. She needed all of him.

Minutes or hours later he pulled away and left an aching void in her breast.

"I bought the Windsor Hotel in Denver and moved into the penthouse," he said huskily. "If you like, you can have the adjoining suite."

She hadn't thought that far, her desire racing. "You want us to live in sin?"

"I'm working on a divorce." Those sad lines deepened from his nose to his mouth. "It's private in the penthouse, and you'll have a suite to yourself, sitting room, kitchenette, bedroom…"

"My own suite?" Away from leering men, away from gossiping church ladies, away from… "Jake." Her hand flew to her mouth.

"What about Jake? He can find another manager."

She stood and put on her shawl. "Jake's been so good to me."

Tabor pulled her down and kissed her until his beloved face and blessed lips and strong arms engulfed her and everything else fell away...

Except Jake.

She pulled back, her guilt tainting everything. "I'm sorry, Horace. I can't. I cannot do this."

Baby Doe let herself into the store and set the gift she'd ordered for Sands on the table. Looking around for the last time, she was proud of the handsome displays and spotless housekeeping. She straightened a tweedy sleeve, the texture rough on her fingers.

Sands miserable note waited under her hotel door this morning, wondering where she was.

The door squeaked, and she turned. "Jake. You surprised me."

He brushed past her, his brown curls smelling of rosemary. "You don't owe me an explanation." Grabbing a feather duster, he fluffed invisible dust.

"Jake, can't we talk about this? You've been like a brother to me."

"Now I'm a brother?" He spat the words. "I did everything for you, Baby."

"I appreciate that." Pain pulsed behind her eyes. "Without you, I wouldn't have survived."

"I gave you time to heal. Didn't pressure you. But I wasn't enough, was I? You wanted more from the time you came to Central City."

She straightened a suit on its hanger, hoping he'd calm down.

"You loved me, Baby Doe." His accusation hung like icicles on the roof.

"I never told you I loved you."

"Of course, you did, Baby." His feather duster trembled. "Every day I looked in your eyes, I saw your love. When I nursed you back to life after your baby died. When I brought you here, lent you money, gave you a job."

"I owe you so much."

"It's not about the money. Or maybe it is? He has more money than I do."

"That's not fair." She sat him down at the oak table, taking his hands. "You're the best friend I've had but you must have known I didn't love you that way."

"William Bush, really? How could you?" His mouth contorted. "He's slippery."

Her head ducked back. "Not Billy. I'm in love with Horace Tabor."

His eyes widened. "That rich bastard? He'll toss you out like a losing poker hand."

"His marriage is over, Jake. We're meant to be together. Can't you be happy for me?"

Sands' eyes followed a milk wagon clanging past the display window.

"I will be okay, Jake." She squeezed his hand. "And so, will you. It will all work out."

He closed his eyes. "My God, Tabor is a lucky son-of-a-gun."

She slid the leather box across the table. "This is for you."

Inside the box he found the gold pocket watch and turned it over. "To Jake, until the very end, I'll remember my best friend. Love, Baby Doe." Placing the watch in the box, he shoved it back. "I don't need Tabor's consolation prize. And I don't want to be friends." He walked away.

Whatever she said to stop him would be a lie. As Emily Dickenson wrote, *the heart wants what it wants.* And her heart had never wanted someone more.

22

Denver, Colorado, June 1881

A new life. The first month was a whirlwind of excitement as Baby Doe settled into her Windsor Hotel suite adjoining Tabor's. She marveled at the twists of fate that brought her to this paradise of fuchsia velvet settees, carnation lampshades, and a rose marble fireplace. The perfect pink nest to nurture their new love, whispering together until the embers glowed on the hearth, lolling around in a feather bed cloud, room service on trays with rose buds and linen napkins.

But too soon, the responsibilities of state and business stole Tabor away from their Windsor haven, leaving her by herself for days. After the haberdashery and back-breaking mining, the hours alone stretched out as endlessly as the vast Colorado horizon.

She wrote her family about her move to Denver which prompted a surprising flurry of letters. Mam questioned why she left Leadville. How would she support herself now and could she send money because Da had a chance to open a new haberdashery?

Finally, she could help her parents in the substantial way she'd come west for. She wrote Mam that she'd taken Tabor as a partner in her mine and they'd produced a handsome profit. Mam didn't need more details until they were engaged. *Engaged*? She pushed the thought away, enclosing a thousand-dollar check for Da's haberdashery, feeling ambivalent. It felt better not to worry about money, but money mucked things up, too, like her feelings for her parents. Instead of their daughter, she'd become a source of income.

Not allowing her thoughts to pickle, she threw herself into creating a detailed scrapbook about Tabor's career, scouring *The Denver Tribune* for articles about good things he did for Colorado.

"Lt. Governor Tabor is no hanging judge regarding criminal pardons. He listened to the death-row prisoners and made fair, compassionate judgments."

Pasting articles to the pages, she pondered the difference between the Tabor in the newspaper and her own attentive lover. She bit her lip. He was *not* hers alone. They couldn't be seen together in public. She'd found true love, yet she was secreted away.

Bored with the scrapbook, she began to sketch ideas on a pad, drawing a grand theater in exquisite detail, as splendid as she could imagine. Over the next few days, she rose early and stayed up late drawing. The idea became so beautiful and real, she couldn't wait to show Tabor.

Friday came, and the mantel clock struck four. A key twisted in the lock, and he stepped inside, handsome and dignified in his long coat and top hat. She buried her face in his vest, smelling of cherry tobacco and the bracing mist of Creed.

He stroked her hair. "You're a glorious sunset at the end of a long day."

His poetry was as corny as his jokes, but it touched her. She untied his four-in-hand and poured him a sherry. "I was reading about your pardons. How does it feel to have the power of life or death in your hands?"

"It's not in my hands. It's in their eyes." He sipped the sherry. "Sometimes their eyes beg to end their miserable ways. Sometimes, they beg for another chance."

"I wouldn't want to be in your position," she said.

"I can make a real difference in people's lives here." His face shone with satisfaction, then his brows knitted. "Don't get me wrong, I could never give up mining. We discovered a new silver vein at the Matchless Mine. Biggest vein they've ever seen."

She hugged him. "And you said the Matchless made you pin money."

"This vein alone will yield twenty-five thousand dollars a month."

Silver dollars piling higher every month. Never going hungry, never wearing rags, never living in a shack. "That should make stockholders happy."

"I'm the sole stockholder. The Matchless stock was never worth selling, so I kept it myself."

"What will you do with all that money?" *Money*, that two-edged sword.

"What will *we* do with the money?" His amber gaze sparked.

She took her sketch pad from the desk. "What if we build an opera house for Denver?"

"Like in Leadville?"

"Only grander. The Tabor *Grand* Opera House." She showed him her drawings. "Red brick and white marble, six-stories high and a block long, massive cupolas on the corners. A center rotunda with stained-glass ceiling. Spires rise from each peak in the roof."

"I didn't know you had this talent." His fingers grazed the sketches. "Not a bad idea… A grand theater to bring culture and entertainment to the West…I'll look at real estate next week."

"I'll come with you." She needed the chance to leave the suite.

"Too close to the election. People will talk." He rubbed her neck. "You're better off here."

His rejection tasted harsh as chicory.

Tabor embraced her idea, purchasing land, hiring an architect and building crew. A tornado of activity, fueled by Matchless Mine profits, whirled around her. So different than with Harvey or Jake, when she'd worked for their vision. Horace used his money and influence to make *her* dream come true. Still, doubt niggled her, having never done anything this big. What if it failed? Would their relationship survive?

While Tabor was in Leadville, she searched Larimer shops for books and periodicals about palaces, estates, museums, architecture, and had them delivered to the Windsor.

"Where would you like these, Missus?" The young Chinese bellboy peered over a stack of books weighing down his thin arms. His mandarin-collared shirt with black frog closings reminded her of Chin Lin Sou in Central City.

After the Fourth of July closed, she heard Chin had opened a laundry in Denver's Chinatown, on Hop Alley. She wanted to visit him, but Hop Alley was not a place for women, notorious for opium dens, illegal gambling, prostitution. Someday, she'd brave it.

"Pile them beside the others, Bin-Bin," she said.

As the boy bent over, the books tumbled to the floor. "So sorry. So sorry." He shielded his head as if she'd hit him.

"It's all right." She piled them up. "They're only books."

He averted his eyes and bowed.

"You've been a great help." She gave him a silver dollar, a habit gleaned from Tabor.

"Lady kind to Bin-Bin." He handed her an envelope. "This came for Mr. Tabor."

Beautiful penmanship caught her eye, then the signature. Augusta Tabor. "I'll give it to him." Bin-Bin closed the door, and she slid a knife under the seal, pushing second thoughts aside.

"Dear Husband,

Believe me that no one will be prouder of the Tabor Grand Opera House than your broken-hearted wife. God knows I'm truly sorry for our estrangement and will humble myself if you will only return. Whatever I said was in the heat of passion and you know the awful condition I was in. I beseech you, let us bury the past and commence anew, and my life shall be devoted to you forever.

Your loving wife,

Augusta"

The door knob rattled, and she stuffed the letter under her mattress.

"Hello-o-o Baby." Tabor set down his bag and spun her around. "Oh, I missed you."

She kissed him like he'd been gone months instead of days. His powerful presence filled the room, and her lonesome suite became their home again. Settling him into the loveseat, she poured sherry and snuggled into his arm.

He dug in his bag and presented her a large rock. "Solid silver from the Matchless."

"It must weigh twenty pounds." She set the rock by her drawings which he picked up.

"You've been busy." He leafed through the pages.

"Belgian carpeting, English furniture, French tapestries," she explained.

He smoothed his mustache. "What would you call this style?"

"Over-the-moon," she joked.

"Perfect. Because I told the newspaper it was a mix of Rococo, Moroccan, and Egyptian, and it's making me Baroque."

She hugged him, peering at the mattress which concealed Augusta's letter. Should she give it to him? She squeezed him tighter, her love outweighing her guilt.

Months later, Baby Doe went to see the progress on the Tabor Grand. Billy Bush waited for her in the Windsor lobby, resplendent with wood paneling rising to deep crown moldings. He hadn't changed much for Denver, still the gambler skimmer, emerald brocade vest, diamondback cane, and jet-black widow's peak.

"Mrs. Doe, how mysterious you look. Though, personally, I prefer your mining togs."

She pulled a black mantilla over her face, disguising her identity from reporters. "Shush. See that old woman in the hat behind the column? She spies on me whenever I'm in the lobby."

"Don't you recognize Augusta?" He pointed his cane. "I'll tell Maxcy to keep her away."

"Maxcy hates me as it is, why rub it in his face?" She jerked his arm toward the door. "Why Horace insists on you taking me everywhere, I'll never know."

"He doesn't want any trouble," Bush said. "And *you* are trouble."

"Pshaw." She helped herself into the scarlet carriage hitched to grey Percherons.

Bush closed the door behind him, and the carriage jolted off. She flipped the suffocating mantilla off her face, hating the thing, but so far it had worked to diffuse rumors.

"What was all that in the newspaper about you and Tabor raising a ruckus in Leadville?" she asked, heat rising from her corset. "You seem hell-bent on ruining his reputation."

"You think you're the only pretty girl to turn his head?" he said. "Last week, Gladys Robeson performed on stage with those lace tights and red bustier, and Tabor tossed a bucketful of silver dollars across the footlights."

"Poppycock." But what if he told the truth? The carriage stopped, and she jerked the door open. Her kitten heel stuck between cobblestones and Bush bent to release it.

"Gladys took his money and disappeared." He jiggled her heel, but it held firm. "Tabor just ordered more champagne, and we woke up in the same spot, a girl in each arm."

"I won't hear another word of these lies." Baby Doe pressed her hands on her ears and squeezed her eyes shut.

"Hear no evil, see no evil." Tabor said, behind her.

She pulled the mantilla over her face to hide her fury. "Better to cover up in public."

"Always a step ahead of me, Baby." Tabor walked with them into the lobby. "The stone masons need to be paid, Billy. Take care of it, will you?"

"Sure, Boss." He tipped his hat.

She'd love to slap the smirk off his face. "I don't want Billy at the Tabor Grand."

"Whoa, hold your horses." Tabor laughed. "Billy's been with me before the Tabor name meant beans."

"You can't trust him," she said.

Tabor turned to her. "He's like the brother I never had a chance to know."

"You had a brother?"

He flinched, and the old sadness returned to his face. "Let's save that tale for another time?"

"Of course." She didn't want to ruin the moment they'd see their creation together. "You found my green and red marble." She ran her hand up the column.

"Italy, just like you thought. They found your Louis XIV chairs in Paris, too."

Everywhere she looked, her drawings had become real: leaded windows, Italian cornices, and Shakespearian tapestries. Fifteen hundred plush seats from the stage to the curved balconies. The domed ceiling displayed a panorama of billowing clouds to twinkling stars.

In the past, when she'd designed stage sets, with her brother's poor painting skills, they never lived up to her imagination. But the Tabor Grand was more glorious than she dared imagine. How astonishing that Tabor had supported her idea. He endorsed her, collaborated with her, invested in her. There could be no greater love than that, and that love was hers.

They climbed the spiral staircase to the private Tabor box, surrounded by stage sets. On stage, a painter on a ladder dropped his palette, clattering to the floor.

"Mr. Hopkins," Tabor called. "We came to see your masterpiece."

The painter turned to him. "This is the last curtain I'll ever paint, so help me God."

The curtain depicted tragic ruins of buildings crumbling to dust in a shroud of gray mist.

Baby Doe read the poem painted on the bottom.

"So fleet the works of men, back to the earth again;

Ancient and holy things fade like a dream."

Despair seeped into her bones. "We could have picked a cheerier poem, don't you think?"

"I'm not so good at profound, I guess," Tabor said.

Bush's cane tapped across the marble floor.

"Billy, I'm glad you came back." Tabor gripped his shoulder. "I've thought about it till I'm off the chump, but I see no way around it. I want you to accompany Baby Doe opening night."

"What?" All her gratification was ripped from her.

"I'd be honored to accompany Mrs. Doe." A smile curled Bush's lip.

"You understand, don't you, Baby?" Tabor asked.

"Oh, I understand," she said. "You can't be seen with a harlot."

"Don't be like that." He hugged her. "It won't be like this forever."

"Only one thing." She looked at him squarely. "Augusta cannot sit in our private box."

23

Denver, Colorado,
September 1881

Just as Baby Doe clipped a jeweled ornament into her hair for the final touch, a bellboy delivered a May Company box with a note in Tabor's scrawling hand.

"To my darling Baby Doe,

At least if I can't be with you, I'll know I have the most beautiful woman in the theater.

Sweetest Love, Horace"

Her heart plunged. The most important night of her life, and she'd had to live it in secret.

Lifting the tissue, she uncovered a confection that made her gasp: violet organdy edged with silver filigree, so much finer than the dress she'd planned to wear. Fingers shaking, she tried on the gown.

A low neckline framed a creamy expanse of shoulders and chest. A rigid corset created fullness at the bosom and hips but cinched her tiny waist. Ribbons tied up the outer skirt, revealing an underskirt of cornflower blue. An elaborate bustle extended in a profusion of frills and swags.

She heard a knock and swung open the door. "Horace."

Bush's mouth fell open, and she laughed.

"Billy, you're drooling." Cornflower blue peeked from his black dinner jacket, annoying her. "Your cummerbund matches my dress."

"Tabor sent it," he said.

"He wants people to think we're a couple."

"He can't afford a scandal to ruin his nomination for U.S. senator."

She considered the circumstances. Tabor needed Augusta to get elected. "Is Augusta coming tonight?" she asked.

"I'm not sure." Billy passed her a silver flask.

She shook her head.

"Drink it. You're acting all possessed-like."

She took a long drink, Irish whiskey burning her throat.

"Now listen to me." He grabbed her chin. "Everybody who is anybody will be there. Be discreet."

Defiance surged from her gut. "If Horace wanted to keep me under wraps, he wouldn't have chosen this dress."

"That's Tabor for you." He ogled her breasts. "He wants to have his cake and eat it, too."

"I don't appreciate being the cake." She took another swig of whiskey.

Baby Doe saw Tabor at the entrance, striking in formal coat and top hat, a line of people waiting to thank him. At least Augusta wasn't standing next to him.

The corner tower of the Tabor Grand soared like a beacon of pride. The streets were jammed with people arriving in buggies and on foot. Fine carriages with handsome livery lined up at the entrances. Cowboys, miners, trappers, buffalo hunters, railroad men, cavalry, gunslingers, and gamblers came for opening night.

In the lobby, a rotund man smoking a cigar approached Bush. "I need to talk to you."

"I'll explore the lobby," she said.

Thick Brussels carpet cushioned her feet. She studied the moiré silk wall-covering, wood paneling with gilded molding, gaslights twinkling under cut-glass globes. Marble, mahogany, brocade… every surface spoke of opulence. Two immense gilded mirrors reflected an enormous Baccarat crystal chandelier. A fresco of cherubs hovered above them on the ceiling. The perfume of gardenias and tuberoses mingled with expensive tobacco.

A bell chimed, but Turnbull and Bush continued their heated debate. She waited close by, so he'd see her.

"Stop worrying. Tabor will win hands down," Bush said.

"If he gets divorced, he'll lose," Turnbull said. "And I'll lose my puppet at the Capitol."

"Then he won't get divorced."

Bush's words hit hard. Had she given her heart to a man who valued politics over her?

"See to it." Turnbull stuffed a hundred-dollar bill in Bush's pocket and waddled away.

"Tabor won't divorce?" she asked Bush.

"I'm paid to tell people what they want to hear," he said.

"And I'm a smudge on Tabor's shining armor?" She couldn't bear it.

"I wouldn't worry about it if I were you. You always land on your feet." He took her arm and walked through massive mahogany doors into the grand rotunda, buzzing with excitement.

An usher led them down to the front seats, fashioned from smooth Japanese cherry and brushed mohair upholstery. Patrons gaped at the stained-glass dome, colored facets dancing in the gaslights, dramatic murals decorated with laurel garlands.

She stared at the stage, the backdrop curtain looming like a specter.

"So fleet the works of men, back to the earth again;
Ancient and holy things fade like a dream."

Sweat dampened her tendrils. She'd ignored these warnings before, but now?

Maxcy Tabor and his fiancé sat in their proscenium box, waving to the audience. Tabor's box stood empty, save for the *TABOR* placard of Matchless silver she'd had engraved.

Panic prickled her spine. If Tabor walked in with Augusta right now, she would die on the spot. She stood, but Bush pulled her down in her seat, squeezing her hand until it hurt.

"Is this your idea of discreet?"

The lights dimmed. A small, studious man entered the stage. "Welcome to the opening of the Tabor Grand." His large ears flapped from the sides of his head. "I'm Eugene Field, editor of *The Denver Tribune*." His sing-song voice sounded comical.

So, this was the mighty Mr. Field, his powerful pen a lightning rod of controversy.

"I'm not always kind to Mr. Tabor in the newspaper. But here's the truth. Without Horace Tabor, Denver would be downright boring."

The audience laughed.

"Who else through blind persistence could lasso culture and lay it at our feet?" Field flung his arm. "Ladies and Gentlemen, our host and benefactor, Mr. Horace Tabor."

The applause deafened Baby Doe.

Tabor walked to the microphone, towering over Field, his top hat making him taller yet.

"Many people worked tirelessly on the Tabor Grand and deserve our heartfelt thanks," he said. "But there's one person without whom none of this would be possible." He held out his hand from the stage.

Tabor's courage to publicly recognize her pumped adrenaline through her veins.

"William Bush," he said. "Manager of the Tabor Grand. Stand up and take a bow."

The spotlights crisscrossed, hunting them down, blinding her with their glare. How could she be so stupid? Of course, he wouldn't introduce her. She was his mistress, nothing more.

"Now, without further ado, we welcome the famous opera star, Emma Abbott, to sing *Regnava nel Silenzio*."

The soprano appeared under the spotlight, costumed in lace and chintz, her hair in long curls. Though Baby Doe couldn't comprehend her Italian, arrows of tortured love shot through her.

What was she starting here? A life of lies and secrecy?

Glancing up in the darkened theater, she found Tabor taking his seat and waved a handkerchief to catch his eye. Augusta appeared behind him, ghostly face above her black dress. Baby Doe snatched her hand down, and Augusta glared her victory.

Emma Abbott hit an ear-splitting crescendo, and Baby Doe sprung from her seat. Bush grabbed for her, but she tore away and scaled the stairs.

A blast of cold night air hit her scorching face as she bolted from the opera house.

"Baby Doe," Bush yelled from the doors.

She ran down the boardwalk, holding up her skirts, relieved to be out of there. Turning into an alley, her slippers slid on cobblestones, twisting her ankles every which way.

Where could she go? Union Station. She would catch a train home to Oshkosh, escape this shame and start over.

"Baby Doe," Bush called.

Hearing his footfalls behind her, she jutted down another passage, narrow as a canyon and reeking of sewage. A black cat pounced from above. She looked up to see where it came from.

A woman leaned over a window sill, blue smoke curling from a thin pipe. A shock of white ran through her raven hair falling past her waist. Her broad cheekbones tilted up, almond eyes reflecting the moon. A Celestial.

"Which way to Union Station?" Baby Doe asked.

But the woman touched a long red fingernail to her mouth.

Baby Doe backed into a barrel, toppling it over with a hollow racket. Stumbling on in the darkness, she felt the Celestial's eyes on her back.

Chinatown's Hop Alley. Union Station lay on the other side, she needed to keep going.

Feeling her way along a winding brick wall, the only light came from the night sky. Pungent smells of cardamom, ginger, and earthy fungus wafted from baskets on a stoop. She peered in the next window and flinched. Dead ducks hung to dry, dripping blood.

Running the opposite direction, she smashed her forehead against a low-hanging sign. Blood trickled into her eyes. She pulled a handkerchief from her purse, embroidered with *TABOR*. How foolish to think he would choose her? Not when she stood in the way of his ambition.

The swinging sign said CHIN LIN SOU LAUNDRY & IRONING. Chin? Seeing a light in the back gave her hope. She banged on the door until her hand bruised, but no one came.

Holding the handkerchief to her head, she stumbled farther down the passageway toward a dim red light from a basement window. High-pitched nasal voices floated to her ears. Through filmy curtains, a woman lounged on overstuffed pillows, sucking a long bamboo pipe and puffing circles of smoke. Black hair strung out behind her, exposing a white neck; a diaphanous gown hung low with one nipple exposed.

Celestial men sat around her on floor cushions, half smiles framed betelnut-stained teeth. Some sucked bamboo pipes, eyelids drooping. Black braids hung down their backs like bell clappers.

"Can someone help me?" She waved, but they sat in a stupor, watching the woman.

A train whistle blew, and she moved toward the sound, wary of a brightly-lit doorway ahead. Boisterous voices clamored in her ears, and a strange mix of Chinese, Irish, and Black men clustered around pool tables. Crouching in the shadows, she waited for a chance to pass without notice.

"You cheated me, Chink." A red-faced Irishman threw a punch at a Chinese man. Other Irishmen joined the fracas, pummeling the Celestial and hurling him out the door.

His body ploughed into Baby Doe, her skull hitting the

cobblestone street with a sickening crack. Lightning bolts jolted through her brain with excruciating pain.

An enormous rack of antlers rose against the starry sky. Bear claws hung from its neck, fish scales undulated on a fiery body. *Pixiu, the protector.*

"Chin, you're here."

The beast picked her up and hurled her over a bony shoulder, running through a crowd of white men bashing doors down, swinging clubs, and throwing Chinese out of second story windows.

"The Chink took a white girl," an Irishman yelled. "Run after them."

A few drunken brutes chased them but as they passed alleyways, hordes of angry men joined in, clutching burning torches, spewing a cacophony of foreign curses. Chin ducked into a darkened doorway, sheltering her with his wings.

"Why are all these men here?" Baby Doe asked.

"White men finished with Chinese. Kill them now," he said, huffing.

A mob pulled an iron gas lamp out of the street and heaved it into a window. Shattered glass spewed on her as gas exploded into flames. A stream of shiny black heads jumped through the broken window. Rioters caught the Chinese by their braids, sawing them off at their bloody nape. The Chinese yowled like the terrified mules at the mines.

Chin picked her up again, his hooves clomped down the alley away from the crowd.

"There he goes. Catch him," a man yelled and chased after them.

Struggling to hold on to his scaly ribs, she drifted in and out of awareness, her throat drowning in metallic liquid. Chin ducked into a dark tunnel, and the sweet stink of decaying rats gagged her. Drifting, bouncing…in the sewers.

"Chin, get in here." Her voice was vaguely familiar. "They'll slaughter every last one of you."

Baby Doe smelled her cloying gardenia and heard the out-of-sync plunk of a player piano.

"Who've you got there? Lordy, who split her head open?" An orange-haired woman lifted Baby Doe's curls, sopping with blood. "Hold the stage, I've seen that face. That's Tabor's floozy."

The insult brought her to the surface, but pain kept her under.

The Irish gang caught up to them. "Told you the Chink would come here." Torch-lit faces seethed with rage.

Chin ran with her down a hallway of gilded mirrors in every size and shape. Hadn't she seen this before? *House of Mirrors.* Harvey's naked body splayed behind orange-haired…Mattie Silks.

A gun fired, and a bullet flew past her head, jeers and snarls edging closer. Chin opened a wardrobe and laid her on a pile of gaudy dresses. "Stay here. Lady safe." She drifted into darkness.

Sometime later, the door opened, and a meaty Irishman grabbed her shoulders and shook her until her teeth chattered. "Where's that Yellow Plague?" Her neck snapped about in his hands, then he flung her across the hall like a rag doll. Her bruised head smashed against a gilded frame. The mirror shattered, raining silver spikes on her body.

"If she dies, they'll blame Chin Lin Sou," a woman said, her voice husky. "She's barely breathing."

Warm fingers touched Baby Doe's nose, her mouth. She inhaled the musky smell of snake oil. She tried to open her eyes but couldn't. Her hand flew to her face, hitting something.

"Baby, it's me." Bush's warm hand covered hers. "Don't move. You're hurt."

"I have to…" *leave.* "Why can't I…" *speak?* "Have to go…" *home.*

She saw herself running down the train tracks after a locomotive. The Pullman porter leaned out the door, grabbed her hand, and heaved her aboard.

"You're safe now, Baby. I'll take care of everything." Bush's voice confused her.

George's face changed—terrifying horns and red lion mask. "Chin?"

William Bush headed for the bar off the Windsor lobby. He couldn't let Tabor know Baby Doe had been attacked. Not until he was sure she would make it.

He pictured Baby Doe's small lifeless body, battered and bruised, blood still seeping through her bandages. She laid still as a corpse…then, without warning, she babbled, then silent again. As soon as this meeting was over, he'd go back and comfort her somehow.

He ordered a Walker's Old Highlands and waited for Tabor. The Windsor bar was nicknamed *The Office* by patrons, with handsome wood and leather interior and, colorful liquor bottles lining the mirrored bar front.

Tabor slumped into the stool beside him.

"I've searched everywhere." Bush hung his head. "She must have caught a train home."

"Tell Turnbull to find himself a new candidate for senator."

Bush's lungs collapsed. "Don't be hasty. The Republicans are counting on you."

"What if she's dead?" Tabor plucked hair from his mustache. "What if she died because I wouldn't accompany her to the opening?"

"Running for senator means everything to you."

"I'm not doing anything until I find her." Tabor walked out the back door.

Bush's fingers gripped his Scotch. Turnbull wouldn't like this.

Augusta peered into the bar, face splotched purple. "Is Horace in here?"

Bush shook his head. "Just missed him."

"Did you see him turn me away from the Tabor box? It was

humiliating sitting in Maxcy's box like poor relation."

Bush whistled, tapping his cane in time.

"I saw that Little Baby woman." She narrowed her eyes. "Did she think I wouldn't recognize her with that veil? The nerve. Who wouldn't notice a painted hussy?"

He whistled louder, striking his cane on the side of the bar.

"Horace wants to be senator more than anything, doesn't he?" she said.

"Really couldn't tell you." His grip on his cane tightened.

"Tell Horace to come home." Her beady eyes gleamed. "He won't win without me."

Bush's temples throbbed. "I'll be sure to tell him."

24

Denver, Colorado, October 1881

Burning sage permeated Baby Doe's sinuses. Someone chanted sounds she could not understand, minor notes floating like a haunting lullaby. A blur of black hair streaked with white. Broad cheekbones. The Celestial woman from Hop Alley. A rainbow of colors radiated around her.

"Tell me your dream. Quickly, before it escapes." She waved a wand of smoldering sage.

"I dreamed of Horace." Baby Doe fought through a paralyzing fog, her body shivering and naked under a silk kimono. "His hair and mustache were black and his face perfectly handsome. Magnificent looking, tall and happy. A high silk hat and velvet collared coat."

"What next?" The woman's black eyes pried into her soul.

"His face leaned to mine…he kissed my lips…" Her mouth trembled, the feeling so real. "Then, he said, I do."

"Your spirit has spoken." The Celestial woman shook a rattlesnake rattle.

"Where am I? How'd I get here?" Her voice croaked.

Spanish moss dangled from wires strung across the ceiling. A pot boiled at the fireplace, smelling musty. Lacquered boxes were filled with bones, feathers and teeth.

Pain shot through her head. Gunshots whizzing past. Fiery

scales. Enormous horns. Hooves breaking on cobblestones.

"Pixiu, the protector saved your life." The woman reached into a lacquered chest and pulled out a black jar.

"Chin." Baby Doe drew her knees up and rocked, her confusion dark and wild.

The Celestial rubbed her back, radiating warmth. Gently, she removed the bandage on Baby Doe's head and applied salve from the jar smelling like an arnica bush. Though her vision was blurry, the Celestial's black eyes seemed to shine from within.

"Are you Chinese?" she asked.

"My mother is Chinese; my father is Ute. They named me Two-Spirit." One hand patted a small drum, her other shook the rattle, and she started to chant again.

Two-Spirit's hands mesmerized her, large and masculine, nails stained blue. A dragon brocade dress stretched tight over broad shoulders and flat chest.

Baby Doe pulled back. "You're a man."

"Man and woman. Two-Spirit." He smiled with stained teeth. "Witch doctor."

The door opened, and a rattlesnake cane preceded Bush. She sat up, happy to see him. "Yeoww." The pain in her head made her recoil.

Two-Spirit laid her back on the cushions. "Not ready."

Bush kneeled beside her. "I thought we'd lost you."

The humiliation of opening night replayed in her head. "Augusta came." Claiming her rightful place. "Everyone will talk."

Bush shook his head. "Nobody's thinking about the theater after the bloodbath in Hop Alley. Three thousand white men raided Chinatown to destroy the Yellow Plague. Hacked off their braids. Slit their throats. I heard the mob yelling about a Chink kidnapping a white girl and followed them to House of Mirrors."

"My fault." Baby Doe collapsed, guilt crushing her.

"Nothing to do with you." Bush rubbed her hand. "They want to deport the Chinese."

Two-Spirit chanted at the altar where incense burned above a bear claw necklace.

A memory flashed to her, bear claws against a smooth chest. "I need to see Chin."

Two-Spirit's vibrato soared to a scream.

"What is he saying?" Baby Doe gasped the smoky air. "Where's Chin?"

He turned away, and she grabbed his arm.

"He didn't make it, Baby. Leave it at that."

"What happened?"

"Damn, you're stubborn." He snorted. "The mob put a noose around his neck and dragged him through the streets."

A feral yowl convulsed through her body and did not stop. Bush held her until she fell into a dark sleep.

The tinkling water of the Windsor lobby fountain and perfumed smell of flower arrangements welcomed her home. *Used to be home.* Baby Doe hesitated, unable to see beyond a narrow tunnel of vision. Her back shook, it wouldn't hold her much longer.

"Sure you want to stay at the Windsor?" Bush said. "I can get you a room at the American Hotel until you go."

"I won't hide from Horace," she said. "I'm finished feeling ashamed. Besides, my things are here. I'll be fine in my own apartment." The back of her neck cricked, her body brittle and achy.

The blue silk dress Bush bought hung on her gaunt frame. She tripped, and he caught her. As usual, he'd been so good getting her ready, holding the mirror while she smudged rouge on her cheeks, brushing her hair into curls. Though he raved about the results, the reflection in the mirror told the truth. Her shoulders slumped forward, hurting too much to draw them back. Her right eye veered outward, and her skin was dull under rouge, making her look like an antique porcelain doll.

"The doctor said you can't travel for months." Bush tightened his grip.

"I'll stay until I recover, then I'll go home." Denver would never be the same after the Hop Alley riots. White men had destroyed Chinese homes and businesses, attacked innocent victims.

And Chin. Pixiu, the protector, was dead.

Bush pushed the elevator button.

"Oh, no. I don't use this Otis contraption." She took a step toward the wide staircase.

"You will today. You're wobbly as a colt." He ordered the operator to take them to the penthouse suite. The door closed, then the brass gate, like a tomb closing for the last time.

"Let me out of here, Billy." She yanked at the gate. "I need to get out."

He put his arm around her and his strength calmed her.

The elevator finally opened, and they walked down the hallway to her old suite. Her heart skipped, then raced. Their beautiful nest, away from everyone and everything, was where they'd deepened their love, respect and appreciation for each other. She had cherished Tabor's voracious advocacy for regular folk and how he used his knowledge and new-found wealth to improve their lot. And, he seemed to delight in her creativity and love for theater, encouraging her ideas. All this love fought with the stark reality that he belonged to someone else.

The door swung open and there was Tabor, grayer at his temples, deeper lines around his mustache. "Baby." His arms cradled her like a fallen bird. "Where have you been?"

"She was in Hop Alley." Bush cleared his throat. "They found her unconscious and nursed her in a room over a Chinese laundry. She's in rough shape, Boss."

"You were there during the riots?" He held her shoulders, inspecting her.

Hard to look him in the eye, her vision was so blurry. "I was going to Union Station."

"I've wired her brother," Bush said. "He's coming to take care of her."

"Until the doctor says I can handle the trip home to Oshkosh." There she said it. "I'm sorry, Horace, I just can't live in secret anymore. It's not good for either of us."

Tabor's jaw went slack. "You've been through so much."

"I'll stay in my suite until I can travel." She spoke slowly to emphasize the words. "I'll be out of your way in a month." Her knees gave out, and she sat in the closest armchair, not wanting him to see how weak she'd become.

He opened the front door. "Thanks for bringing her home, Billy."

Bush turned to her. "Will you be all right?"

"I'll take good care of her," Tabor said and ushered him out.

Sitting on the arm of her chair, his familiar smell surrounded her. She wanted to lay her head on his lap, feel him close. But she had to be strong. "I'm sorry I ruined your opening night."

"You think I care about that?" He caressed her hair, no longer matted with blood. "What matters is how unhappy you were. I should have realized how it hurt you."

"It's not your fault." Her head throbbed, too heavy on her shoulders. "But after I leave, everything will return to normal."

He kneeled in front of her, took her hands in his. "Would you marry me?"

She smiled, but felt sad to see him act like this. "You *are* married."

"What if I wasn't? Would you marry me then?" He kissed her hand, held it to his mouth and kissed it again.

"You are running for the senate. It's not our time."

He studied her for a few moments, brows pulled together. Then he stood and stretched. "Who took care of you in Hop Alley?"

"A woman. A man. Two-Spirit." Tabor's image spiraled away to a pinpoint, then a pain sliced through her head and she fell backward, into Hop Alley, reeking of rotting meat, rats, and pungent spices. "Chin," she cried out. Her head smashed against a brick wall. Torches chased her down wretched alleys. Men leered at her, grabbed her, beat her. She lashed out, fighting off the animals.

"What is it, Baby?" Tabor said. "What's happening?"

Her mind reeled with all Chin Lin Sou had done for her. Saving her from freezing in Blackhawk, and then again in Hop Alley, carrying her through the opium dens and hiding her from the lynch mob. Chin's mysterious blue eyes. Pixiu, the protector. Sobs racked her chest, her tears soaking Tabor's shirt. "He died for me."

25

Denver, Colorado, November 1881

Denver's great Romanesque Union Station stretched for acres. The humidity of steam engines made Baby Doe woozy. She planted her feet wide to stop her vertigo. Trains arrived and left, people hugged and kissed. Porters rolled trolleys teetering with luggage in every direction, wheels whirring like gears gone haywire. Too many comings and goings for her muddled mind.

"Go ahead and catch your train." She swayed, unsteady. "I'll just sit here on the bench and wait for Peter."

"I'm not leaving you here to fend for yourself and I want to meet your brother."

"You can meet him when you return from Durango," she tried again, her anxiety growing. She hadn't seen Peter in four years. He hadn't even written after her divorce, but now he wanted to take care of her? Suspicious. Peter always had an angle.

Tabor sat beside her. "I'll wait."

"My family doesn't know about us," she admitted.

He winced. "Then Peter will be the first to know."

"It's none of their business, now that I'm going home."

"I'm not giving up on you." He drew her to him and her resistance melted. How could she leave him? Yet, she wouldn't live as his mistress.

"You never said why you were going to Durango," she said.

His smile was mysterious. “I just might have an ace up my sleeve.”

The Chicago train pulled into the platform, spraying steam in their faces, brakes grinding and screeching. The doors opened, and passengers streamed out. She saw his strawberry blond curls clashing with his green-tweed suit and waved. “Peter.” Through her clouded vision his hair appeared darker and his violet eyes harder. She hoped she hadn’t changed that much.

“My partner-in-crime, my leading lady…how I’ve missed you.” He hugged her, then stood back. “You don’t look so hot, Lizzie.”

“Same old charmer, huh, Peter?” Her speech sounded slow even to her stuffed-up ears.

“I’m Horace Tabor.” He shook Peter’s hand, towering above him. “Your sister was caught in the Chinese riots. We’re lucky she’s alive.”

Peter cocked his head to the side. “You’re my sister’s partner, right?”

“That’s one way to put it.” A train whistle split the air.

“You’ll miss your train,” she said, not wanting to discuss this with Peter.

Tabor kissed her gently, until the last whistle blew.

“I expect you to take good care of Baby Doe,” he told Peter. “She’s been through the ringer.” He jumped onto the train as it pulled away.

“Baby Doe?” Peter said.

“My new name.” Her eyes followed Tabor’s train as it pulled out, her heart hurting.

“You’ve got it bad, sis.” Peter waved a cocky finger at her. “I’m guessing Horace Tabor is not just a partner.”

“My old sparring buddy.” He might be the only family member who would understand. “How would you like to see the biggest theater west of the Mississippi?”

Baby Doe took him into the Tabor Grand Opera House. Peter ogled the marble columns, crystal chandeliers, and cushioned Oriental carpets.

"You're telling me Tabor let you design this?" his voice echoed in the vast auditorium.

"We had architects and designers, of course." Her hand grazed the mohair upholstery. "I drew up ideas and gave them photographs for reference."

"*We.* You said it again. If you are a *we*, then why are you going home?"

A lump formed in her throat. "It's complicated."

For once he didn't quip back, just gazed at the theater. After a while he broke the silence. "Lizzie, I've never seen anything so magnificent."

"I'm Baby Doe now, Peter."

He grimaced. "What happened, Lizzie? Harvey said you took up with a Jewish tailor."

"He doesn't know a thing about Jake." Heat flushed her chest. "Harvey abandoned me and went home to his momma."

"Why didn't you come home, too?" Peter squeezed her hand and opened a floodgate of anger and sorrow.

She swallowed it back. "He said he'd be back by Christmas and left me with no money. We were expecting a son."

"I'm an uncle?" He laughed. "Where is the lad?"

She dropped his hand. "He died in childbirth."

"Why didn't you tell us? We could have sent you money."

"Hah. I've sent money home for years." She loathed her bitter tone. "After Harvey left, Jake Sands gave me a job and an apartment."

"And what did you give in exchange?"

She rolled her eyes. "Jake was a friend."

"And what about Tabor? He's old enough to be your father."

Her head pounded, she'd done too much, too soon. "What's it matter now? When I'm well enough to travel, you'll take me home, and I'll forget this ever happened."

"That kiss at the station doesn't look like you can forget."

"I have to leave, Peter." She rubbed her throbbing temples. "He's married."

He gasped theatrically, hand over his mouth. "Tell me something I don't know. You're better off without him. *The Chicago Tribune* exposed Tabor for a rich philanderer who throws silver dollars around like rice at a wedding."

She smacked his leg. "He's nothing like that. After Harvey, I swore off men. But, when I met Tabor, his passion for making things better inspired me. Not just big things, like this theater, but he supports the little people, like the Masons, Elks, the firemen. In fact, he helps anyone who needs it." Light shone through the stained-glass rotunda throwing prisms of color on the walls. "Horace Tabor is like a beautiful, benevolent rainbow."

"Got it." Peter grinned. "Tabor's your pot of gold."

"Why is it always about money with you? I *love* Horace."

"You're banished to the Windsor tower like Rapunzel? Does that sound like love to you?"

The truth hurt. "Stop it, Peter. The walls have ears."

"Hello walls," he bellowed and jumped to the arms of his theater seat. "I've come to save sweet Lizzie from a life of lies."

"You are no savior." She thought of Chin and how he sacrificed his life to save her.

Bush swung open the auditorium door. "Are you alright, Baby Doe?" He speared his cane at her brother. "Who's this lunatic?"

Arms outstretched for balance, Peter walked across the seat backs like a tightrope.

She couldn't tell which was more humorous, his acrobatics, or Bush's astonishment.

Reaching the end, Peter somersaulted into the air and landed on his feet, bowler hat intact. "Peter McCourt, at your service." He bowed with flourish. "And who, handsome devil, are you?"

"William Bush, the devil who sent for you. Try that again and I'll have you run out on a rail."

Peter clapped. "Bravo. I love thrill rides. But you needn't bother.

As soon as I get my sister packed up, we'll head back to Oshkosh."

"Over my dead body." His cane poked Peter's chest. "You have no idea what she's been through." He swung his cane to the carpet. "Baby Doe said you're a stage manager."

"Uptown Theater in Chicago," Peter boasted.

"Come with me." Bush walked with his cane to the stage, and Peter followed.

Baby Doe sat back, exhausted. When would her energy return?

"I'm told the riggings aren't as complicated as they look." Bush gazed at the ropes, pulleys, and curtains.

"Grand Drape. Austrian. Tormentor." Peter pointed to the riggings like an expert. "Stage backdrop, traveler, tableau, contour, borders, scrim, cyclorama." Pulling the ropes in succession, a flurry of curtains flowed into place.

"Impressive." Bush's eyes narrowed.

She clapped from her seat. "You've come a long way since McCourt Theater."

"I didn't wither up and die when you abandoned us for a gold mine." His caustic tone seemed to cover his hurt.

"You seem to forget I went to support our parents," she bristled.

"Children, quit bickering," Bush said. "Peter, how would you like to be my stage manager while you're here?"

She shook her head. "We'll be going home too soon."

"I need this job, Lizzie," Peter pleaded. "The theater fired me when I came to get you."

She sighed. "A month. Then we go back." Her head pounded. "And call me Baby Doe."

A rare fog obscured the imposing façade of the Tabor Grand. "I lied." Peter huffed big clouds of breath. "I wasn't a stage manager in Chicago. I swept floors. I have no idea how to host a performer."

"Why aren't I surprised?" She frowned. "If you have trouble, leave it to me."

"But Oscar Wilde as my virgin debut?" He held his wrist to his forehead. "I adore the ground he walks on."

He'd stirred himself into such a tizzy, she couldn't help but tease him. "Remember what Mam says about fog?"

"Bad weather?" He blew into his clasped hands.

"Fog foretells that something hidden will soon be revealed."

"Just the type of blither-blather I need right now." Peter unraveled the fringe of his scarf. "What if I say the wrong thing? I've never met an Englishman."

Thigh-high boots cut through the mist followed by a sweeping cape and wide-brimmed Cavalier hat adorned by an ostrich feather.

"Is that him?" Peter asked.

"Who else would it be?" Baby Doe giggled, astonished by the exotic creature who towered above them by a good two feet.

Under his whirling cape, the famous English poet wore velvet knee-britches and a lace collared shirt. Long hair curled about his shoulders, framing a long, horsey face. His sensuous mouth and languid eyes promised wit, charm and something decidedly wicked.

"Mr. Wilde, welcome to Denver." Peter bowed, looking rather like a court jester. "I'm Peter McCourt, stage manager of the Tabor Grand. I'm to be your escort."

"Well, tra, la, la." He held his hand out for Peter to kiss.

Peter's mouth pursed, then he offered a handshake.

Wilde lowered long lashes. "You're adorable, Peter. May I call you that? And who is this divine creature?"

"This is my sister, Lizz— This is Baby Doe."

Still dizzy from her cracked head, she curtsied best she could, holding her plumed hat, remarkably like Wilde's.

"The Almighty broke the mold when he made you two." His half-lidded eyes goggled them. "So pretty. And bite-sized." He snapped his large teeth, making her smile.

"I hope you'll like your dressing room." Peter cocked his eyebrow.

"Lead the way, pretty boy." Wilde took his arm while his coachman pulled a trolley of trunks.

"I see you plan to teach Denver about fashion, Mr. Wilde," she said.

"Only one thing to know, darling girl. Fashion is what one wears oneself. What is unfashionable is what other people wear."

"This way, Mr. Wilde," Peter said.

Wilde leaned so close to her brother's ear, he could have nibbled it. "Call me Oscar, dear boy. My closest friends do."

Peter's cheeks burned bright as he led them into the Tabor Grand.

Wilde pirouetted, his cape swirling around him, taking in the magnificence of the theater. "Flourishes, upon flourishes, upon flourishes."

"One can never have too many flourishes." She pointed out their plumes. "I like your hat."

"You're the only woman in the world who'd have known the right hat to wear on an occasion like this, Mrs. Doe."

"Not Mrs. Doe. Just Baby Doe." So tired of slurking around, she told the truth.

"She's divorced," Peter boasted. "And recovering from a horrible trauma."

"I prefer women with a past." Wilde winked. "They're always so damned amusing."

Peter inserted a long skeleton key into the dressing room door.

"Don't give up on love, darling," Wilde advised her. "One should always be in love. That's the reason one should never marry."

"Oh, I'm in love, all right," she confessed. "But he's already married, so I'm living incognito."

"Incognito is my favorite word besides outrageous." He twirled a lock of hair on his finger. "We must continue this conversation over absinthe, later?"

"I know just the place," she said, thinking of Gahan's.

Peter opened the dressing room door. "We've booked a full house for your show tonight. Mr. Tabor was sorry to miss your show but promised to meet us at his theater in Leadville."

Wilde circled the dressing room Peter decorated, stopping to sniff the sunflowers. Spreading goose-liver pâté on a toast point, he ate it and groaned with pleasure. He draped his body across a Parisian sofa with a salacious grin. "Someone did his homework. All my favorite things."

Peter twisted the cage off champagne, and Wilde cackled.

He held up his glass. "To charming siblings."

"To charm." She clinked his glass and set it aside. Champagne added to her wooziness.

"I don't know that women are always rewarded for being charming," Wilde said. "I think they're usually punished for it."

Peter read the *Denver Tribune*. "Regardless of what you have heard about Mr. Wilde's character, he is more famous than any English celebrity except Charles Dickens."

Wilde's fingers fumbled tying his silk jabot. "The public has an insatiable curiosity to know everything except what is worth knowing."

Peter helped him tie his jabot. "Don't worry, Denver's ready to hear your advice."

"It is always silly to give advice." Wilde bit his lip. "But to give good advice is fatal."

"On that note, we'll let you rest before your performance." Baby Doe gestured to her brother.

"Won't you stay, Peter?" Wilde plucked a sunflower petal and held it out. "It would really help my jitters."

Peter took the petal and waved her away. "We will meet you after the show."

We. She shut the door behind her. *Fog foretells that something hidden that will soon be revealed.* Mam's superstitions proved true more often than not.

Peter abandoned her for Oscar. Not that she wasn't cared for. Tabor brought in a special doctor for her head injuries, who prescribed rest and quiet. With any luck, he said, she'd improve over time. Tabor still had to hold her arm when she crossed the room. He brought her periodicals to read but the typeface jumbled. The chance she may never improve haunted her. He brought her nosegays, chocolates, a lace negligee. But the more she relied on him, the more she couldn't live this way. The next time he left on business, she planned to board the train without Peter.

"Thank you for taking me to the station, Billy." Her hands shook as she tried to fold a shawl in her trunk. "Peter has forgotten all about taking me home. He wants to stay with Oscar as long as he's here."

Bush steadied her shaking hands. "I came to talk you out of leaving. You shouldn't travel yet, not alone at any rate."

"I just don't know what got into Peter. His behavior goes against the way we were raised. He is positively gooey over that man."

"Like watching you with Tabor," he spewed words like venom.

"I suppose I looked just as ridiculous. My heart took over all sense of reason." Packing the negligee Tabor gave her hurt too much to look at it. "I've got to get out of here."

"But not now, Baby." His grip tightened. "Tabor won't run for senator if you leave and he'll lose his shot."

"And you'll lose your payouts from Turnbull?" she asked slyly. "I heard the two of you at the Tabor Grand."

"We're so alike, you and me." He drew her close, pressing his lips on hers, his heart hammering against her breast.

Her mind skittered with confusion. He'd rescued her and nursed her back to health. She'd come to see him as a trusted friend. Given that, she might have forgiven this indiscretion until his passion rose hard on her stomach, clear he wouldn't stop with a kiss.

She slapped his face, leaving a white imprint. "You need to leave, Billy."

He pinned her shoulders on the bed and kissed her the French way. She twisted and bucked but her struggle threw kerosene on the fire, his rough beard scraping her face.

She dug her fingernails into his back, adrenalin surging through her. "Get. Off. Me. Now."

He propped himself up. "Don't you know how much I love you?"

She darted from under him, running to Tabor's suite, locking the door behind her. Ragged breaths tore at her throat, chest pounding. She looked through the peep hole.

Bush straightened the bed, then walked to the door where she stood. "I will leave my wife for you, Baby. I swear. I've waited so long."

"Go away, Billy." She leaned her back against the door.

"I'm sorry I sprang on you like that. Stay with me, Baby. Tabor will throw you away."

"He'll throw *you* away when I tell him about this." She squeezed her eyes closed.

His fist pounded the door. "I couldn't help myself."

She slid down to the floor. "How could you do that, Billy? You're like a brother to Horace."

Silence. Then, the scuff of his boot heel and the click of the closing door.

More reason to leave. She'd hire a buggy to Union Station. Her ears whirred with an irritating ringing, head spinning. When she tried to stand, her legs wouldn't hold her. Shivering with cold and shock, she pulled the bedspread down around her. The train trip would have to wait until she could walk on her own. She had to be patient. Not her strong suit.

Billy Bush drank tequila shots in The Office. He should've waited until Baby Doe healed, but then she may have left before he told her how he felt. He had to get another chance with her.

The double doors swung open and Tabor entered, snow piled on his shoulders and boots, face aglow. "I've done it, Billy." He sat on the barstool, waving an envelope. "The judge in Durango issued divorce papers. All I need is Augusta's signature and I'm a free man."

"That can't be legal. You're a Denver resident," Bush said. "Besides, a divorce right now will ruin the election." Turnbull paid him plenty to manage the situation.

"Sarsaparilla, please?" Tabor asked the bartender.

"You need the Republican wives behind you to win." Bush dug in his pocket and pulled out two locks of hair tied with a ribbon. "Augusta asked me to give you this."

Tabor clasped the strands between his palms. "She cut locks of hair on our wedding day and bound them together."

"All Augusta wants is to be a Tabor," Bush said. "Hasn't she earned the right?"

Tabor fanned the hair with his fingers and watched it drift to the floor. "Twenty-two years I worked for that woman's blessing. When I ran the store, she said I was simple-minded. When I prospected, she called me lazy. When elected mayor, she called me a blowhard. And Maxcy…she's degraded me so much my son would rather have *you* as a father." He gummed the words like a tequila worm. "She took my manhood, Billy, and I want it back."

"As your best friend, I'm telling you, you're throwing away the senate for a gold digger."

"Why, Billy, I detect a note of jealousy." Tabor thrust the envelope into his hand. "Take this to Augusta."

Pointing his cane toward the door, Bush walked out of The Office, and dropped the papers in the nearest spittoon. Damn if he'd turn Baby Doe over to Tabor that easily.

Tabor asked Baby Doe to accompany him to Leadville for Oscar Wilde's show, and was overjoyed when she agreed. She was so antsy cooped up in the Windsor, a change of scene would do her good. After the show, he planned a special celebration at the Matchless Mine, but by the time Wilde and Peter arrived, they were downright soapy-eyed.

"Ow, Ow, Ow, Owwwooooo." Wilde howled at the full moon.

Tabor helped him into the ore bucket with Peter. "Watch your step. It's a long way down."

"Admiral of the Red, at your service." Wilde saluted. "Hold me steady, Peter, won't you? My tail is down, I'm afraid."

The crank screeched, and the hoist man lowered the bucket into the shaft. Tabor climbed into the next bucket and held out his hand for Baby Doe, her complexion pale in the moonlight. With her by his side, maybe the mine wouldn't close in on him like it usually did. He kissed her in the darkness, and the taste of her lips revitalized him. He hoped his surprise would revive her, too.

A peculiar melody wafted up through the shaft, making him smile.

"Bagpipes?" she asked.

"Not exactly."

When they reached bottom, she gasped. A hurdy-gurdy player cranked a rosined wheel against cat-gut strings. The whine wormed into his bones. Her beautiful face was lit by hundreds of candles illuminating the underground chamber. Oysters, smoked pheasant, venison, a cheddar wheel, and crusty bread filled an ore cart.

"How exotic." She clapped to the music, and her joy delighted him.

Wilde and Peter danced amongst half a dozen hurdy-gurdy girls, gyrating to the music, striking and colorful in their clashing satins of orange, purple, and green.

She chucked her chin toward the boys, grasping each other's elbows and kicking up their heels. "Apparently, Peter likes long-haired poets."

Tabor grimaced. "In that case, we need more whiskey." He doled out fresh shots.

"To all things Matchless," Wilde toasted Peter. "Forever immortalized by their perfection."

Tabor took her hand. "Can I tempt you with a sight you've never seen?"

Wilde butted in. "I can resist everything except temptation."

Tabor boarded them into an ore cart and pumped the handle, gliding on the rail into blackness, shadows leaping on the hewn stone. The hurdy-gurdy faded into the distance. Musty smells closed in like dirt thrown on a coffin. Stopping the cart, he helped Baby Doe out.

"Raise the lantern over on the other side of the tunnel, Peter, and you'll see the biggest silver vein ever discovered." He turned away from the stupendous sight which spurred his fears.

"Now I've seen the elephant," Wilde exclaimed.

Baby Doe gulped. "You said the vein was giant, but I never imagined this…" Her voice hushed. "Magnificent."

Even with his back turned, Tabor pictured the monstrous vein like a bolt of lightning through the midnight sky. "I always had faith that something better lay just around the bend. Then one day, I discovered a mine like none other."

"The *Matchless*," she said, and he knew she understood.

"Rub it like the Blarney stone for good luck," Peter wailed.

"There's a bloody fortune here, I'll wager," Wilde said.

"I need another drink," Peter said. "Oscar, do you have the whiskey jug or do I?"

The boys drank, dropped the jug, and cracked it to pieces, laughing.

Baby Doe's hand groped for Tabor. "Hey, where'd you go?"

He pulled her close, trying to calm his breath.

"What's wrong? Why aren't you looking at the vein?" she asked.

"Not sure I understand it myself, but it's something like this: We chisel silver out of God's mountain like it's our right and before we know it, all the silver is gone. Gone forever...not a glorious speck left where God hid it." Acid ate his gut. "When I look at that silver vein, I know it will be gone someday. It makes me crazy."

"Silver makes you crazy?"

His thumb found the dimple in her chin. “Would you love me if I was crazy?”

She broke free. “You’re scaring me, Horace.”

“Would you love me if there was no silver?” he whispered.

A laugh escaped her throat. “Why are you speaking in riddles?”

He brought her hand to the rock wall opposite the vein. “Push here.”

The rock gave way, and she cried out. “Heavens, what is this?”

“My vault. No one else knows it’s here. Feel anything?” His heart stopped as she patted the bottom and found the velvet box. “I got a divorce in Durango. And I found a lawyer in St. Louis to marry us.”

Peter called across the tunnel, “I had no idea you were this rich.”

She handed him the box without looking inside. “Billy says your secret divorce is worthless without Augusta’s signature. And I won’t be married by a St. Louis lawyer.”

His heart sunk. “Baby, sweetheart—”

She sealed his lips with two fingers, leaning so close he smelled her skin. “My first wedding was a shameful affair just to marry me off to a gold mine. When I divorced, I swore on the Bible that if I married again, it would be for love, and I’d have a proper wedding in the eyes of God.”

He kissed her fingers. “Give me time, Baby. Just until the election.”

“A big Catholic wedding, with a priest, my family, flowers, a cake, and a real wedding dress.”

“Peter. Peter.” Wilde’s voice echoed. “I have a nose bleed. Can money give you a nose bleed? I’m dying. I’m dying.”

“It’s the altitude, Oscar.” She walked toward the boys. “Let’s get something to eat.”

“Supper? This was a bloody feast,” Wilde said. “The first course was whisky; the second course was whisky; the third course was whisky. Though, I have little recollection of dessert.”

As they ascended the Matchless shaft, black pines rose above

Tabor like apparitions against the starry sky. At the top, Baby Doe walked ahead, not waiting for him.

Oscar Wilde swept his arm to the full moon. "A dreamer finds his way by moonlight and his punishment is that he sees the dawn before the rest of the world."

Tabor found her at the carriage. "Catholic wedding, huh?" First, he had to finalize the divorce.

26

Denver, Colorado, June 1882

After their trip, Tabor stole away to the quiet of the Tabor Grand, hoping to forge a new plan. If he won the election, everything should fall into place with Baby Doe. As he walked across the marble lobby, another set of footfalls echoed after him. A spindly figure bent around a column.

"What're you doing here?" he asked.

Augusta had dressed in her Sunday best, even a hat. Still, her face seemed worn as shoe leather after Baby Doe's glow. The realization made him feel guilty.

She tugged her jacket. "I needed to talk to you."

Augusta drew him in like a sad song that kept playing in his head. Memories flooded him. Augusta's forthright manner and no-nonsense ways had been refreshing. She knew her way around a butter churn and spinning wheel, planting gardens and raising chickens, compared to his bohemian mother.

"How did you find me?"

"Mr. Bush told me you'd be here."

They entered the auditorium, sunlight streamed through the stained-glass.

"Mind if we sit a spell?" she said. "My back's acting up."

"Get someone else to milk Black Beauty." He sat in a mohair seat.

She laughed. "You have a point."

He sighed, he hadn't seen her laugh in twenty years.

She cleared her throat. "Horace, I made you a home. Raised our son. Followed you all over God's green earth. Even waited patiently while you took up with women." Her shoulders heaved. "And, now in plain sight of your son and the entire city—"

Her sobs touched a soft spot, but he couldn't console her, wouldn't be fair now. When had his love dried up and blown away?

"It's time you came home now, Horace."

He wouldn't lead her on. "I can't come back."

She huffed. "Father is right. You're just like your thieving, whoring mother."

His hackles raised. "What's your father got against my mother?"

She scoffed. "Thirty-eight years ago, your mother ran away with Aunt Flossie."

"Come on, that's ridiculous." But the smug look on her face, told him it was true.

"That's why Father was mad at the funeral. Flossie left millions to your mother."

"My mother is still alive?" Emptiness and shame mixed with shock. "It can't be. Where is she? Why haven't I heard about her?"

Her lips crimped to one side. "Your mother is a poet in the Hamptons."

"What happened to my brother? Is he there, too?"

"He's a drunk like your pa. Never made a nickel on his own, sponges off your mother."

He rubbed his stiff neck. "Any more good news?"

She nodded. "If you want to be senator, you need to come home. Otherwise I'll ruin you."

Her poison crept through his veins, any sympathy he had for her was wiped clean.

"Never been fond of blackmail," he said. "Do what you have to do." He left her in the theater, feeling free for the first time in years.

27

Denver, Colorado
September 1882

Bush walked Augusta and Maxcy down the courthouse hall, their heels clicking on the hardwood floor. Just a few more yards, and Tabor's dreams of the senate and Baby Doe would be blown sky high. He swabbed his neck with his handkerchief, his nerves getting the best of him.

When he'd told Turnbull about Baby Doe, the banker dumped Tabor as his senate candidate, and wanted Tabor divorced before the election, so he'd lose. Bush would make that happen in the most public way.

"Why should I rush into a divorce?" Augusta said. "Horace will come home after he's elected senator, I'm sure of it."

"After the election, Tabor will sell the mansion out from under you when he moves to Washington. You need the judge to grant your settlement now."

"Liss..ten to Billy, Ma," Maxcy said. "He wouldn't lead us wrong."

"All right, all right. Quit browbeating me." She kicked her dress out of the way.

"Th-thanks for getting her a l-lawyer, Billy," Maxcy said. "I don't know what we'd d-do without your help."

He wiped his neck again, wondering why his conscience kicked up now. Hell, Tabor deserved this, carrying on with Baby Doe.

At the courtroom door, Augusta turned to Maxcy. "Go back

to work. If I must do this, I can't do it with my son watching me."

"Ma, no—"

"Go on, now." She swatted him.

"Take c-care of her, Billy." Maxcy walked down the long hall alone, shoulders slumped.

Bush shrugged off his guilt. It wasn't his fault Tabor wanted to throw away his family. He took Augusta's arm, but she jerked away.

"I'm not crippled." She walked to the first row and sat with Amos Steck.

Bush nodded to Eugene Field from *The Denver Tribune* by the door. Good, he took the bait. Turnbull will pay extra for nasty press before the election.

Darn if Rockwell, Tabor's lawyer, wasn't sitting across the aisle. Would he stop the divorce?

Judge Harrington called Augusta to the stand. "On what grounds do you request a divorce from Lt. Governor Tabor?"

"On grounds of desertion and non-support, your honor." Augusta's voice shook. "Horace left our home in June of eighteen eighty-one."

She should have charged adultery. Would have made juicier headlines.

"It's unprecedented for this court to grant a woman a divorce." Judge Harrington squirmed in his chair. "Mr. Steck, what settlement do you propose for your client?"

Steck took out a ledger sheet. "By our calculations, Tabor has assets of ten-million dollars."

Bush sweated. Ten million, sure, without Tabor's debt which outran his income.

"And what support has he given you, ma'am?" the judge asked.

Augusta wrung her handkerchief. "I have a house, but I take boarders to pay the mortgage."

Tabor hated she took boarders when she didn't need to.

The judge addressed Rockwell. "What does Tabor have to say about this?"

"Mr. Tabor has not been informed of today's proceeding," Rockwell said. "I just learned of it when I came into court this morning. But previously, he instructed me to give Mrs. Tabor whatever she needs."

The judge peered over his glasses. "I see Tabor procured a divorce in Durango in March?"

"Did you know about that?" Augusta glared at Bush.

"Doesn't matter," the judge said. "It's illegal to file in any county other than one's domicile."

"I told Tabor it was not worth the paper it was written on—" Rockwell said.

"Enough," the judge said. "Mrs. Tabor has seen fit to clean up his mess. So, if there's no more testimony?"

Augusta stood. "May I say something for the record?"

"Of course, Mrs. Tabor," the judge said.

"This divorce is not willingly asked for." Her shoulders shook. "Not willingly, not willingly."

Like an Edison lightbulb exploding, Bush realized what was bothering him. Now, nothing stood in the way of Tabor marrying Baby Doe.

Baby Doe worked with the Windsor staff to decorate the ballroom for Tabor's victory celebration when he won the senate. She surveyed the room for last-minute touches.

Red, white, and blue banners festooned the walls, hot-house carnations filled vases, and the bar was stocked with Kentucky whiskey and champagne. She filled the humidor with fresh Virginia cigars, a touch Tabor's cronies would appreciate.

This party would pay tribute to Tabor's generosity, wisdom, and hard work. The grandest celebration she'd ever planned, yet she couldn't attend, ever the disgraceful mistress. She'd made up her mind what she had to do, now she had to find the courage.

Tabor strode toward the ballroom, a rolled newspaper in his fist.

"You can't see this yet," she said, keeping him in the hallway.

"All I see is red." He gave her the newspaper. "Augusta filed for divorce. She knows this will kill my chances."

"Vulgar. Cruel. Shocking," she read the headline. "Horace Tabor deserted his wife without a penny while beguiling Denver with shiny baubles like the Tabor Grand."

"Governor Pitkin called me morally corrupt." He winced.

"People will see right through that blowhard, since he's running against you for the senate."

"Along with Thomas Bowen," he said.

"But Bowen defended you in the paper." She read, "What goes on with a married couple is between them and God. Mr. Tabor gave her a generous settlement."

"Bowen's a straight arrow. If I can't win, he should," Tabor said. "If Pitkin is senator, he'll vote for the gold standard. Silver will be dead, and so will the economy." He looked spent, every wrinkle of his fifty-three years.

"You'd win hands down, if it wasn't for me," she said.

Bush walked toward them, and she met his guilty gaze. She'd never forgive his ravishment but would wait to tell Tabor 'til after the election. He had enough to worry about.

Bush's rumpled suit had seen several sunsets, and a heavy beard bristled over an oily complexion. "Met with every Republican voter." He handed Tabor a ledger. "Greased more palms in the past two days than I have in a lifetime."

"You paid for votes?" Baby Doe asked.

"Charitable contributions," Bush said, with a crooked smile.

"Wouldn't have to break the bank to win, if you'd kept Augusta out of court," Tabor said.

"The woman has a mind of her own, Boss." Bush scowled.

Baby Doe sensed his fingerprints all over this disaster.

"Fireman's fund, good." Tabor scrolled the ledger. "Kennedy is influential. The Elks, the Archdiocese, Denver Pioneers...What's this check for ten thousand to Mine '73?"

Bush yanked back the ledger. "Don't remember that one. Let me look into it."

"Haven't heard of Mine '73," Tabor said. "But if it's an important mine, we need him."

Bush buried the ledger under his arm. "Almost forgot. Thomas Bowen's waiting downstairs in The Office."

Tabor squeezed her hand. "Wish me luck. I'm off to catch a weasel asleep."

She watched them walk down the hallway, heads together. Tabor said something, and Bush laughed. Scheming and dreaming, friends for twenty years. Tabor would hate Bush when she told what he'd done to her. But, first Tabor had to win.

She closed the ballroom doors and went to find Peter. He better be packed.

A towheaded barmaid brought their drinks, bending over the table for a perfect view.

Thomas Bowen placed a coin between her breasts. "That's what I'm talking about." He swigged his whiskey.

"Who would have guessed we'd be running against each other for senator?" Tabor drank his sarsaparilla, sweet and satisfying, hoping to stave off his nerves.

Bowen hooted and shuffled cards. "You're a shoo-in. Don't give it another thought."

"Read the paper today?" Tabor shook his head. "And I quote: 'Tabor's divorce is unacceptable, but deserting his wife is unforgivable.' Only, I didn't desert her, Tombo."

Bowen held up his palm. "Don't need to tell me what kind of man you are."

"Pitkin will win unless we outplay him."

"Why cut me in, Tabor?" Bowen dealt cards. "It's your race to lose with all you've done."

Tabor finished his drink. "If the press kills my chances, I want a miner in Washington D.C. to protect silver."

"You don't trust a Wesleyan Crew paddler?" Bowen laughed and drank his whiskey.

"Here's the plan," Tabor said. "As soon as you or I win the majority, the other swings his votes to the leading candidate. Pitkin gets stiffed, and one of us goes to the Capitol." If it worked to his advantage, he and Baby Doe would board the train for Washington D.C. tomorrow. If not, at least Bowen was better than Pitkin.

Bowen shook his hand. "Just like you to raise the ante when everyone thinks you're busted."

"Better head over there." He thrust his hand in his pocket, rubbing his silver dollar, praying for a lucky streak.

The auditorium was full when they arrived, and they took seats. No time to talk before the ballots were passed. Across the room, Pitkin glared at him. The final showdown with the easterner.

Senator Chaffee conducted several rounds of voting with Tabor in the lead, but he needed two-thirds of the votes to win.

The senator called for a break. While everyone else headed to the bar, Tabor took Bowen aside. "Time to execute our plan."

Bowen smiled and left to talk to his people.

Tabor's stomach churned with nerves and he popped a licorice. And then another. Durn stuff wasn't working.

A page rang the bell and the delegates returned, smelling of tobacco and liquor. Several men stopped and shook Tabor's hand. Bowen sat next to him and gave him a thumbs up.

Ballots were collected. Tabor rummaged in his pocket for his silver dollar. Cold as ice.

Senator Chaffee stepped to the podium. "We finally have a two-thirds majority. The new senator from Colorado is…" He smiled at Tabor and tore open the envelope.

Tabor braced himself to stand and acknowledge his supporters.

"The new senator from Colorado is…Thomas Bowen?" Chaffee

turned to the accountants. "How is it possible? Tabor was in the lead."

Bowen leaned to him. "Swear to God, I had nothing to do with this."

Across the room, Pitkin cocked his hand like a pistol and shot a bullet of clarity between Tabor's eyes. He'd thrown his votes to Bowen rather than let Tabor win.

Everything he'd fought for…defending silver, taking Baby Doe to Washington…destroyed by the man with the make-believe gun.

28

Denver, Colorado, November 1882

Just a few final touches before she left: pouring champagne for the opening toast; directing the pianist to play Tabor's favorite tunes; lighting a dozen candelabra around the room, setting fire to her own desires. She'd almost destroyed him, and he would have let her. What was it about love that obliterated good sense? The last match scorched her fingertips before she blew it out.

The party would last all night. Everyone too drunk to give a second thought about her. By morning, she'd be halfway to Oshkosh.

Delegates poured into the ballroom. She had to leave before Tabor arrived. If she saw his face aglow with victory, the spark in his eyes, her courage would vanish.

She smelled Creed cologne, then his mustache tickled her cheek.

"I lost." Tabor kissed her ear.

"No." She expected his joking eyes, but the gleam had been snuffed. His mouth drooped, and his shoulders slumped. Somehow, she'd believed he'd survive the scandal through sheer will.

Hugging him close, her heart bled for him. She'd single-handedly taken down this great man.

Senator Chaffee called from the bar. "Come join us, Tabor."

He lowered his head. "I have to congratulate Bowen."

"I can't stay. I just came to say—"

But he walked away.

She hated to leave him now, but if she stayed, the newspapers would only make it worse. The least she could do was say goodbye.

Tabor whisked champagne off a waiter's tray and walked to the crowd, neck ties undone, a good-time glow on their faces.

"Congratulations, Senator Bowen." He shook his hand. "Best damn card player won."

Bowen raised his glass. "To Horace Tabor, for a race well run." They all drank, their sheepish smiles betraying the irony.

"You'd do us an honor to accept the interim short term, Tabor," Chaffee said. "Senator Teller was elected Secretary of the Interior, leaving the senate chair empty before Bowen takes office. We'd like you to fill it."

"Throwing me a bone, Chaffee?" His anger flared.

"Get off your high horse." Pitkin sneered. "You lost. Get over it."

Baby Doe waited at the entrance wearing the blue cape he'd given her. Her face glowed like a full moon in his darkest hour.

"On second thought, I *will* go to Washington," Tabor said. He'd take her with him, away from all this scandal.

Chaffee held up Tabor's hand like a prizefighter. "Presenting Horace Tabor, senator from the great state of Colorado." The delegates whistled and guffawed at his pitiful fate.

Bad Luck Tabor. Shame and anger burned his gullet.

"Speech, speech," Bush and Maxcy heckled.

"Now you want a speech?" Tabor huffed. "I went in for the big prize and received one seventy-second part of it."

Baby Doe waved a scarf from the door. Peter tugged at her arm.

"Yet, I'm satisfied, since you've secured a capable gentleman for the long term." He clapped Bowen's shoulder and left the crowd.

Maxcy stopped him. "Ma had to file for divorce, or she wouldn't get the mansion."

"You and your mother cost me the election. Haven't I always provided for you both?"

He pushed past, but Baby Doe no longer stood at the doorway. By the time he reached it, she was running down the curved stairway to the lobby, her cape billowing behind.

"Where are you going?" he called to her.

"I refuse to destroy you, Horace." Her wet cheeks reflected the glow of the chandelier. "And, I cannot live in shadows."

Tabor started after her, but Maxcy caught his sleeve. "Pa, I'm so sorry. I thought..."

"Baby Doe wait."

Her violet eyes hardened. "Your family needs you."

She escaped through the lobby doors and into the carriage.

"Let her go, Pa."

Maxcy sounded so forlorn, Tabor followed him back to the ballroom. The sweet smell of Virginia tobacco, the lilies, the champagne, a million candleflames burned like that night at the Matchless Mine. Baby Doe's grand tribute for him. Now he understood it was her farewell.

"Never Mind the Why or Wherefore" played on the piano.

Snow drifted aimlessly from a leaden sky as Tabor's train pulled into Washington D.C. Bush had booked him a room at the Willard, the most elegant hotel in the city, a stone's throw from the White House.

"Welcome to The Willard. Do you have a reservation?" asked the young man behind the reception desk. His name tag read Mr. James Ryan, Manager.

"It should be under Horace Tabor."

"Ah, Mr. Tabor. We received a letter for you."

He recognized Augusta's penmanship and stuffed the letter in his pocket.

"I'm sorry," Ryan said. "I don't have a reservation for you and all rooms are booked."

"I'm sure you'll find something." He flashed a twenty-dollar bill.

"Sorry." Ryan wagged his finger. "The only room left is Abraham Lincoln's Suite."

"That'll do."

Ryan coughed. "It's one thousand dollars a night."

"I like to stretch out." Tabor tucked the twenty in Ryan's breast pocket.

"Very well, then. Make yourself comfortable while we prepare your room."

Walking through the towering marble columns, Tabor found a leather wing chair and tore open Augusta's letter.

"Jan. 31, 1883

Dear Husband,

This is the 26th anniversary of our wedding. Just such a storm as we're having today, we were married in. And surely, we didn't live in a storm all those 24 years that you were at home. Now you're enjoying the honors of senateship, for which you deserted me. When your month is out, come home and let us live in harmony. There is no need having our case dragged through court again.

I subscribe myself your loving wife, Mrs. Horace Tabor"

He crumpled the letter.

"Mr. Tabor, your room is ready." Ryan waited.

"Will you bring me stationery and a pen?"

"The Lincoln suite has a beautiful writing desk, fully stocked."

"This can't wait."

"Certainly, sir." Ryan left and returned with a fountain pen, ink and paper.

Wind howled outside, and snow drifted on the window sills. Tabor dipped the pen in ink. He started several times, crossing out the words, crumpling paper, and beginning again.

"Dear Baby Doe,

From the moment I met you, I knew we were two of a kind. You've lived through things that crush most folks. Yet, you've come out stronger, showing a brave and beautiful face with each new challenge.

I've been a gambler, taking it to the limit to see if I can beat the odds. But win or lose, I need someone to share life with, and it has to be you. You fill the empty hole inside me, one I never knew I had.

The day I lost the election, I thought the game was over, but sometimes, you have to let it ride. The world changes, and we change with it or die. I'm not ready for that. I can start life over with you.

Marry me in Washington or stay in Oshkosh and I'll come there. I'm not letting you go.

Your devoted Horace"

After Tabor's letter, Baby Doe went straight to confession, asking Father Bonduel to steer her away from temptation. But more letters came each day, piling up on the mantle. She kept up confessions until she thought Father Bonduel would lock her out of church.

She worked with Da at his new haberdashery, much smaller than his original. Working helped pass the hours, which moved at a snail's pace in Oshkosh, so unlike lively Denver and the boom-or-bust mining towns.

She missed working toward her own goals, whether at the Fourth of July mine or designing costumes or the Tabor Grand Opera House. Most of all, she missed Tabor, his big ideas and bluster, his silly jokes and hearty laugh. She even missed his deep, rhythmic snore that made her feel everything was right with the world.

One morning, she caught Mam reading her letters to her sister, Claudia, both moon-eyed over Horace Tabor.

"He's a United States senator," Mam said. "And he's so rich."

"It's over, Mam." Her mouth tasted sour. "Your little Lizzie is not marrying a rich man, so please, get used to it. Is that all you ever wanted for me?"

"It's just as easy to marry a rich man as a poor one." Mam smiled slyly.

"Chasing money made a mess of my life, Mother." She never called her that.

Claudia piped up. "I don't care how much money Senator Tabor has. He's head-over-heels for you and doesn't give a plug nickel what people think. So, what's standing in your way?"

Baby Doe drank coffee from a chipped cup, rereading Tabor's letter, her breath bottled up in her chest. He'd faced the firestorm after his divorce, lost the senate election and still wanted her as badly as she wanted him.

Da popped his head around the corner. "I'll meet you out front with the buggy, lass."

Baby Doe put on her coat and slipped out the door. The bitter wind froze her face by the time she got in the buggy. Winter in Oshkosh was brutal compared to Denver, where the sun melted a blizzard the next day. Hardly a soul braved the icy streets. The old mare's hooves skidded on the ice, while Da struggled to keep her steady.

"Senator Tabor wrote to ask my permission for your hand," he said.

Her insides churned. "Did you tell him off?"

Da shook his bowler, ever the dapper gentleman. "Wasn't sure what you wanted me to say."

All her dammed-up feelings broke loose. "Oh, Da. I've made such a mess of everything." She gripped his arm. "You and Ma tried to give me the best, and what did I do but fail at the gold mine, get divorced, then take up with a married man? I've prayed night and day, confessed to Father Bonduel, but I can't get him out of my mind."

"If we confess our sins, He is faithful and just to forgive us our sins, and to cleanse us from all unrighteousness," Da quoted.

"You think God will forgive me?"

"That's what the good book says. Now you have to forgive yourself."

The sun burned through the morning clouds making the snow sparkle.

God had given her this life to live, and it was up to her to live it the best she knew how.

First day as United States senator. Tabor flipped his lucky silver dollar and caught it in his palm. Lady Luck smiled on him once again. Bet the limit. So much to discuss with President Arthur.

Dressing carefully, he fastened his French cuffs with diamond and onyx cufflinks the size of postage stamps. A matching jeweled stickpin decorated his lapel. Unable to decide on which ring, he wore a couple on each hand. Wouldn't want to come off as a mountain ruffian.

When Henry Teller met him, he shielded himself from the glare of diamonds. "Couldn't you dress more subtly, Tabor?"

"I am who I am, Teller." He threw back the jibe. "And broke I'm not."

"Highly unusual for President Arthur to ask to meet you. Apparently, President Grant suggested he not miss your Wild West stories." Teller glared. "They think westerners are trouble. Don't make it worse."

"Indian massacres, railroad wars, Chinese riots, trigger-happy guards at silver mines?" Tabor teased. "Why would they think we're trouble?"

"They think Colorado men pack six-irons on their hips and mining picks in their back pockets." The elder statesman shook his head.

"Relax. I took the spurs off my boots."

The White House entrance hall gleamed with a rainbow of stained glass.

"President Arthur wouldn't move in until Louis Tiffany redecorated it top to bottom," Teller whispered.

A baby-faced page led the way, gloved hands pointing out

details. “The windows, lampshades, and wall motifs were also designed by Tiffany.” He disappeared behind double doors, then returned. “The president will see you now.”

The Yellow Oval Room radiated sunshine with goldenrod walls, marigold draperies, and oriental rugs woven in shades of ocher. Tabor wished Baby Doe could see this.

President Arthur rose from his executive desk, emblazoned with an American eagle. A jabot embellished his fly-away collar and four-button suit, and mutton-chop sideburns puffed grandly from well-fed jowls. He emanated affluence and style.

“Welcome, gentlemen.” The president shook their hands and gestured to wingback chairs under an enormous painting of George Washington.

“President Grant told me about the Indian uprising during his Leadville visit,” he said.

“Tabor shouldn’t have let them perform war dances,” Teller said. “Riles up their killing instinct.”

Tabor’s hackles bristled. “Utes don’t have war dances. That kind of ignorance started the Meeker Massacre.”

“I like your passion, Senator Tabor.” Light reflected off the president’s round glasses. “I’m sorry you’ll be with us such a short while.”

“I’m better in small doses.” He smiled.

“How many silver mines do you own now?” the president asked.

“More’n a hundred, I guess. Most mines run in the red, just a handful make the other holes worthwhile. The Matchless Mine alone yields four thousand dollars a day.”

Teller cleared his throat. “The economy needs western silver, Mr. President, but eastern bankers support the gold standard. They want miners to focus on gold.”

“Well, fellas, I instruct my boys to keep the gold rocks, too,” Tabor joked.

“You don’t chuck gold on the rubbish pile?” The president laughed. “Seriously, though, minting all this silver into Morgan silver dollars causes inflation.”

"The economy needs inflation," Tabor argued. "Prices are so low now; farmers and factories can't make money. Silver raises wages and prices."

The page interrupted. "Mr. President, an urgent matter has come up in the Blue Room."

"I'm sorry we don't have more time." The president smoothed his lamb-chop sideburn. "Your views are refreshing, Senator Tabor."

"May I buy you a drink at the Round Robin?" Tabor offered. "I'm staying at The Willard."

Teller's eyes bugged out.

"You don't cut up didoes, do you?" President Arthur ran his finger down his calendar.

Teller stepped forward. "Please excuse Tabor, sir. He—"

"I have time for a nightcap at nine," the president said.

"Nine at the Round Robin, then." Tabor shook his hand longer than he meant to, but he was the president after all.

Outside the White House, a new snow squall had blown in.

"Watch yourself. You're alone on this one." Teller walked off, leaving him to find his way.

"You're just miffed I didn't invite you." Snow swirled around him, making it hard to distinguish the street from the lawn. When he reached The Willard, his fingers and toes were frozen.

"How was your meeting with the president, sir?" Ryan asked.

"He's meeting me for a nightcap in the Round Robin."

"We'll have his table ready." Ryan handed him a telegram. "This came for you."

His numb fingers fumbled with the seal.

I DO, the telegram said. **I DO.**

"Something wrong, sir?" Ryan asked, taking his elbow. "You better sit down."

"She said yes." Tabor clapped his hand down on Ryan's shoulder, shaking his head. "I'm getting married!" Today, he'd met the president of the United States, but Baby Doe was all that mattered.

"That's wonderful, sir." Ryan shook his hand. "Congratulations."

"How are you at planning weddings?" Tabor asked.

Plain-suited Pinkerton agents hovered around The Round Robin's circular bar, their dark suits standing out like black ducks in a pond of mallards. The legislators, congressmen, and senators were the mallards, gussied up in foulard ties and muttonchops, gold pocket watches and cigar cases. They leaned over brass railings, feigning indifference, a thin disguise for their fascination for President Arthur and the Silver King huddled by the back door.

The president swirled a mint julep, specialty of the house, sent over by Mr. Ryan, who stood in the shadows scanning the room for trouble.

"So, what drives the richest man in the country to politics?" the president asked.

"Just opinionated, I guess," he said. "When something's not right, I tend to jump in. Usually up to my neck in quicksand."

"Well, you can't get into too much trouble in a month or two."

"Might as well raise a ruckus while I can."

"Defending bi-metallism?" He sipped his mint julep and made a face.

"Someone has to stand up for silver, and it sure ain't the bankers. This country became rich from silver mines. Silver inflates the money supply and means more cash for everyone. Silver allows the farmers, factories and mines to keep running."

"My advisors say so much silver depresses the economy, and we need to adopt the gold standard to restore prosperity." He pushed aside his cocktail.

Tabor called to the bartender. "Two Gibsons, extra onion."

The president smiled. "We see eye-to-eye on drinks, at least."

When the cocktails arrived, Tabor toasted. "To your mentor, Senator Gibson."

The president gulped. "Ah, that's more like it. Gibson would like a self-made man like you. He built the transcontinental railroad, you know."

"You mean the Chinese built the railroad for Gibson."

"Your point?" His voice raised and Pinkertons closed in.

"If it weren't for the Chinese, the railroad wouldn't have crossed the Rockies." Tabor gathered his nerve. "Yet, you signed the Chinese Exclusion Act that treats them like prisoners. They're banned from workplaces. They can't even get mining jobs anymore."

The president emptied his glass, and another Gibson was delivered.

"If you'd done your homework, you'd know I vetoed the Chinese Exclusion Act, but Congress overrode it."

"Stuck my foot in it, didn't I? Not unusual for me, I reckon." He loosened his noose of a tie.

"No one can say this country has not profited by Chinese work." The president's voice boomed like he was making a speech. "Furthermore, trade with China is the key to national wealth and influence." He leaned in and lowered his voice. "You're a straight-shooter, Senator Tabor. A rare breed in Washington, I'm afraid. Nothing's easy here. Don't expect to get the smallest item passed in the senate without some serious boot-licking." Tapping his glass on the table, another drink appeared. "Like another?"

Tabor shook his head. "I have enough trouble keeping my head on my shoulders."

The president circled his forefinger around the room. "These hypocrites asked me to ban liquor in the White House, but dammit, what I do with my private life is my own damned business." A Pinkerton held his overcoat for him. "Apparently, I hit my quota."

Tabor stood. "There's more I'd like to bend your ear about."

President Arthur huffed. "You cross-lots, don't you?"

The Pinkertons opened the back doors, flurries blasting through The Round Robin. The president stepped into the snowstorm and Tabor followed him.

"Thousands of acres of forests are being clear cut out west. It will take generations to grow back, and disease is rampant, Bubonic Plague from the prairie dogs, Tuberculosis, Bright's Disease."

"Mighty lofty plans for a short term. Good luck with it," the president said as the doorman closed the carriage door, and the horses slogged through slush.

Tabor sighed. Shot his wad and came up empty. He expected more from the president. Wet and shivering, he returned to the Round Robin. The entire bar clapped and jeered, mocking him.

Teller puffed a fat cigar. "Give you enough rope to hang yourself and you do. Just dangling in the wind." He blew smoke in his face.

Tabor waved it away. "A hanged man is at the end of his struggle. But I've just begun."

The senate page handed him files. "Senator Tabor, here are the files you requested for the Forest Land committee and Epidemic Disease committee."

Regular nightcaps with the president had given him access to the information and influential contacts he needed to accomplish something without the rigmarole of the senate.

Tabor wrote a quick note and gave it to the page with a silver dollar. "Please deliver this to the president." He leafed through the files.

Teller nudged him. "The president should've thrown your tail to the curb."

"Catch up, Teller. We're having dinner Friday night."

"You invited the president to dinner? Gutsy move."

"I'm closing down Ebbitt's Grill for him and a few friends."

Teller shook his head. "I thought they exaggerated about you."

Senators around them began to stare.

Tabor leaned to him. "Shorty Scout is sending buffalo, venison, and Canadian snow geese."

Teller's wattle turned rooster red.

The senate session droned on, weighed down with minutia.

When did they get to the issues? Bored with the glacial pace, Tabor wrote another telegram to Baby Doe.

Feb. 20, 1883 "My darling girl, it seems like an age since I saw you last…what if we had never met? This world would have been blank to me."

Finally, the bell rang, and senators filed out of the chamber. Eager for recess, they lit cigars and cracked sophomoric jokes. Is this all they came for? Where was their dedication to solve issues?

"Eight o'clock Friday, Senator Tabor?" asked the rusty-haired senator from Vermont.

"Formal attire, I assume?" asked another.

"See you at Ebbitt's. Wouldn't miss it."

"Watch yourself," Teller warned. "The more they envy you, the more they'll crucify you."

"Don't be a spoilsport, Teller." Tabor slapped his shoulder. "You can come too."

29

Washington D.C., March 1883

Baby Doe's stomach leapt like a trout swimming upstream as she stepped out of the Washington D.C. train station, her brother, sister, and parents in tow. Two days on the train had made them all cranky and catawampus. She'd get them settled into the hotel, cleaned up, and rested before introducing them to Tabor.

A clean-shaven coachman in a long black coat held up a slate chalked with curlicue script: McCOURT. He loaded their trunks into the landau.

"Should've known Tabor would send a carriage," Peter said.

She shook her head. "Horace doesn't know we're here, yet. The hotel sent the coach."

"You didn't tell him we were coming?" Mam clucked her tongue.

"What if he doesn't want us here?" Claudia bit a ragged fingernail.

"What if he wants the bride price back?" Da said. Tabor had sent him a big cashier's check for a bride price, ignoring the fact he was owed a dowry.

"Enough." Her hands sliced through the air, trying to control their panic. "Horace will be thrilled that we came early for the wedding. You read his letters."

Mam held up the bundle of letters bound in a pretty ribbon. "The senator is so smitten with our Lizzie he wouldn't take no for an answer."

Claudia giggled. "As you quoted for the Oshkosh Gazette."

"Lizzie, isn't the senator too old to call him my son-in-law?" Da asked.

"Don't talk about his age," she said. "And don't call me Lizzie, call me Baby Doe."

"Better be a proper Catholic wedding." Da straightened his tie.

"With a priest and all the sacraments," she answered.

"Impossible since you're both divorced," Peter said.

She made a face at Peter. "Nothing's impossible for Horace."

Claudia clasped her hands together. "Read us his last letter, again."

"Quit pestering her," Mam said.

"I don't mind, I'd read it a hundred times. 'Now comes the crowning event of my life, my marriage to the woman I love and love to death. It seems almost too much happiness for mortals, but it belongs to us. We give ourselves to one another and whose business is it? We do not rob anybody of anything that belongs to them."

"Take the pot of gold while you can, Lizzie," Peter said. "Billy says once Tabor owns you, he'll be off to the next prospect."

"Don't you dare quote Billy Bush to me." She wished she'd left him behind with the rest of the McCourt clan.

As the carriage drove through Washington D.C., telegraph lines buzzed overhead. Brick buildings towered five and six stories high, dwarfing those in Oshkosh. Businessmen bustled down the streets in distinguished coats and top hats instead of Denver's dusty mash of cowboy, miner and peddler. Horse-drawn streetcars ran down center tracks. On the horizon, a colossal structure appeared, shining white and magnificent in the spring sun. A row of marble Corinthian columns supported a heroic dome.

"Looks like a wedding cake," Claudia said.

"Our nation's Capitol." Mam said, eyes filling with tears.

Da grasped her hand. "Little Lizzie is marrying a senator."

Baby Doe's throat ached hearing them, not sure what she felt, but whatever it was overwhelmed her with emotion. Maybe it was being this close to happiness and having them here with her.

The carriage turned into a street flanked with government buildings, restaurants, and bars. At the intersection, policemen stood shoulder-to-shoulder blocking traffic in front of Old Ebbitt Grill. A tall gentleman in a dinner jacket and top hat greeted men at the door.

"It's Horace." Baby Doe leaped from the carriage. "Horace."

His eyes met hers, eyebrows arching, then he turned and walked away. A crowd of men in suits stared at her with judgmental eyes.

Why had she been so impulsive? She'd embarrassed him. Her family stood by the carriage looking as motley as hoboes.

Then, Tabor reappeared, face beaming and a fashionable gentleman by his side. "President Arthur, I'd like to introduce my fiancé, Baby Doe."

Head whirling in relief and surprise, she curtsied to the president.

He reached for her hand and kissed it. "What a lucky fellow Senator Tabor is to be marrying you," he said. "When is the wedding?"

"Why, next Friday afternoon, five o'clock," she said, pleased she could even speak. "Would you like to come?" Her hand covered her mouth.

Mam and Claudia gasped.

"I would be honored." He smiled.

"I'll be sure you get an invitation, Mr. President," she said.

Tabor squeezed her hand, beaming down at her.

The world is your oyster, he'd told her long ago, and she didn't believe him. But, if this wasn't a pearl of a moment, she didn't know what was.

Tabor greeted her family and sent the carriage around the corner to The Willard, promising to meet them the next day for dinner.

Invitations. Nausea waved through her. What kind of invitations? Thick parchment, letter pressed in bold black ink. No, silver. Actual silver.

At the hotel, a gloved hand helped her down from the carriage. "Welcome to the Willard Hotel. We hope you enjoy your stay." Doormen opened the hotel doors. Brass buttons gleamed on scarlet uniforms, even more glorious than The Windsor.

If this was something out of a dream, she prayed she'd never wake up.

"My lands." Mam gawked at ceilings painted with noblemen on horseback chasing foxes.

"You really outdid yourself this time, Lizzie," Claudia whispered.

Da tipped his head back to see and backed into an urn.

A man caught it and steadied it on the pedestal. "You must be Senator Tabor's family. I'm Mr. Ryan, manager of The Willard." His curly black hair contrasted with his pale skin.

"You have any whiskey?" Da raised bushy eyebrows.

"The Round Robin is right over there," Ryan said.

Peter and Da crossed the lobby.

"I was wondering if you might recommend a printer for my wedding invitations?" Baby Doe asked Ryan. "Oh, no, I don't even know who to send them to."

"Senator Tabor gave me the guest list, but there won't be time to print and mail them before the wedding."

"Then, I'd like the finest stationery notes sent up to my room."

"Still, the post office will never get them there on time."

Her chin collapsed to her chest.

"I *could* have them hand delivered," Ryan said.

"Really? You'd do that for me?" His kindness touched her.

"A pleasure to be of service to such a beautiful bride." He bowed and left.

She raised her tired eyes to the frescoed ceilings. Legions of angels frolicked on billowing clouds. Handwritten invitations would be beautiful.

A gawky young man with orange hair and a big camera approached her. "Say, are you Senator Tabor's fiancé? I'm McGee from the Washington Post. Mind posing for a picture?"

She looked at her rumpled traveling suit. "Won't you let me change?"

He clicked the shutter, and the flash powder exploded in her face. "The Washington Post is very curious about the lady who nabbed the Silver King."

"I don't like the sound of that."

He shrugged. "Fame has a price."

Up in her suite, she wrote out the invitations in her finest penmanship, while Mam and Claudia folded them and inserted them into envelopes.

The maître d' led the McCourt family through the Willard's Peacock Alley to meet Senator Tabor for a celebration dinner. Baby Doe lagged behind, light-headed and hiccupping, not wanting to see Tabor in this nervous state. Mam had laced her corset so tight, her chest felt like a hot-air balloon ready to burst.

Colorful flags of the world hung the entire length of the dining room. Ladies sipped tea with gloved hands and crooked pinkies. Pointy high-heeled boots wagged as fast as their tongues. In comparison, Mam's and Claudia's muslin dresses looked drab as field mice as the family followed the maître d'. Tomorrow, she'd take them shopping, and they'd be the toast of Washington D.C.

"Psst. Over here." Tabor pulled her behind a potted palm and wrapped his arms around her for the first time in months. A new suit skimmed his broad shoulders, and diamond rings gleamed on his fingers. He'd changed so much since she met him, from mountain mayor to distinguished senator. Was his heart the same? Inhaling his scent, fresh as alpine air, she knew. This precious man who had first become her partner, then friend, then lover, would soon be her own husband.

"I knew you wouldn't give up on us," he said, voice thick with emotion.

"I didn't want to leave, but I just couldn't live like that in Denver."

"You deserved better." His finger traced her lips. "That was no life for a woman like you. But all that will change after we are married."

As they kissed, the brittleness in her chest broke like an egg, pouring out the love she held inside. Reluctantly, she led him to their table.

Tabor shook her father's hand and greeted her mother and sister. Then he turned to Peter. "We have some unfinished business."

Peter shifted in his chair, face coloring. "I know I shouldn't have left the Tabor Grand without giving notice. But I couldn't let her travel alone."

"Actually, I was hoping you'd be my best man." Tabor's tone sounded peculiar.

"What about Maxcy?" Baby Doe asked. "Or Billy?"

"They couldn't break away from the Windsor." He frowned. "In fact, after the wedding, Peter, I'd be obliged if you'd manage the Tabor Grand. It's getting too much for Billy to handle the theater and all my other businesses."

"I'll be on the train Monday morning." Peter turned to Da. "Manager of the Tabor Grand."

"Don't mess it up," Da said.

"Did you see the Washington Post?" Ma read from the front page. "The Silver King's bride is a perfect blonde with magnificent golden hair reaching to the floor when uncoiled. There never was a more beautiful set of teeth than the smile which her lips disclose, while her eyes are large and full of expression. A beauty among beauties."

"Ahhh, the legend grows." Peter rubbed his hands together. "Beautiful Baby Doe, richest bride in America. If that doesn't turn people green, nothing will."

"Wait until they hear President Arthur is coming to the wedding," Tabor grinned.

Claudia squealed like a piglet, and everyone in Peacock Alley stared at them.

Baby Doe yanked her arm. "Lower your voice. Everyone's staring."

"Then let's give them something to stare at." Tabor gave her a velvet case the size of a Bible, heavy in her hands.

"What's this, Horace?" she asked.

Claudia leaned closer, smelling of talcum. "Open it, Lizzie."

"What are you waiting for?" Peter asked.

Tabor started to take it away. "Maybe she doesn't want it."

"Can't a girl savor the moment?" She opened the box and pressed her hand against her pounding heart.

Folks at surrounding tables gasped, and Mam whiffed her smelling salts.

Stark and shining against black velvet lay an enormous ruby pendant surrounded by diamonds. She'd never seen anything like this in her life.

Tabor draped the chain on her décolleté. "This necklace was owned by Queen Isabella of Spain." He caressed her neck, sending a thrill down her spine. "Now it will grace *my* queen."

The ruby felt warm and substantial on her chest, a talisman of his love. She kissed him unabashedly in front of God and Washington society. Never again would she hide her love for Tabor. Once they were married, her honor would be restored, and no one could disparage them.

Her family gathered around. Da and Peter laughed at Tabor's anecdotes. Claudia's eyes never left the ruby, as if it held her in a trance. Mam grasped Baby Doe's hand across the table, tears in her eyes. "This is everything I ever wanted for you."

"I know, Mam." Squeezing her mother's hand, she finally knew what happy felt like. One rare moment where everything was right. She'd struggled so in her life, but would always keep this moment in her heart, family gathered around, accepting Tabor, accepting their marriage.

Ryan approached the table and bent down to her. "May I have a word with you?"

"Excuse me, everyone." She followed him, giddy with excitement. Her hand grasped the pendant, hard and real.

As soon as they were out of sight, Ryan stopped. "I'm deeply sorry but I wanted to save you embarrassment." He handed her the wedding invitations, some torn in pieces, others crumpled.

She cried out, covering her mouth. Her mind skittered like butter on a hot skillet. She looked through them one by one, senators, congressman and their wives...Tabor would be shamed, and the happiest day of their lives, ruined.

"What would you like me to do?" he asked.

"Dispose of these, please, Mr. Ryan." She handed back the rubble. "I'm sure I can count on your discretion."

At the table, she kissed Tabor's cheek. No one would ruin their wedding. "Mr. Ryan wanted to know about wedding flowers."

Claudia stuck another hairpin into Baby Doe's scalp.

"Ow, that smarts." She rubbed her head feeling more like a voodoo doll than a bride.

Strains of organ music drifted through the door. "They've started, Claudia. You should be up with Peter by now."

"Oh, no. Oh, no." Her sister swooped up her aqua tulle skirt and ran. "I've ruined your entrance."

Nothing could ruin her entrance more than her own black mood. She'd demanded a proper Catholic wedding to heal their transgressions. Divorce was the gravest of sins. But the mangled invitations had brought her fresh shame and anguish.

The silk damask bodice of her wedding dress squeezed her like a used tube of Crème Angelique Dentifrice. You'd think, for seven-thousand dollars, they could have made the dress more comfortable. Viewing her billowing bustle in the mirror, her diminutive derriere looked enormous.

Tabor snuck up and kissed her neck, handing her a bouquet of wildflowers. “Claudia forgot to bring you this.”

The scent soothed her. “Isn’t it bad luck to see the bride before the wedding?”

He took in every detail from her arctic fox stole to her silk slippers. “I may be the luckiest fool on earth, but if I couldn’t see you, I’d just be a fool.”

She laughed. The organ began the Wagner march. “Last chance to elope.”

His eyebrows shot up. “You want to?”

“Might disappoint the president.”

“It’s you I don’t want to disappoint.” His fingers interlaced hers. “This wedding is for us, nobody else. We’re choosing each other, and that’s all that matters.”

Her father came and shook Tabor’s hand, tears in his eyes. “It’s time.”

Leaning down to kiss her, Tabor hesitated and held his finger to his mouth. “Don’t forget. I’m first in line to kiss the bride.” One last look and he left.

Her father walked her out front. “Sure about this, lass?” His wayward eyebrows twitched.

“I love Horace, Da.” She took his arm and strode through the flowered archway, the perfume of white jasmine, gardenias, and tuberoses intoxicating her. Tabor’s face shone at the altar, smiling not only with his mouth, but with dancing eyes and tapping toes.

Claudia and Peter stood on either side.

Most of the Tiffany chairs in the ballroom were empty, save for a few in the front. She faltered, and her father supported her. She stepped forward, allowing the organ cadence to guide her feet down the carpet.

On the left, surrounded by black-suited Pinkertons, President Arthur smiled at her. She smiled back. Behind him, she saw familiar faces of Senators Bowen, Chaffee, and Teller. No wives were present, not another woman besides her sister and mother. You’d think they would have come, if only to see the president.

Pain throbbed behind her eyes, threatening to black out her sight. She felt for her ruby necklace, solid and consoling, and focused on Tabor, radiating confidence and pride.

At the end of the aisle, Da kissed her cheek and sat next to her mother.

The Irish-Catholic priest with ferocious eyebrows stepped in front of them, asking the congregation to bow their heads. Tabor slipped his hand in hers.

After the prayer, a soprano sang her first passionate notes, and panic rose in her chest, recalling her shameful flight from the Tabor Grand. But the aria expressed love found, instead of love lost, and she breathed a prayer of thanks.

"I do." Tabor's oath penetrated her thoughts.

The priest turned to her. "Do you take Horace Tabor as your lawful wedded husband, to have and to hold, for better or worse, for richer or poorer, in sickness and health, to love and cherish until death do you part?"

The devotion in Tabor's eyes steadied her.

"I do."

"If anyone knows of a reason why this couple should not wed, speak now, or forever hold your peace."

Senator Teller cleared his throat and Mam glared at him.

"Any one?"

Coughs and rustling…but no one spoke up.

Finally, he raised his hands in blessing. "What God has joined together, let no man put asunder. You may kiss the bride."

Tabor's heavy brow brushed her forehead and his mustache tickled her mouth. All that existed were his lips, his arms, his scent.

The organ recessional resounded as they walked back through the flowered arches, smiling to men on the aisle, and formed a reception line with her parents. The first to congratulate them was President Arthur, who took her hands in his.

"You are the most stunning bride I've ever seen, Mrs. Tabor."

Mrs. Tabor. "We're so honored you could come," she gushed.

Thirty-two dignitaries and senators followed, bidding them good wishes and piling presents on the reception table. Try as she might to ignore it, the absence of their wives needled her.

The newlyweds took their places at the head table, and she was grateful when the waiter poured champagne. Tiny bubbles slipped down her throat, and she marveled at the wonderland around her. A massive wedding bell of white roses hung in the center of the room, surmounted by Cupid's bow, his arrow tipped with violets. A canopy of foliage surrounded the wedding cake. She snuggled into her husband's arm and kissed his ear. Not even the reporters and photographers at the ballroom doorway bothered her on this splendid night.

Peter made the first toast during dinner. "May your love be as deep as Tabor's mines."

Politicians laughed and ate their steak. Waiters refilled their glasses.

The champagne emboldened her to speak to the president. "Horace tells me you've redecorated The White House with Louis Tiffany's work."

The president nodded. "I would be honored to arrange a White House tour. Then I'll have the pleasure of seeing you again before you leave."

"We may never leave, Mr. President," Tabor said. "I like being in the thick of things."

Senators exchanged glances.

"May I be so bold as to request a white rose from your bouquet?" the president asked. "My daughter takes interest in weddings and such."

Touched, she pulled a rosebud and handed it to him.

The orange-haired reporter called to her from the doorway. "Congratulations, Mrs. Tabor. Remember me?"

She nodded. "Mr. McGee from the Washington Post."

"Mr. Tabor," he said. "Maybe you can clear something up for me."

"What's that, son?" He smiled, puffed his cigar.

"Why did you apply for a marriage license in St. Louis before you divorced your former wife? And what about the illegal divorce papers you filed in Durango?"

The cigar dropped from Tabor's mouth, and senators leaned back in their chairs. Her perfect wedding party disintegrated before her eyes.

She stood and addressed him. "Mr. McGee, have you ever been in love?"

"No ma'am." His cheeks flushed.

"Love is a wild horse, impossible to tame," she said. "The horse takes you places you never thought you'd go. But if you hold on tight, it always leads you home."

"Here, here." The president raised his glass and politicians followed his lead.

Tabor nuzzled her ear. "Shall we end this shindig on a high note?"

"Why not?"

He swept her up in his arms, bustle, train, veil and all, and she laughed.

"My bride and I thank you for coming." He gazed at her. "But it *is* our wedding night, and we're going home."

The president applauded and tipped the rose she'd given him. She tossed her bouquet to Claudia who hugged it to her heart. Tabor carried her past tables of politicians, who nodded congratulations as they ordered fresh cocktails. When they reached the ballroom doors, McGee stood behind his camera igniting a tray of black powder, with a loud bang and blinding light.

"Goodnight, Mr. McGee," she called. "I hope you'll find love someday."

Tabor had nodded off, his head against the railcar, rocking with the chugging train up to New York City. The Silver King had shown those bigwigs a thing or two about how to get things done. He'd written forest conservation bills, fought for miner pensions, and lobbied for Chinese rights, while other senators passed *him* the restaurant bill.

She was glad his term was over, and they could escape for a honeymoon, no senators and wives to spoil it. She admired her diamond solitaire, symbolizing promises kept. But at what price? Pulling rosary beads through her fingers, she asked forgiveness for the broken hearts left in their wake. Augusta, Maxcy, and what about Jake? He'd closed his haberdashery, and she had no idea where he was now.

Picking up *The Washington Post* from the opposite bench, she admired their wedding photo with President Arthur on the front page. Underneath was an interview with Senator Teller.

"Tabor is gone," they quoted Teller. "I thank God he was not elected for six years. Thirty days nearly killed us. I humiliated myself to attend his wedding since he was from Colorado, but Mrs. Teller wouldn't. Tabor made a great fool of himself with that woman. He ought to retire and attend his private affairs."

People could be so cruel and spiteful, only the president had been kind after the wedding, entertaining them at the White House.

Tabor started snoring in that peaceful murmur she loved, blending with the rhythm of the train tracks. They didn't need Teller's blessing now that they were married. They didn't need anyone's blessing, except God's, and she was certain they had that. She stuffed the newspaper under the seat, out of sight, vowing not to worry about it again.

Part Three

I dreamed today that my darling Tabor threw
his pants & vest on a rocking chair
and he said "life without you is unbearable"
and he disappeared from me.
He had gone
I put my hand in his pants pocket
& pulled out two grand pure gold pieces.

—Baby Doe Tabor Diary, Colorado Historical Society

30

New York City,
April 1883

The bellman piled Baby Doe's new leather trunks high on his cart at the Chelsea Hotel. Their expansive shopping trips delighted her, as did the symphony of solicitous voices.

"May we help you with anything, Mrs. Tabor? Your coat is ermine, isn't it, Mrs. Tabor? May we get you an umbrella, Mrs. Tabor? It's raining you know..."

Raining? What did that matter? She was Mrs. Horace Tabor and it was glorious. Doormen, waiters, chambermaids, hotel managers, theater and restaurant owners: all made a fuss over her. She had her own purse full of silver dollars to dole out generously. She loved New York City, with its fast pace and smell of roasting chestnuts.

Most of all, she loved the theater district, with its stimulating writers, actors, musicians, and artists. They attended Tony Pastor's Vaudeville Theater where Lillian Russell starred in *The Mulligan Guard Picnic*. She and Lillian had hit it off when she played *H.M.S. Pinafore* at the Tabor Grand. After the show, Pastor took them backstage.

Lillian opened her dressing room door, hair pinned up and holding a newborn. "Oh, my goodness. Didn't expect visitors." Her face lit up and she kissed her cheek.

"Baby Doe."

"You were outstanding tonight, Miss Russell." Tabor tipped his top hat.

"I never thought I'd see you on a New York stage." Baby Doe squeezed her hand, and Lillian stared at her Tiffany diamond ring.

"Let me show you our new pulley system," Pastor said, and took Tabor into the riggings.

Lillian's baby reached for Baby Doe's cheek. Those fingers, pink and moving, made her yearn for her own lost son.

"Would you like to hold her?" Lillian handed her the baby. "Her father's still married, unfortunately. But I'll be starring in his new play, Pocahontas."

Detecting sadness under her pride Baby Doe stroked the baby's hair. "What's the play about?"

"An English gentleman who agonizes about marrying an American heathen." Lillian huffed. "I'm the heathen."

She laughed. "I've been called that myself." But now she was Mrs. Horace Tabor.

"Will you have children?"

"Horace is past all that. His son is almost my age." She kissed the baby's wiggling toes, smelling like baby powder.

Tabor returned, tapping his watch. "We're late for Delmonico's."

She handed the infant back. "Isn't she the sweetest thing you've ever seen, Horace?"

"*You're* the sweetest thing I've seen." He took her arm. "Ready, Babe?"

She couldn't help but feel let down.

A week later, Baby Doe took deep breaths to calm her nerves as they walked into the Vanderbilt's new Metropolitan Opera House. She had every right to be nervous given the newspapers escalating the scandal of Tabor's immoral divorce, illegal marriage license, unholy Catholic wedding, and those ridiculous charges of polygamy. How would the Vanderbilts receive them?

"How do you know the Vanderbilts?" she asked Tabor.

"William Vanderbilt invests in our mines," he said. "His wife can't wait to meet you."

"What if I'm not dressed right?" She checked her outfit. Her ermine coat and pale-blue gown embroidered with seed pearls gleamed under the chandeliers.

Tabor smiled. "You never have to worry about that again, Baby."

The theater's seven stories loomed overhead, box seats cantilevered from the sides. A haughty usher checked their invitation twice before leading them to the private box. Their hosts, Alva and William Vanderbilt, arrived five minutes later, followed by a spotlight and applause.

Mr. Vanderbilt looked as if he'd stepped off a yacht, jaunty ascot at his neck, tussled curls parted in the middle, sunburned face. A scarf billowed from Mrs. Vanderbilt's princess-gown of green silk. Frizzled bangs jazzed her top knot. The couple waved at them just as the lights dimmed.

Baby Doe had expected English opera, but *Faust* was performed in Italian. She sat back in her cushioned seat and allowed the music to take her away.

An hour later, the lights went up for intermission and waiters served champagne.

Tabor guzzled his. "I'd rather wrestle a grizzly than sit through Italian opera."

"Senator Tabor, you've been holding out on me," Vanderbilt said. "May I?" He kissed Baby Doe's hand, his lips lingering. Mrs. Vanderbilt moved toward them, dragging another woman, with a fierce glint in her eye.

Vanderbilt leaned to Baby Doe. "The eagles are circling, and you look like lunch." He tugged Tabor's arm. "Join me for a cigar in the salon?" The men left.

"I'm Alva Vanderbilt, and this is Patricia Reese." She shook her hand with a firm grip. "You're a stunner, aren't you?"

Patricia nodded her approval.

"The opera was remarkable, wasn't it?" Baby Doe said.

"Liar." Alva cackled. "It's in Italian, and no one has a clue what's happening, but my word, aren't we cultured? At least we have seats." She adopted a nasal, high-brow tone. "The Astors said the Academy of Music had no seats left for the Vanderbilts. Like new money doesn't spend like old? The Astor money's so old, it crumbles to dust." She called for more champagne.

"I'm sure the Astors would love your theater," Baby Doe said. "It's magnificent."

"Who needs the Astors when I've got the Tabors." Alva and Patricia toasted her. "If old society doesn't accept you, make your *own* way."

Patricia nodded. "Alva tells me you were married at The Willard Hotel?"

"Details. Tell us details." Alva fingered the beads on Baby Doe's neckline. "What did I read? The bride wore a seven-thousand-dollar gown and Queen Isabella necklace."

"Was the wedding enormous?" Patricia asked.

"Small, actually," she said. "Just my family and a few politicians."

"Don't be so modest," Patricia said. "President Arthur attended your wedding."

"What did the wives wear?" Alva asked, too innocently.

Awful images sprung to mind: shredded wedding invitations, empty Tiffany chairs, Senator Teller's judgmental quote.

Alva sniggered. "We heard the wives didn't come. Forget the old biddies. Their loss."

Baby Doe held her glass up for more champagne, not caring if she appeared uncouth.

"Old society always shuns new society." Alva waved her glass around. "But you can beat them at their own game. Living well is the best revenge."

"I'll keep that in mind," Baby Doe said. Surely, Denver would never be so punishing.

The *Idle Rich* were not idle at all, Baby Doe discovered. They spent their time seeking out the finest things made, a new sport Tabor wanted to share with his bride. Not unlike prospecting, she suspected. He swept her up in his enthusiasm for dazzling silver tea service, fine Belgium linens, goose-down featherbeds. If she showed the slightest interest, Tabor bought it.

"You'll never see this back in Denver," he explained.

They visited Haughwout's, specializing in crystal and silverware, farther north along Manhattan's fashionable shopping stretch, followed by Alexander T. Stewart's department store, America's palace of trade. They bought clothing, art, and furnishings, enough to fill two railcars.

The extravagance made her feel guilty and indulgent. "I used to count pennies to buy a loaf of bread."

He kissed her nose. "You've suffered enough for one lifetime."

"It's enough, now, Horace." She'd had her fill.

"But I saved the best for last," he said as the carriage stopped and he helped her out.

"Here?" She looked for a store, but only foundries lined the dingy Manhattan street. Burning chemicals tinged the air. Whirring and clanging machinery reminded her of the ore smelters.

Tabor opened a heavy warehouse door, and she walked inside. It took a minute for her eyes to adjust to the darkness. A large cast-iron furnace spewed flames, as a man shoveled sand into a cauldron. Once it melted, he spun the molten liquid onto a long metal tube and blew into one end, then pulled the bubble into a pear shape.

The man propped goggles up on his forehead. "Sorry, we don't accept visitors."

"I believe we're expected. Mr. and Mrs. Horace Tabor?"

"Ah, the president's friends. I'm Louis Tiffany."

Louis Comfort Tiffany. She squeezed Tabor's hand. "Your work at the White House was stunning. What inspired you to work with glass?"

"I was awestruck by the Moorish mosaics in Spain." He led them through the worktables. "It seemed natural to interpret mosaics in glass."

A craftsman cut shapes into an opalescent sheet of glass, his hands butchered with cuts. Another man fit the pieces like a puzzle, forming magnolia blossoms against a brilliant blue sky.

"Lately, I'm inspired by Edison's light bulb shining through colored glass," Tiffany said. "Lamps as beautiful as they are useful."

Her hand followed the shape of a lampshade. "Dragonflies dancing in the cattails."

"Pick out the ones you like." Tabor stroked her back. "The world is your oyster."

His curious phrase had come true. She'd left behind a life of struggle and replaced it with love and abundance.

A page bounded through the door, ruddy and breathless. He searched the room, then ran to Tabor, handing him a telegram. "This came for you at the Chelsea. Says it's urgent."

Tabor ripped it open.

Baby Doe looked over his shoulder. "It's from Peter."

BUSH EMBEZZELING STOP **NEED TABOR IMMEDIATELY** STOP

She jumped to conclusions. "One of Peter's jokes, you know how he is." On second thought, not even Peter would pull a stunt like this.

31

Denver, Colorado, June 1883

Jerking open the Tabor Grand door, Tabor strode across the lobby, his mind in turmoil. Either Bush or Peter was lying and either way would end in disaster.

Baby Doe ran to catch up. "Why would Billy embezzle from you? You're like brothers."

A turn of a blade in his festering wound. Two brothers lost in one lifetime. He stormed Peter's office. "McCourt, what's the meaning of your telegram?"

Peter held up his palms, speaking fast. "I was looking for a tax record and found checks made out to Mine '73. Seemed strange, since Tabor Grand books are separate from mining operations, so I telegraphed Lou Leonard. He never heard of Mine '73."

Peter showed him the ledger with regular withdrawals in Bush's penmanship.

"There must be an explanation," Baby Doe said.

"Mine '73? '73 was the year I met Billy at the Republican Convention." His gullet burned something fierce. "Have you confronted him about this?" He popped a licorice.

Peter's face reddened. "I assumed you'd want to do it, since he's your friend."

"We'll see about that."

Tabor and Baby Doe crossed the street to their offices in the

First National. He'd loved Bush from the time they met, a kindred spirit who grew up without a father, in need of a second chance in life. Had he really turned on him?

Confused and remorseful, Tabor opened the door for his wife. "Why don't you wait for me in the lobby? It could get ugly."

She marched past him. "Then we'll face it together."

Bush jumped up when he saw her. "You're back. I missed you."

Tabor followed. "That's funny, because we missed you and Maxcy at the wedding."

His mustache twitched. "Someone had to hold down the fort."

"Tell me about Mine '73," Tabor said.

Bush swabbed his neck. "Haven't had time to look into it."

"Let me guess," Tabor said. "'73 was the year of the convention when you counted the votes, and no one questioned the outcome after the crash."

"And, *you* won by a landslide." Bush polished his nails on his shirt.

"That's just it," Tabor said. "You've always been there to *help* me with some sly deal or another, to which I turned a blind eye because of our friendship."

"My pleasure, Boss."

"And Mine 73 is your payback." He held out his hand. "Give me your keys."

"Which one do you need?" Bush held up a large ring.

"All of them." Tabor jerked the keys away. "You're fired." He swung his fist into Bush's jaw with a crack.

Baby Doe gasped.

Bush staggered backward, wiggling his jaw. He pulled his cane handle and unsheathed his sword. "This is because of her, isn't it?"

He slashed the blade through the air, swooping around until the tip indented Tabor's abdomen. "She's lying. I never touched her."

"Liar," she said, and Tabor knocked his sword away.

Bush lunged for the blade, slicing through his fingers. Crying out, he grabbed his hand, blood spurting. "You bastard. I gave you everything, including her."

Peter and two guards rushed in and strong-armed Bush, pushing him down the hallway.

Heart thrashing against his ribs, Tabor staggered back against the wall, breathing hard. "Billy touched you?"

She trembled, her face pale. "He tried to seduce me, but I locked myself in your apartment."

He rubbed his tired eyes. "Why didn't you tell me?"

"I thought it would kill you." Her shoulders caved.

"No, Baby, it would have killed him." He held out his arms, and she came to him.

The loud tock-tock of the grandfather clock in his suite drowned out Rockwell's yammering.

Tabor loved that clock. Bush gave it to him when they opened the hotel. Good times.

Rockwell slid the file into his briefcase. "The Pinkertons discovered checks identified as *Donation* funneled into Mine '73. Bush siphoned off a fortune."

The grandfather clock chimed five times. Most likely, Bush was drinking whiskey with Maxcy at The Office. Tabor had lost them both along the way.

"Settle out of court with Billy." He'd lost his appetite for revenge.

"He's counter-suing for malicious prosecution and back wages," Rockwell said.

Another rabbit punch. "How's he figure that?"

"He says you owe him five-thousand for senate campaign services, ten-thousand for acting as your divorce liaison, and seventy-five-thousand for defamation of character."

Rockwell's words gutted him.

"But your case is solid," he said. "I feel confident we'll win in court."

"Pay Billy." Tabor lost his best friend; what consolation was revenge? He heard the orchestra warming up in the penthouse ballroom. “If you’ll excuse me, my bride is waiting for our wedding party to begin. You and Mrs. Rockwell are coming, aren’t you?”

The lawyer cleared his throat. “We had a previous engagement.”

“I see.” Tabor walked toward the music. All afternoon, they’d taken cancellations of regret, illness, unexpected trips, and catastrophe. He told himself it didn’t matter, but it mattered to her.

The orchestra played his favorite waltz. Bone china and silver service adorned two-dozen empty tables. A small figure swathed in organdy danced alone under the chandelier.

Baby Doe.

He pressed his mouth to her ear. “You are the most beautiful woman in the room.”

A slow smile dawned on her face, violet eyes glistening.

He took her hand and held the small of her back. “May I have this dance?” They moved as one to the waltz, his disappointments shrinking to grains of sand.

32

Denver, Colorado, July 1884

Another agonizing wail reached Tabor's ears from the other side of the carved wood door.

"Something's wrong." Six hours since he'd sent for Doctor Lemming. Six hours hearing his wife in torture.

"The doctor's doing all he can," Peter said. "These things take time."

Tabor tore at his mustache. "After Bush's trial, I wanted to start over, have a son. I should never have asked her to go through this."

"Yeooow." The sound sliced through his eardrums. He banged on the locked door to no answer, then spun around. "I can't stand this. If I lose her, I'll die."

Peter took him downstairs. "You won't lose her, she's tough. She's been through it before."

He stopped on the stairs. "What are you talking about?"

Peter blanched. "We need whiskey for this one."

They reached the masculine den Baby Doe had created for him in their new Sherman Street mansion, but the room held no comfort now. She'd decorated the fifty-eight rooms herself, layering rich textures in warm colors, creating a comforting cocoon to compensate for the cold shoulder Denver society dealt them.

Peter handed him a whiskey. "She had a son in her first marriage."

The news stunned him. "Where's the boy?"

"He died."

A lump choked his throat. "But she lived."

"And she'll be fine today." Peter poked his head out the door. "Miss Jillian, come stoke this fire. It's freezing in here."

The first-floor housekeeper came and tended the fire, her hair tied in a kerchief.

They sat in Tiffany throne chairs with medieval symbols and Celtic upholstery. The fire did nothing to warm Tabor's bones. He remembered the day Maxcy was born. Now Maxcy was married, and he hadn't even been invited to the wedding.

"You need a distraction," Peter said. "What do you think if I start a theater circuit for Broadway shows? We'd start at the Tabor Grand, loop down to Colorado Springs, Pueblo, Trinidad, Salida, then west to Leadville, Glenwood Springs, Aspen, and Grand Junction. I just need funding."

Tabor smiled. Peter had taken over the theater and profits were up. "You'll have to earn it. I want you to be my business manager."

"You want me to take Bush's job."

Tabor snorted. "Without the embezzlement."

The door swung open. Doctor Lemming held a bundle swaddled in flannel. "It was a tough one, but mother is resting peacefully."

Tears sprang to his eyes at first glimpse of his son's face, so like Maxcy's. "May I hold him?"

"It's a girl." The doctor handed over the baby.

"A girl?" Barely feeling her weight, he tightened his hold. Petite and beautiful like her mother, her skin was translucent over blue veins, their blood intermingled in this gift from heaven. "She's a girl, Peter." He held her up for his brother-in-law.

Peter touched her tiny nose and recited.

A newborn babe brings light to the house,
warmth to the hearth and joy to the soul
For wealth is family. Family is wealth."

"Family is wealth," Tabor repeated and smelled her sweet head.

Had he done this with Maxcy? He couldn't remember. He'd been given another chance at a family and, this time, he'd make it right.

Baby Doe pushed Lily's perambulator down Sherman street. Two women strolled toward her with flowered dresses and parasols over frizzled hair. A perfect chance to meet the neighbors. She pushed back the carriage hood and adjusted Lily's bonnet. How could they resist her beautiful daughter? She'd spared no expense on Lily's exquisite layette: diamond-tipped gold diaper pins, fine French lace gowns, booties and hat tipped with peacock feathers.

As Baby Doe got closer, one woman leaned to the other, whispering. Then, lifting their skirts so they wouldn't sully themselves, they crossed the street.

She held Lily up and showed off her Battenberg lace dress. "Why not come over and say hello? She's a beautiful girl, twenty-one inches long and seven pounds. She has my hair and her father's amber eyes."

They stood on the other side, mouths open, ogling the richest baby in the country.

Would Lily always be shunned for her parent's sins? The rejection wasn't just her imagination. Baby Doe asked every Catholic church in Denver to baptize Lily, and they'd refused due to the Tabors' disgraceful divorces and remarriage.

Miss Jillian waved from the steps of their mansion. "You have a visitor, Missus Tabor. Friar Guido from the Sacred Heart."

Her heart jumped. Had he changed his mind?

The neighbor women strained their necks to get a look.

She laid Lily in the perambulator and started home. "Nice chatting with you, but Father Guido is calling."

In the entryway, the friar gazed at the enormous Tiffany stained-glass window; a river cascaded down mountain ridges, a tiny cross planted on the highest peak, in memory of her son.

"Friar Guido, so good of you to come." She scooped up her angel. "This is my daughter, Elizabeth Bonduel Lily Tabor."

He stroked the baby's arm. "My eyes are not good. Where can I see the child in better light?"

"Let's join Mr. Tabor on the portico. Miss Jillian, will you bring us tea?"

The friar's nostrils flared. "Perhaps some sherry?"

"Miss Jillian, bring the sherry from Madrid." All the better to convince him to baptize Lily.

The friar pointed to gifts on the table. "You're blessed with many friends to celebrate the birth of your child."

"The gifts are from my husband's business partners," she said briskly, not wanting his pity. "You're our first visitor." She opened the portico door. "Horace, Friar Guido's here."

Tabor shook his hand vigorously. "Am I supposed to shake your hand? I'm not schooled in these things. Always preferred a mountain river to church on Sunday."

The friar stepped back, glanced at the door.

"The sherry will be here shortly." Baby Doe placed Lily in the pram.

"Should I call you Father?" Tabor asked.

"Only Catholics may call me Father." His rheumy eyes sparked.

"Now I've stuck my foot in it. Only my wife speaks Catholic."

When Jillian came with the sherry, the friar finished the glass in a gulp.

"Leave us the bottle, Jillian," Baby Doe said.

Tabor presented the friar a gold coin. "I minted a hundred of these for Lily's christening."

"Baby Tabor is born," the friar read. "May I offer a better badge of consecration?" He gave Baby Doe a Saint Christopher medal. "Blessed by the Holy Father in Rome."

She kissed the medal, her heart welling with gratitude. "This means the world to me."

Lily's fingers curled around the friar's thumb, wrinkling her nose as if smelling new hay. “Then you’ll christen Lily?” Baby Doe asked.

“I would, but the rectory roof is ready to cave in, and the church has no money to repair it.” His eyes glazed over their Oriental carpets, mosaic tables, and grandfather clock.

“I had no idea Father,” she said. “Forgive me, I haven’t been to church lately.” Last time she slid into a pew, the other women moved to another row. Now, she prayed at home.

The friar patted her hand. “As the Bible says, fish are caught in a cruel net, or birds are taken in a snare, so men are trapped by evil times that fall unexpectedly upon them.”

“If you listen to the Bible, we’re all doomed.” Tabor laughed and shook his head.

Baby Doe wiped her finger across her mouth. “We would love to repair the chapel roof, wouldn’t we, Horace?”

Tabor opened the secretary and wrote out a bank draft. “That should build a new roof and a new wing besides.”

Father Guido finished his third sherry. “I’ll be in touch to set a date for the christening.”

“That’s wonderful, isn’t it, Horace?” She squeezed his hand. At least Lily would be baptized a child of the Lord.

33

Denver, Colorado, May 1886

A new roof on the Sacred Heart chapel did nothing to change the attitude of Denver society. Neighbor ladies still wouldn't speak to Baby Doe, let alone allow her to join their charities. The first couple years, when Lily was a baby, she had little time for anything else. But now, Lily was walking and playing on her own.

When Tabor traveled to the mines, time came to a standstill cooped up in their mansion, which she called the mausoleum. She wasn't joking. So cavernous and rambling, she and Lily stayed in her sunny parlor all day, having tea parties and playing dolls.

Still, she longed for her own cause, praying her rosary dozens of times before it came to her. She'd open her parlor to hear requests from Friar Guido's flock.

The word spread through the congregation. Folks lined up at her door every Wednesday: teachers, miners, mothers with babies in tow...anyone who needed a helping hand. Neighbor ladies gathered across the street watching her mansion, arms folded and tongues clucking. Mad Hens.

Baby Doe heard people's requests in her parlor of tapestry, bird's eye maple furniture, and leaded-glass windows, while Lily played blocks on the Persian carpet.

Times were tougher since bankers were pushing for the gold standard, and silver prices continued to sink. Hearing people's stories brought up rough memories of her own hard times, and the people who helped her: Chin Lin Sou, Mr. Doe, even Billy Bush. At least she could be kind to others.

White-capped Jillian brought in the next man to her parlor, hat in hand and wearing an oil-cloth slicker, shifting weight from one foot to the other. “Jed Smith, ma’am, fire chief of Hook and Ladder number three. I’m here because of the fire on the east side.”

“*The Denver Tribune* said it was brutal.”

He crushed his hat into a ball. “Lost seven men.” His head dropped down, watching Lily play. “Their children and wives are pretty bad off.”

She took a halting breath. The Oshkosh fires had started her journey west. “Nothing can bring back their husbands and fathers, but maybe we can help them get back on their feet.” She wrote out a bank draft and handed it to him. “Bless you for keeping Denver safe.”

“Thank you, Mrs. Tabor. Thank you.” He backed out of the room, just as Tabor walked in.

“Papa.” Lily’s chubby legs wobbled toward him, and he picked her up.

“Mr. Tabor.” The fireman shook his hand. “Jed, from Hook and Ladder.”

“Did she give you enough, Jed?”

“No need to raise the ante, Horace,” Baby Doe said. “This isn’t a poker game.”

“Say hello to the boys at the station, won’t you?” He tickled Lily and she giggled.

“Sure will. And thank you again.” He bobbed his head and left.

Tabor kissed her, his lips tasting of black licorice. “So, while I’m out making money, you’re home, giving it away.”

She smiled, knowing he approved. “How’s Lou Leonard?”

“You know Lou. Pessimist by nature. He thinks all the mines are tapped out.”

Doubt nagged her. “Maybe this isn’t the time for charity work?”

“Balderdash.” He sat down with Lily. “If I listened to Lou,

we'd never buy another mine. Mining's a gamble. Remember, it only takes one mine like the Matchless to make all the other holes worthwhile." He spun a silver dollar for Lily on the coffee table.

She slapped the spinning coin.

"You landed on Lady Luck," Tabor said.

The toddler clapped. "Luck-y. Luck-y."

Baby Doe picked up his silver dollar. A sharp twinge under her ribs made her buckle. Lady Luck had nearly rubbed off.

A couple months later, Jillian delivered mail to Tabor. One of the envelopes smelled of lilacs. The return address said Montauk, New York. He didn't know anyone in Montauk.

"Dear Horace,

Please read this before you throw it away. But why should you? I threw you away like yesterday's newspaper and it's the only regret of my life.

I passed by a newsstand yesterday and saw your baby girl on the cover of Harper's magazine. You had those same soulful eyes, wiser than your brother's—so much wiser. You have no reason to forgive me for abandoning you, but I want you to know, I believed it was best at the time. God, I'm lying even as I try to come clean. I wanted a new life. A glamorous life. I wanted nothing to do with being a quarryman's wife. Why did I take your brother instead of you? He was a baby and you were already so smart and tenacious. I knew you'd grow up fine.

In truth, I've not looked back often. I've enjoyed my freedom and made a name for myself, if only in literary circles. But I have followed your life in the headlines. You were destined for greatness despite me.

Now to the point. I'm dying. Some kind of stomach tumor, doctors say. I beg of you to have mercy on me and let me see my granddaughter. If you consent, I'll be on the next train.

Your mother,

Sylvia Austin Warner Tabor"

He loosened his collar, sweat pouring down his back. Searching for feelings for his mother, he found none. All he felt was the bruised and battered heart of his pa when she lied and cheated and left with his younger brother. Had Pa known she'd left for another woman? Of course he did. She ripped his heart out.

Tabor lit a fire, though the shutters and curtains were closed against the summer heat.

34

Denver, Colorado
1888

Ever since Tabor was asked to speak at the European Mining Conference in Paris, they'd been planning their trip. Baby Doe read to Lily about the sights they'd see.

But, a week before the trip, something went wrong. Sluggish and feverish, nothing felt right in her body. She called Doctor Lemming. When he told her she was pregnant again, she was overjoyed. But then he said, if she wanted to keep this child, she'd have to stay in bed until the birth.

When she told her family, Tabor reached for her hand. "We'll stay home with you."

"You have to go." She shook her head. "The conference is crucial to gaining new silver investors. And Lily has been looking forward to France, haven't you darling?"

Her daughter slathered lemon curd on a biscuit. "Can we visit the Eiffel Tower, Momma?"

"Papa will take you to the very top." It would be good for Lily to have a sibling, so she wouldn't be alone. No one had attended her last birthday party, even though they'd brought in Shetland ponies to ride.

"The doctor needs Momma to stay here," Tabor told Lily.

Her daughter's forehead crumpled. "Is the baby why you can't come to Paris?"

Tabor's chair screeched against the marble floor. "I can't leave you here alone."

"Who'll take care of Momma?" Lily wailed.

"I'll have Peter move in to keep you company," he said.

"As if Peter will be of any help. I have Jillian and Samson, and the rest of the staff."

Lily laid her small hand in hers. "Why do you need another baby when you have me?"

She drew her daughter close. "I wouldn't trade you for all the silver and gold in the world. You need to take care of Papa over in Paris, and when you come back, you can tell me all about it."

Such a long time to be apart from them.

As she predicted, Peter was no help. He used the Tabor mansion to entertain his friends downstairs while she was banished to her third-floor bedroom, bored out of her mind.

Week after week, she couldn't sleep, waking up sweating, lower back aching, belly growling. She longed for Tabor's arms around her, little Lily's sweet face.

One of those endless nights, Peter's horrific scream woke her. "Stop. You're killing me."

She stumbled from bed, woozy and disoriented. Her body had swelled beyond recognition. She felt for the Winchester rifle under her bed and grasped it under her arm.

"I'm coming. I'm coming, Peter. Hang on."

A deafening shriek pierced the air. She waddled out, bare feet slipping on the floorboards.

Voices and hysterical laughing drifted from below. Her skin flushed hot and sweat sprung from her pores. Stumbling, she hit the wall with her shoulder and reeled to the railing. Grasping for balance with one hand, the Winchester in the other, she forced herself to the landing.

Another shriek echoed, followed by a maniacal laugh. The Tabor ballroom was littered with men, shirt sleeves rolled up, ties loosened. Cigar smoke choked the air. Women in garish gowns danced with each other. The sideboard groaned with Tabor's fine liquors and champagne.

"You in or out?" Her brother played faro at one of the tables, shirt open at the neck, a young man rubbed his naked chest.

"Peter!" She banged the butt of the rifle on the floor to get his attention. "Peter, what's going on? Who are these people?"

"Everything's fine. Go back to bed, Lizzie." He drank straight from a champagne bottle.

His insolence made her head throb. "So you can steal us blind?"

"Pay her no mind." He shrugged. "She's off her duff with the baby due soon."

She pushed the rifle through the banister. "You and your friends need to clear out."

People scattered out of range.

"You have no right to speak to friends that way," he yelled.

"They're not *my* friends, are they? And they're not Horace's. So, what are they doing in our house, drinking our liquor and eating our food?"

Peter ran to the staircase. "You're not yourself, Lizzie."

She aimed the rifle at the ceiling and pulled the trigger. The recoil threw her against the wall.

Seventy pounds of chandelier dropped through the air, crashing to the marble floor, smashing the crystal prisms.

Gas rippled through the carpet, exploding with fury as it reached the lamps. People running, screaming…the smell of singed wool and terror…

Her belly cramped, back and legs smarted as Peter reached her with a dozen men behind him, leering at her organdy nightgown.

"Get out of here. Out of here, all of you," she shouted. The baby kicked, and she buckled.

Peter grabbed for the rifle, but she jerked it back and aimed at the gaping crowd. "You and your fancy friends clear out."

Jillian shooed revelers toward the front door. Chilly air blew on Baby Doe's feverish skin.

"And don't come back." She waved the gun at them.

Peter closed the door, throwing daggers with his eyes.

When she tried to get up, she collapsed on the landing, her legs too weak. Waves of pain convulsed through her. "Lillian, call Doctor Lemming." She wouldn't lose this baby.

Jillian and Samson carried her to bed, and Doctor Lemming gave her something to sleep.

35

Denver, Colorado, 1890

Baby Doe prayed for guidance and formed a plan to turn her brother away from sin. First, she'd take him to confession with Friar Guido. "When Peter comes back, have him come see me," she told Jillian. "And alert the staff. He's not to have parties here."

Miss Jillian's feather duster paused atop the piano keys. "You won't have to worry about that, Missus. He moved out."

Her arms prickled. "Left me here alone?"

"Good riddance, if you don't mind me saying," Jillian said. "The downstairs staff barely got his party cleaned up."

A ghastly scream punctured her eardrums, and the whole garish party scene replayed in her mind. But through the window, she saw Samson prying open a large crate. Dozens of peacocks strutted out on the lawn as Lily ran through them.

With Jillian's help, she lumbered down the stairs, velvet peignoir trailing behind her.

Lily romped and giggled among the peacocks, her face lit with joy. Her curls bounced on her shoulders, burnished by the late afternoon sun. Every time a peacock shrieked, she put her hands over her ears and laughed. When the birds jumped into the garden fountain for a long drink, Lily pulled off shoes and socks to join them.

Tears flowed down Baby Doe's cheeks.

Tabor embraced her from behind, kissing her temple. "Do you like them?"

"Peacocks. You brought me peacocks." Leaning into his chest, the sight and sounds overwhelmed her. "There must be a hundred."

"They seemed to have multiplied since France." Tabor scratched his head, grinning under his sweeping mustache, amber eyes never leaving her face.

Lily ran toward them, so much taller than when she left.

"Lily." She held out her arms, aching to hold her. "I missed you so much."

"Come see. Come see." Lily led her toward Sherman Street.

Three life-sized statues stood in naked glory, white marble sparkling in the sunlight.

"Dionysus, Hera, and Aphrodite." Lily introduced them like she'd practiced a million times.

Tabor joined her. "Peter met us at the train station," he said.

"That bastard deserted me," she said.

He chucked her chin. "Peter left you with a houseful of servants and Doctor Lemming."

"Uncle Peter said the baby made you crazy." Lily spread her hands on her belly. "I hate the baby." She ran to the house.

"Come back here," Tabor called.

"Let her go, Horace." Baby Doe placed her hands on her stomach where Lily's had been. "She hasn't had it easy, has she? She'll be all right after the baby is born."

Rose Mary Echo Silver Dollar Tabor was born December 17, 1889. Refusing to let Tabor mint commemorative coins, Baby Doe sent understated announcements to a small circle of business and political acquaintances. She tried not to notice which families ignored them and what parties they weren't invited to, though it hurt to think she brought this fate upon her children. She focused on making a warm and loving home, albeit spectacular.

She redesigned the nursery, involving Lily every step of the way, wanting her to love Silver Dollar. How couldn't she, with those enormous brown eyes and all that dark hair?

The result was worth the extravagance. A rose-painted tea service sat on a mosaic tea table, next to an English rocking horse. Porcelain dolls, dressed in eyelet dresses and large flowered hats occupied tiny chairs, ready for a tea party.

Silver Dollar's crib was cast of pure silver, piled with down pillows and angora blankets. Baby Doe scooped Lily up and leaned over the side. "Isn't your sister just the most precious doll?"

Lily squeezed the baby's arm until she cried.

"Careful. Babies are delicate," Baby Doe said, calmly. "Miss Sally, can you give Silver Dollar her bath?"

Miss Sally handed her an envelope. "Just delivered, Missus." She scooped up the squalling baby and took her out.

Baby Doe took Lily to the window seat. "Let's read this together, shall we?" She traced the words, so Lily could recognize them. She was as smart as she was stubborn.

"Dear Mrs. Tabor,

Capitol Hill has established itself as the arbiter of taste in Denver neighborhoods. With due respect we approach the matter of your statues. Their lack of clothing is not in keeping with our atmosphere of propriety. We respectfully ask you to remove the indecent statues for the reputation of the neighborhood.

In addition, the noise and filth of the peacocks is unconscionable. We expect you to remove them as well.

The Capitol Hill Neighborhood Committee"

"But I love the statues," Lily whined. "Papa brought those statues all the way from France."

A bolt of obstinance prodded her. No matter how she tried to fit in, society would never accept them, so why try?

"You're right, Lily," she said. "How would you like to play dress up?"

Tabor heard his daughter's giggle and the sound pulled his heavy heart out of the quagmire. Mining had become tedious as silver lost more value on Wall Street.

Following a flutter in the garden, he saw Lily tying a sash around Dionysus's tulle gown. Baby Doe crowned Hera's head with a flower wreath that matched her apricot satin gown. Only Aphrodite remained naked, a pile of chiffon fabric at her feet.

Lily skipped to him. "The neighbors don't like naked statues, so we dressed them up."

Seeing them together like this, having fun, lifted his spirits. "I'd love to stay and help you, but I have to meet with my lawyer."

"I want to be a lawyer when I grow up," Lily said. "Then I won't have to be a gold digger like Momma."

Tabor caught her shoulder. "Why would you say such a nasty thing?"

"The kids at school say it." She pointed at Baby Doe. "Gold digger. Gold digger."

"Apologize to your mother."

She jutted out her chin.

"Lily, darling, don't listen to their insults." Baby Doe tried to hug her. "They're just jealous."

Lily tugged on his sleeve. "Take me with you, Papa. Please, please, please?"

Baby Doe sighed. "Go ahead and take her, she's been cooped up all day."

"Not until you apologize." He held Lily's shoulders.

"Sorry, Momma," she said, then tugged his arm.

"I'll see you two at dinner." Baby Doe draped fabric around Aphrodite's waist. Her nonchalance didn't fool him.

As Rockwell and Peter presented the pending lawsuits, each one weighed on Tabor like a sandbag. If a mine produced well, neighboring mines sued him for infringing on their territory. If a mine didn't produce, stockholders sued him for fraud. No matter what, Rockwell got paid.

"Uncle Peter, can you help me build a house of cards?" Lily asked.

He joined her, and Tabor smiled, grateful for his brother-in-law. After all, he'd managed the businesses and endured Baby Doe's pregnancy. He'd be valuable in his new Honduras venture.

As the lawyer droned on, Tabor grew more interested in the conversation on the floor.

"Are we going to lose all our money, Uncle Peter?" Lily balanced cards on their edges.

"Don't worry," he said, building a second story. "Your papa has more businesses than you can count, and his silver mines support them all."

"Like your theater circuit?" Lily formed a peaked roof.

"I wouldn't have the circuit without your father."

"You have the concentration of a grasshopper, Tabor." Rockwell slammed his briefcase closed. "You had no business donating a city block for the new post office, with your empire crumbling. And your solution is digging mines in Honduras? You're a bigger idiot than I thought." The lawyer huffed out.

What did Rockwell know about divining riches from the earth?

Peter joined him at the table. "I'm with Rockwell. Honduras sounds too risky."

"It doesn't pay to mine silver now, but Honduras has gold," Tabor said. "Besides mining, we'll control the entire logging industry."

"But Honduras is a jungle," Peter argued. "We'll have to bring in our own transportation, buildings, supplies and labor."

"Leave that to me. Your job is to find two million, at least." Peter could be lazy.

Lily added another story to her house, higher and more intricate.

"We'll have to mortgage the Tabor Grand for that much money," Peter said.

That stopped him. "I wouldn't go that far."

"Trust me," Peter said. "I've been over the numbers a million times. That, and the Matchless are the only two pieces of collateral left."

"Matchless silver is almost worthless," Tabor thought aloud. "No choice, then, mortgage the Tabor Grand." Nervous, his foot kicked Lily's house of cards, and it tumbled to the floor.

"You've ruined everything," Lily cried.

"I hope not," he told her, picking up the cards. Honduras would save them.

The spotlight tracked the Tabors as they made their way to their private box one last time before he left for Honduras. Silver Dollar was dressed like her mother in gold damask. Peter held Lily's arm high and regal like the princess she pretended to be. Opera glasses glinted in the footlights, following them. Denver society exchanged gossip behind their programs.

When they got to their box, Baby Doe turned and kissed him long and fully. A ripple of gasps spread through the crowd like the rumble of thunder. Got to love a woman like that.

The house lights dimmed. Their steward popped the cork and poured them champagne, the last bottle of Veuve Clicquot they'd afford for a while. A man in the audience peered up with theater glasses, sketching on a pad of paper. Tomorrow Baby Doe's gown would be copied by seamstresses all over town, despite society shunning her. Their rejection still hurt her, but he tried to make it up to her by entertaining actors from the Tabor Grand: Sarah Bernhardt, Maurice Barrymore, Lillian Russell, Oscar Wilde...and, he made sure society heard about it.

"Miss Lily, you look lovely." He squeezed her hand. "And, Silver, you look scrumptious."

She pointed to her family. "Crumpshus. Crumpshus. Crumpshus."

The auditorium lights went down. His cue to leave for the stage.

"Be sure to laugh at my jokes," he said.

"We will, Papa," his girls said.

The new governor addressed the audience. "We're here tonight to thank Senator Horace Tabor, who donated an entire city block for the new Denver Post Office, the largest facility in the West." The audience applauded.

Tabor took the microphone, looking out to the full house. "When I was postmaster, about a hundred years ago—" They laughed. "Seriously, when we opened the post office in Leadville, we served one hundred people and that was tough. But the Denver Post Office will serve *one-hundred-thousand*, so, I am overjoyed to announce that I will *not* be the postmaster."

The entire audience stood and applauded. His daughters pressed against the railing, smiling down at him. Baby Doe blew him a kiss, radiant as when he first saw her. God, how he loved that woman.

Honduras better pay off.

36

Denver, Colorado, 1892

Why hadn't Tabor answered her letters? Even her telegrams received no answer.

She'd spent weeks with Rockwell, dealing with lawsuits against their companies. And Peter. How could he leave her with piles of unpaid bills and past-due mortgages?

Lily chased Silver into the room, knocking a porcelain ballerina off the table and smashing it to bits. They'd been on each other's nerves since a snowstorm closed their Catholic school early for Christmas break. Time for a lesson in goodwill.

"Girls, ask Jillian to get you dressed, and I'll take you out," she said, determined to show them true Christmas spirit.

She helped Samson load boxes in the back of the Morgan. The girls ambled in beside her on the bench, dressed in velvet dresses and Persian lamb coats. She should have told Jillian to tone it down, but too late now. Samson snapped the reigns, and the horses pranced to East Denver, buffeted by brisk wind. A gloomy sky pelted snow on a shabby schoolhouse.

"That school looks haunted." Silver's breath hung in the air.

"I thought we were going to have fun," Lily whined.

The bell rang, and children poured from the doors.

Baby Doe got out into the snow and the girls followed. "Can you laugh like Santa Claus?"

They bounced up and down on their toes. "Ho, Ho, Ho. Ho, Ho, Ho."

A crowd of children gathered, mimicking Santa's laugh. A girl rubbed her bare hands together, sticking out from frayed coat sleeves.

"Would you like a present?" Baby Doe asked.

"Get away from my daughter." A woman trudged toward her, hands red and chapped.

"We meant no harm. We have Christmas gifts." She held out a basket of cheese, bread, canned ham, and dried fruit. "For you, mother."

Anger drained from the woman's face. "Bless you, Missus. Bless you."

"Ho, Ho, Ho. Merry Christmas," Lily said. "We have presents for good boys and girls. Are there any here?" Her wit was so like her father's.

"Trucks for boys, dolls for girls," Silver chimed.

Seeing her daughter's generosity should have made her happy, but a vile taste crept up her tongue. Tabor should be here with them. What if something had happened to him down there? Why did he always choose adventure over his family?

That night, while Jillian bathed the girls, Baby Doe slumped at the Chippendale secretary, shuffling through the mounting bills, searching for things to sell to keep them afloat.

Late January, Tabor finally came home. Unnatural yellow mottled his skin like old bruises, and his hair had grayed in the months he'd been gone.

"I was so worried when I didn't hear from you." She pressed her cheek to his chest.

"The government shut down the telegraph office."

"You must be tired." She held his waist and climbed the stairs. His hipbones protruded.

"It was a sinkhole for a million dollars, Baby."

Her knees buckled but she forced herself to stand straight. "Rest here, Horace. I'll be right back." She poured him a snifter of brandy and asked Jillian to draw him a bath.

Tabor huddled on the sofa, spent and ancient, drinking the brandy while she held his hand.

"Welcome home, sir." Miss Jillian curtsied, her face dewy with steam. "Your bath is ready." Baby Doe unbuttoned his shirt and recoiled from the angry pustules on his back. "What happened to you?" She helped him into the warm bath.

"Mosquitoes, millipedes, grasshawks, mantids. The varmints love American blood."

Still had his humor, thank God. Lathering a sponge, she gently washed his sores.

"One hundred and fifteen degrees, suffocating humidity." He wheezed. "Jungle so dense it could only be cut with machetes. It all grew back in a month, dense as ever."

She kneaded his shoulders, remembering the shoulders of another discouraged man. "Horace, they're going to foreclose on the Tabor Grand unless we pay off the lien."

"Sell off all the businesses, just keep the Tabor Grand." Kissing her hand, he looked at her with rheumy eyes. "I have to go to Washington to fight for silver. President Cleveland's campaigning for the gold standard. If silver goes down, we go down, and the country with us."

She laid her head on his chest, listening to his heart. The same heart that worked so hard for all of them. Selling the Queen Isabella necklace would hold the bank off for a while.

Tabor's speech before the senate would make or break the future of silver in this country. Nothing had changed, not the pomp of flags nor the impressive senate seal, marble columns, leather chairs, and handsome wood desks. A sea of faces fighting for power.

"The United States is the greatest producer of silver in the world." He rubbed his lucky silver dollar in his pocket. "And our economy thrives when we have unlimited silver coinage."

Democrats cheered, but eastern Republicans sat in staunch defiance.

"The mining industry produces this country's wealth; it is our undeniable right to mint silver into dollars." His notes blurred in front of him, and he spoke from the heart.

"Why do eastern banks advocate the gold standard? In a word… greed. If you wipe silver out, gold will double." Sweat ran into his eyes. "But that's not all that will double. Factory and farm debt will double, and they'll have to repay their debt in gold when they only have silver."

He wiped his forehead with his handkerchief. "I believe in the American dream that rewards hard work, not banker's get-rich-quick schemes." Senators nodded. "To adopt the gold standard is a conspiracy by rich bankers to keep the working class under their thumbs."

Western Republicans joined Democrats' applause.

Best damn job he could do. Walking up the aisle, he leaned down to Thomas Bowen. "Heads says we convinced them, Tombo." He flipped his lucky silver dollar in the air, spinning slowly in the dim light, slapping it on the back of his hand.

Bowen frowned. "It's blank."

Tabor stared at the dollar on his hand. Lady Luck had completely disappeared, rubbed out from years of betting on her.

President Cleveland stepped to the podium, his rotund figure commanding the stage. "Whether you're Democrat or Republican doesn't matter today. We're facing the worst depression in our history. Five railroad lines have gone bankrupt. Hundreds of banks have closed their doors. Thousands of companies failed, causing seventeen percent unemployment."

The gallery fell silent.

"The U.S. Treasury has been forced to borrow sixty-five million in gold bullion from Wall Street banker J.P. Morgan to keep from bankruptcy." Cleveland stared them down. "I implore you to save this country. We must repeal the Silver Purchase Act and support the gold standard."

A thundering applause deafened Tabor. His stomach churned, and he popped a licorice, not likely to save him from the pain to come. He left the gallery and caught the next train home.

If poker taught him anything, it was when to fold.

37

Denver, Colorado,
1893

Since Baby Doe arrived at Union Station the temperature had dropped twenty degrees. She'd worn her best outfit to cheer up Tabor, but now felt frivolous and foolish as the wind whipped through her tiered skirt and blew off her wide-brim hat blossoming with flowers.

"President Cleveland repeals Silver Purchase Act," the newsboy cried, his voice carried away in gusts of wind.

The train arrived, and Tabor stepped off, his face etched with defeat.

"Horace." She pressed her body to his and kissed his lips, sweet with licorice.

He held her tight against the whirling leaves, the sky blackening.

"Why wouldn't they listen to reason?" she asked.

"The president believes the gold standard is the only way to stop the depression."

"Has he lost his mind? As soon as silver fell to half value, the stock market collapsed." A wild gust blew her skirt high, and she yanked it around her. "What are we going to do?"

A giant anvil cloud rose vertically in the sky with a blue-green shelf looming underneath.

"Where's the carriage?" He raised his voice above the buffeting wind.

A torrent of muddy water rushed over their feet, rainbow trout flopping in the currents. Startled, she wished she hadn't worn her pearl-button boots.

"The Platte River's flooding," he yelled, taking her arm. "We have to run for it."

An ear-splitting crack preceded a huge cottonwood tree falling right in front of them exposing bare roots. Tabor swooped her up in his arms just as hailstones hammered their heads, rooftops, carriages, and every surface bold enough to face the furious sky.

"Repent, heathens, while there is time." A priest stretched out his arms to the maroon sky. "The Lord is strong as a tempest of hail, a flood of mighty waters overflowing." He shook his fist while hail battered his face.

Tabor lifted her into their white and gold carriage and slammed the door behind them. Samson jerked the reigns. The horses swayed and whinnied. Out the window, long streamers of hail fell through murky clouds, ripping leaves off the trees.

As quickly as it appeared, the anvil cloud moved off. A brilliant light streamed on Denver's buildings like a spotlight.

"How's that for a homecoming?" She laughed nervously.

"I can't come home yet, Baby." He shook his head. "We need gold and we need it now. I'm going to reopen the Cripple Creek mine."

"That mine went bust long ago." Reaching in her pocket, she grasped her rosary beads, warding off the fear creeping into her body. "We need you at home, Horace."

"I wouldn't leave unless I had to, Baby. I have to try." He took her hands, eyes pleading. "Can you be strong a little longer?"

She wanted to tell him how the girls needed him, how she missed him, how lonely and afraid she was. But his eyes pleaded for a second chance, like the men he'd pardoned. The world he'd created was crumbling around him and he needed to shore it up. He'd be a broken man if he didn't.

"We'll be fine, Horace. Just come home as soon as you can."

"That's my girl." He kissed her. "Now, I need you to sell the silver mines as quickly as possible. They'll be worthless by the end of the month."

"*All* the silver mines? There must be a hundred." The enormity of the task daunted her.

"Except the Matchless Mine." Tabor chuckled. "Keep the Matchless for pin money."

Baby Doe gathered up all their deeds, notes, and certificates to meet with Tabor's partners at the First National Bank. Glancing in the lobby mirror, she prayed they wouldn't see the desperation in her eyes. She took a whiff of smelling salts to clear her head.

Turnbull and Senator Chaffee sat at the far end of the conference table like aging fat cats, all sagging jowls and wayward whiskers.

Turnbull blew cigar smoke her way. "Is Tabor with you?"

She sat across from them, spreading her skirts and taking her time, as if the sky wasn't falling. "I've taken over as our business manager."

Chaffee raised his eyebrows. "You'll need to go full chisel on that."

"I beg your pardon?"

"Look Mrs. Tabor, we go back fourteen years with your husband. Tabor's a great man, but he's a disaster with money."

"Explain, gentlemen," she said evenly.

"He's over-leveraged, borrowed on everything he owned to buy more silver mines."

She fanned the deeds in front of them. "I'm willing to sell all these properties at seventy-five percent of market value if you pay cash." She tilted her head and smiled. Turnbull picked up a deed. He picked up another and another, passing them to Chaffee.

She had them drooling over the profits already. But their silence dragged.

"There are other banks." She reached for the deeds.

"No, there aren't." Turnbull slammed his hands down on them. "The First National Bank foreclosed on these properties since payments were not made. We've been waiting for Tabor to surface to give him notice."

She struggled to understand. "But *you're* the bank. You can reverse the foreclosures and help us sell the properties to pay the loans."

"Too far gone." Turnbull gathered up the deeds. "Thank you for these, though. It will save you an embarrassing visit from the sheriff."

"Tabor's a good man," Chaffee said. "And the luckiest S.O.B. that walks the planet. This is just a hiccup for him."

"A hiccup." She wanted to snatch the deeds and run. "What about the Matchless?"

"It's yours, free and clear," Chaffee told her. "It's the only mine Tabor didn't mortgage."

"By rights, the Matchless should be confiscated to pay our expenses," Turnbull argued.

Her gut buckled.

"Turnbull, a silver mine is as worthless as your rotten soul on judgment day," Chaffee threatened. "Leave the Tabors alone."

"For pity sake." Turnbull bit his cigar. "Let us know if we can do anything else for you."

She stood, anxious to leave these thieves. "I certainly will… unless I have the hiccups."

"Dear Baby Doe,
I need you to wire me ten thousand dollars from the sale of the mines to keep Cripple Creek operations going. No shopping excursions at May's. Ha, ha. When we strike it, I'll take you and the girls to Chicago, and we'll have Marshall Field set you up with the latest finery..."

Blood pulsed behind her eyes. Tabor didn't know the mines had been foreclosed.

She wrestled with the widening fissure between stark reality and his optimism, growing harder to reconcile. But she couldn't allow herself to be swallowed by the futility of it all.

There was more than one way to win a poker game.

She dressed in a frock of apricot and cream with a décolleté cutout. Applying rouge to her cheeks and lips, she brushed her long lashes with black ash, then studied her image in the Tiffany mirror purchased on her honeymoon, ten years ago. Her curls still gleamed gold, but she didn't like the puffiness under her eyes. Tilting her head, she grinned coquettishly. Come now, she could do better than that. She threw back her head and laughed, ending with her best disarming smile. Rusty, but it would have to do.

She marched into the Windsor, down the hallway to Bush's office. The plush Brussels carpet and gilded moldings did nothing to soothe her nerves. Bush was flipping through the ledger on his desk, leaning on his diamond rattler cane. She cleared her throat, delicately.

His eyes went liquid. Then he came around and sat on his desk, ever the cavalier.

"Billy." His smarmy grin repulsed her, but she focused on her goal. "Reviewing the deeds, I see we still own part of the Windsor." She dangled the carrot.

"Oh, yes." His voice crimped with disdain. "Tabor made it clear he'd never sell the whole thing to me and Maxcy."

"I've decided to sell. You and Maxcy can own the Windsor outright."

"That's why you came? To sell us the Windsor?" He fingered the rattler's head on his cane. "Would you care for a sherry, or perhaps champagne?"

Not as hard as she thought. "Champagne is in order, isn't it?"

Bush ordered it on the house phone.

It had been so long since she'd tasted champagne, her tongue ached.

"Shall we move over to the sofa, where we can be more comfortable?"

"Why not?" She'd flatter his ego.

Bush fell into the leather chesterfield with his stiff leg, patting the seat next to him.

Smiling sweetly, she sat in the chair.

A waiter arrived and poured champagne. "Anything else, sir?"

"Close the door on the way out."

Alarm bells sounded in her head, and she took a long sip.

"Not so fast," he said. "Let me make a toast. To the Windsor… and its new owners." He drank the entire glass and poured another.

"Not exactly new owners. You and Maxcy owned part of the Windsor from the beginning."

"You don't know the new owners." He sipped champagne. "A company back east bought the Windsor. Your shares had liens on them, so the bank sold them."

Her mouth went dry. "Maxcy wouldn't do that without consulting his father."

He cocked his head. "Funny, Maxcy never mentions his father."

She leaned forward. "We need that money to keep afloat until the gold mine starts paying."

"Too late, Baby." He poured more champagne in her glass.

She watched the bubbles burst. No witty comeback. No crafty move. No more cards to play.

Baby Doe wrote letters to their mine foremen, harsher than a school marm's punishment.

We regret your mine will be closed until further notice.

We regret your mine will be closed until further notice.

We regret your mine will be closed until further notice.

She imagined the foremen's eyes when they opened the letters. Bitter or brave, it didn't matter. There'd be no work anywhere after the silver crash.

"I sold the last of the peacocks." Samson handed her the money.

"The girls are still wringing their eyes out to see them go."

"Remember the day you unloaded them?" She sighed. "Lily in her red coat dancing around with her hands on her ears?" It seemed like a golden dream that disappeared upon awakening.

"I don't feel right leaving before Mr. Tabor gets home." Samson's brown cheeks hung in sad folds. "He'll never forgive me."

"The girls and I will be fine. It's better this way. Mr. Tabor would be saddest to see you go."

"Oh, no, Missus Tabor. He'll be saddest that you sold his carriages and horses."

Samson was right. Tabor had spent most Sundays at the riding park, showing off his latest carriage and liveries. The Landau, the white and gold, the crimson enameled...she'd sold them all. They are just *things*, she reminded herself, her temples throbbing.

"I promised Mrs. Lawrence you'd be to her house by seven." She shooed him.

Lily came and threw herself at him. "Papa would never let her do this if he was here."

"Samson has to leave, Lily." She took her daughter into her arms as he slipped out.

38

Cripple Creek, Colorado, 1894

Surface ore samples showed promise, but after three months, Tabor still hadn't located a major vein. The second lien on the Tabor Grand had been spent. He couldn't face telling Baby Doe he needed more. She'd gone from bestowing money to charities to fending off lawyers in court.

He entered a saloon in Cripple Creek, noticing a poker game at the far table.

"Senator Tabor is that you?" The man left the table and shook his hand, gold rings gleaming. "Remember me from Leadville days? Winfield Stratton."

"Stratton, you dog." Tabor smiled. "Finally struck gold, didn't you? Independence Mine?"

"Thanks to you," Stratton said. "You grubstaked me twenty years ago when I couldn't afford beans. I remember you said; 'cut me in when you strike it rich.' Just like that." He shook his head. "Those were the days, weren't they?"

Tabor sighed, aching for that bygone feeling that something was about to happen, his whole life ahead of him.

"Whiskey for me and my friend," Stratton told the bartender and sat next to him.

"Much obliged." He nodded.

"Heard you were working Cripple Creek again. How's it going?"

"The gold is there, alright." He had no energy to bluff. "But my money's run out."

Stratton studied him with blood-shot eyes. "How much you need?"

Where was he going with this? "Fifteen thousand should get us there."

Stratton raised his glass to Tabor's. "Cut me in when you strike it rich."

Adrenaline pumped through his veins. Tabor Luck was back.

Baby Doe couldn't believe how Rockwell's law offices had grown, employing a dozen lawyers and twice as many secretaries and assistants, paid for with Tabor's hefty retainers.

"Colorado Mutual is calling in the second lien on the Tabor Grand," Rockwell said to Peter, as if she wasn't in the room.

"Hold them off." She fluttered her fan to hide her shame. "We should have enough money to make a payment by the end of the month."

Peter glared. "Horace took out a *second* lien on the Tabor Grand?"

"The new owner's taking over the theater as we speak. These are the foreclosure papers." Rockwell handed her an envelope and cleared his throat. "I resign. I've been working for the past year without payment. Consider the twenty-seven thousand you owe me as a parting gift."

Her brain scrambled. "You have to see us through this. You owe Tabor that much."

"There's nothing more I can do." His chin waddled pompously.

Peter stormed out, and she ran after him.

"If you'll just make this payment to Colorado Mutual, they'll stop the proceedings." Peter kept walking, and she grabbed his arm. "Don't you hear me?"

He pulled away. "My money would be an umbrella in a tornado, Lizzie, sucked into Tabor's vortex like everything else." Walking into the Tabor Grand, he let the doors close in her face.

She jerked open the handle and yelled, "You're dead to me, Peter McCourt."

Her brother turned back. "I'd die a thousand deaths for you if that would help, Lizzie. It's over. Face it." He walked into his office.

Feeling faint, she grabbed the lobby wall. The taffeta wallcovering slipped past her fingers like it had never belonged to her. Her knees fell on the Oriental carpet, and she stayed there, praying, though, even God couldn't help them now.

An older woman with a cane walked over to help. Baby Doe looked up, and the dowager's pince-nez glasses conjured a memory gone hazy with time. "Augusta?"

"I prefer Mrs. Tabor." Her stingy mouth released the words.

Prayer answered. Augusta could save the Tabor Grand. Her divorce settlement made her a millionaire several times over. "They foreclosed on the theater," Baby Doe said. "It means the world to Horace."

"I didn't buy it for Horace, if that's what you think." Her nostrils flared.

"You bought the Tabor Grand?" A mixture of regret and relief washed over her.

"You stole my husband, but you cannot steal my name. My name is on that door. Mine and Maxcy's. I couldn't let it fall to someone else." She rapped Baby Doe with her cane. "Get up, I can't stand your groveling. You deserve every misery that befalls you. You ripped my family apart and took Horace for all he was worth. Get out of here before I call the manager." Augusta walked triumphantly toward Peter's office.

She dragged herself to see the auditorium one last time, the domed ceiling painted with puffy clouds and cherubs, mohair and crimson plush seats, the stunning gold and white Tabor box. Memories of her daughters' laughter, champagne corks flying, stolen kisses.

The backdrop curtain with its scene of ruin and decay, taunted her with its inscription.

"So fleet the works of men, back to earth again,
Ancient and holy things fade like a dream."

Tabor's old back seized up when he lifted the pick. Waiting for his muscles to release, he read Baby Doe's letter again, hearing her sweet voice in his head, so hopeless and final.

"Dear Horace,

After doing everything I could, I find that I have done nothing.

All I can bequeath my little ones is honor and my fidelity as a mother and wife. I have tried to be as near perfect as we mortals can be. I alone have made me what I am, but all my good work is forgotten.

Yours,

Baby Doe"

What was he still doing here?

With a whinny and the crunch of buggy wheels, Winfield Stratton jumped down from his shiny rig. Taking off his top hat, he scratched wisps of white hair.

"You're out of luck if you came for your money," Tabor said.

Stratton picked up a rock, shining in the sunlight. "This ore looks rich. Has that glimmer."

"That's the problem." Tabor leaned against his pick, back screaming. "As long as it glimmers, I've followed it. Thirty years… that glimmer is always just an arm's length away."

"You can't give up."

A bitter laugh escaped his throat. "I never give up. But my family pays the price." He shoved his pick away. "I appreciate what you did for me, Stratton. Take the mine to repay what I owe you."

"You don't mean that."

"Never meant anything more in my life."

The closer he came to Denver and seeing Baby Doe, the more that prickling sensation coursed through his body, urging him toward her. What a selfish fool he'd been all these years, leaving her to fend for herself. Had he forgotten that she was the treasure he was searching for?

As his buggy reached downtown, a fountain of flames shot into the sky south of the state Capitol, his neighborhood. His heart leapt to his throat, and he forced the old bay to gallop.

Turning onto Sherman Street, flames imprinted his retinas. His house. He jumped down and pushed through throngs of people mesmerized by the fire. A pair of girls, similar ages to his own, hid their faces in their nanny's nightgown.

"Make way." Men heaved wooden tubs, water sloshing over the sides.

An old woman with a long white braid held a candle, casting a deathly glow on her face. "Pride goeth before destruction, and a haughty spirit before a fall."

Flames devoured the shingles of his roof. Sirens wailed from all directions. A team of horses pulled a fire wagon rounded the corner. Firemen in red slickers and hats reeled a hose from the water tank. Neighbors ran with buckets of water from nearby wells.

Tabor's chest tightened as he scanned the crowds for his wife and daughters. Light flickered on petrified faces, none belonging to him.

A horrific crash riveted his attention. The main beam of his house had burned through and the roof caved into the top floor. He ran to the fire chief. "Where's my family?"

The chief pushed him back. "Stand behind the truck. You're in the way."

The fire exploded with a deafening roar. "Baby Doe, Baby Doe." His voice swept away.

"Senator Tabor, it's me, Duffy," a young fireman yelled. "Your wife's not here. I heard she moved down to Cripple Creek."

Tabor ducked past Duffy and jumped onto the flaming portico. His family must be inside.

Duffy ran after him. "It's not safe."

Flames jutted through the siding. Waves of heat seared his face. He cupped his hand to the window and looked in. No furniture, must have sold it off. A rat lumbered across the floor.

"Baby Doe." He banged on the window pane.

Another crash came from above, fire shrieking like coyotes. He reached the padlocked front door. Pulling off his boot, he hacked the lock with his heel. Wouldn't budge. With a ferocious howl, he heaved into the door, the impact cracking his shoulder.

Duffy and another fireman strong-armed him and carried him off the portico, depositing him behind the fire wagon.

"Horace." Baby Doe called from behind a tree, motioning to him. She'd wrapped an old coat around her and tied gunny sacks over her feet. "You're supposed to be in Cripple Creek."

She took him away from the chaos, trudging through the overgrown west garden. Macabre shapes of neglected plants and trees hung like skeletons against the glowering sky.

In the empty carriage house, moonlight shone on the girls' sleeping faces, huddled under a blanket on the floor. He squeezed back tears. Safe. They were safe. Through no help from him.

Baby Doe hugged him. "When do you have to go back to Cripple Creek?"

"Ran out of money." He stroked her blonde hair and gazed at her face, that beautiful face engraved in his mind, much braver in person.

"But now you'll have the insurance money from the house." She smiled mysteriously.

"You burned the house to pay for the mine?" The irony skewered him.

She buried her head in his chest. "Don't be angry. I knew you needed it."

"Only, the mansion isn't insured," he said. "I cashed it in to pay for Cripple Creek."

Her face went pale. "Horace, no."

"Doesn't matter. I gave up the mine, too."

"You can't give up." She beat on his chest. "You can't. You can't. You'll die if you give up."

He grasped her fists. "What I can't give up, is you, Baby. I stood alone in that Godforsaken hole and it came to me…why in the world was I there, when you're here?"

She squeezed her eyes closed. "The world is spinning out of control."

He rubbed her back. "We still have each other."

Pulling a worn deed from her bosom, she handed it to him. "And the Matchless Mine for pin money."

He laughed and kissed her temple, fingering the feathery pages of the deed. "Ah, the Matchless."

39

Denver, Colorado, 1896

"Senator Tabor, sir." Shorty Scout Zeitz saluted him. "It'll be an honor to have your family at the Buckhorn Exchange."

"Thank you, Shorty. I can help out here, until I find work." He took the game tracker's hand in his, shaking it long and hard. He'd hired the Shorty Scout whenever he needed to impress easterners with the western treasure of elk, beaver, and buffaloes. Shorty hadn't changed, fringed buckskin shirt and trousers, bandana around his neck. He'd settled down with Dolly and opened the best damn steak house in the West.

Lily and Silver hid behind their mother, embarrassed to be looking for a place to spend the night after the sheriff evicted them from the carriage house.

"Mrs. Tabor, these can't be your daughters," Shorty Scout said. "You don't look old enough to be their mother."

The glimmer of pleasure on his wife's lovely face only depressed Tabor. Once he'd regaled her with silly jokes and extravagant presents, but now she'd lost everything due to his foolhardiness. He had to find a way to make it up to her.

The girls gazed at the knotty pine walls, mounted with Shorty's conquests: rabbits, elk, moose, coyotes, beavers.

"Mr. Zeits is a famous game tracker, girls," Tabor said. "Look at that buffalo."

"I've been called many things." A buxom woman presented a fishnet-glove. "But buffalo isn't one of them." Rhinestone hair combs held back bleached curls. Vivid colors painted her face, black eyebrows drawn above her own, and a red smile boasted a gold tooth.

"Dolly," he rasped, choked up to see his friend. "I see you and Shorty finally got together."

"Can I buy you a drink, Senator?" Shorty handed him a whiskey.

"Such a tragedy your house burned down," Dolly said. "Where are you living?"

Shorty jumped in. "They're bunking upstairs for now."

"Yippee." Silver bounced on her chair.

Dolly eyed Baby Doe. "Say, ever tended bar? A looker like you would bring in big tips."

"I could learn."

"She's got our daughters to raise," Tabor said, not about to see her as a barmaid.

A hefty man in a suit leaned in the front door. "I was told I'd find you here, Tabor."

"What do you want, Turnbull?" The turncoat banker was the last person he wanted to see.

"This came for you." He waved an envelope. "From a law firm in the Hamptons."

Tabor snatched it away, old anger surfacing. The only one he knew in the Hamptons was his mother, a fact he hadn't shared with anyone after Augusta told him, not even Baby Doe.

"If that's money, Tabor, it must go to satisfy your debt," Turnbull said.

"You'll have to leave now." Dolly pushed the banker out the door.

"You owe millions to the First National Bank. Don't forget that." He wagged his finger.

Tabor ducked into a storeroom smelling of salt and borax and opened the envelope.

Last Will and Testament of Sylvia Austin Warner Tabor

She died. Years of pent-up rage dissolved in an instant. *My mother's dead.* After everything he'd lost, it seemed plain stupid to bear a grudge against her.

For my one true son, Horace Austin Warner Tabor, Two million, five hundred thousand dollars.

He placed the document in his inside pocket and called out the door. "Shorty, can you take a trip with me? I'm going to need your help."

The sun dipped below Mount Massive, sky streaked orange and pink, reflecting on the abandoned Matchless Mine like a tinted photograph.

"She's seen better days, Shorty." Tabor patted the head frame, weathered and rotting, the iron fittings rusting together. He yanked on the hoist bucket, but it refused to budge. "Give me a hand, will you? Let's get this thing moving."

Shorty squirted oil on the joints of the rig, and they pulled the hoist reel together. With a terrific groan, it finally gave way.

Tabor thrust his claustrophobia aside and climbed into the bucket. Baby Doe had married the Silver King and ended up with a poor and broken man. Wouldn't she be surprised with this silver lining to their troubles? Even though he hadn't forgiven his mother for abandoning him, this gift went a long way toward redemption. He just had to keep it quiet until Turnbull and his vultures stopped circling for his flesh.

He jerked the rope. "Lower the boom." The hoist wheel squealed, and the bucket descended. Raising his eyes to the first star winking in the sky, he made a wish. More like a prayer.

Holding the lamp high, he dropped through chiseled rock walls glistening with ground water. Dankness cloyed at his nostrils. His head throbbed from lack of oxygen. Inhaling fiercely, he sucked in the meager air. "Hold on, old boy. You can do this."

The bucket splashed into water before hitting rock bottom; the mine needed to be pumped out. "Bull's eye. I landed," he yelled up to the navy sky, four stories up. Stepping out of the bucket, cold water soaked up to his ankle. The lamp flickered. Don't go out.

He sloshed down the deserted tunnel feeling the sides closing in, hearing rocks dribbling down. Memories flashed, the clank of picks and chisels, the laughter and insults, the smell of burning candles and Nobel's blasting powder.

There it was. Holding the lamp up, he gazed at the monstrous vein, no longer afraid: the huge lightning bolt of silver ran through multiple layers of bedrock. He touched its gleaming surface, fortifying his strength. Silver hadn't let him down, politics had. Silver would rise again, and when it did, he'd be ready.

Turning away from the vein, he searched the back wall where he'd shown Baby Doe his secret vault so many years ago. Water streamed down, melding the crevices together. He put down the lantern and felt along the wet wall, digging into every crack, breaking his fingernails. Lack of oxygen forced him to pant. Finally, he caught a groove. That was it. Shoving the rock with all his strength, it gave way. Reaching into his pocket for his mother's will, he placed it inside, and pushed the rock back in place. Relief flooded him. Once Turnbull stopped tracking him, he'd come back for his inheritance and build their empire again.

"Yooo-hooo." Shorty's voice bounced off the shaft walls. "You still down there?" His laughter filled the cavern.

Tabor picked up the lamp and started back. "Coming, Shorty." He climbed into the bucket and jerked on the rope. "Going up."

The crank groaned as the bucket ascended. Tabor whistled like a lark.

40

Denver, Colorado, 1898

"Couldn't this wait until morning, Horace?" Baby Doe herded her drowsy daughters into Shorty Scout's buggy.

"Trust me," he said, eyes sparking like she hadn't seen in a long time. "I know I don't deserve your trust after all I've put you through, but this will be worth it."

"I can't wait." She squeezed his hand, never able to resist his enthusiasm.

Her anticipation grew until he drove up to the Windsor. The hotel harbored secrets, so many shameful secrets. The happiest and loneliest time of her life.

Baby Doe followed Tabor through the lobby, a daughter on each hand, memories crashing in on her. The column Augusta hid behind, noxious gardenias in vases, the terrifying Otis elevator to the penthouse.

"What are we doing here, Papa?" Lily whined as the elevator ascended.

"We're on an adventure, silly goose," Silver Dollar chided.

Baby Doe's stomach quaked and sweat misted her bodice. Why would he rub her nose in the painful loss of their private nest, where they'd begun their lives together, and she'd drawn up Tabor Grand plans. Now taken away from them, like everything else.

He inserted the long key and unlocked the door. "Welcome

home, girls."

"Home?" Baby Doe repeated, unable to make sense of it.

He smiled the giddy smile of faith restored and promises kept.

She wanted to feel what he felt but the past overshadowed the future. Sweeping her hand along the chesterfield settee where they'd spent hours talking, looking out at the twinkling streetlights of Larimer Street, raising her gaze to the snow-capped mountains lit by the moon.

Tabor watched her and waited.

She opened the door that connected the two suites. A step-stool rose to their high mahogany bed with paneled headboard and featherbed. So many nights of love.

The girls climbed up on the bed, squealing and laughing.

"Do we get to stay, Mamma?" Silver Dollar danced a jig.

"Don't be a nincompoop." Lily sniffed. "Who lives in a hotel?"

The girls jumped down to explore, their voices mixing with Baby Doe's emotions, ultimately scouring her clean. She crossed the room to Tabor.

"It's home, Horace. You brought us home." She spread her hands on his chest. "Can we afford it?"

"I start Monday as the new postmaster of the Denver Post Office." He laughed. "They ought to let me run the place since I donated the land."

Her stomach fell. "That's crazy. You hated being a postmaster."

"What could be crazier than chasing after a rock that glimmers? Now *that's* crazy." He huffed. "I wouldn't blame you if you want to leave me. This is not what you signed up for."

Heat rushed to her chest. "You believed them, didn't you?"

"Who?"

"People said I'd leave you when the money ran out, and you believed them." Her limbs shook with disgrace she'd tried to leave behind.

"I'm just saying I was old when you met me, but at least I was rich. Now I'm a lowly postmaster and even older." He turned her to face the oval mirror she'd gazed in so many times before. "Look at you. You're young and beautiful. A million men would love to take care of you."

"That's an insult to both of us, Horace. Do you think I married you to take care of me? I can take care of myself."

"You've taken care of *all* of us, while I took stupid risks and lost everything." His chin dropped, his deep-set eyes disappearing in the shadows.

Her careless words had cut him down when he needed building up. "We haven't lost everything. We have our family and a new home." She kissed his cheeks, forehead, and nose. "You...have... me. It was never about money, Horace. It was how you played the game. I'd win and lose a thousand fortunes, if we played the game with the heart and courage you've shown me."

He caressed her cheek. "You go-for-broke gamblers are dangerous."

"Come to think of it, you were a postmaster when you struck it rich the first time." She kissed him. "Don't you see? Tabor Luck is back."

His eyebrows arched, eyes crinkling. "I think you're on to something, there, Baby." She nestled under his arm. "Right now, I feel like the luckiest man alive."

Their one-year anniversary at the Windsor was something to celebrate. They'd never been so happy, living out of the limelight like normal folks. Baby Doe took in mending to save for a special family dinner. Wouldn't Mam just croak if she knew?

Returning with the groceries, she hoped Tabor wouldn't be working late again. He worked at postmaster just like everything else in his life. Full bore.

But, he was home, sitting in a chair by the window, his complexion sallow.

She kissed his cheek and handed him the newspaper. "They discovered gold in the Klondike. They sail up from San Francisco to Skagway, then take the White Pass Trail to the Yukon River."

Peeling off the newspaper pages one by one, Tabor fed them to the fire, staring blankly as they burned.

"Don't hold back how you feel, now." She laughed, then frowned and felt his forehead. "You're burning up."

"An old friend came to see me at the post office." He cradled his stomach. "We grabbed a hotdog at Louie's, and now it's biting back. In fact, it's a dogfight in there."

"Come lay down." She took him into their bedroom. "I'll bring you some ginger tea. Fix you right up." Pulling a crocheted blanket over him, she closed the door. The post office was hard work at his age. If only they'd kept Cripple Creek, which struck a motherlode after Tabor gave it to Stratton. He wouldn't have to work at all.

"What's wrong with Papa?" Lily asked.

"Can you read to Silver Dollar?" Baby Doe said, trying to distract her.

"I want to see Papa."

"Your father might have the flu, and I don't want you girls catching it."

Lily pushed past her. "I don't care. I'm seeing Papa."

Why was it always like this between them?

Baby Doe read Silver a poem by Eugene Field, a kinder exercise for his poison pen.

"Where are you going, and what do you wish?
The old moon asked the three.
"We have come to fish for the herring fish.
That live in this beautiful sea;
Nets of silver and gold have we!
Said Wynken, Blynken, And Nod."

Lily came back, pale and shaken. "Papa's talking crazy."

Baby Doe reached for her, but she flinched. "He'll be all right, Lily. You'll see. He'll be fine." She went to check on him.

Tabor was clammy and yellow, sweat plastering his nightshirt to his chest. "We've got to secure the mine walls. The river's filling the shaft with water."

She wiped his brow, much hotter than earlier. "Horace, I need to call the doctor."

"We need a pump, or the shaft will fill up with water," he said, frantic. "Do something."

What should she do? "I'll get the pump."

"Tell Lou we need more men."

Lou Leonard died years ago. She rang the front desk. "Send Doctor Hayden immediately. Mr. Tabor is sick."

Lily eyed her from the doorway.

"Take care of Silver until the doctor comes, okay?"

Lily made a face.

Baby Doe stroked his flailing arms, trying to calm him, but it was no use reasoning with his delusions. His agitation grew while she waited for the doctor. Helpless, she watched her brave husband adrift in his own mind.

"Man the pump. Water's caving in the mine. I must save the vault. Important."

"Okay, Horace. Hold on." What else could she do but be there for him?

"Go up in the bucket, damn it. You'll drown down here." He waved maniacally. "Raise the bucket. You'll die."

"We're going up now." She calmed his quaking hands. "Keep your arms inside the bucket, or you'll break them off."

"I need to get something in the vault." He groped her face. "Is that you, Baby Doe? I can't see you. Don't leave me." His eyes were wide open.

Panic choked her. "Horace, can't you see me?"

"Too dark. Baby Doe, never let go of the Matchless." He let out a howl that pierced her core. "Oh, my God. My gut's on fire. I'm on fire. Put out the fire."

She heard a gasp at the door. Lily's eyes bulged at her father's histrionics.

"Go ask the front desk where the doctor is. Run."

He didn't let up. "There are more cracks in the rock. Damn it, Baby, close the cracks. The water's coming through."

Cracks? Her heart cracked watching his torture. Nothing soothed him.

"Spackle the cracks, Baby." His eyes bugged from their sockets, ringed purple.

"I'm mending them, Horace. The water has stopped."

"Billy, Maxcy, get the men dressed in uniform. There's no more time." He threw a long leg out of bed, his bones showing through thin skin.

Lily rushed in with Doctor Hayden, smudged eyeglasses askew.

"I'm sorry. The hospital was bedlam tonight." He pulled a stethoscope out of his bag. "I got here soon as I could. What are his symptoms?"

"He's dizzy, delirious, cramping muscles, and pain. He's in so much pain."

"Could it be arsenic poisoning?"

Baby Doe shook her head. "Maybe influenza? He had lunch with a friend. When he started to feel sick, he came right home."

"If it's influenza, it's contagious. Put the girls to bed." He looked her in the eye. "I'll come out after I examine him."

Baby Doe walked with Lily to the girl's bedroom. "Is Silver Dollar sleeping?"

"No, Momma, she's praying."

"Let's all pray, girls. Papa needs our help." They recited the rosary to the moving beads.

"Sing that song Papa likes," Lily demanded.

Silver's eyes closed as Baby Doe sang the Irish lullaby she'd sung since they were born. When it was finished, Lily hugged her fiercely.

"Don't worry, darling. Papa can get through anything." Tucking her in bed, she kissed her forehead, then closed the door.

She waited for the doctor to emerge and tell her Horace would be fine. Sure, he'd need rest, and there would be medicine to take.

But he'd be fine.

Doctor Hayden appeared, wiping his glasses on his white coat. "I can't sugarcoat this, Mrs. Tabor…he's too far gone. I can't imagine how he made it home in all that pain." His despondent attitude sent waves of shock through her.

"Does he have to go to the hospital?"

"Nothing we can do there. I gave him a shot of morphine to keep him calm. Can I call someone for you?"

"Horace will pull out of this, he always does. He's strong."

"Mrs. Tabor, the end is near. You should not be alone. Who can I call?"

Her mind went numb. Should she call Peter? She hadn't spoken to him since he refused to help them. "I have Horace. All I need is Horace."

Doctor Hayden shook his head. "Get some rest. I'll send someone to help you." He closed the door behind him.

Angry with his ridiculous prognosis, she screamed into a pillow to stifle the sound, howling and sobbing until her ribs ached. The doctor had no idea who he was dealing with. Tabor had weathered scandal, political ruin, and economic collapse. He would not die of the flu. Spent and exhausted, she returned to their bedroom.

There, she saw it. The specter of death hung above him, ominous, yawning, and hollow as her life would be without him.

Crawling in beside him, she shielded his body with hers. Horace Tabor could not die. Not now. She fell asleep breathing in the scent of Creed.

Tabor stirred. "Baby Doe."

Hope leaped in her chest. "I'm here, Horace."

"Hang onto the Matchless."

She put her cheek on his. "I'll never let it go."

"I c-came to see my father."

Maxcy Tabor. The boy she'd avoided all her married life, now a man standing at her door. Hatred spread through her like spilled ink.

"It's not a good time." She closed the door, but he stuck his foot in the jam. Shiny black shoes and white spats.

It had been sixteen years since Maxcy sided with his mother in the divorce. Tabor hadn't spoken his name since Maxcy failed to attend their wedding, but she'd seen the regret on his face.

"Doctor Hayden said he doesn't have much longer," he said.

"He's sleeping. Come back later."

"No." Maxcy took off his top hat, sweat beading his broad forehead…Tabor's forehead. His amber irises mirrored his father's. His suit of tailored pinstriped wool was the sort Tabor used to afford. The pocket watch Tabor gave him on his twenty-first birthday hung from his vest pocket. "I need to t-tell him…"

"Maxcy?" Tabor called weakly from the bedroom. He hadn't spoken since yesterday.

Her heart heaved in surrender. "He's in the back bedroom."

Maxcy's face lost its bravado, his eyes brimming with tears.

"None of that." She wiped his eyes like he was her own child and led him back.

Reaching the bedroom, Maxcy turned back. "I shouldn't have come."

She grabbed his arm. "You owe him this."

Maxcy entered the room and sat close to the bed, gripping his top hat with white knuckles. "Father, I'm so s-sorry."

"Don't worry, Maxcy. It looks like a chipmunk to me." A spark in Tabor's vacant eyes. "Just keep whittling, and it'll get better."

Maxcy squeezed his eyes shut. "Okay, Pa. I'll keep at it, I promise."

"Good boy." Tabor reached for him, but fell short, his hand landing on the blanket. His eyes fluttered closed.

Maxcy grasped his hand, a lost boy. Tabor moaned, but his eyes didn't open.

"I c-could have helped him," Maxcy said. "I should have helped."

Her jaw clenched against her resentment, unwilling to deepen his pain. "Horace loved being postmaster again."

Maxcy scoffed. "He said he'd rather be six feet under than to ever be a postmaster."

The truth of his statement built inside her like a boiler ready to blow. She grabbed her rosary, the beads worn shiny with use, and pulled them through her fingers. The strand snapped under pressure, beads scattering on the floor. The silver Jesus medallion dropped to the threadbare rug, but Mother Mary remained in her hand, dangling threads bereft of beads.

"Let me help you." He bent over and gathered them up.

"You're too late, Maxcy. Too damn late."

Tabor let out a labored sigh and his mouth fell open.

Baby Doe held his frail wrist. No pulse under her fingertips.

"Is he—"

"Quiet." She pressed her hand under Tabor's chin, her cheek close to his. No throb of blood. No whisper of breath.

She closed her eyes and stopped breathing. Grasping at the vestiges of his spirit as it left his body. Leaving her.

"H-he's gone. My father is gone," Maxcy sobbed.

Her fingers lingered on his mouth, feeling for a last breath.

Gone.

41

Denver, Colorado, 1899

The words blurred on the newspaper page, unintelligible to Baby Doe.

"What do they say about Papa?" Lily snatched the paper out of her hands and read aloud. Silver Dollar sat beside her, round face attentive.

"Horace Tabor came to Colorado during the Gold Rush and dedicated his life to mining. He came into great fame and fortune in 1878 with the discovery of the Little Pittsburg Mine, followed by hundreds of other mines, most notably, The Matchless. He invested his money to benefit the people of Colorado, building Leadville's Tabor Opera House, public utilities and companies. In Denver, he built the Tabor Grand Opera House, the Tabor block, and donated land for the Denver Post Office. Horace Tabor was a leader in politics, business and mining. A true legend."

Baby Doe gazed at the mountains, snow blanketing their purple peaks, wishing she was there. Her ribs tightened like a vise around her heart.

Sympathy flowers choked the air with sickening aroma. Telegrams and letters of condolences littered their suite, sent by senators, governors, city council officials, mayors, churches, business associates, fraternities, actors, and acquaintances. People who abandoned him during the silver crash, when he needed them most.

She opened the window and gulped cold air.

"Mr. Bush is at the door, Momma," Lily said.

"Send him away," she said, but changed her mind. "Check on Silver Dollar, won't you?" Her oldest nodded, shocked into obedience by the loss of her father.

Bush stood in the hallway, leaning on his serpent's cane and holding a crystal vase of lilies. Once her favorite, now they signaled death.

"I want you to know I never wanted...never meant to hurt him," he said.

"Of course, you did. You should have come clean. He would have forgiven you."

"It was like getting caught cheating at poker," he smirked. "I couldn't admit my mistake, so I upped the ante."

"You bastard." She leaped at him, beating his chest. "You lying, cheating, thieving crook. You sent him to the grave."

Bush dropped the crystal vase, and it shattered on the marble floor. Large shards gleamed among broken lily stems. Her hand trembled. She could take a piece and slit his throat or slit her own and end this misery.

"Momma, do you need help?" Silver called from the bedroom.

"Everything's all right." Her head throbbed.

Bush stepped over the shambles. "It didn't turn out the way you planned," he whispered hoarsely. "But *your* life isn't over. I'm here for you, Baby."

His nerve repulsed her. "Slithering in for his spoils, Billy?"

"Don't be that way. You know I've cared about—"

Her hand reeled back, and she slapped him. "Thank you for reminding me how much I despise you."

He held his cheek. "You need someone to help you through this."

He was right. There was no one else. Tabor had been her someone.

She pushed him out, needing peace, needing solitude, knowing she'd get neither.

Peter opened the doors to the street, as loyal and loving as if there'd never been a strained word between them. Under the circumstances, Baby Doe appreciated his support as she stepped into the crowds wobbly as a lamb.

"Oh, my word." She pulled the girls close. Throngs of people closed in on them.

"I should have warned you," Peter said. "The chief of police estimated ten-thousand people for Tabor's funeral."

Her grief mixed with gratitude, strengthening her to face the day. "Girls, your father would be so happy to be remembered like this." She pulled off the black mantilla and greeted the crowds bare faced, proud to claim her place as Mrs. Horace Tabor. A dozen photographers captured the famous Tabor widow and her daughters. Peter hustled them into the carriage.

Lily held Silver's hand, their tearful eyes opened wide at thousands of mourners lining the streets. After the silver crash, people had discarded Tabor like yesterday's newspaper. But in his death, they venerate him? Bitterness tinged Baby Doe's pride. Fear, too. Tabor was such a commanding force in her life; she felt small and hollow without him. She missed his arms around her and his unstoppable attitude through impossible odds. Where would she find strength now?

At the state capitol, Peter helped her down from the carriage. The snow had melted, and columbines bloomed on the pathway to the capitol. How Tabor loved columbines.

The white granite building with its majestic dome was so like the nation's capitol where they'd married. With shaky legs, the steep stairs were a tough climb, so she counted steps to get through it. On the fifteenth step, she paused to read the inscription to the girls. "One mile above sea level. Your papa used to say he was halfway to heaven here in Denver."

"Does that mean heaven is two miles high?" Silver Dollar's eyes pleaded.

"I suppose so." She smiled. "*Leadville* is two miles high."

"Then Papa is in Leadville?"

"I wouldn't be surprised if he was. He loved Leadville so."

Billy Bush waited for them at the top of the stairs, as he had for the three days Tabor's casket had lain in state. He'd weathered her anger and grief, insisting on helping her through the funeral. Truth be told, she couldn't have done it without him. As uncertain as she felt about the future, Bush had been a rock through this ordeal.

Officers of the state militia stood at attention around Tabor's ornate casket, carved in Brazilian mahogany and gilded as if he died a rich man. Floral arrangements lined the halls to the Governor's Salon. The state of Colorado sent a six-foot cornucopia, overflowing with carnations, roses, chrysanthemums, and a bounty of fruit.

Peter read the placard to the girls. "Here is the horn-of-plenty signifying all that Horace Tabor gave of his heart and riches to the people of Colorado."

The glory unfolding for Tabor at his death astonished Baby Doe. If only he could see this tribute. Maybe, he could. She ached for a tangible sign of his spirit.

The state militia carried the casket down to a shiny black wagon adorned with flower garlands. Eight black horses wore red rose wreaths on their necks. Maxcy Tabor climbed next to the captain, and she flinched, still angry at the way he treated his father.

"He's Horace's son, he deserves to be there," Bush told her.

She knew he was right, Tabor would be happy to have Maxcy at his side.

Their own carriage followed the wagon down Broadway, in a mile-long procession of marching bands, police, state militia, firemen, and miners.

The procession stopped at Sacred Heart Cathedral, where Father Guido gave the mass, black eyebrows above imploring eyes.

"May the turf lie lightly on his breast that pulsed with such a big heart. God, like man, loves the great heart. Surely he loves Tabor."

After the service, people lined up to pay their respects.

Bush dragged over a chair. "You better sit down. This will take hours."

Peter, Lily, and Silver stood by the casket, brave and silent, as mourners expressed their condolences. The miners came first, clenching hats in their earth-stained hands.

"Jimmy Fisher, ma'am. I worked at the Matchless." He handed her a silver dollar. "Mr. Tabor shared his luck with all of us."

She flipped the coin over to Lady Luck, stamped proud and strong as a lady ought to be.

Hundreds of miners followed, giving her silver dollars until Bush had to find a brass caldron to hold them all.

Glamorous in blue velvet and feathers, Lillian Russell pressed a silver dollar in Baby Doe's hand. "You and Senator Tabor were so happy after your wedding. It gave me hope to find that kind of love." She broke into a sob.

The next mourner handed Baby Doe a silver dollar, and the next.

When the cauldron was filled, Bush found a wooden crate.

"Winfield Stratton, ma'am." An old man handed her an ore bag of silver dollars. "I'll never forget how dedicated Tabor was to you, giving up his gold mine just to get home."

"The Cripple Creek mine," she said. Her throat choked up, unable to speak.

No one left the church without placing a silver dollar in her hands, a tribute to Horace Tabor's generosity and optimism that made the impossible, possible.

The enormity of life without him whipped through her like a zephyr.

After the service, Bush took the silver dollars to the Windsor, and Peter drove their family to the cemetery. At least she'd insisted on a private burial. She couldn't have faced the crowds now. But without the music, the wafting incense, the warm handshakes and heartfelt words, the silence closed in. She gasped to fill her raw lungs with oxygen. Her fingernails dug into the silver dollar she kept in memoriam of Tabor's strength. God knew, she had none left of her own.

Gravediggers dug a deep hole, sounding like miners shoveling slag. Then, too soon, Tabor's casket was lowered into the ground.

Silver Dollar tore at her dress. "Don't let them, Momma. Don't let them put Papa in the ground."

Baby Doe hugged her close. "Papa's in heaven, now, remember? Two miles high. He'll be all right." She held out a hand for her older daughter. "Lily, darling, come."

"I can see from here," she said, sullen and pale. Peter put his arm around her.

Baby Doe swayed and locked her knees. She'd never hold Horace again. Never hear his bad jokes. Never feel him nuzzle behind her ear.

The last dirt was heaved on the mound. Father Guido gave a final benediction and bid them a peaceful night.

Peter held out his hand. "I'll take you back to the Windsor."

"I need time with him," she said. "Take the girls and send the carriage back later." She watched until they were out of sight, gathering courage to face the grave.

Her heart was locked in that casket with Horace. He had been her Morning Star, nourishing her ideas and ambition, enriching her life. Even after losing their wealth, they'd created a rich life with their family. As wonderful as the silver dollar tribute was, it wouldn't pay the Windsor rent for long.

What to do? What to do? Her parents wanted her to move back to Oshkosh, but she couldn't leave Horace here. Maybe she could get a tailor job in Denver. Or wait tables at The Buckhorn Exchange.

She had to support her family somehow.

Her ribs contracted, forcing a wail she swallowed back. Feeling sorry for herself wouldn't feed or clothe them. Leaning her head back, she inhaled fresh air. The mountains rose to the west, majestic and magnificent. Horace would love this view.

A lark hovered nearby, dressed for mating season in a sharp black and white tuxedo. He shot up into the turquoise sky, straight as an arrow from a bow, pouring out the most impassioned song of chirrups and trills. She followed his ascent until he was a tiny speck.

Then, the lark plunged toward the earth, spiraling, wings outstretched. Just before the ground, he swooped up again, his mating song warbling in her ears.

"Hold onto the Matchless."

The words startled her. So clear and unmistakable.

The Matchless Mine had meant everything to Horace, with that remarkable silver vein, now worthless. But what else lay in those tunnels? She'd seen zinc, copper, lead, even gold, and when silver came back, which it surely would, she could support their family.

The Matchless was a symbol of everything they stood for: tenacity, courage, and most of all, luck. Was that why he never let it go? He'd kept it for her.

Once again, the lark soared into the sky, stretching its wings wide and free, then joyfully plunged to the ground, singing to burst his lungs.

Baby Doe laid her hand on Tabor's headstone, knowing where she would go.

Matchless dreams. Matchless love. Matchless life.

Afterword

Baby Doe Tabor captured my imagination from the time I was five years old, when my family moved to Colorado. We spent weekends driving through the Rocky Mountains exploring ghost-towns and camping alongside mountain rivers. We panned gold and explored the mines of Central City and Leadville and other mountain towns. It was easy to imagine Baby Doe and her daughters, Lily and Silver Dollar working at the Matchless Mine in the still-wild mining town of Leadville. Baby Doe Tabor surprised everyone with her loyalty and determination. *Gold Digger,* is only half the Baby Doe Tabor story. For the rest, sign up to receive notice of the sequel, *Silver Dollar,* at http://www.rebecca-rosenberg.com

Please leave a review for
Gold Digger, The Story of Baby Doe Tabor

Goodreads https://www.goodreads.com/book/show/40018748gold-digger-the-remarkable-baby-doe-tabor

Bookbub https://www.bookbub.com/profile/rebecca-rosenberg

Amazon.com

Download the *Gold Digger* Reading Group Guide, https://www.rebecca-rosenberg.com/mybooks/

Sign up for Rebecca Rosenberg's email list for the sequel, *Silver Dollar.* https://www.rebecca-rosenberg.com

Connect with Rebecca:

Website: http://www.rebecca-rosenberg.com

Facebook: https://www.facebook.com/rebeccarosenbergnovels/

Amazon: https://www.amazon.com/Rebecca-Rosenberg/e/B075WGKJ3Y/ref=dp_byline_cont_ebooks_1

GoodReads: https://www.goodreads.com/author/show/7652050.Rebecca_Rosenberg

BookBub: https://www.bookbub.com/profile/rebecca-rosenberg

Pinterest: https://www.pinterest.com/rebecca7487/gold-digger-the-remarkable-baby-doe-tabor/

Other books by Rebecca Rosenberg:

THE SECRET LIFE OF MRS. LONDON

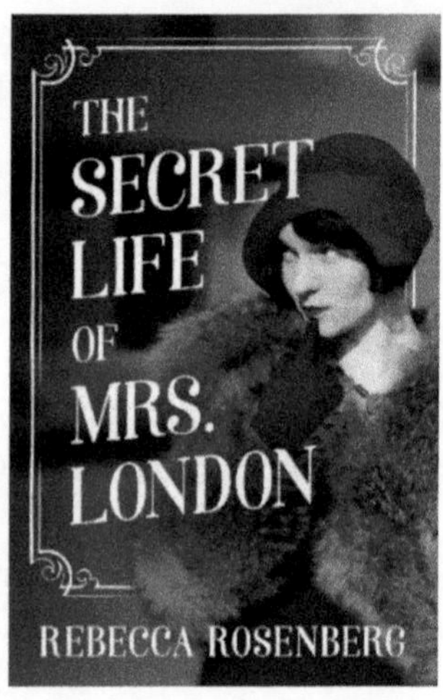

San Francisco, 1915. As America teeters on the brink of world war, Charmian and her husband, famed novelist Jack London, wrestle with genius and desire, politics and marital competitiveness. Charmian longs to be viewed as an equal partner, but Jack doesn't see it that way…until Charmian is pulled from the audience during a magic show by escape artist Harry Houdini, a man enmeshed in his own complicated marriage. Suddenly, charmed by the Houdini's attention and entranced by his sexual magnetism, Charmian's eyes open to a world of possibilities that could be *her* escape.

As Charmian grapples with her urge to explore the forbidden, Jack's increasingly reckless behavior threatens her dedication. Now torn between two of history's most mysterious and charismatic figures, she must find the courage to forge her own path, even as she fears the loss of everything she holds dear.

BUY NOW : https://www.amazon.com/dp/B072KRP7MN

SILVER DOLLAR (2020)
THE SEQUEL TO **GOLD DIGGER**
by Rebecca Rosenberg

Baby Doe Tabor is left a penniless widow when her husband dies in 1899, leaving her with two daughters to raise in Colorado. On his deathbed, he urges: "Hang onto the Matchless Mine", the only possession left of their silver fortune. She moves the family to Leadville, Colorado to work the silver mine, haunted with memories of her husband. The bank forecloses the Matchless and a mysterious investor takes over. Through furtive hunches and pure determination, Baby Doe encounters new love, devastating loss and discovers what her husband meant when he told her to "Hang onto the Matchless."

CHAMPAGNE WIDOWS SERIES (2021)
by Rebecca Rosenberg

The true story of five French widows (from 1800 to 1950) who fight heartbreak, war, economic disasters, and bad harvests, to head their own Champagne wineries during times when it was unheard of for women to own any business. Through their intelligence, perseverance and creativity, they create wildly successful champagne wineries and ignite an explosive world-wide market for champagne.

Acknowledgments

Gold Digger has been a decade-long journey. How can I begin to thank all those who helped along the way? First, I thank my husband who has listened to *Gold Digger* through a hundred revisions. Thank you, Gary Rosenberg. Then, I appreciate my early readers; Pam Schlossberg who started writing with me, Lori Fantozzi, Marchelle Carleton, Ginger Parnes, Diane Brown, Beth Mink, Kathleen Fitzgerald, my parents Peggy and Jim Cramer and Jim and Paulette Fisher, my children, Marissa and Mark Rosenberg, my sister-in-law, Diane Rosenberg. And I can never forget the help of my writing group, Darling Buds, Anne McMillan, Kirsten Lind, Maryann Shepard, Ralph Smith and Robin Boord.

Special thanks to Cindy Conger who juggles our many balls with flair, and Gail Kearns, my book Sherpa!

I appreciate the diligent and discerning eyes of my editor, Lorin Oberweger.

Thank you to my author friends who have been wonderfully supportive; Patricia V. Davis, Martha Conway, Thelma Adams, Camille Di Maio.

Lastly, thank you to the fiction gurus who create enthusiasm for novels and provide a great service to readers and authors on their websites, blogs, and facebook pages. Especially, Kathy L. Murphy, Tiajuana Neel, Linda Levack Zagan, Amy Bruno, Susan Peterson, Kayleigh Wilkes, Tonni Callan, Kristy Barrett, Sharlene Martin Moore, Kate Rock, to name just a few of these dynamic women.

About Rebecca Rosenberg

Rebecca grew up in Colorado exploring old mines, ghost towns and honky-tonks with her family, sparking her life-long love of the Rocky Mountains and obsession with the Tabors. Now, Rebecca lives and writes on a lavender farm in Sonoma, California.

CPSIA information can be obtained
at www.ICGtesting.com
Printed in the USA
LVHW031457030619
619985LV00001B/135

9 780578 427799